DANCE
OF THE
JAGUARS

Other Books by Lee E. Cart

Born in the Wayeb: Book One of *The Mayan Chronicles*
Rise of the Jaguar Woman: Book Two of *The Mayan Chronicles*
Tumbling Triangles
Birds in the Backyard
The Cracker Book: Artisanal Crackers for Every Occasion
The Paper Trail: Useful Charts to Organize Your Writing

The How to Do Anything Series ™ Kindle Books
How to Revise Your Writing
How to Lose Weight without Much Effort
How to Save Hundreds in Editing Fees

DANCE
OF THE
JAGUARS
BOOK THREE
OF
THE MAYAN CHRONICLES

Lee E. Cart

Ek' Balam Press
Wellington, Maine

Ek' Balam Press
15 Taylor Cenetery Road
Wellington, Maine 04942

Cover design by 100 Covers

Printed in the United States of America
Library of Congress Control Number: 2022909748
ISBN: 978-0-9906765-6-0

To my grandchildren, Jenson and Riley,
you fill my heart with love and joy

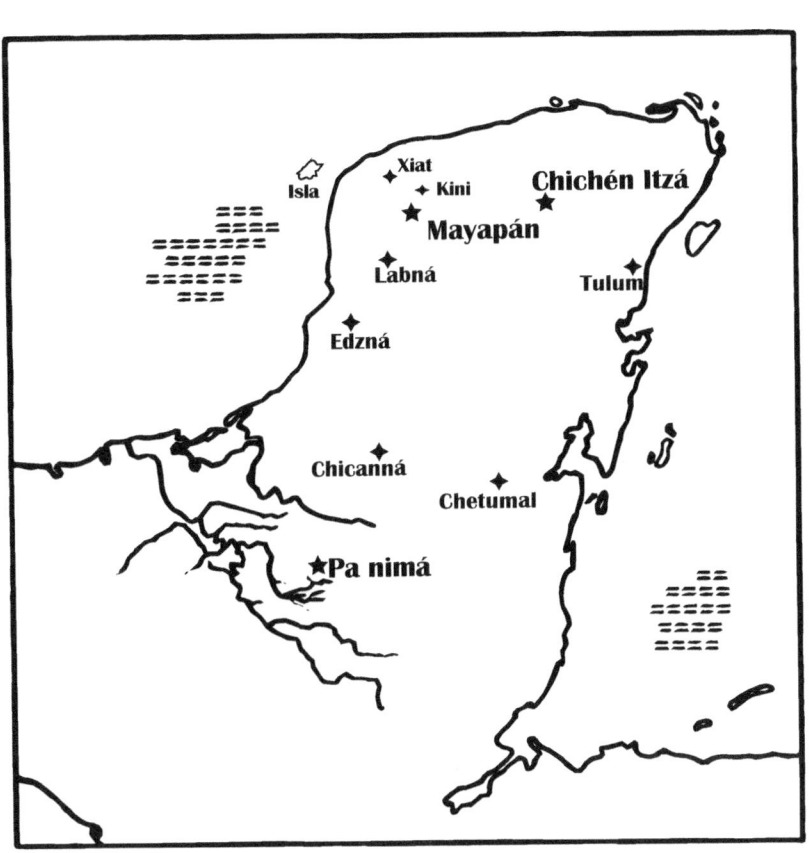

Xiat
Isla
Kini
Chichén Itzá
Mayapán
Labná
Tulum
Edzná
Chicanná
Chetumal
Pa nimá

CAST OF CHARACTERS

The city of Chichén Itzá

Ajelbal: Member of the Xiu tribe betrothed to Satal, died of old age; a flutist.

Alaxel: Chachal's secret lover; a prince.

Chiwekox: One of Satal's personal shamans; a boa constrictor.

Ch'o: One of Satal's personal shamans; a rat.

Ixtzol: One of Satal's personal shamans; a centipede.

Kämisanel: Head of the warriors; killer, murderer, assassin.

K'oy: One of Satal's personal shamans; a spider monkey.

Koyopa: One of Satal's personal shamans; lightning.

Pataninel: One of Satal's personal shamans; a servant.

Sachoj: Great-grandmother to Satal, reduced to a shrunken head; a viper.

Satal: Leader of the city, wife of Q'alel, mother to Chachal, member of the city council, presumed dead after falling into Mayapán's cenote; a black wasp.

Sina'j: One of Satal's personal shamans; a scorpion.

Tewichinel: One of Satal's personal shamans; a priest.

Yuxba': One of Satal's personal shamans; to bow.

The city of Mayapán

Alom: Mother to Yakal, second wife to Q'alel; a servant.

Binel ja': Younger sister to Yakal; a river or brook.

Biribik: Guard to Na'om, husband to Mok'onel; tall, well-built.

Bitol: Commander of the Gates and uncle to Yakal; a builder of ancient pyramids.

Box: Young man who works at the pottery workshop and friend to Tz'; to build a fire.

Ilonel: Lead raider employed by Satal, killed in the attack on Pa nimá; a spy.

Imul: Younger sister to Yakal; a rabbit.

Kubal Joron: A member of the city council and partner to Matz'; a water jug.

Kux: A member of Ilonel's group of spies; a weasel.

Mayibal: Infant son of Yakal and Uskab; a miracle or marvel.

Masat: Younger sister to Yakal, worked as servant to Satal; a deer.

Matz': A member of the city council and partner to Kubal Joron; an ear of corn with few grains.

Memetik: Houseboy to Kubal Joron and Matz'; to bleat like a goat.

Najtir: Shaman who helps trained Tz'; ancient.

Nil: Son of Q'abarel, works at the Silowik Tukan; a waterfall.

Nimal: Head of the regiment; a leader.

Nima Winaq: Head of the shamans in Mayapán; old man.

Q'abarel: Owner of the Silowik Tukan bar, father to Nil; a drunkard.

Q'alel: Father to Yakal and husband to Satal, died of suspicious circumstances; a military leader.

Puk'pik: Owner of the pottery workshop; a person with a pot belly.

Tarnel: Owner of the slave market; a bodyguard.

Tikoy: Younger brother to Yakal, died in the attack on Pa nimá; a frog.

T'ot: Cook and seller of seafood in the marketplace; shellfish.

Uskab: Second wife to Yakal, mother of Mayibal; a honey bee.

Xik': The fletcher of fine arrows; a feather.

Yakal: Father to Naòm, son of Q'alel and Alom, half-brother to Chachal; a stonemason.

The village of Pa nimá

Ajchak: Husband to Tzalon, father to Tuney, a new member of the village; a peasant farmer.

Ajkun (Ati't): Grandmother to Naòm, the village midwife and herbal healer; a witch who heals.

Ala: Infant son to Witzik' and K'ale'n, twin; young boy.

Ali: Infant daughter to Witzik' and K'ale'n, twin; young girl.

Banal Bo'j: A village member, died in the attack on the village; a pot maker.

Chachal: Mother to Tz', wife of Chiman, died in the attack on the village; a necklace of colored stones.

Ch'imil: younger of Naòm's twin sons; star.

Chiman: Father to Tz', husband to Chachal, leader and shaman of the village; a shaman.

Ek' Balam: Black jaguar, friend to Naòm; dark or black jaguar.

K'ale'n: Husband to Witzik', father to twins, Ali and Ala, a new member of the village; a bundle of firewood.

Kemonel: Mother to Mok'onel, Poy, and Tze'm, died in the attack on the village; a weaver.

Kab: Infant son of Xoral and Tzukunel; sweets or candy.

K'ab Balam: older of Na'om's twin sons; jaguar hand.

Kon: Young friend to Tz', died in the attack on the village; a stupid person.

Lintat: Grandson to Noy and Mam, befriended by Na'om; a young boy between three and eight.

Mam: Grandfather to Lintat, husband to Noy; a grandfather.

Mok'onel: Older daughter to Kemonel, stays in Mayapán after the attack on the village; a robber or thief.

Na'om: Granddaughter to Ajkun, daughter to Yakal, presumed dead after falling into the cenote in Mayapán; to have felt or sensed something.

Noy: Grandmother to Lintat, wife to Mam; a grandmother.

Pempen: Wife to Setesik, mother to Sijuan; a butterfly.

Potz': A village member, died in the attack on the village; a blind or one-eyed person.

Poy: Younger daughter to Kemonel, died in the attack on the village; a doll.

Setesik: Husband to Pempen, father to Sijuan; a large round basket.

Sia': Female jaguar who lives near Ajkun's hut; a cat.

Sijuan: Daughter to Pempen and Setesik, friend to Mok'onel; a female friend.

Tajinel: Husband to Ajkun, died of old age; a farmer.

Tu'janel: Mother of Na'om, first wife to Yakal, died in childbirth; a new mother.

Tzalon: Wife to Ajchak, mother to Tuney, a new member of the village; a gladiola flower.

Tuney: Infant daughter to Tzalon and Ajchak; dahlia flower.

Tz'ajonel (Tz'): Son of Chiman and Chachal, friend of Na'om; a painter.

Tze'm: Newborn son of Kemonel, died in the attack on the village; a laugh.

Tzukunel: Husband to Xoral, father to Kab, a new member of the village; a hunter.

Xoral: Wife to Tzukunel, mother to Kab, a new member of the village; a flower garden.

Witzik': Wife to K'ale'n, mother to twins Ali and Ala, a new member of the village; a corn flower.

In the countryside

Alixel: Daughter to Kärinik and Chapal Kär, mother to Mial and Ukabal; a princess.
Be Anim: Twin brother to Tik Anim in the village of Xiat; to run.
Chapal Kär: Husband to Kärinik, father to Alixel, presumed dead; a fisherman.
Ch'awinel: Shaman and leader of the village of Xiat; a person who talks a lot.
Eqomal: A young shaman on the island; apprentice.
Josol Che': The carpenter in the village of Xiat; a carpenter.
Jumumik: Twin brother to Jututik in the village of Xiat; to run fast.
Jututik: Twin brother to Jumumik in the village of Xiat; to run fast.
Kärinik: Mother to Alixel, aids Na'om on the beach; to fish.
Kunaj: Grandmother to Kärinik, died of old age; to cure, to heal.
Mial: Granddaughter to Kärinik, daughter to Alixel; firstborn daughter.
Tatá: Leader of the shamans on the island; old man, honored person.
Tik Anim: Twin brother to Be Anim; to run.
Tikonel: Husband to Alixel, father to Mial and Ukabal; sower, farmer.
Ukabal: Grandson to Kärinik, son to Alixel; second child.

The Mayan Gods and Creatures of the Underworld

Acan: The god of wine, belching, and intoxication.
Ahalgan: The god of pus.
Ahalpuh: The god of pestilence.
Ah-Cun-Can: A war god related to snakes and serpents.
Ah-Pekku: The god of thunder.
Bajbik: Leader of the were-jaguars; thick-lipped.
Buluc-Chabtan: The god of war, violence, and death who likes to roast people on skewers over a fire.
Camazotz: The god of bats and friend to Satal.
Chac: The god of rain and lightning.

Hunahpu and Xbalanque (The Hero Twins): The twin ball players who were able to outwit the gods of the Underworld and survived the numerous trials set before them so they could return to the world of the living.

Hun-Batz: The god of howler monkeys.

Itzamná: The supreme god of the Maya who taught the people to grow maize and cacao.

Ixchel: The jaguar goddess of midwifery and medicine.

Kukulcan: The plumed serpent god.

Hun-Kamé: One Death, one of the gods of the Underworld who protects the sacred fire.

Poxlom: The god of diseases.

Vucub-Kamé: Seven Death, one of the gods of the Underworld who protects the sacred fire.

Tlacolotl: The god of evil and dark places.

Xaman Ek: The patron god of travelers and merchants.

Xojol: A female were-jaguar; dancer.

Yum Cimil: The god of death.

Na'om

The sun had barely crested the high walls surrounding Mayapán when Na'om stepped outside the hut she was staying in. She frowned, then reluctantly nodded to the four guards dressed in leather body armor and loincloths who stood on either side of the small doorway. Each carried a large obsidian knife in a leather scabbard at their side and a wooden stave with a sharpened point. Na'om motioned for them to lead the way. The city council members, which now included Chiman and Ajkun, insisted she have an escort at all times. She sighed. She knew her grandparents meant well, but they didn't understand that the guards made her feel like a prisoner rather than someone who needed protection. She knew she could defend herself against any mortal enemy better than anyone, but she had agreed to the chaperones to appease Chiman and Ajkun's fears.

She felt Ek' Balam's wet nose push into the palm of her hand, and she patted the black jaguar. "They worry too much about me," she whispered as she leaned down and gave the cat a quick kiss on the top of the head. *At least Ajkun has finally agreed to let us sleep in our own hut,* Na'om thought as the group crossed the courtyard and entered the alley in front of the house. Looking both ways, Na'om could see the street was deserted, a fact that pleased her as it meant she could walk to the Temple of the Warriors in relative peace. Ever since she'd arrived in the city, the citizens had lined the streets whenever she appeared, begging for her attention. It had made it so difficult to go anywhere during the day, even with her attendants, that Naʼom had spent most of her time in her hut, only going out at first light or at dusk. She longed for the freedom sheʼd experienced in Pa nimá where the villagers had actively avoided her, and sheʼd been able to roam the jungle with Ekʼ Balam at will.

Naʼom exhaled slowly. *I suppose those days are over*, she mused as she nodded at a small group of people who had stopped in their tracks to watch her pass. One elderly woman held out an amulet, and Naʼom took the piece of jewelry and kissed it before handing it back.

"Maltiox, maltiox, Lady Naʼom, may Itzamná bless you, jaguar woman," the woman mumbled.

Naʼom nodded and continued on her way. *I should have left even earlier*, she thought as she looked ahead toward the marketplace. The area was already humming with activity. Where the booths had not been damaged in the attack on the city, the stall owners were busy arranging their wares while calling out their prices to the groups of women who waited impatiently to purchase the freshest meats and vegetables of the day. Nearby, several men worked on clearing some remaining debris, while others were chopping small fiddlewood trees into poles of various lengths to be used for new stall structures. Farther ahead, she could see several tamales vendors meandering through the people on the outskirts of the market. Steam wafted out from the large oval baskets covered with clean white cotton cloths that hung from hemp ropes tied over their shoulders.

"Iguana, turtle, peccary, and deer," they called in their singsong cadence. "Iguana, turtle, peccary, and deer." Naʼomʼs stomach grumbled in response, and she almost stopped to get something to eat. *No, I must get to the temple; thereʼs time to eat after the meeting.*

Suddenly the crowds caught sight of her, and the people pushed in on all sides, jostling and shoving to get closer to her. A hand reached out and snatched at Naʼomʼs deep blue skirt, and Ekʼ Balam whirled around and growled. The man quickly withdrew into the back of the group, his eyes opened wide in fear. The guards tightened their circle around her and used their wooden staves to physically push the men and women back so she could get through. They rushed her past the remaining throngs and into a smaller side street where she was able to walk freely again.

"Maltiox," she said to the guards as she straightened her skirt. *Maybe*

I do need an escort after all, she thought as they hurried onward.

A few minutes later, the group arrived at the temple, and the guards took up spots on either side of the main entranceway. Na'om stepped into the dark hallway and let her eyes adjust to the dimmer light. She walked down to the council room and peered in, but the room was empty of people. She sighed. She was once again too early. A long wooden table surrounded by leather chairs filled most of the room, and she smiled when she saw a stack of small ceramic plates and several ceramic mugs at one end of it. She knew then that Ajkun would stop at the market and purchase breakfast for everyone to enjoy after the meeting.

While she waited for the council members to appear, Na'om paced up and down the hallway. She needed to move and burn off some of the anxiety she felt. During the night, she'd dreamt of the Underworld yet again, of being trapped in the blackness, stumbling about in the dark on her own, with no sense of which direction to go in order to escape. When she'd banged her bare foot one more time on some unseen obstacle and cried out in pain, Ek' Balam had been the one to gently wake her with a quick brush of his tongue against her cheek. Fearing her dreams would return her to that horrid place, it had taken Na'om a long time to drift back to sleep. When she finally did, she'd had vague dreams about Tz'. She sensed he was alive but in some kind of danger. He was about to do something that would change the course of everything, but every time she concentrated on what that might be, the dream dissipated. She took a deep breath and let it out slowly, willing the knot in her stomach to unwind.

As she walked, her leather sandals made a pit-pat sound that echoed off the high limestone walls. The repetition burrowed into her mind, and Na'om felt a rush of anger and frustration filter through her body. She quickly slipped off her shoes and threw them into a corner of the hallway and continued to pad bare foot on the cool tiles. Meanwhile, Ek' Balam lay on the floor near the doorway to the council room. Each time she approached him, the black jaguar lifted his head and looked at her, before placing his head back down on his paws.

"How can you be so calm?" Na'om said as she paused in front of the big cat. "It's been almost a moon's time since the city was attacked. We need to get to Chichén Itzá and find Tz'. Who knows what Satal has done to him while we've been waiting here." She bent down and stroked the cat's head and instantly felt calmer as his energy mingled with hers.

She turned when she heard footsteps enter the corridor and hurried to greet her grandmother. Ajkun had a large pottery jug in her hands. Behind her were Noy, Kärinik, and Alom. Each woman carried a platter of food covered with a cotton cloth. Na'om reached out to take the heavy pitcher from Ajkun and led the way into the council room where the women placed the food in the center of the table. Na'om gave each of the women a kiss on the cheek and an extra hug to Ajkun.

"Any sign of the men yet?" Na'om asked. "I don't want to eat until we get done with our discussion this morning, but I don't want the food to grow cold either."

"I saw Chiman and Yakal leaving the observatory building as we entered the courtyard outside, so they should be here any minute," Ajkun replied. She patted Na'om gently on the forearm. "I'm sure they'll have answers today."

Just then, Na'om looked down the hallway and saw Chiman, Yakal, and the other men of the council enter the building. She was pleased to see Chiman held a document in one hand. She turned and pushed the plates of food to the end of the table so there'd be space to unfold the parchment.

"*Saqarik*," she said in greeting. Chiman gave her a long hug, and then Yakal stepped forward. She embraced her father, but she still felt uncomfortable in his arms and was glad to move away from him.

The scent of fresh jasmine blossoms wafted into the air as Kubal Joron and Matz' took their places on the opposite side of the table. Na'om smiled when she saw the men were wearing matching indigo blue tunics and loincloths. She didn't quite understand the relationship they had, but she'd quickly learned in the short time that she'd known them that they were generous, kindhearted men. They had volunteered to help pay for anything that might be needed in the counterattack against Satal.

Kubal Joron lifted the corner of one of the cloths covering the food. "Hmm, cornmeal and raspberry pastries," he said, "one of my favorites." He reached for one of the small plates stacked nearby, but stopped when Matz' touched him lightly on the arm and gave him a look.

"All right, I'll wait," Kubal Joron said. He dropped the cloth and settled back in his chair.

Na'om turned to Chiman. "*Mam*, what did the shamans say? Do they have the dates when we can launch the assault on Satal?"

Chiman nodded. He stepped to the table and unfolded the fig-bark paper he held in his hand. Yakal helped him place small plates in each corner to weigh them down so the paper would lie flat on the table. Everyone leaned in to better see the black ink drawings sketched on the page. Na'om saw a large, four-sided pyramid standing at one end of a massive open courtyard. The pyramid's stepped sides were covered with dozens of howler and spider monkeys. Hundreds of snakes and scorpions filled the square in front of the pyramid, and she gasped when she recognized the were-jaguars from the Underworld standing guard around a small figure of a woman. "That must be Satal," she stated while she pointed to the drawing. "But I don't understand," she said as she continued to point. "Why are they in the picture?" The scroll depicted Hun-Kamé and Vucub-Kamé, the skeletal gods of the Underworld, and Camazotz, the bat god, who hovered in the air above the pyramid.

"It appears Satal's going to call forth all the forces she used against the people here in Mayapán, plus many more," Chiman said.

"How is that possible?" Ajkun asked. "What kind of dark magic is this?"

"The same as she used before, except more of it, as the shamans have determined we must strike Chichén Itzá during the Wayeb," Chiman said.

Ajkun gasped and sat down abruptly in one of the many chairs near the table. "Satal will be at her strongest at that point."

"Yes, I'm afraid so," Chiman replied. "However, we must remember that Na'om was also born during the Wayeb."

Na'om gave a small laugh. "Just barely. It certainly doesn't provide me with enough ability to combat Satal when she has all of the Underworld at her bidding."

Kärinik looked up from the drawing. "Na'om, you forget one important thing; you passed all the trials in the Underworld and were transformed by that experience, a feat no one else alive, including Satal, has ever done."

"Maltiox, Kärinik," Na'om replied. An awkward silence filled the room.

Finally, Kubal Joron coughed, breaking the stillness. "Even so, Satal will muster the same army she used here, and we almost didn't survive the attack, even though we had this city's walls to protect us. Now our army will be vulnerable and exposed since we'll be going onto her territory. How will we defeat her when she has all the advantages on her side?" He pulled a lavender cloth from inside his sleeve, swiped at his brow, and nervously began tapping his fingers on the tabletop.

Naʼom turned to look at the drawings again. "Do we attack on the first day of the Wayeb or any of the five days?"

"The shamans haven't deciphered this," Chiman said.

"I suppose the timing doesn't really matter; we have to defeat Satal whenever we can and at whatever cost," Naʼom said. She looked at the group. "So, we have a little over three moons' time to prepare." She pulled a chair up to the table and motioned that the others should sit as well. "Will the fletchers, knife makers, and leather workers be able to produce enough weapons and armor in that amount of time?"

Nimal grimaced. "Not with the number of men employed right now."

"Then we need to get more help. You'll have to hire men and women from outside the city, anyone willing to work," she said. Naʼom turned to Kubal Joron and Matzʼ. "We'll need more cacao beans to pay for supplies and for the extra workers. Can you do this?"

Matzʼ nodded at Kubal Joron, who cleared his throat and spoke. "Yes, Lady Naʼom, our coffers are at your command. If Nimal and Bitol can come by our palace later today, we can give them several more satchels of cacao beans."

"Good. Maltiox." She looked at Yakal. "Can your stonemasons work longer days to repair the damage done to the city's walls? We'll need to make sure everyone left here is safe from any retaliation Satal might attempt while the main army is on the march to Chichén Itzá."

"Of course, Naʼom. I'll take men away from repairing the destroyed houses and put them on wall-building detail at once."

Naʼom smiled and turned to look at Nimal and Bitol. "How are we doing on stockpiling salt?"

Before Nimal could answer, Kärinik interjected. "My daughter says every woman in every village loyal to Mayapán has a basket or more of salt on hand, ready to be used whenever you need it."

"Excellent."

Nimal spoke. "And the warriors will carry bags of salt with them for protection, as you requested, Lady Naʼom."

"Good. But I'm afraid that still might not be enough."

Ajkun looked around the room. "What if the men wore the salt in bags under their leather vests? That would create a shield against anything Satal might use against them."

Chiman smiled at Ajkun. "What a wonderful idea."

"Who will make the bags and fill them?" Nimal demanded. "All my men are already busy preparing other weapons."

Kärinik spoke up. "We women will weave the cloth, fill the bags, and stitch them shut. If the leather makers can provide us with some scraps, we'll even sew straps on them so they can be worn over the shoulders and hang down each man's chest and back."

"I like the idea," Na'om said. "I leave you and Ajkun and Alom to coordinate this."

Alom looked up from her place at the table. "I've heard rumors from some of the women at the market that there are many in Chichén Itzá who are unhappy now that Satal is in power there. She's sacrificed too many innocent people in order to gain favor with the gods. Perhaps there are some willing to fight against her?"

Na'om nodded. "If we can find these people and trust that they'll be on our side, then we must engage them as well. Mam, can you speak to Ch'awinel and learn what he might know?"

Chiman smiled. "I'll ask him to call a meeting of all the shamans and leaders from the nearby villages and have them cautiously spread the word."

"Good. If we can get more households closer to Chichén Itzá to stockpile salt, we might just have a chance against her in this battle." Na'om slumped back in her chair. "We still must wait three moons, though."

Bitol shifted in his seat. "We can't attack if we're not ready, Lady Na'om. Even with that amount of time, it will be difficult to be sufficiently prepared *and* make the long trek to Chichén Itzá."

Nimal nodded. "And I suspect many of the men will be fearful of making the long journey once they know we'll be arriving just in time for the Wayeb."

"Then we must convince them that there is no other choice," Na'om replied.

"Must we attack?" Alom asked. "After all, Satal has retreated and has shown no signs of coming here again. Perhaps if we leave her alone, she'll leave us alone."

"No!" Na'om said as she hit the table with her fist. "She has taken Tz' from us; Itzamná only knows what she's done to him in all this time."

"There must be a counterattack so we can avenge the many lives Satal took from us," Nimal added.

"And we must ensure that Satal is killed, so that we no longer need live in fear of her," Yakal said. "I for one will gladly give my life if it will end hers."

Chiman nodded. "Yes, but first we must ensure that Tz' is safe."

Nimal interrupted. "It's my understanding that Tz' left the city of his own free will several days before Satal attacked. Whether we find him or not is inconsequential. We mustn't lose sight of the true objective, to defeat Satal, as you said earlier, 'at whatever cost.'"

Na'om scowled at the older man. "What are you suggesting?" she demanded.

Nimal leaned back in his chair, then glanced at Kubal Joron and Bitol for support. But both men looked down at the table. "Since Tz' is Satal's grandson, perhaps we should be more fearful of him rather than for him. If the cost includes this boy, so be it."

Chiman stood up abruptly, knocking over his chair, which hit the tile floor with a loud thwack. "I won't have you speak that way about my son," he cried.

"Chiman, please, sit down," Ajkun implored. She tugged on the long sleeve of his green tunic and helped Yakal right his chair. "We don't know what prompted Tz' to go to Chichén Itzá; perhaps as her grandson, he thought he might influence her in some way. But until we actually speak to him, please, let's keep our speculations to a minimum." She looked directly at Nimal as she said this.

The older warrior dipped his head in acknowledgment. "As you wish, my lady. I meant no disrespect."

"Chiman, have you spoken to the shaman, Najtir?" Yakal asked.

"Yes, and learned nothing new, I'm afraid. Tz' was attempting to shapeshift under Najtir's tutelage and when he couldn't do it, he left the city. We don't know for certain he even went to see Satal, but Najtir suspects he did since she is a true master of that art."

"I've known Tz' my whole life; I can't imagine he wanted to study under Satal, even if she is his grandmother. That's just doesn't sound like him," Na'om said.

Ajkun reached over and touched her arm. "When he learned of your 'death,' I'm afraid he changed quite a bit. He was not himself when he left

Pa nimá and returned here."

"Well, I'd like to speak to this shaman," Na'om said. "Perhaps he'll remember some more details that might be helpful."

"I'll make the arrangements," Chiman said.

"I don't care if Tz' is Satal's grandson; he's my friend, and I'll do anything in my power to bring him back where he belongs," Na'om stated.

"All of us can only do so much, Na'om, and then it's in the hands of the gods." Ajkun stood up, pushed the parchment to one side, and pulled one of the food platters into the center of the table. "Come, let's eat; perhaps some food will help us think better."

Noy and Alom hurried to help her arrange the plates while Kärinik poured everyone a mug of juice made from infused hibiscus flowers mixed with honey.

"Excellent idea, Lady Ajkun," Kubal Joron said as he helped himself to three of the fresh pastries. He bit into one and sighed. "Wonderful, wonderful, I must know which vendor you purchased these from; they truly are delicious."

Na'om avoided looking at anyone while she picked at the food on her plate. The mere thought that Tz' might want to be with Satal had made her lose her appetite. It can't be true, I don't care what anyone else thinks, she thought as she poked at a lump of honey beaded on the edge of her pastry. The sticky mixture stuck to her fingertip, and without thinking, she stuck her finger in her mouth and sucked on it to remove it. I can't believe Tz' would voluntarily choose to be with Satal even if she is his grandmother. Why, she's responsible for the attack on Pa nimá, when Chachal was killed! "That's it!" Na'om said as she placed her plate on the table. "Satal was responsible for the attack on our village, so Tz' went to confront her and to avenge his mother's death." She looked eagerly around the table for confirmation that she was right.

Chiman nodded. "Yes, that's possible. Even though he didn't speak about it much after we returned to the village, I know Tz' was very hurt by Chachal's death."

Yakal cleared his throat. "Maybe or there could be another reason why he left." He looked at Chiman. "Tz' knew you weren't his father by blood; he might have left to go find his real father and just happened to be in Chichén Itzá when Satal struck this city."

Na'om looked at Yakal with surprise. "What are you implying?"

Chiman smiled at his granddaughter. "It's all right, Na'om, your grandmother told me the truth many moons ago. Chachal had a love relationship before I married her, so Tz' is not really my son."

Stunned, Na'om sat back in her leather chair. "Then we're not related by blood?"

"No, which means when he returns, you're free to follow your heart, as I did mine," Ajkun said and smiled as she looked at her granddaughter and then at Chiman.

"When were you planning on telling me this?" Na'om demanded. But no one would answer her. The she blushed as she felt a wave of emotions rush through her body. She had always loved Tz' but hadn't realized it was so obvious to those around her.

In the silence, Kubal Joron reached for a fifth pastry to put on his plate, but Matz' gave him a stern look that made him return the delicacy to the platter. "All right, all right, I'll save some room for lunch," he muttered. He wiped his lips with his lavender-colored cloth and tucked the fabric inside his large sleeve.

Na'om took the interruption to change the topic. "I'd like to speak to anyone else who knew Tz' while he was living here," Na'om said. She turned to Alom. "Didn't you meet one of his friends at one point?"

"Yes, Box, who works at the pottery workshop owned by Puk'pik. Box seems like a nice young man; I'm sure he'd be happy to tell you whatever he knows."

"Then I'll go speak to him today." Na'om took a small bite of the pastry on her plate. "Now that we know when we can begin the counterattack, there's much to be done." She stood up and pushed her chair back, a signal to the others that the meeting was over.

Everyone stood, and Nimal, Yakal, Bitol, Kubal Joron, and Matz' quickly left the temple.

"Would you like us to accompany you to the pottery workshops?" Ajkun said as she slipped her arm into the crook of Na'om's elbow.

"No, Ati't, maltiox. I think I need to meet Box on my own."

Ajkun nodded and gave her granddaughter a hug before taking Chiman's hand in hers. "You go on then; we'll send servants to clean up here, won't we, Chiman?"

"Yes, of course," he replied. "I'll have some guards summon them immediately."

Na'om nodded, slipped on her sandals, and motioned to Ek' Balam. "Ready, boy?" she asked. The two hurried down the long corridor and out into the bright sunlight. Na'om looked right and left and noticed the guards had changed.

"Take me to the pottery workshop run by Puk'pik," she commanded.

"At once, my lady," the tallest guard said, and the group set off into the city streets.

Tz'

A bright greenish light appeared from one of the many limestone tunnels at the bottom of the cenote near the Akab Dzib, the large building where the shamans practiced their arts. The light flowed swiftly through the water, illuminating the murky bottom, and hovered over the prone and lifeless body of Tz'. He was still tied at the hands and feet by the pieces of sisal rope that Satal's guards had wrapped tightly around his limbs before pushing him off the edge of the well, and his head had fallen to one side, pressing his cheek into the mud. The light gathered around Tz', encasing him in its embrace, and lifted him from the muddy sand before surging through the water, deeper into the labyrinth of caves and caverns that lay hidden under the city of Chichén Itzá.

Despite its heavy burden, the light swooshed forward until it reached a narrow, rocky shelf that protruded above the waterline. It gently placed Tz' down on his back, and then it pulled into a tall column of green energy that drove itself directly at Tz's chest, slamming into his body with a loud crack that reverberated throughout the tunnel. The impact shook the ledge, sending a shower of small pebbles into the water.

A large spurt of water erupted from Tz's mouth as he bolted half upright, took a deep gulp of air, and crashed back onto the hard, rocky surface. He rolled onto his side, curling into a ball as he coughed and coughed, hacking up more water. His eyes leaked tears from the force of his coughing, and they mingled with the water dripping from his hair. When he was finally able to catch his breath, he noticed the green light hovering just a few inches above the surface of the dark water just in front of him. He sat upright again, hitching on his butt to place his back against the rough wall of the tunnel.

"What are you?" he cried. "What do you want?" He coughed into his tied hands, feeling a steady ache in his entire body. His ribs hurt where he'd been punched in the chest, and his shoulders were sore from landing roughly in the bottom of the cenote. He grimaced and shoved with his feet to raise himself higher against the wall, scraping his bare back against the rough stones.

The hazy green light didn't answer, but began to shift and reform, twisting and bending until individual body parts appeared. A hand, a leg, the torso of a woman, and finally a face.

"*Chuch*, is that you?" Tz' leaned forward, trying to ascertain if the shape in front of him really was his mother or just a figment of his imagination. He shook his head and wondered where he was. *My last thoughts were of Na'om and of how I'd never see her again. And then I died.*

"No, Tz', you're not dead," Chachal replied.

"But how did you find me? I don't understand." Tz' coughed up some more water. "Satal's guards threw me into the cenote, and I stopped breathing."

"I heard your cry for help and fortunately was able to get to you in time." Chachal held up one translucent green hand to stop Tz' from speaking. "But you are stuck in the Underworld, at least for now."

"I still don't understand." Tz' studied his mother's rough, ragged appearance as her image faded in and out. "What happened to you? You don't look. . .." Tz' hesitated, searching for the right word. "Whole."

Chachal sighed. "I've used quite a bit of my energy of late, especially just now to bring you back to life. It'll take time for me to regain my strength, so I need you to listen carefully to what I'm about to say, so I don't have to repeat myself."

"All right."

"Na'om has passed the trials the gods set before her and has returned to the land of the living."

Tz' smiled when he heard Na'om's name. Instantly, he pictured her in his mind and felt his heart fill with love.

Chachal drifted closer to Tz'. "Listen to me, Tz'. Na'om still faces the biggest challenge of her life; she must defeat Satal."

"Then I have to get out of here, so I can be with her and help her," he said.

Chachal shook her head. "It's not that simple. Na'om is the only one who can release you from here, but she must find the strength to destroy Satal before she can rescue you. In the meantime, you have to remain here."

Tz' looked around him, at the deep, dark water that flowed silently by in front of him and the small ledge he sat on, and he knew he would quickly die if he had to remain indefinitely in that spot. "But there must be something I can do to get out on my own! I'm not a little boy without any skills." Tz' stood up, moaning with the pain that penetrated his chest. He peered into the darkness beyond his mother's light, searching for something, anything that would help him reach the surface. But the gloom only revealed dark tunnels and water, and Tz' quickly realized his mother was right; he was trapped below ground.

Chachal's legs began to disappear, and Tz' could see the effort on his mother's face as she pulled herself back together.

"The only place I can think of where you might have a chance of surviving is in the House of the Jaguars. There you'll be surrounded by your distant cousins, the were-jaguars."

At the mention of the were-jaguars, Tz' felt a quick thrill ripple through his body, and he shivered. "You know about them?"

"Of course; you're my son. I know many, many things now, Tz', things I couldn't possibly understand when I was alive."

Tz' hung his head and his wet black hair fell over his eyes. "Then you know I haven't been able to shapeshift into a were-jaguar since that time with Tat axel in the temple." He thought back to the countless hours he had practiced with Najtir in Mayapán and again while locked in Satal's cage. He hadn't shapeshifted at all, so how was he supposed to do it now?

"You'll need assistance to change into your spirit animal, and I've expended too much energy to help you. There is someone you can call on, but the price might be too high."

"Who is it?"

"Camazotz."

At the mention of the bat god's name, Tz' groaned. He was the last creature he wanted to see. "Considering he tried to kill me many moons ago, I'm not sure that's such a good idea."

"It's the only option I can think of for now. Bear in mind, though, that if you want to return to the surface, you have to remember you're not really one of those creatures." Chachal's legs and arms began to dissipate into the deep gloom of the tunnel. "I have to go," she said as her body continued to fade away. Only her face floated in front of Tz'. "Make your decision soon, Tz', before it's too late."

Tz' reached out with his bound hands to touch his mother, but he grasped only air.

Chachal was gone, and he was left sitting in the complete dark. It pressed in on him like a weight, and he opened his eyes wider, searching for the tiniest point of light, but there was only blackness. He couldn't even see his own hand when he held it directly in front of his face. Dizziness swirled through him, and he scrabbled backward on the narrow ledge until his shoulders were firmly against the wall again. *I'm not calling on Camazotz to help me*, Tz' thought. *Surely, I can get out of here on my own.*

Searching with his hands, Tz' found a large, sharp rock by his side that he used to cut the sisal cord between his feet. Then he held the rock between his feet and sawed back and forth on the braided rope tying his hands together until they were free. He sat for hours, listening to the water gurgle by, hoping for a speck of light to appear, but it remained dark. He had no idea if it was day or night. *All right, I can't sit here forever*, Tz' thought. *I must find my way back to the surface.* He slipped into the cool water, easing himself down from the ledge until he could grip the sandy, silty bottom with his toes. He was surprised to feel the water came to his chest. Holding one hand against the wall to his left, he inched forward into the gloom, deeper and deeper into the Underworld. The water pressed against his sore ribs, but he kept moving, determined to locate an exit. For hours, he followed the turns and twists of the tunnel he was in, expecting at any moment to see a speck of light coming from a crack or an opening in the tunnel roof, but it all remained dark.

Suddenly, his fingertips on his left hand touched empty space, and Tz' stopped. He turned to the wall and searched the area with both hands. The wall curved away from him, into another tunnel. He didn't dare leave the passageway he was in, so he faced forward again, took a step and then another. Open space continued on his left side. He inched forward again. On his fifth step, his foot dropped downward, and he plunged over his head into the water. He kicked and swam upward, blowing and spluttering water out of his mouth as he gulped in a breath of air. He paddled forward, searching for the tunnel wall, but found nothing. He turned to his right and again swam ahead, but still had no luck finding his footing or any sense of the tunnel. Panic raced through him as colder water circled around his feet, tugging at his ankles, and Tz' imagined it was some horrid creature trying to pull him to his death. He thrashed and spun in a circle, kicking and swimming back the way he thought he had come. Finally, he felt his feet bump into a ridge of sand, and he hurried to stand up. Water drained off him as he stretched out his arms and found the passageway wall. He hugged the rough surface, grateful to feel something solid in the blackness.

Afraid of falling into the abyss again if he continued forward, Tz' reluctantly placed his right hand against the wall, ready to retrace his steps toward the ledge he had left so long before. As he pushed through the water, the ceiling pressed down from above, catching pieces of his hair, and the water rose higher and higher on his body until it was just below his chin. *I'm not in the same tunnel as before,* he thought, and panic sent a shiver through his body.

"Chuch, are you there? I need your help," Tz' shouted. His voice echoed off the walls, bumping and bouncing over and around until it finally faded away. There was no reply. Tz' felt his chest tighten with fear. *Itzamná, what am I going to do?*

"Call on Camazotz," an unfamiliar woman's voice said.

Tz' swung around in the dark, searching for the person who'd spoken. "Who's there, what do you want?"

"I'm Sachoj, one of your distant relatives," the voice continued. "I'm here to help you."

Tz' peered into the darkness and then jolted backward into the wall behind him when a shrunken head appeared just in front of him. He stared at the wizened face and wisps of long, gray hair floating above the surface of the water.

"Joining the were-jaguars is the only way you'll survive; ask Camazotz for help." Then Sachoj's face disappeared as quickly as it had popped into view.

"Wait, come back," Tz' cried. But there was no answer.

He took four more steps forward and felt the top of the tunnel against his skull. The water brushed at his lips as he took one more step and then another, and he stopped again as the water rushed up his nose. Spluttering and coughing, Tz' put out his hand. Solid rock was in front of him, to his left, and to his right. He twisted his head sideways, took a deep breath of air, then ducked under the surface. He quickly explored the cave wall, but there was no opening in the jagged surface. *A dead end, and I have no idea where to go from here. . . .* He rose to the surface, banging his forehead against the wall as he blew water out through his nose.

Fear tingled through his body, the chill settling deeper into his bones than that created by the cool water. His stomach cramped with hunger, and he whimpered with the pain. He knew he needed to eat and to get someplace warm and dry if he were ever to see Na'om again. Tz' called out to his mother once again, but the only response was his echo as it dissipated into the obscurity.

Shaking with fear, Tz' whispered, "Camazotz?" He counted to twenty in his mind and then whispered again.

Suddenly, he heard a swooshing noise and then smelled the unforgettable stench of must and decay that he remembered from his first encounter with the bat god. He sensed the giant creature was floating mere feet from where he stood, but he couldn't see him.

"Ah, dear boy, I've been waiting and waiting, wondering when you'd called for me," Camazotz said. "You could have been feasting on fresh meat with your cousins in the House of the Jaguars, if only you'd sent for me sooner."

"What do you want in return for helping me?"

"When the timing is right, you'll know the price," Camazotz replied.

"No, I must know now," Tz' said.

"Dear boy, if you don't want my help, I can leave you here." Camazotz fanned his wings, and Tz' coughed as the fetid air reached him.

"No, wait, I can't find my way in the dark."

The bat fluttered his wings again and quickly sank his talons deep into Tz's shoulders.

"*Ahh*, you're hurting me!" Tz' cried. He raised his hands to push the bat, but Camazotz swiftly lifted him into the air. Tz's lower body still hung in the water, and his head was just below the bat's chest. He tried not to breathe.

"This will be over soon," Camazotz said as he beat his wings and flew swiftly down the tunnel.

Tz' had no sense of where they were headed. His feet and legs dragged through the water, and he raised his hands to cover his face and mouth from the spray. Within minutes, Camazotz had dumped Tz' onto a gravel beach. He felt around with his hands and crawled away from the water's edge. It felt good to kneel on solid ground.

"Follow the tunnel in front of you; it will lead you to the were-jaguars' lair." The bat flicked his wings, ready to depart.

"Wait; what tunnel? I still can't see anything," Tz' cried.

"Once you shapeshift, it will all become clear."

Tz' hung his head. "I can't do it," he mumbled.

"Ha, you're the grandson of Satal, the darkest witch in the land, and yet, you can't perform a simple task like shapeshifting." The bat chortled again. Then he took a deep breath and let it out slowly, filling the area with the putrid scent of old blood and rot.

Tz' coughed, and tears welled in his eyes, as much from the rank air around him as from shame at not being good at the task he needed if he was to survive.

"No wonder Satal threw you into the cenote," Camazotz said. "Well, I'll assist you this one last time, but only because I still think there's a hint of potential in you." The bat reached out with his wings and encircled Tz's body, wrapping himself tightly around his chest, legs, and arms. "Imagine you're a were-jaguar," the bat commanded.

Tz' felt a strong tingling run through his limbs and body. He concentrated on becoming a were-jaguar, and almost instantly, his body morphed and flowed, pushing and pulling in multiple directions all at once. Camazotz let go as Tz's legs and arms foreshortened and grew thicker and stronger. The pieces of sisal rope still wrapped around his wrists and ankles broke apart and fell to the ground. Tz' groaned with pain as his forehead flattened and widened, and his jaws grew heavier, filled with two sets of razor-sharp teeth. He lifted one hand and watched with fascinated horror as it finished transforming into a wide paw with a thick claw at the end of each digit. Power and energy surged through his body. Through his yellow jaguar eyes, vague shapes sharpened into focus, first the tunnel, then the water, and finally, he saw Camazotz hovering nearby. Tz' laughed, and the roar echoed throughout the chamber. He heard a distant growl in response.

"They know you're here. Hurry and join them before they eat all the new meat," Camazotz said, then he fluttered his wings and disappeared into the dark tunnel behind him.

The thought of fresh, bloody meat made Tz' salivate, and he bent forward, sniffing the ground. A hundred different smells flooded his nostrils, each distinct scent making him drool even more. He turned his broad head toward the tunnel, where the air brought more tantalizing smells. He padded forward several steps and realized his feet, legs, and shoulders no longer throbbed with pain. He was massive, all sinews, muscles, and bones, a creature of power and freedom. He knew he could rip the throat from a peccary in an instant, and he longed for the chance to do so.

He heard distant growling again, followed by several jaguar roars. *They definitely know I'm here*, Tz' thought, and he exposed his upper fangs in a wide grin as he loped into the tunnel in search of his cousins.

SATAL

Satal sat on a soft mattress stuffed with ceiba fluff with multiple pillows placed against the stucco wall at her back. She had watched for hours out of her one good eye as daylight slowly crept from the closest window opening and across the tiled floor. Even as the sunbeam slid up the wall on the far side of the room, she made no move to get up. Occasionally, she shifted her weight, tugging at the thick, woolen blanket that covered her legs with her right arm, pulling the soft, dark brown fabric closer to her chest and face. Despite the covering, she still felt cold; it was deep in her center, and she knew no blankets would penetrate that chill. At that moment, with no one about, with no one watching her or expecting anything from her, Satal felt old. She felt older than the lush bougainvillea vine that covered the entire wall outside with a rich array of bright pink flowers, older than the tiles and stones that made up the floor beneath her, older, perhaps, than death itself. Death, brought upon those around her, had always generated a tinge of excitement and energy for Satal. She enjoyed watching the life-force bleed slowly from anyone who stood in her way; the sight always brought her pleasure. But now, Satal was still weak and wounded, blind in her left eye, with a left arm that hung useless at her side. She was tired, and she knew she grew more vulnerable with each moment that she allowed these feelings of uselessness and age to last.

Yakal's to blame, for all of it, she thought. *I should have killed him as a child when I had the chance.*

Ha, Sachoj hissed in her ear. *Then he wouldn't have conceived the jaguar girl, the source of power you need if you're to continue to rule the region.*

Satal sighed. She knew her great-grandmother was right. Her spies had told her of the throngs of people who had rallied around Na'om as she'd traveled across the land and of her triumphant return to Mayapán. The fact that she had survived the trials the gods had set before her in the Underworld only proved to Satal how strong Na'om's power really was. It was a strength that Satal ached to possess. With it, she would be unstoppable, able to command vast areas in this world and the Underworld. She would no longer be beholden to Camazotz and the other gods, for her power would rival theirs. She had only to defeat Na'om, and the girl's energy would pass to her. But until she found a way to generate more strength, she had little hope of shapeshifting and engaging with Na'om when she and her army finally advanced on Chichén Itzá.

The citizens of Mayapán *would* attack, of this, she was sure. But her elite group of shamans had yet to reveal *when* they would come marching across the arid lands to the city. Without this knowledge, Satal was unable to formulate any magical methods of defense. Of course, Kämisanel, head of the warriors, was hard at work regrouping his men after the numerous losses they'd incurred at Mayapán. The fletchers, tanners, and stonemasons were busy rebuilding their supplies of bows and arrows, leather armor, and obsidian knives and spearheads, but none of that helped Satal. She needed strength of a different kind, one that came from within, but her reserves were depleted, and she didn't know how to proceed. She had asked the gods for help, but none of them were answering her cries for aid. Hun-Batz, Ah-Pekku, and the others had disappeared as soon as the battle in Mayapán had been lost. Even her old friend, Camazotz, had not answered any of her recent requests for aid. She had guaranteed the gods of war and death a feast and had provided them with only a fraction of that. It was no wonder they were ignoring her.

I warned you about promising them too much, but would you listen? Nooo. . . . Sachoj said.

"Quiet, old woman, I'm trying to think," Satal replied. She looked around the large room when she realized she'd spoken out loud. But she didn't need to fear. After their return to the city, Tewichinel and the other shamans had learned very quickly to leave Satal alone when she was in this kind of mood. She smiled, thinking of how they'd all cowered in front of her after the retreat. Despite her physical wounds, which included her inability to shout because of her damaged vocal cords, she'd conveyed her displeasure to each and every one of them at the outcome of the attack on Mayapán. They'd reacted as she'd anticipated, simpering and whispering to do better the next time around, even though she knew the result of the battle had been as much her fault as theirs. *If Yakal hadn't wounded me with that salt water, we would have taken the city easily.* Satal frowned and allowed her anger to begin to fester inside. *Any* feeling was better than the emptiness she had carried with her since the army had retreated.

And the citizens of Chichén Itzá still fear you, my dear, Sachoj crooned.

This brought another smile to Satal's face, instantly feeding her waning confidence, and she straightened her back a bit against the pillows. *As well they should, since I hold their puny and almost insignificant lives in the palm of my hand. With one snap of my fingers, I could have anyone sacrificed to the gods to help repay the debt I owe to them.* Her temperament lifted even more as she thought about it. *Yes, some bloodletting is well overdue.* She nodded to herself. *I'll order Tewichinel to take some of the prisoners to the pyramid for sacrifice tomorrow.*

Just as she thought of him, Tewichinel appeared in the doorway, carrying a lit candle stuck in a pottery vessel in his hand.

Startled out of her reverie, Satal looked with her one good eye at the old shaman. She suspected he sat just out of sight so he could respond to anything she might need within seconds.

Tewichinel bowed to her. "My lady, is there something you desire?" the man asked.

"Yes, tomorrow we must sacrifice some of the men we captured in Mayapán. The gods need to be paid with blood; perhaps then they'll answer me when I pray to them."

"As you wish, Lady Satal. I shall make the arrangements immediately. Is there anything else you desire?"

Satal looked at the older man. In the candlelight, his body was cast in shadow so his dark brown eyes blended into his deeply lined face. She felt she was looking into a deep pool of liquid brown cacao, and the thought made her hungry for the first time in days. She attempted to smile and grimaced when the newly formed skin on her face pulled tight at the corner of her mouth. "Some food, something soft and sweet, perhaps a bit of hot cacao to wash it down," she whispered. Her throat still throbbed whenever she spoke.

"At once, Lady Satal," Tewichinel said and started to back his way through the doorway.

"Wait, is there any word from the other shamans?" she rasped.

"Nothing, my lady. Rest assured, I will bring you news as soon as they've deciphered the movements of the stars in the sky and know when the counterattack will take place." The man bowed again and left the room.

Satal drummed her fingers on the bedding. She hated waiting, and even more so, hated being dependent on anyone. However, she was grateful for Tewichinel. He was the most loyal of all her shamans and had been the one to tend her wounds over the past few weeks. He'd applied healing ointments and salves to her face and arm, carefully bandaging the blistered skin until it had begun to heal, and he'd been the one to bathe her and help her dress since the attack. Just as Tewichinel had patiently prepared her to die prior to the cenote ceremony so many moons ago, now he assisted her in returning to the living. All the same, Satal was frustrated by her inability to do anything, and she wriggled on the mattress, trying to find a more comfortable position.

Patience, Satal, you must have patience, Sachoj said. *In the meantime, feed your body's needs, all of them. Only when the soul is sated is the mind able to do its best work.*

Satal leaned back on the pillows and closed her eyes, praying once again to Camazotz, Buluc-Chabtan, Tlacolotl, and Yum Cimil for some image or sign that she could use to start building her inner strength again. But there was only darkness and the endless circling of mindless and random thoughts that led her nowhere.

Tewichinel reappeared shortly thereafter carrying a lacquered wooden tray. He knelt and placed it on the mattress next to Satal. Bite-size pieces of mango, pineapple, and custard apple filled a small ceramic bowl. Beside it, a plate held several small, fried corn patties drizzled with honey. Beside them stood a large, dark-green earthenware mug filled with frothy cacao. Satal leaned over and breathed in the steam and scent of the bitter chocolate, and she felt her mouth water. She reached out to lift the heavy cup, then thought better of it.

"Help me," she commanded.

Tewichinel lifted the cup and held it to her lips, tilting it so she could sip the hot liquid slowly. She felt the warmth slide down her throat, coating the soreness that still bothered her. The shaman placed the mug carefully on the tray, then fed her bites of the fruit, one piece at a time, until the bowl was empty. Then he moved on to the corn pastries, and Satal had the nerve to suck his fingers clean of the sticky honey that threatened to drip onto the woolen blanket still tucked around her chest. Satiated, Satal leaned back against the pillows and closed her eyes. She heard Tewichinel shift his feet and prepare to rise.

"Don't go," she ordered. She opened her eyes and pointed to the open space beside her. "Sit here, next to me," she said. She felt a twinge in her belly.

"As you wish, Lady Satal," he replied. Silently, the shaman moved the tray out of the way and sat on the mattress next to Satal. He crossed his arms across his chest and bowed his head.

Satal felt a warmth growing inside her. She enjoyed being able to command this man to do her biding. "Do you find me attractive?" she asked. She waited, but there was no response. She pushed the shaman with her good hand and watched his body rock back and forth.

"My lady, I, I. . . ." he stammered. He cleared his throat. "My lady, I honor and respect you and will willingly give my life for yours if the gods demand it." Tewichinel fell silent.

Satal looked at the shaman's bent figure, at the knobby bones protruding from his back, his sinewy arms that showed his age in the wrinkles evident in the dark skin, and at the small puddle of flesh that formed where he once had a taut stomach. *Ha, why would he think me desirous after taking care of me as if I was an infant?* Satal felt all sense of desire suddenly flee, and she began to laugh.

"Ah, what fools we are, eh, my friend?" she said, and she patted him on the shoulder. "Go on, get up." She poked him in the ribs with her fingertip.

Tewichinel hurried to slide off the mattress and bowed deeply. "Of course, Lady Satal," he said.

"Why are you so good to me?" she asked as she picked at a loose thread on the blanket.

"My family has been honored to serve your house for many, many generations, my lady," the shaman said. "My grandmother was the personal servant to your great-grandmother, Sachoj."

Satal stopped fiddling and looked at Tewichinel. "I had no idea. Tell me more."

"I'm afraid there's little more to tell, my lady. Each generation of my family has worked in some manner for your ancestors, but alas, the work shall stop with me as I have no offspring. I do remember being taken to the cave where your family members have been buried throughout time. I was a very young boy, but the place made a deep impression on me as it was filled with all manner of snakes that slithered among the urns that contain the bones of the deceased."

"Ahh, yes, the snakes Sachoj was so fond of. Someday, I wish to be buried there as well."

"I will do my best to honor your request, Lady Satal, but I fear I shall join my ancestors long before you do. Is there anything else?"

Satal waved her hand, dismissing him. "No, no, go. I need time to think."

Tewichinel bowed, picked up the tray, and hurried from the room.

Satal lay back on the pillows. She had never understood the shaman's devotion, but it all made sense now. But he was right; he was old and prepared to die, while she still had years ahead of her, if she could capture Na'om and seize her young energy. She closed her eyes and tried to imagine a way to defeat Na'om and her army that wouldn't entail direct combat. But her mind remained blank. She blew out the candle and sat in the dark, searching the shadows in the room for any ideas. But nothing came to her.

Satal was in better spirits the next morning when she marched with Tewichinel and two other shamans to the Temple of the Warriors. A small group of citizens had gathered on the parade grounds below the stone building to watch the ritual sacrifice. She looked up the steep flight of stairs and saw the other shamans were already in position near the chac mool at the top. Several young men bound hand and foot with sisal rope lay at the base of the statue. Nearby, pottery braziers sent clouds of smoke into the air that drifted down to where she stood. She breathed in the sharp scent of burning eucalyptus leaves mixed with copal and smiled. She loved the intoxicating elixir. With Tewichinel's help, she ascended the stone steps until she stood alongside the captured warriors.

"Come now, don't look so grim," she chided the man nearest her. "Soon, you'll be among the ancestors, feasting with those who have died before you."

"My lady, I beg you," the man implored. "I have three small children at home. Spare me and I pledge to fight for *you* in the battles to come."

"Ha, you dare to address me? No, no, my boy, your blood has become a valuable commodity, making you worth more dead than alive." She nodded to the four shamans nearby who grabbed the young man by his arms and legs and thrust him onto the stone chac mool. His bare chest lay exposed to the sky, and Satal waved to Tewichinel.

The senior shaman stepped forward, a large black obsidian knife in his hands. He towered over the youth, then plunged the blade deep into the man's chest. He quickly cut a circle through muscle and bones as blood poured onto his feet and the stones of the temple. Then he reached down and yanked out the man's still beating heart. He held it up to the sky, and blood ran down his arms, soaking into the sleeves of his green shirt. The crowd cheered. Then Tewichinel gently placed the organ in a large reed basket. He nodded to his fellow shamans, who removed the corpse and placed another man on the altar for sacrifice.

After the first few deaths, Satal had had enough of the scent of fresh blood and smoke, but she wanted to appease the gods, so she waited impatiently until all nine men had been killed. When the last body was removed from the chac mool, she reached into the basket nearby and carefully placed each heart into the stone platter held between the stone sculpture's hands. "May the lords of Xibalba accept these tokens of my devotion," she said. The crowd yelled and stomped their feet. *And give me some renewed strength*, she thought. *The gods should have plenty to eat now. And after the bodies have been dumped into the underbrush outside the city, the wild jaguars and other nocturnal creatures that lurk everywhere will have their fill as well.*

Wearily, Satal walked with Tewichinel back to her palace where she rinsed the blood from her face, hands, and feet before retiring to her room for the night. She lay on the bed and closed her eyes, hoping for some sign from one of the gods that her sacrifice had been received. After many minutes, she imagined a stream of bitterness flowing through her limbs, moving from her fingertips and toes inward to her center where it pooled in the pit of her stomach. It swirled among the cornmeal and chocolate she'd eaten the day before and mixed with the seed of anger she'd planted earlier. In her mind's eye, she pictured the seed taking root in that rich mixture, a seed that sprouted tiny black leaves, vines, and tendrils that interlaced and twined together, reaching, growing from her core into each extremity, filling her arms, legs, fingers, and toes with gnarled and knotted shoots and sprigs. Flower buds appeared on the thick vines, slowly unfurling into deep-throated blossoms so black they reflected the darkest shades of purple and blue. Satal inhaled deeply, filling her lungs with their pernicious fragrance that hung in the air around her. As she continued to meditate, the blossoms slowly opened wider, exposing long, black filaments and bulbous anthers that suddenly popped open, dispersing a noxious cloud of mustard-yellow pollen.

Startled, Satal opened her eyes, expecting to see herself enveloped in the yellow dust, but she was surrounded by the deep gloom of the room. Through the window opening, she could see the night stars high in the sky. She closed her eyes again and saw the yellow haze still floating inside her. The fog slowly warmed her and began to feed her strength; her notions of feeling ancient and spent quickly dispersed. She smiled and whispered, "Maltiox, Tlacolotl." The god of evil still had faith in her, and she now had a powerful weapon in her arsenal.

AJKUN

Ajkun looked around the hut she and Chiman had moved into for the duration of their stay in Mayapán. She was glad they were no longer sharing a place with Na'om and Ek' Balam, but she wished they had a little more space. One large hammock hung diagonally from one corner to the other, which left little room to move on either side of it.

"Good thing these are so easy to move out of the way," Ajkun said as she slipped one knotted end of the hammock off its hook and moved the whole thing to the opposite side of the room. She turned around and smiled when Chiman slipped his arms around her.

"And easy to move back into place," he said as he unhooked the hammock, "in case we want to go back to bed," he added while he stretched the fabric back into place.

Ajkun laughed. "Not now, my love, I have many things to do this afternoon, or you shall have no supper!"

"Yakal and Uskab have invited us all to eat with them tonight." Chiman looked at the frown on Ajkun's face. "Yakal is trying to correct the errors he made in his youth. You must let go of the past and forgive him, my dear." He held out his arms and Ajkun stepped into them for a hug.

With her face pressed against Chiman's chest, she whispered, "I'll make more of an effort, I promise. Uskab is a lovely girl, Mayibal is a sweet boy, and I'm glad Yakal has found happiness in his life. I just wish he'd been there for Na'om during her childhood; she's struggling to accept him as her father, and so am I." She squeezed Chiman around the waist. "You were always there for her, though, for which I am so grateful."

Chiman gave Ajkun a kiss on the top of her head. "You did a wonderful job raising her. But we must let Yakal be a part of the family too, especially while we're living in this city." Then he smiled and rocked the hammock with his hand. "You're right, this has to wait. I must speak to the shamans and see if they have any other news about the counterattack." He handed the knotted cord back to Ajkun.

"I long for the day when we may go home again. I miss the peace and quiet of Pa nimá. And the children. And the access to all that water; oh, I shall never take water for granted again," Ajkun said. "I long to swim in the river and to take a hot shower with buckets of water, not the small baths we must endure using only the water we can carry in the gourds."

"I miss our home too, my love. I pray that Setesik and Pempen are managing to keep the village in order." He reached out and swept Ajkun up in a big hug. "I especially miss our lovely, solid bed," he whispered, kissing her cheek. "How anyone can make love while hanging in these hammocks is beyond me," he added as Ajkun laughed.

"Come now, we don't do so badly, do we?" Ajkun said. She kissed Chiman back and then stepped away. She brushed her hands off and straightened a stray sprig of hair. "Off you go," she said as she gently pushed Chiman toward the doorway. "I must go stand in line for water while you discuss important matters with the shamans."

Chiman turned around. "You know I would bring you with me to the observatory if I could, but the people here are much stricter about what their women are and aren't allowed to learn. The fact that you can read glyphs have many asking questions. If you were to come with me and speak to the shamans, I'm not sure what might happen."

"But Satal was a woman and was involved in everything," Ajkun stated.

"Yes, and she ruled by fear, which wasn't very productive," Chiman said. "The city council would much rather have had a man in control all these years."

"I think Kubal Joron and Matz' might be all right with my speaking to the shamans, but I can see Bitol and Nimal have a difficult time accepting a woman as their equal."

Chiman leaned in and kissed the top of Ajkun's head. "Not their equal, by any means."

Ajkun looked up. "What does that mean?" she demanded.

"Oh, my love, you are far superior to those men," Chiman said. "They know of war and revenge and bloodletting and sacrifice, yes, but you, you know of the healing properties of plants, of how a woman must give birth, of love and kindness and generosity. Those are far more valuable than anything those men might know." He hugged Ajkun again. "I'll meet you at Yakal's house when the evening star appears in the sky," he said as he left.

Ajkun took a deep breath and let it out. The mention of Yakal always made her tense. She didn't know if she could ever forgive him for abandoning Na'om after Tu'janel's death and leaving the village. *I must let my old feelings go*, she thought as she tidied up their few belongings and set out with the empty water gourds toward the cenote. *Na'om will never embrace Yakal if I don't set an example. And Uskab is a wonderful wife and mother; I must be thankful that Yakal has found a new wife.* But the loss of her daughter sat heavily in Ajkun's heart. No matter how many years had passed, and despite her best efforts to push her grief aside, her passing still hurt. Particularly during the Wayeb when the anniversary of Tu'janel's death arrived. Then she always felt vulnerable to the pain. *I must be especially vigilant this year to not let her death bother me*, Ajkun mused as she approached the cenote. *My focus must be on helping Na'om defeat Satal and nothing else.*

A long line of women encircled the edge of the cenote, waiting for the young boys who tended the buckets to fill their gourds with water. Ajkun noticed that several young women had large earthenware pots with handles that they carried in tandem. It took two of them to lift the jar once it was full, but Ajkun could see that they would then have enough water for several days. *I must talk to Chiman about providing me with one of those*, she thought as the line inched forward. The sun beat down, and sweat glistened on the shoulders and backs of the boys as they threw their buckets into the water several feet below the cenote's edge. Their sinewy arms strained with the effort of pulling on the hemp ropes attached to the full buckets. Water sloshed on the ground as the boys filled gourd after gourd; rivulets of murky water trickled back into the cenote, and

Ajkun was glad she had arrived as early as she had. *Otherwise, we'll be bathing and drinking muddy water.* And once again, she longed for the crystal-clear river that gurgled and burbled past Pa nimá.

When she'd safely delivered her precious water back to the hut, Ajkun went to see Alom. Together, the two women walked to the central plaza where a large awning had been erected to provide shade from the hot sun. Several large baskets filled with reddish salt stood in a row, and beside them were stacks of colorful cotton bags that the women of the city had woven and sewn. They would provide a protective layer of salt for each warrior under his leather vest. Several women were busy filling the bags, which they passed to others who sat in a semicircle and sewed them shut. Alom picked up a stingray needle and some fine thread from a pile and joined the women and girls who were sewing.

Ajkun approached a very pregnant woman who was bent over, filling a bag. "Let me do this," Ajkun said as she took the wooden salt scoop from the woman's hand. "Go and rest before we have to call your midwife."

"Maltiox, Lady Ajkun," the woman replied, and she waddled over to the sewing group and took her place next to the others.

Ajkun looked around, mentally counting the piles of filled bags. *We'll need two for each person*, she surmised, *so we don't have nearly enough. And I must tell Chiman that they should be moved indoors. The last thing we can afford is that they get wet!* She picked up one of the filled bags and noted with dismay how all the salt moved to the bottom, leaving most of the sack empty. "Alom, take a look at this," she said as she held up the cotton. The salt slumped downward.

Alom stood up and took the sack. "We'll have to spread the salt out and then stitch horizontal and vertical lines in the fabric, making pockets that will hold the salt in place." She looked at the piles. "I'll have two of the women help me with this right away," she said as she began to move the filled sacks.

"We might as well add the leather shoulder straps and ties while we're at it," Ajkun said. "Then we'll have each completed vest moved to a safe place indoors."

The hours passed as the women stitched and filled bags. Some ladies and their children left, but others soon arrived to take their places. Each household knew it was vitally important to have enough for everyone to wear.

When the sun was low on the horizon, Ajkun and Alom walked back to their respective houses, with the promise of meeting for dinner at Yakal's house. Ajkun washed up and brushed her hair and was surprised when Chiman appeared. "I thought we were meeting at Yakal's house," she said as she gave him a hug.

"This is for you, my dear," Chiman said as he handed Ajkun a small parcel tied with hemp string.

Ajkun looked at Chiman and smiled. "What, a present? Why?"

"No reason other than to say, 'I love you,'" he replied.

Ajkun untied the string and unfolded the piece of cloth. Inside was a pair of turquoise earrings and a necklace to match. "Oh, Chiman, they're beautiful," Ajkun exclaimed. She quickly put the earrings on and had Chiman help her with the necklace.

"Now you look like a proper lady of Mayapán," Chiman said as he placed a kiss on Ajkun's forehead. "And if I had more cacao beans, I would buy you even more pretty things."

"Maltiox, my love, but I don't need gifts to know that you care for me," Ajkun said. She took Chiman's arm as they reentered the street. "We've made many more vests for the warriors today; you must find a safe place indoors to store them."

"Yes, all right, I think there's room in the Temple of the Warriors," Chiman said. "I'll bring a group with me tomorrow to collect the ones you've finished."

They entered the small street where Yakal lived, and instantly, Ajkun felt her anxiety increase. She swallowed and forced herself to relax. *Focus on the here and now,* she reminded herself. Although she was tired, she was eager to see Mayibal and play for a bit before they sat down to eat. She was very fond of the little boy, and playing with him helped her overcome her dismay at not being in the village with the children she had helped birth. She hoped given time that Na'om would learn to love Mayibal as well. Even though they were separated in age by many years, they were still half sister and brother. *I must set the example and forgive Yakal,* she reminded herself. But she struggled with her mixed emotions the whole evening and was glad when Chiman finally motioned that it was time to leave.

YAKAL

Yakal woke up before the dawn and listened as the older women in the huts nearby began their daily chores of lighting fires, tending children, and making breakfast. His thoughts drifted back to the evening before. *Ajkun was not unfriendly,* he decided, *but she wasn't exactly friendly, either. At least she got Na'om to play with Mayibal for once. Uskab says I must give them all more time to adjust, but I wonder if Na'om or Ajkun will ever forgive me for leaving Pa nimá all those years ago.* He shifted his weight in the large hammock he shared with Uskab and Mayibal and slowly managed to extricate himself from the jumble of arms and legs. As he ran a peccary bristle brush through his shoulder-length black hair, he heard Mayibal begin to cry and mumble in his sleep.

"Shush, little one," Uskab whispered. She pulled up the corner of her cotton shirt and let Mayibal suckle her right breast. She glanced over at Yakal as he put the brush back on the shelf. "He's getting too old for this, but it's the only way to keep him quiet at this hour."

Yakal nodded. "Stay here; I'll light the fire and warm some porridge for him. He needs to eat real food if he's to grow into a strong young man and come help me with my stone sculptures."

Uskab smiled. "Maltiox, Yakal, but I should be preparing the meal for you both, not lying here." She gently pulled her nipple from Mayibal's half-open mouth, dropped her shirt, and stood up. Mayibal whimpered, but Uskab set the hammock rocking, and the boy drifted into a deeper sleep.

She walked over to Yakal and gave him a hug. "He needs a younger brother or sister to take his place at my breast. Then he will grow rapidly into the helper you want him to be." She playfully ran her fingertips down Yakal's bare chest, but he grabbed her hand before it passed his belly button.

He kissed Uskab on the top of the head and stepped away. "You know how I feel about bringing another child into this world while Satal still lives."

Uskab sighed. "Yes, I know, but Mayibal needs a sibling. And life is so uncertain, we should prepare for the future now."

"That's exactly why I don't want to bring another child into the world at this time. None of us knows what will happen when we confront that old witch." Yakal walked back over to Uskab and wrapped her in his arms. "I want to make sure you and Mayibal are safe for all time before I add to our family."

Uskab nodded, but Yakal could see she was still unhappy. "When we've returned from the counterattack, then I promise I'll make you smile, all right?" He patted her playfully on the bottom. "Now, where's that porridge you promised, eh?"

Uskab scurried from the hut and set about lighting the fire while Yakal lingered inside. He looked at Mayibal. The boy had tossed the woolen blanket off his chunky toddler body and thrown his arms wide, claiming the entire hammock for himself. Yakal leaned over and pulled the blanket up to his chin. He felt his heart swell with love as he leaned in closer and placed a little kiss on Mayibal's forehead. "I will do anything for you, little one, even give my life, if necessary, if it means you are safe." He studied his child. He had grown rapidly in the past few months, and Yakal knew Uskab was right; it was time for his son to have a sister or brother. Yakal felt his body flush at the idea of making love to Uskab. *No, we must wait,* he thought. *I can't run the risk of having Uskab with child if something should go wrong during the confrontation with Satal. Only when I know Satal is dead will I allow myself that luxury.*

Yakal took a deep breath and then went outside. The sun had risen above the buildings, the lane in front of the hut was filling with people going about their day, and he had more work to do on rebuilding the city's walls. He took the pottery bowl Uskab offered him and stirred a large dollop of honey into the corn porridge. He ate quickly, barely tasting the food as he watched Uskab prepare a bowl for Mayibal. She wore only her night shift, and he could see the outline of her body through the thin cotton fabric. He sighed. *The sooner we defeat Satal, the quicker life can return to normal.*

He handed Uskab his empty bowl and wiped his mouth with a cloth before turning to kiss her. "I'll be in a meeting with the other builders for some time, so I won't be home for lunch today."

Uskab nodded. "I'm going to take Mayibal over to Ajkun and Alom later this morning. They can fuss over him while I go shop at the market and attend to some things here." Mayibal began to babble inside the hut, and Uskab went indoors.

Yakal followed, and while Uskab took care of his son, Yakal reached into the rafters of the hut and removed a small leather pouch from the palm fronds. He extracted four cacao beans and held them in one hand while he tucked the bag back into the thatching. He handed the beans to Uskab. "Buy yourself something nice to wear at the market today and something for my little one too," he added as he tickled Mayibal's chubby belly. The boy laughed and batted at Yakal's hand.

"Maltiox, my love," Uskab said and kissed Yakal on the cheek. "Say '*matzaqik*' to Tat," she whispered to Mayibal.

"Matzza," Mayibal prattled and laughed again.

"Good-bye, little one, I'll be back later," Yakal replied with a smile. He quickly left the hut and headed to the city walls. He needed to make sure Mayapán was well fortified before they marched on Chichén Itzá so that everyone who stayed behind remained safe while the army was gone.

Na'om

Na'om did her best to ignore all the people who stopped in their tracks to watch her pass by, but there were just too many of them to avoid. She sighed and then reached out one hand to touch the amulets and necklaces held in her way. She brushed them with her fingertips, hoping the act was sufficient to appease all the people who needed something from her.

Once they reached the area where the potters worked, the crowds thinned, and Na'om was grateful for the relative silence when she stepped into the courtyard that housed Puk'pik's pottery workshop. She watched as several young boys with bundles of sticks balanced on their shoulders pushed past her guards and hurried forward to dump the wood in an ever-growing pile near one of the pottery kilns. She heard the *slap, slap, slap* of clay as it was worked, and she turned to see a row of potters sitting at small tables lined against one of the courtyard walls. They were forming and shaping a variety of housewares, including pitchers and plates. Nearby were long wooden tables filled with formed wares ready to go into the kilns for firing. Beyond, she could see another section of tables filled with glazed plates, dishes, and small figurines, waiting to be taken to the market and sold.

In the far corner of the courtyard, under a wooden portico that partially blocked the hot afternoon sun, a middle-aged man with a large belly that hung over his deep green cotton loincloth was in deep discussion with a tall, muscular youth with shoulder-length black hair. As soon as the older man noticed her, he pushed himself up from the stool he was sitting on and hurried over to greet her.

He bowed low to the ground. "Lady Na'om, to what do we owe this great honor today? I am Puk'pik, owner of this workshop. How may we be of service?"

"Ajaw Puk'pik, I'd like to speak to a young man named Box. He was a friend to someone very dear to me," she said. She felt eyes gazing on her and was surprised to see the young man was watching her very closely.

Puk'pik snapped his fingers and beckoned to the youth he'd been talking to. He came over to the group, and Na'om smiled as she looked into his deep brown eyes.

Puk'pik shoved the boy toward Na'om. "This is Box; he'll tell you anything you want to know."

Box bowed deeply and smiled back at Na'om, but he didn't say anything.

"I want to know everything you learned about Tz' while he worked here," she commanded.

"As you wish, Lady Na'om," Box replied, and he bowed again.

Na'om looked around the courtyard and noticed a series of small rooms located off to one side. "Perhaps we can talk in private in one of those areas?"

"Yes, an excellent idea," Puk'pik said while he motioned for the group to follow him to an empty chamber. "I'll send for some refreshments while you two chat." He glowered at Box for the briefest of seconds when the youth settled into one of the two chairs in the room before Na'om had taken her seat. "Please, take all the time you need, my lady," Puk'pik added as he left them.

The guards with Na'om took up stances outside the doorway, Ek' Balam settled on the floor, and Na'om sat down in the remaining leather chair. She sniffed the air, which was filled with the scent of wet clay, and she noticed the lump of clay under a damp cloth on a nearby table. After an uncomfortable stretch of silence, Na'om asked, "What do the potters do in here?"

"Our artisans meet with clients to have their likenesses sculpted onto these clay figurines," Boz said as he removed the towel and showed Na'om the basic sculpture underneath. "Once the basic figurine's shape has been transformed to mimic the purchaser, they bury the likeness alongside their loved ones so they are joined forever in the Underworld." Box returned the damp towel. "Actually, your friend made a sculpture of you, but you're even more beautiful in person, Lady Na'om."

"What do you mean?"

"Tz' made a pottery statue of you, but it didn't capture the true beauty of your face, my lady. I meant no disrespect."

Na'om felt her face flush, and she had to look away for a second. Growing up, she'd received a few compliments from Ajkun and Chiman for work well done, but she'd never been noticed by a boy before. Even Tz' had never said she was pretty. She looked at Box and studied his angular face. Tiny lines framed his eyes, and she wondered if that was from laughing, squinting at the sun, or if he was really older than he appeared. He had black obsidian ear plugs in both earlobes and a small tattoo of what looked like a bird on his upper chest. She leaned forward for a closer look, but stopped when Box laughed.

"I'm sorry, that was rude of me," Na'om said. She sat up straight in the leather chair and looked away.

"It's all right, I don't mind. People are always trying to figure out what the design is," Box said. "It's supposed to be a bird, but I made the mistake of letting the tattoo artist drink balché while he was working on me, so it didn't come out the way it should have."

Na'om laughed. And then fell silent. It had been a long time since she'd enjoyed anything, and she instantly felt guilty for it. She shifted on the uncomfortable stool and finally blurted out, "Tell me what you know about Tz'."

Box nodded and looked straight into Na'om's eyes. "I met him in one of the shops we sell pottery censors to; he had just purchased an old book and was looking for a jaguar censor, but the ones I had just delivered were already sold, so I told him to follow me here so he could order one. Old Puk'pik thought he had come to apply for a job as a general laborer and wanted to hire him. Tz' accepted the position as soon as he heard there was an opening. I think he was glad to have something to do that would fill his days. He was a good worker, and we often went for a drink after work at the Silowik Tukan."

Na'om frowned at the name.

"It's a local bar, my lady, where a good friend works. Tz' and I went there after work to relax and chat. Often, he didn't say much at all, but once he'd had a glass of balché, he'd spend time talking about the village he'd grown up in and of the girl he had been going to marry. He was so unhappy and unsure of his future, though, once he knew you'd fallen into the cenote." Box looked past Na'om toward the doorway to the room.

"I was sad to see him leave, but he said he needed to return to his village and work with his father. So, I was even more surprised to see him back here only a few moons later. He was convinced you were alive, but trapped in the Underworld. Nil, he's my friend at the Silowik Tukan, suggested Tz' find a shaman to help him." Box sighed and shifted his weight on the stool he was sitting on. "We . . . I didn't see much of him after that. He was too busy working with the old man he found." Box picked up a dry lump of clay from the table and crumbled it between his fingers, letting the dust drift to the floor. "He was convinced he could save you from the Underworld if he learned how to shapeshift into some other creature. I didn't really know what to say once he started trying that. So, I kept away for a bit, and then the attack came on the city. I went to find Tz', to see if he was all right, and that's when I learned he'd left before the attack even started." Box dusted his hands together and then placed them on his thighs. He looked back at Na'om. "I know that he loves you, yet he went to study the dark arts with one of the worst people I've ever heard of. Even though Satal is his grandmother, she's created too much misery in the world for one person. Frankly, I can't wait until she's joined her ancestors!"

Na'om smiled at Box. Even though she'd just met him, she liked him. He was honest, fearless, and earnest, not to mention good-looking. "Maltiox, Box, for telling me all this. I had no idea Tz' was so wrapped up in the idea of learning to shapeshift." She looked down at the jaguar spots embedded into her skin, a relic of her time underground. "I hope he fares better than I did. We know he went to Chichén Itzá to train with Satal; what we don't know is what happened to him after he arrived in that city."

Box leaned forward on the stool and placed his hands on the table in between them. "If he went to study with Satal, would she have accepted him as her grandson and agreed to train him, or would she have locked him up? If he went there with any idea of helping you, then I suspect she's put him in bonds." He reached out a fingertip and lightly touched a spot on Na'om's hand. "I can't imagine him wanting to do anything except what would bring him closer to you, my lady."

His touch sent a shiver of energy through Na'om, and she quickly withdrew her hand from his reach. She looked down at the area where his finger had gently brushed her hand and was surprised to see a bright blue spot on her skin. She vigorously rubbed at it with her other hand and watched as the energy dissipated into the air.

"I'm sorry," Box said as he sat back on his stool. "I meant no disrespect in touching you." He dropped his head down and scuffed his worn sandals on the floor.

"No, no, it's fine," Na'om said. "It's just. . . ." she didn't know how to explain what had just happened. So, she waved her hand over her jaguar spots. "I'm sensitive to any kind of physical contact now, thanks to all of this, and am not used to anyone really touching me." She blushed again as she heard the lie for what it was and suddenly reached forward and grabbed one of Box's hands. "I don't mind you touching me, really I don't." Just as quickly as she'd clutched his hand, she let it go. Suddenly, she didn't know what to say or do.

"Did it hurt?" Box asked. He pointed to the marks on Na'om's skin.

"No, it happened while I was in the Underworld. Once I reemerged on the beach and washed off all the dirt and grime, the design appeared. I don't know when it happened or why, but I guess I'm stuck with looking like this from now on."

"I like it," Box said, "it's far better than any tattoo."

Na'om blushed again. Fortunately, at that moment, Puk'pik reappeared with a tray. On it was a plate full of small cookies and two mugs of fresh lemon water. The older man bowed as he placed the tray on the table between them. "My lady, some refreshments for you." He nodded at Box. "Have you told Lady Na'om everything she needs to know?"

Box stumbled to his feet and nodded. "Yes, Ajaw, I'd best be getting back to work." He hurried to the door and left the room before Na'om could say good-bye.

Puk'pik sank down onto the stool Box had vacated. He motioned toward the plate and handed one of the mugs to Na'om before taking the second one. "To your continued success, my lady," he said as he drank some of the flavored water. He picked up a cookie and took a big bite.

Na'om nodded, placed her mug back on the tray without drinking anything, and stood up. "Maltiox, Ajaw Puk'pik. I must be going now."

Puk'pik struggled up from the stool, almost knocking it over in his haste to stand. He bowed, and a few pastry crumbs fell to the floor.

"If I need to speak to Box again, will that be all right?"

"Yes, yes of course, my lady, anything you need, if we can help in any way, feel free to ask or come by any time."

"Maltiox, I'll remember that." Na'om nodded and walked through the doorway. Her guards straightened up from leaning against the wall and fell into place around her as she prepared to leave the courtyard. She swept her eyes around the area, searching for Box, but she was disappointed to see the young man had disappeared. She looked down at her hand and could still feel the tingling residue of where he'd touched her, and despite herself, she smiled.

Tz'

Within minutes of leaving the underground river, Tz' noticed a stench in the air. He stopped to inhale deeply, sucking in the potent smell with his wide nostrils, and he grinned. Musk, urine, rot, and underneath all that, meat, something he craved with an intensity he had never known before. He hurried forward, his large paws leaving tracks in the dry dirt, and he paused when he rounded a slight corner in the tunnel. In the gloom, he could see hundreds of old bones lying on the ground, their ends gnawed and chewed by the were-jaguars. Rib cages, leg bones, and animal skulls of all shapes and sizes lay heaped together in a vast jumble, blanketing the tunnel floor as far as he could see.

Tz' climbed nimbly over the rickety layer of bones, feeling them crunch underneath his thick, padded paws. As he moved deeper and deeper into the passageway, the air grew more fetid, and the scent of decaying meat made Tz's stomach cramp with hunger. He stopped to tear at some small bits of dried tendon on the leg bone of a deer. The tiny bites only amplified his hunger, though, and he pawed at the pile of bones in front of him, hoping to discover another that might give him more sustenance.

Deep growls forced Tz' to lift his heavy head, and he saw multiple pairs of reddish-orange eyes peering at him in the darkness. He crouched low to the ground and swished his thick tail a few times, but quickly stopped when the growls intensified. Jagged edges of old carcasses pressed into his belly, and he tensed his muscles in case any of the were-jaguars attacked. The pairs of eyes drew closer, and Tz' could see that the twenty or so animals in front of him were even bigger than he had imagined. They were far larger than a normal jaguar, with long, razor-sharp fangs protruding past their upper and lower lips. He quickly assessed that even the smallest of them was superior in strength and body to the animal he had shapeshifted into, so he forced himself still lower to the ground, quickly showing obedience to one and all around him. Within minutes, the snarling stopped, and he felt many of the were-jaguars sniff him from head to tail. A few of the cats even began to purr. He slowly stood upright, sniffing around the tails of those that would let him. Several of the larger animals quickly lost interest in Tz' and receded deeper into the tunnel, but the largest were-jaguar swatted at his head with its huge paw, scratching him along his left cheek. He whimpered from the sudden pain and arched his back, but immediately backed down when the giant cat hissed at him. Tz' dropped his head, but he refused to let the old male fully intimidate him. He looked from the corner of his eye at the ancient were-jaguar. Covered in scars, his fur scruffy and ragged, the jaguar hissed and spit on the ground, then spun around and lifted its tail, spraying Tz' with a noxious stream of putrid-smelling urine. Tz' howled as it hit his face, and he swiped at his eyes with his paws, trying in vain to quell the sudden pain. Blinded, he swatted at the air around him and stopped only when he felt the rasp of a thick tongue lick the side of his face. Another wet tongue licked the other side of his face, and a soft purring filled the air around him. Tz' lay down, letting the females clean him from head to tail. When he finally could, he opened his eyes and saw that the four smaller were-jaguars had surrounded him on all sides and were ready to gently herd him back the way they had come.

When they reached the center of a larger cave filled with many more piles of bones, Tz' could see the males in the pack lying around in groups of two or three. Several of them raised their heads and hissed at Tz', and the leader growled as Tz' approached. He stopped in his tracks, as he didn't want to get sprayed again, but the females motioned him forward toward a large, half-eaten deer in the middle of the cave. Tz' sidled over to the carcass, and after casting one more glance toward the groups of males, he ripped and tore at the bloody meat. He managed to break off a hind leg and dragged it to a more private spot where he lay down, the leg between his front paws, and happily gnawed on the bones until he felt satiated. Pushing the remaining meat to one side for later, Tz' cleaned his face with his tongue and paws, then lay back down, where he quickly fell into a deep sleep.

He woke hours later to feel two of the females sprawled out next to him, flanking him on either side. He liked the heat their bodies gave off and moved closer to the jaguar on his right, nuzzling her with his nose before drifting back to sleep.

The next time he woke up, the cave was empty of were-jaguars, including the two females. He stood and stretched, chewed some more on the deer leg, and then paced around the cave with his nose to the dirt, trying to discern where the pack had gone. It was difficult to pick up the scents they had left among the many piles of rotting meat, but he eventually found one trail that led away from the cave. Nose to the ground, he followed the smells for several hundred paces before pausing. He lifted his head, looked back the way he had come, and realized he could barely see the cave of bones. Then suddenly, he caught a whiff of something that instantly made him salivate and he rushed forward, sniffing the air, following the elusive scent. He raced around each bend and curve in the tunnel, hunting for the source that brought tantalizing thoughts to his mind while droplets of saliva filled his mouth. He went farther and farther away from the House of Jaguars, following one passageway and then another, until he had no idea where he was. He sat down to think, but the smell was too strong; he had to find it. He turned another corner in the tunnel and in the distance, he could barely see an eerie green glow that flickered and wavered in the air. Tz' padded forward, sniffing and growling as the scent grew even more intense, and he entered a large cave. Several skeletal figures stood around a strange green fire. Bits and pieces of fabric hung off their old, browned bones, and each skeleton was holding a stick to the flames. Tz' growled. Skewered onto the end of each piece of wood was a human heart. Droplets of blood and fat splattered into the fire, giving off the luscious smells that threatened to drive Tz' mad. He growled again and stepped forward. One of the skeletons turned at the noise and almost dropped his stick.

"Hun-Kamé, Hun-Kamé," the skeleton shouted. "Look who's here!" He waved his stick excitedly, and the roasted heart bounced and jiggled about.

"Shush, Vucub-Kamé, we know who it is," Hun-Kamé said. The elderly skeleton turned to stare at Tz' with his bulging eyes. He wore an ancient headdress made of tattered and dusty feathers on his skull. "Come, join us in our feast." He held out his half-cooked human heart to Tz'.

It was the invitation Tz' had been waiting for; he pounced, knocking the heart to the ground. Blood splattered onto his muzzle and paws as he ripped into the chewy meat, tearing it into bite-sized pieces that he swallowed whole. He looked at the other hearts with longing, but none of the other skeletons offered him any.

"Well, that didn't take long," Hun-Kamé laughed. "Now that you've feasted, we should discuss what you owe me. I'll speak and you'll answer me with your thoughts."

Tz' nodded. He suddenly didn't feel so well, and he almost emptied his stomach on the spot, but he gagged a few times and managed to keep the food down.

"Now that you've partaken of the feast Lady Satal provided for us, I believe it's within my right to demand that you stay here with us."

What? NO, that's not possible! I've made a terrible mistake. I have to return to the surface and resume my life as a human. But even as Tz' thought this, he could feel the effect eating the god's food was having on him. The memories of his life above the surface were slipping away, and the more he tried to grasp them, the quicker they disappeared. He struggled to retain some sense of his humanness but knew he needed help. He crouched low at the bony feet of Hun-Kamé. *Please, my lord, I beg you, I made a serious mistake.*

"You're a quick learner, at times," Hun-Kamé said. He chuckled, and the rib bones in his body jiggled up and down. "I'm feeling generous right now, thanks to this wonderful food. What if in exchange for staying here in the Underworld, I make you the leader of the were-jaguars? Then you'd have all the power you crave, any female you wanted, and all the meat you could eat, as the other males would have to pay you tribute. Bajbik is old and feeble; it's time the blood lines were renewed with younger, more vital energy."

Tz' tried to word his thoughts carefully. *My lord, you honor me with this idea, but my life and heart belong to . . .* Tz' suddenly realized he couldn't remember the girl's name and the more he struggled to say it, the further it receded into the back of his mind.

"If you can't recall this girl's name, she can't be too important," Vucub-Kamé cackled.

"Shush, Vucub-Kamé, let's give him time to respond," Hun-Kamé said. He nodded to the other skeletons around the fire, and they scuttled from the cave, their bones clicking and clacking as they walked. They took their blackened hearts with them. "Come, sit by the fire and look into its flames; perhaps that will evoke a memory or two," Hun-Kamé said.

Tz' padded forward and sat down on his haunches. He expected to feel heat emanating from the fire, but there was only a cool breeze as the flames flickered and danced. He stared into the green light, but the longer he looked, the less he remembered about anything before his time as a were-jaguar.

"He can't think of her name; he can't remember," Vucub-Kamé laughed. "It's Na'om, you fool," he whispered.

"Quiet!" Hun-Kamé said as he instantly smacked Vucub-Kamé in the ribs.

"Ow, oh, that hurt," Vucub-Kamé yelped as two bones detached from his sternum. He thrust them back together and sidled away from Hun-Kamé and Tz'.

Tz' shut his eyes against the glare. He knew he had had a life before becoming a were-jaguar, he must have. He had been a man and in love with someone, but who she was or where they had lived, he couldn't recall. The details were so hazy, and the more he tried to connect to them, the quicker they receded. He sighed; his memories were too far away to catch. Then he thought of how the other were-jaguars looked at him, at the way they'd been treating him. If he were the leader of the pack, they would have to obey *his* commands. A rush of power flowed through him, and he felt his muscles swell and his bones grow larger. He knew he would be a great leader. He opened his eyes and looked at Hun-Kamé. *You have a deal.*

"An excellent decision," Hun-Kamé said. He reached over, grabbed the heart from Vucub-Kamé, and tossed it to Tz' who caught it easily in his mouth.

"Aye, that was mine," Vucub-Kamé said, but he quickly shut his jaws when he saw Hun-Kamé make a fist.

"Return to your lair and call upon me if you should need assistance," Hun-Kamé said. He nodded to Vucub-Kamé, and together they left the cave, disappearing into one of the many tunnels that connected the cave to the labyrinth of passageways that comprised the Underworld.

Tz' lay down with the heart between his paws and took his time eating it. He had never tasted anything quite so rich in his life, and he fell asleep as soon as he was done.

The strange green fire was out when he finally awoke. The darkness pressed in on him, blacker than a moonless night, and he wasn't sure where he had entered the cave. He spent many minutes sniffing the dirt until he caught a whiff of his own fetid footsteps. Nose to the ground, he loped through the passageways, twisting and turning as the limestone walls pressed in on him, but he came to a sudden halt when he saw an odd green glow in front of him. *I know I didn't run in a circle,* he thought. He growled and advanced toward the light, which gradually took the form of a human.

"Oh, Tz', what have you done?" the woman cried. "I warned you to remember who you really are." She reached out to touch him on the head and he growled and backed away.

Let me be, he cried as he sidled around the apparition. He didn't recognize the woman and wondered how she knew his name.

"You've been tricked by the gods and forgotten yourself already," the woman lamented.

Tz' peered again at the hazy light, but he didn't acknowledge her. A slight breeze brought the smell of the were-jaguars' lair into the tunnel and he ran and ran until he was back in the cave. There was still no sign of the others.

He paced among the bones, his tail swishing from side to side. *I should know who that woman was,* he thought as he scrambled over another jumble of ribs and leg bones. *But I just can't remember.* He reached the end of the cave, turned around, and wandered back to the center, but he felt exposed and vulnerable out in the open. He headed to the nearest cave wall, scratched out a secluded spot among the bones, and settled down to wait. Placing his big head on his front paws, he allowed his eyes to close, but he didn't sleep. He kept his ears tuned for the slightest noise, and time passed, although Tz' didn't know how long. Finally, he heard the were-jaguars return. Opening his eyes, he watched as the males dragged in carcasses and body parts, which they dumped on the ground. The whole pack lay down and began to feed, and Tz' warily approached the group. The old male hissed at him and struck out with one large paw, which grazed Tz' across his side. He winced and backed up, then approached again from a different angle, slinking forward until he could wiggle his way in between a young male and a female who had one side of a rib cage ripped open. He lapped at the blood dribbling from the opening and then yanked on some of the bones with his powerful jaws. He ate the stringy meat in three bites, then moved away to wash and groom.

He lay down, his head propped up by a peccary skull, and watched as the other animals settled into small groups. One female and male slunk away into the darkness. Their growls and roars echoed in the enclosed space and brought a flush of heat to Tz's body. He felt the urge to mate deep inside and got up to nudge one of the young females lying nearby. He wanted nothing more than to release the tension he felt throughout his body, and the only way to do that was to become one with the female. Without a glance behind, the female started toward the entrance to a narrow tunnel, with Tz' close on her heels, but he stopped when one of the males blocked his way. The were-jaguar arched his back and bared his teeth. Spittle oozed from between his fangs, dripping into the packed dirt under his feet.

Tz' instantly felt the hackles on his back rise, and he growled back. The young male stood up, his tail swishing from side to side, and Tz' arched his back and spit in the cat's direction. The were-jaguar growled, then without warning, he jumped, crossing the distance to Tz' in one leap.

Tz' felt the were-jaguar's claws clamp into his neck and he twisted and turned, trying to get the cat off him. The two tumbled and rolled about, crashing and crunching over the old bones underneath as they spit and hissed, scratching and clawing, first one on top and then the other. They collided into the wall of the cave, and Tz' planted his hind feet against the solid limestone, pushed, and managed to flip the other were-jaguar onto his back. He quickly stepped onto the other cat's chest with one of his front paws while straddling the were-jaguar's belly with his own body. He hissed into the male's face and the other cat spit back, hitting Tz' in the cheek. Tz' growled and slashed with his free paw, striking the cat across the face, leaving a trail of bloody claw marks from the cat's ear to his chin. The were-jaguar whimpered and Tz' felt the fight go out of his body, so he let go. The cat rolled onto his belly and slunk away without another glance toward Tz'. Suddenly, Tz' realized the entire pack had been watching the skirmish, so he arched his shoulders and proudly walked to his spot in the cave. He urinated around the whole area to mark it as his own and then wedged himself between a pile of old ribcages and the limestone rocks behind him.

He closed his eyes, striving to shut out his immediate needs and wants of food, mating, and companionship. Eventually, he slept. In his dreams, he wandered the paths outside a village, following the tantalizing smell of something or someone. With his nose pressed to the ground, he discovered the scent was everywhere. He knew if he could locate the source, it would help him remember so many things, but no matter how fast he moved or how far he went, he was never able to catch the source creating such an alluring aroma.

SATAL

Satal was already awake and waiting when Tewichinel arrived to help her bathe and dress. She extended her good arm, and he half-lifted her off the mattress, then helped her down the hallway to the small bathing room where she removed the cotton shift she'd been wearing for the past two days. She tossed the garment into a corner before sitting down on a large earthen pot to empty her bladder. When she was done, the shaman entered the room with a large turtle shell full of warm water, which he carefully placed on the floor. He left and returned with a ceramic container of jasmine-scented soap and a pile of clean cotton towels. He dipped a rag into the warm water, wrung it out, then applied a small amount of soap to the cloth, before proceeding to scrub Satal's back. She quickly took the cloth away from him, though, as she was determined to regain her strength and dignity as soon as possible. "I'll finish," she said. "Bring me clean clothes and undergarments."

"Right away, my lady," Tewichinel said while he backed out of the room.

Once clean, Satal felt refreshed and invigorated, as if she'd shaken off a serious illness. She momentarily closed her eyes and imagined the yellow cloud still inside her body. The haze was thicker than the night before, and she felt the pressure of it pushing against her skin from the inside, filling her, plumping her stringy limbs with renewed vigor and vitality.

When Tewichinel returned, she allowed him to help her dress, then handed the shaman a brush for her long, graying hair. Each stroke against her scalp sent a tingling sensation down Satal's spine, and she laughed.

"My lady, is everything all right?" the shaman asked. He put the brush down.

"Never better, my friend, never better," Satal replied.

The old shaman walked with Satal to the main room of her palace and helped her to sit at the large round table where a breakfast tray awaited her.

Just as Satal was finishing the last crumbs of a deer meat tamale, there was a knock on the wooden front door. Tewichinel hurried to open it. Two of his brother shamans, Koyopa and Ixtzol, stood on the tiled floor outside the door. Koyopa carried a scroll in his right hand.

"Come in, come in," Satal motioned to the two shamans. "What news do you bring?"

The two men bowed deeply and edged into the room, keeping their heads down as they approached Satal at the table. Their sandaled feet shuffled across the tiles, creating the only noise in the large room.

Koyopa bowed even deeper, bending at the waist so his shoulder-length black hair grazed the floor. "My lady, the shamans have determined the time of the counterattack," he said, and he offered Satal the scroll.

She quickly pushed her plate out of the way and stood up to unroll the parchment. She held one corner down with her hand, then grabbed the plate and placed it on the edge of the scroll to prevent it from rolling up on her. Quick ink sketches showed a young woman standing near the main pyramid of the city, surrounded by hundreds of snakes, centipedes, scorpions, and monkeys. A pack of were-jaguars stood behind these creatures, and beyond them was a solid wall of soldiers armed with spears, obsidian knives, and bows and arrows.

Satal laughed. "It appears our enemy, Na'om, will be severely outnumbered."

Ixtzol moved forward and bowed deeply. "My lady, the best news is still to come. Our brother shamans have determined their attack will come during the Wayeb. With the portal to the Underworld wide open, and your supreme abilities to entice the gods to rejoin our cause, our enemies will have no chance at survival."

Satal felt her heart leap at this unexpected news. She would be at her most powerful during the Wayeb and her enemies at their lowest ebb. It was almost too good to be true. She turned and smiled at the three men in front of her. "We have a little over two moons to prepare, and much must be done in that time. Tell Kämisanel to increase production in all areas, and any person who refuses to work shall be sacrificed at once."

The men nodded, bowed, and left the room with Tewichinel behind them. Satal felt a thrumming inside her as the poisonous yellow cloud she'd created billowed and swelled in her body. She hummed a little tune as she turned to look at the scroll again. Then she leaned in to focus on the drawings of the were-jaguars. It had been a long time since she'd interacted with these creatures. She frowned, trying to recall the name of the leader of the pack. "Sachoj, are you there? What is that creature's name?"

Bajbik, her great-grandmother replied. *But he is old, and another is ready to take his place.*

Satal looked up from the drawings, turning her head as if she might see her great-grandmother, despite knowing her shrunken head was at the bottom of the cenote in Mayapán.

"What do you mean? You know I hate riddles, old woman!"

The boy is with them, she hissed.

"But he should be at the bottom of the cenote where I threw him," Satal said. *I might have been rash to do that,* she mused. *He was my grandson, after all.*

Never fear, your daughter Chachal managed to rescue the boy from drowning.

"Ha, now that is a bit of good news," Satal interrupted.

Oh, it gets better. Chachal instructed the boy to ask Camazotz for help in shapeshifting into a were-jaguar.

"Excellent," Satal said smiling. "My daughter's being more useful in death than she ever was in life."

Oh, but there is still more to tell, Sachoj cackled. *He found his way to the sacred council fire and has been fed sacrificial foods by Hun-Kamé himself!*

"In all my days, I could never have planned something so wonderful," Satal cried. "Now he won't be able to return to his human form without help from someone extremely powerful. The only one with that much strength is Na'om, and I'll make sure she never goes near him."

Hun-Kamé suggested the boy become leader of the pack, an idea he readily accepted. And he's shown an interest in one of the females, a desire

I recommend you foster as quickly as possible.

At this news, Satal danced a few steps in place while holding onto the leather-topped table with her good hand. "Excellent. I'll make sure this female were-jaguar uses all of her abilities to entice him by performing some magic today."

She snapped her fingers, and within minutes, Tewichinel reappeared. "Bring me my bag of dried mushrooms and my pipe," she ordered. The shaman turned without a word and left the room.

Satal made herself comfortable in one of the many leather chairs and waited impatiently for Tewichinel to return. *Sachoj, how long has this female been a were-jaguar?* she thought.

Not too long; she hasn't forgotten some of her human ways, including the ability to speak and think as a woman, Sachoj replied.

Good.

Tewichinel entered the room carrying an old canvas bag, Satal's carved jadeite pipe, a lit candle, and a piece of straw. He set the items on the table next to Satal, then proceeded to pack the bowl of the pipe with dried mushrooms. "Shall I stay and help you, my lady?" he asked as he handed the pipe to Satal. He lit the piece of straw and held the burning flame to the bowl as Satal sucked on the stem of the pipe.

"No, I'll be fine, maltiox. Go now and get some rest and return in a few hours' time."

"As you wish, my lady," Tewichinel said. He bowed and silently left the room.

Satal drew in a few more deep breaths of the mushroom's potent smoke before placing the pipe back on the table. She leaned back in her chair, closed her eyes and imagined the entrance to Xibalba and the many tunnels that spread throughout the land. Within minutes, she had found her way to the lair of the were-jaguars. Her spirit hovered high above the creatures, and she searched them one by one, until she found Tz'. He was asleep, curled up among a rubble of bones, several paces from where the rest of the pack lounged about. Satal then turned back to the pack and studied the females until she found the youngest one. She concentrated her energy on the were-jaguar and slipped with ease into the animal's mind. *Xojol,* she commanded, *you'll go and speak to the new were-jaguar, become his friend, and teach him how to hunt and kill. You'll encourage him to test his strength against the other males, reminding him he should be the leader of the pack. And when the time comes and I summon you all, you'll be by his side as we face our enemies.*

Xojol nodded her big head and bared her fangs in an attempt to smile. *As you command, my lady.*

Satal popped back out of Xojol's mind and hovered once again near the ceiling of the cave. She watched as Xojol stood up and stretched, then went over to Tz', nuzzled him in the paw, then sprawled on the bare ground next to him.

Satal grinned and quickly returned her spirit to her own body. She felt the stiffness of the leather against her back and the solidness of the tiles under her feet before she opened her eyes again. *When Na'om finds out Tz' has completely turned against her, it'll be easy to capture her and drain her of her powers.* Satal chortled. She couldn't wait until the Wayeb arrived.

Tz'

Tz' shuffled through the piles of bones closest to him, looking for something he could sink his fangs into, but all he found were some dried pieces of gristle stuck to the end of one hip bone. *Where is there some meat?* he thought. The memory of the hearts he'd eaten came to mind, and he drooled as he envisioned eating another one. Then his empty stomach cramped, and he angrily pushed aside a rickety tower of gnawed remains. The pile fell over with a crash, and the noise echoed through the underground chamber. The male were-jaguars stopped their grooming and feeding and turned as a group to stare with their reddish-orange eyes at Tz'. A low growl began deep in the chest of the largest were-jaguar, and he rose, towering over the others. With the hair on his back on end, and his tail bushed out to twice its normal size, he slowly advanced on Tz'.

Come on, let's do this. Tz' braced his body, preparing for a fight.

The old were-jaguar stalked onward, a deep growl emanating from his throat. Saliva pooled in the corners of his mouth and dribbled down his chin, and he flicked his head, sending droplets of spit into the air. He bared his fangs and hissed at Tz'.

Tz' tensed his leg muscles, ready to spring forward and grabble with the old jaguar, when suddenly, the youngest female bounced up directly in the path of the old male cat, blocking his way to Tz'. She rubbed along the elder were-jaguar's flank, offering him her tail to sniff, before darting into the darkness. The male snarled at Tz', exposing his brownish yellow fangs, and Tz' sucked in a deep breath before crouching lower to the ground. He shivered from head to tail, ready to wrestle and roll with the pack leader when he attacked. The were-jaguar leaned forward and growled, baring all his teeth, and a wave of rancid air hit Tz' in the face. He backed away while the old male turned and loped after the female. Tz' went to his spot near the cave wall and lay down with a sigh. He knew he was destined to be the leader, yet he continued to hesitate and didn't push his position as head of the pack. *What's wrong with me? Why don't I just demand that the others respect me?* Confused, he allowed himself to sleep.

When he woke again, he had no sense of low long he'd been out, only that he was ravenous. With caution, he slunk to the center of the cave where the were-jaguars were lounging and dozing singly and together, as they had been before his sleep. He looked around for the fresh kills the male were-jaguars had brought into the cave and was surprised to see only a few bits and pieces of half-rotten meat still remaining on some bones. He tore at a tendon, swallowing it quickly before any of the were-jaguars attacked, but none made a move toward him. He lay down and gnawed at the remaining meat, then crushed the bones to lap at the marrow inside. He was only partially full, but there was nothing left in the immediate area to eat. He sat on his haunches, licked his front right paw, and swiped at his face, brushing up along his muzzle and behind his ear. But before he could continue, he heard soft purring and turned his head to the sound, pausing in mid-swipe to watch as the youngest female stood and stretched, then walked quickly to another pile of bones where she pawed at a ribcage, revealing some ribs still covered in flesh. She motioned with her head for Tz' to join her in the hidden feast, and he gladly went and ate his fill.

As he sat and groomed again, he wondered how the were-jaguars had eaten so much food in such a short time. *Perhaps they have larger appetites than I do.*

No, you were asleep for many, many days.

Tz' twisted his head to look at her. *I can hear your thoughts!*

Yes, and some of us can hear yours, so you must be careful. The female looked around the cave at the numerous cats dozing. *They didn't want to let you stay, but I convinced them that it would be good to introduce new blood into the pack.* She dropped her head and lowered her voice. *I wanted you to stay.*

Maltiox. Tz' moved a little closer to the female. *My name's Tz'.*

I call myself Xojol. She glanced over at the other were-jaguars. *The leader's name is Bajbik; he's the only one whose name you need to know. He is the one you must challenge in order to be the leader.*

How did you know that's what I wanted? Tz' looked at the young female with even more interest.

I've seen how the others treat you, and I know you'd make a better ruler than the old one. Xojol sidled up to Tz' and pressed her flank against his. *Lie here with me, and I'll tell you all you need to know in order to defeat that smelly old cat!* She licked his cheek with her raspy tongue.

Tz' felt hot blood course through his veins at her touch. His chest swelled. *Yes, I will be the leader of this pack! Then I will have the best meat to eat, a nicer spot to sleep, and the pick of the females as my mate.*

Xojol nipped Tz' on the tip of his ear.

Ow, what was that for? Tz' said as he twisted his head to look at Xojol.

A reminder that I shall be the only female you pair with. When you defeat Bajbik, they will be free to pick any of the other males. Now pay attention!

Tz' nodded and leaned in closer.

Bajbik has a weak front leg from when a peccary rushed him many moons ago. You can use that to your advantage when you fight him. Xojol began to groom Tz' behind his ears. *You should confront him before the next full moon so the others will know to bring their choicest pieces of meat to you,* she purred.

To us, Tz' corrected. He watched the old were-jaguar closely as he moved about the cave and noticed the way he favored his weak front leg. He nudged Xojol. *When is the next full moon?*

Tomorrow night.

So, I need to engage him today, before we go outside, Tz' muttered. He stood up and flexed his muscles, but suddenly felt sick to his stomach as a wave of anxiety and doubt washed over him. He hurried to a dark corner and heaved up some spittle, but whirled around when he heard some of the were-jaguars hissing and mocking him. Tz' could see Bajbik had raised his head and was staring at him with his reddish-yellow eyes.

Then the leader stood up and arched his back, hissing in Tz's direction, as if daring him to make his move. Tz' almost lay back down, but he felt Xojol nudge him.

Do it, do it now, she urged. *You can take him while he's weak with hunger.*

I have little strength myself.

After tomorrow's feast, he'll be so much stronger; now is the time. Xojol pushed him again.

Tz' stumbled into the large open area of the cave where most of the were-jaguars spent their time. As soon as they saw him, they scuttled backward, giving him a wide berth. The only one who stayed in place was Bajbik, who arched his back and bared his yellow teeth. He sent a shot of spittle in Tz's direction, and the glob landed at his feet. Tz' backed away as its rank smell permeated the air. The leader then turned around and sprayed the area with urine, coating everything in the vicinity with its toxic scent. Tz's eyes smarted, but he knew he had to accept this challenge or he'd never be part of the group, let alone the leader.

He dropped his head and charged at Bajbik, aiming for the older male's weak leg. He hit him hard just below the shoulder and felt him wobble. Then sharp fangs dug into Tz's neck, and he whimpered with pain. The bigger cat pulled upward, lifting Tz' until his feet barely touched the ground, and then he began to turn in a wide circle. Tz' felt helpless and stupid as his feet swung below him, his toes just barely scratching the dirt. He watched in dismay as the other males stood up and began to growl, urging Bajbik to continue to spin in place, moving faster and faster. Tz' shut his eyes as the walls began to blur. He knew Bajbik would send him sprawling across the cave.

Do something, Tz', Xojol screamed.

The thought rammed into his brain, and he scrambled to gain a purchase on anything. As he swung around yet again, his claws touched onto a large boulder and he hung on with all the strength he possessed, breaking free of Bajbik's grip. Tz' felt blood trickle down the back of his neck, and he turned and launched himself at Bajbik, landing on the older cat's hindquarters. The two of them crashed to the ground and immediately began to kick and claw each other as they rolled about. Hisses and screeches filled the air as the other were-jaguars hurried to move out of the way. Tz' felt claws digging into his soft stomach area, and he curled inward to protect himself, but this left his neck exposed again, and he felt Bajbik bite down hard. He squinted his eyes closed against the pain and struck out with his paws, time and time again, beating against Bajbik's vulnerable leg until he finally felt something crack. The two collapsed again, and Tz' scrambled to gain an advantage. Bajbik scuttled backward, favoring his broken limb, and Tz' pounced, landing on the other cat's chest. He bit down into the mangy fur around the leader's neck, searching for skin among the folds of fur, and finally tasted blood. He chomped down even harder and was satisfied to hear Bajbik whimper in pain. He shook his head back and forth several times, feeling skin rip between his teeth, and a hot gush of blood filled his mouth. Only then did he let go. His mouth and neck were covered in blood, which dripped down onto the dirt floor of the cave. A rush of energy raced through his body, and he shivered with excitement. Bajbik looked up at Tz' from where he lay broken and bleeding and bared his fangs, then put his head down, and with some difficulty, he managed to scuttle backward into a darker corner of the cave. Two of the older females glanced nervously in Tz's direction, then bounded over the piles of bones to the old leader where they lay down on either side of him and began to lick his wounds with their coarse tongues.

Tz' turned in a wide circle, eyeing each of the males in turn. Every one dropped his head and bowed down to Tz', acknowledging his new power over them all. He filled his lungs with air and let out a roar that echoed through the cave, and the males pressed their bodies to the ground. One of the females bounded up and began to lick Tz's neck, but with a growl, Xojol leaped over a carcass, landing beside Tz'. She swatted the female with her paw and stepped up to Tz', nudging him with her muzzle.

Come, let me tend to your wounds. Tomorrow, when the moon is full, we'll feast on the meat the others bring to you.

Tz' allowed Xojol to lead him to a new spot in the cave, close to the main pile of bones and the largest tunnel leading from the cave to the outside. He could feel the aches in his body where Bajbik had bitten and scratched him, but he knew those wounds would heal. He relished the feeling of power that continued to surge through him, and he sighed with happiness as Xojol attended to him. He closed his eyes, and as Xojol continued to nuzzle him, he drifted toward sleep, secure in the knowledge that he was now leader of the pack.

Na'om

Na'om woke up and swung slowly in her hammock. She had been dreaming of Xibalba again, of wandering through the vast network of tunnels, this time in search of Tz'. The thought of returning to the land of the dead gave her chills, but she knew if it were the way to locate Tz', it would be worth the effort.

What if he's really there and I can find him? she mused as she swayed back and forth. *Could I convince him to return to the surface with me? I must revisit that dream.* She closed her eyes and concentrated on the images that rapidly began to stream through her mind.

She and Ek' Balam were in a dark tunnel, headed to the House of the Jaguars, where Na'om knew she'd find Tz'. She shuddered as images of the snarling beasts she'd faced the last time she'd been in Xibalba came to mind, and for the hundredth time, she couldn't believe that Tz' had shapeshifted into one. She just hoped she'd be able to change him back into his human form, and they could return to the surface and the land of the living together.

As she and Ek' Balam continued to march steadily forward, the air grew more humid, and soon the stench of rotting meat permeated the area. "We must be getting close," Na'om said. "Let's rest for a minute and eat and drink something before we search for Tz.'" She took off her pack basket and set it on the ground. After removing the blanket and the loincloth she'd brought with her, she pulled out an empty coconut shell and a water gourd and filled the bowl for Ek' Balam. Then she unfolded a piece of cotton cloth, exposing a large turkey leg. Using the small obsidian knife Box she had with her, she cut off several pieces of meat for Ek' Balam, and then she took a few bites off the bone. But she found she didn't have much appetite. She was too anxious to be hungry.

She sat down, leaned back against the tunnel wall, and closed her eyes, hoping she could calm her mind. But no matter how hard she tried, her thoughts kept circling back to one thing: the tingling sensation she'd experienced when Box had touched her. She wanted to experience that again. *Stop it*, she muttered, *I'm here to find Tz'!* A spasm of nausea flowed through her, and she leaned over and vomited up the food she'd just eaten. She swiped her mouth with the cloth she still held in her hand, then tossed it to one side. She put her head back again and watched as Ek' Balam started to wash his face. *Why does everything have to be so complicated,* she thought. *My whole life I've felt drawn to Tz' and believed that he was the man I was supposed to spend my life with, but that was before I met Box. . . .* Na'om shook her head and then rapped it against the hard wall in the hopes a bit of pain would help right her senses. *Ajkun was right; I need to take it one small step at a time,* she reminded herself. *First, I must release Tz' from this place, and then we can move forward with our lives, together or separately.* Her heart cramped, and she gasped as tears flooded her eyes. *Itzamná, help me,* she prayed. She didn't know what to do.

Ek' Balam calmly finished washing his face and then looked expectantly at Na'om. "All right, let's go," Na'om said. She picked up the pack basket and set it on her shoulders, then touched Ek' Balam's back to extend their combined circle of light farther into the gloom. She could see chewed bones strewn here and there as they walked, and the piles quickly grew deeper the farther they went. When the stench of rotten meat began to make her stomach queasy again, Na'om stopped, pulled a clean cloth from the pocket in her skirt, and wrapped the fabric around her nose and mouth. Breathing was far more difficult, but it helped reduce the awful smell.

They continued forward, lurching and stumbling over the ever-growing piles of bones until they reached a fork in the tunnel. "Do we go left or right?" Na'om wondered out loud.

A sudden noise from the left tunnel was her answer. She turned and projected her beam of light outward, exposing the area in a dim glow. A large were-jaguar stood facing her, his head lowered, his teeth bared in a snarl.

"Tz'? Is that you?" she asked. She felt Ek' Balam crouch down beside her, his hind legs quivering as if he was ready to pounce. "No, boy, it's okay," she admonished as she placed her hand on his spine. She felt him grow still. "Tz', answer me," she commanded.

The were-jaguar growled in response and spittle dripped from his fangs onto the bones at his feet. The big cat crouched even lower, and Na'om felt sudden panic rush through her as she realized the creature was about to attack. She braced herself and gripped the hilt of her knife, which was still ensconced in its leather scabbard at her waist. "Tz', if that's you, answer me with your mind; I'll be able to hear your thoughts," Na'om said as she slowly pulled the knife out. She held it at arm's length, just in case she was wrong and this was not her long-lost friend.

Then a rush of pain flowed through her as the were-jaguar's thoughts invaded her mind. Image upon image crashed into her, forcing Na'om to gasp and take several steps backward. She saw Tz' sinking into the cenote water, then watched as he summoned Camazotz and shifted into a were-jaguar. She saw him join the pack, the endless time he spent rummaging for food and sleeping, and how the females clustered around him. That's when she shouted, "No!" and finally forced the flow of images to stop. But Na'om still felt Tz's pain, sorrow, and love as these emotions flowed through and around her, and she grasped at the rocky wall behind her to steady herself.

Na'om blinked several times and shook her head, then looked straight into the were-jaguar's eyes. She slowly leaned down and placed her knife on the ground. "I know you won't hurt me," she said as she stepped away from the blade. She extended her hands in front of her, palms up, offering Tz' peace and understanding. "It's time to go home, Tz', let me help you regain your human shape and return to the land of the living."

She stepped forward again, moving ever so slowly as the were-jaguar continued to growl softly. Finally, she was within range of touching the creature, and she tentatively reached out to stroke his muzzle. But the were-jaguar pulled back its big head, bared his fangs, and growled even more.

"Fine, I won't touch you," Na'om said and dropped her hands to her sides. "So, where do we go from here? Do you even want to return to Pa nimá, or have you made this place your home?" Anger coursed through Na'om's body, and she fought it. She didn't want to argue with Tz'. She wanted to return to the surface together and then sort out what their lives might mean.

As she waited for a response, she felt Ek' Balam move closer to her side and heard him growl. She peered into the darkness beyond Tz' and could see several pairs of red eyes looking back at her. "So, you've brought your pack with you, I see. I guess that's the answer I needed." Na'om swung around and took several steps away from the were-jaguar and then felt a rush of air as the big cat pounced. She had just enough time to duck and let the cat fly over her body, but she felt the cat's claws scratch her back, ripping her huipil in several places. She grabbed the knife near her foot and held it out in front of her. "What's it going to be, Tz'? Are you going to fight me or what?" she shouted.

Ek' Balam moved behind her, facing the group of were-jaguars still farther back in the tunnel. "Just let us go and we won't ever bother you again," Na'om said. She shoved the knife back into its scabbard and put her hands at her sides.

The were-jaguar crouched, but instead of pouncing on her, it ran past her, growling and spitting at the were-jaguars hovering nearby. The pack scattered deeper into the black tunnel, and the were-jaguar turned around one more time to face Na'om.

She felt a voice in her head and directed her attention to it.

Don't go, Na'om. I need you, Tz' said. *I've made so many mistakes, though, that I don't know if I can return to the land of the living.*

Na'om nodded her head in response. "The first thing we must do is return you to your human shape," she said as she took off the pack basket again. She fumbled around and found the large piece of charcoal she'd stashed at the bottom. "Chew on this; it will reverse the shapeshifting, restoring you to your normal self."

Tz' shook his big head. *No, I must remain in this form if I'm staying here. Otherwise, the other were-jaguars will tear me apart.*

"But you're not staying here," Na'om said, and she thrust the charcoal in Tz's direction.

Tz' dropped his head until his muzzle almost touched the ground.

I've been down here too long, Na'om, I don't think I can return with you.

"That's nonsense," Na'om said. She took a step toward Tz' and lightly ran her fingers across the top of his skull. A tingly sensation ran up her hand and through her arm.

You don't understand, Tz' said as he twitched his head away from Na'om's hand. He looked up at her with his reddish eyes and then dropped his head. *I've eaten from the hands of the gods.* He hung his head down, avoiding Na'om's glance. *And I've grown fond of one of the females. She's not strong like you; she needs me.*

"I need you too," Na'om said, but she dropped the charcoal on the ground. She couldn't force Tz' to come with her. But now that Tz' had spoken his truth, she knew he was trapped between worlds. And she knew she didn't have the power to bring him to the surface, especially if he didn't want to come.

"So, what happens now?" Na'om asked as she kicked aside a pile of chewed bones and sat down on the rocky ground. She didn't look at Tz' who stood several feet away. She heard Ek' Balam pacing in front of her and watched as he stopped, looked toward his left, and then took off running into the dark tunnel. "Ek' Balam, come back!" she screamed as she jumped to her feet. Her voice echoed around and around, but the jaguar was gone. She slumped to the ground again and cupped her face in her hands. Nothing was going as she had imagined it would. She had thought it would be so simple; she'd find Tz', he'd eat the charcoal, and together, they'd all return to the surface. But now she didn't know what to do or say or what was going to happen.

Na'om only glanced up when she heard chewing sounds and then watched in fear and amazement as Tz' quickly swallowed the charcoal and transformed back into his human shape in front of her. She quickly covered her eyes again as his naked body appeared. Without looking, she reached into her basket yet again and pulled out the loincloth she'd brought. She tossed it to Tz'.

"Maltiox," she heard him mutter.

She jerked her head to one side as she felt him brush her cheek with his fingertips and then reached out to embrace him. His skin was warm and very soft to the touch, as if a thin layer of fur still covered it, and Na'om pulled back to get a close look at Tz's face. There was a fine layer of golden hair on it, and as she looked at the rest of him, she could see his entire body was covered with it.

Tz' smiled briefly at her touch and then dropped his eyes. "I'm not worthy of you, you know that," he said in a semi-whisper.

His voice was rougher, deeper than Na'om remembered, and she shivered slightly. "What matters right now is that we get you back to the land of the living," she replied.

"I can't leave here; the gods have placed me on a new path, and I must follow it."

"But what about the path the gods have always shown *me*, a path that includes having you by my side? No, you have a choice in this, Tz'; I believe we all do." Na'om fought to keep her anger and frustration under control. "You must decide right now whether you want to come with me, be a man, and live in the light or remain here in the Underworld as a were-jaguar."

Tz' shook his head. "I'm so confused. I never really expected to see you again, which is why I let Camazotz help me shapeshift into my spirit animal." He began to pace up and down the tunnel and growl. "I've battled with the pack leader and have taken over. The others bring me food now, and I've made friends with one of the females, Xojol." He paused and growled as he looked at his human hands and body. "I don't have the power to shapeshift again. And I refuse to call on Camazotz to help me. Now I'm forced to be a human, whether I choose it or not."

Na'om's anger rose inside her, and she pushed it outward. It turned the air around her a deep blood red, and in its light, she rummaged around in her basket, feeling for the small leather pouch she had stuffed at the very bottom. She pulled it free from the other belongings and tossed it on the ground toward Tz'.

"What's this?" he asked as he picked it up.

"Jequirity beans, to help you shift back, if that's what you truly desire. I was sure you wouldn't want them. But now I don't know. You seem to have made a good life for yourself down here." Na'om stood up and put her basket on her back.

"Wait, Na'om, don't be angry with me," Tz' pleaded. "You must know I still have feelings for you."

"And it appears for others as well." Na'om's anger made the light around them flicker and dance like flames. She took a deep breath and let it out slowly. She decided to change tactics. She needed answers to so many questions. "Tell me why you went to see Satal."

"When I thought you'd died, a part of me died too. I returned to the village, but everything there reminded me of you. It made me miserable. And then I discovered Satal was still alive. I wanted revenge since she was to blame for your death. That's when I returned to Mayapán so I could learn to use my shamanic powers to defeat her. I worked with Najtir, but I wasn't making any progress with him. I couldn't shapeshift and had no powers that would be strong enough to crush Satal. I foolishly believed she would accept me as her grandson and train me in the darker arts, which I'd then be able to use against her. I never expected her to have me thrown into the cenote."

"So, if all this is true, then why do you want to remain here?" Na'om pointed to the darkness all around them. "Come back to the land of the living, Tz'."

"I can't." Tz' hung his head. "I made the mistake of eating food meant for Hun-Kamé and am now beholden to him. My path has gone in a new direction, one I must follow. One day you'll understand; for now, just trust me."

"So, you'll not return with me, regardless of what I say or do?" Na'om said.

In response, Tz' leaned in close and placed a gentle kiss on Na'om's cheek, then another on her lips. She sighed and kissed back, then kissed him again, deeply, passionately. Her entire body ached for his touch.

She felt Tz's hands move to her shoulders and then one hand cupped her breast through her shirt. But she grabbed his hand and pushed it away.

"What's wrong?" Tz' said.

"Nothing," Na'om lied. Part of her desperately wanted to feel his body touching hers, but something still felt wrong about being intimate with Tz'. Even though she had thought about this moment many times, once again, it seemed he was the one making the decisions. She wanted to be in charge and to have a choice in the matter. She looked at Tz' and felt the urge to kiss him again. *Perhaps if we make love, he'll return to the surface with me.* She smiled at Tz' as she touched his cheek with her fingertips. "It's not you, it's this place; I'm not comfortable in this tunnel, among the bones." She grabbed his wrist and began to pull him toward her. "We must find someplace else."

Together, they ran through the darkness, sensing rather than seeing the twists and turns they needed to take. Finally, Na'om stopped as she smelled fresher air and turned to her left. "Come on, I think I've found a place," she said, and she ran ahead of Tz'. She stepped through an opening in the tunnel wall into a large cave. A cerulean-blue pool of fresh water filled most of the area and there was an opening to the sky in the rocky ceiling high overhead. A patch of sunlight filled the area below it. Na'om smiled. "I've been here before," she said as she walked forward and stooped to scoop some water into her mouth. The warm water was sweet, and she drank some more. Then she stood, quickly removed her clothing, and slipped into the pool, swimming into the sunlight. She treaded water and motioned for Tz' to join her.

He dove in and swam underwater to her. He surfaced and blew outward, sending spray into the air. He reached out to touch her, but Na'om laughed and moved out of reach.

She paddled hard, moving in a circle in the patch of sunlight, with Tz' just behind her, splashing him playfully each time he drew near. But he abruptly turned and swam back to the edge of the pool.

"Wait, don't go; I was just having a bit of fun, like when we were children," Na'om said as she moved through the water to him. She put her feet down on the sandy bottom and reached out to touch Tz's arm.

They embraced, and then Na'om leaned in and kissed Tz' deeply on the mouth. She tasted salt and blood on his lips, but she refused to think about what he'd been living on. She only wanted to be with him in this moment and to feel his arms around her. Tz' swung her around and through the water so her back was pressed up against the edge of the cenote and their kissing intensified. She leaned her head back, bracing it on the dirt, which exposed her neck, and she felt Tz' kiss the length of it from her chin to her chest. Na'om shivered at his touch. He dipped his head and kissed her nipples under the water, then trailed the tip of his tongue up the other side of her neck and kissed her strongly on the mouth again. Then Tz' wrapped his arms around her, drawing her closer to his chest. They kissed again and again, and Na'om parted her lips to taste the tip of his tongue.

And then she abruptly opened her eyes when she felt Ek' Balam press his cold wet nose into her forearm. She blinked several times, letting her eyes adjust once again to the dim light inside the small, thatched hut. *If only the dream were true*, she mused as she rolled out of the hammock and stood barefoot on the cool tile floor. However, the recent images of

Tz' continued to flicker through her mind, and she stood without moving for several minutes, still half-trapped in that reality. Eventually, the dream receded a tiny bit, and Na'om looked around the room. Despite the filtered light, she had no trouble seeing in the dark. After the many months she'd spent trapped in Xibalba, her eyes were trained to use every glimmer of light. The dream continued to flash in her mind, and she longed to know how it would end, but she also knew sleep would not come easily at this point. *I need to take a walk*, she decided and quickly changed out of her night shift and into a long-sleeved, dark-green huipil that hung just below her waist, with a matching skirt that grazed the tops of her feet. She slipped on her leather sandals and wrapped a lightweight gray shawl around her shoulders, then patted Ek' Balam on the head before following him outside.

As she stepped into the tiny courtyard in front of the hut, Na'om inhaled deeply, breathing in the rich mix of smells that permanently permeated the air from the thousands of inhabitants who shared space inside the walls of Mayapán. The tangy scents of peppers and limes mingled with the lush aroma of orchid blossoms and the lingering whiffs of grilled meats and fish. Then she grimaced. Underneath these odors she could still sense the sooty, dank smell of burnt wood, charred stucco, and the sweetly sickening taint of death. Despite the clean-up efforts, including the removal of the hundreds and hundreds of insect and animal bodies left after Satal's massive attack, the city could still smell foul. The reek reminded Na'om of the cave where Camazotz and his legions of bats lived, and she shook her head and blew sharply out her nose. She longed for the sweet smells of the jungle surrounding Pa nimá and wondered not for the first time if she would ever return to her home village.

She stepped into the narrow alleyway in front of the home she was using and headed toward the main gates of the city. The streets were empty of people, the marketplace closed for business, and she was glad. Late at night was the only time she had to be alone, to walk freely in the city without a thousand eyes peering at her jaguar-spotted skin, a hundred persons begging she touch some amulet or necklace for good luck, and an entourage of guards surrounding her who kept most of the people away. When she approached the main entranceway to the city, she nodded at the two guards stationed on either side of the wide copper doors. The older sentry stepped forward, pulled back the massive wooden pin that barred the gates from the outside world, and opened the door just wide enough for Na'om and Ek' Balam to slip through. She walked ahead twenty paces, turned, and saw that the younger guard had reluctantly followed her past the gate, a lit torch in one hand.

Come on, Ek' Balam, I don't want to be followed, Na'om thought as she touched the jaguar on the top of his head. The two hurried toward a narrow path that led to the nearest lime orchard; the trees were in full flower, and white petals were scattered here and there on the ground. She could hear the guard stumbling about, despite the light thrown by his torch and the moon. Na'om hurried onward, putting more distance between her and the man. She didn't want to see him or his light. She needed to believe she was alone, even if she wasn't, and to wander at will under the trees where she felt most at ease. It was the only escape she had from the ever-present sense of responsibility she felt these days. And more importantly, she needed to think about the dream she'd just had.

She could still sense Tz' touch, the firm pressure of his lips upon hers, and she absentmindedly placed her fingertips on her mouth, hoping to mimic the sensation. She closed her eyes, forcing herself to remember any more details of the dream, but the specifics were the same and the dream ended the same way, with them kissing. Frustrated with this lack of resolution, Na'om sat down to concentrate. She would manifest an ending that satisfied her yearning to be with Tz'. She put herself into a relaxed state and pushed her spirit back into the dream, picking up where she had awoken, with them kissing in the cenote.

Their kisses grew more passionate and her body ached in odd places in unfamiliar ways. She pushed Tz' away and awkwardly climbed from the water. She hurried over to her basket, pulled out a blanket, and quickly spread it on the ground. She lay down and closed her eyes as she heard Tz' leap out of the cenote. Droplets of water fell on her body as he moved into position over her, and suddenly, she felt the full weight of his body on hers. Their bodies touched from feet to chest, and Na'om felt the rhythm of Tz's heartbeat against her skin. They kissed again and again, and Na'om parted her lips to taste the tip of his tongue. But then, his body felt so heavy on hers that suddenly she couldn't breathe, and she pushed upward, forcing Tz' to roll off her.

"I'm sorry if I hurt you," Tz' said. His voice was low, almost a growl.

Na'om turned to look at him and she shivered as she looked into his eyes. They had turned deep blood red and a trail of spittle dripped from his lips. "I don't know what just happened; it was all so sudden and not how I imagined it could be," Na'om whispered.

She began to panic. This was not how she had expected Tz' to behave, and she struggled to escape from the daydream, but her spirit was glued to the scene. She didn't want to know anything more, she just wanted to return to her body, but she was trapped and had to follow the dream where it led her. So, she took several deep breaths to relax and fell deeper into that twilight moment.

In her mind's eye, Na'om got up, grabbed her clothes, and put them on, even though she was still wet from swimming in the cenote.

Tz' stood naked in front of Na'om. "You'll bear my child now."

"That's not possible," Na'om said.

"Ah, but it is, for here anything is possible, and I know my son will be born in nine moon's time." He paused and turned away from Na'om. "I also know I can't return with you to the surface."

"What do you mean?" Na'om cried. "I thought this, this," she waved her hand at the blanket still spread on the ground, "that our deep feelings toward one another would make you come back with me." She folded her arms across her chest and took a deep breath.

"The gods have put me on a new path, one that forces me to stay here. So, you must do some things for me once you return to the surface."

Na'om held up her hand and interrupted him. "Why should I do anything for you if you're not willing to come home with me?"

"Because you still love me and will always love me; that's why you came all this way to see me." Tz' began to pace back and forth in a tight line in front of Na'om. "All our lives, we've been governed by what the gods have in store for us; this is my destiny, to be here, to be leader of the were-jaguars." Tz' stood up straighter and pushed out his chest. "I'm the strongest I've ever been when I'm a were-jaguar; I like the feeling of power I have when I'm one of them." He stopped in front of Na'om and stared deeply into her eyes. "I'm meant for more than the life I left in Pa nimá. The gods have set a task before me, and one day you'll understand this."

"And now you prefer the company of these creatures to that of your own family? What about Chiman? What should I tell him when I see him again? That being a were-jaguar is more important than being his son?"

"I'm not his son, not by blood at any rate," Tz' replied.

"But he raised you as his own; can't you see that by staying here you betray the love he feels for you?"

"By staying here, I protect him and you and all the others I love who live among the light!" Tz' shouted. He growled and stopped pacing. "Naóm, I will not return with you, not now anyway. Now, I beg you, you must listen to me and do as I say."

Naóm turned away from Tz' and stared into the waters of the cenote. The sun above had shifted, and the water reflected the darkening sky. Deep down, she knew Tz' was right. Everything he was telling her felt true and genuine in her body. *But where does that leave me?* she wondered. She turned back to look at Tz', at the man he'd become in the many months they'd been separated, and wondered who he really was.

Tz' waited a moment and then continued. "There are three things you must do for me. First, promise me you'll defeat Satal. No matter what sacrifice it entails, you must defeat her."

"That is the plan; go on."

"You must let another man take my place in your heart. Someone like Box."

"Box, what do you know of Box? What makes you think I like him? I've only just met him."

Tz' laughed as he interrupted Naóm. "I know you're fond of him, and he definitely has feelings for you." Tz' stopped walking and looked at Naóm. "It's all right, Naóm. I have feelings for another too; there's no shame in it. We grew up together and are kindred spirits, but our lives are entwined in different ways than either of us imagined. We thought we were meant for each other because we'd never met anyone else outside our village. But then we both discovered the endless possibilities in this world."

Naóm took a deep breath. "And the third request?"

"When our child is old enough, teach him everything you know about the world of the living. All the animals and the birds and what plant heals what ailment. And then, when you've exhausted your knowledge, send him to study with the shamans in Mayapán. He'll become a great shaman and leader one day, I know," Tz' said. He reached out to touch Naóm's forearm, but she stepped away from him.

"There must be something that can be done before all that time passes," Naóm said as she paced around the edge of the pool.

Tz' growled ever so slightly. "I'll not return with you, Naóm." Then his voice softened. "Each month when the moon is full, we're allowed to leave Xibalba to secure the food we need for the month to come. I shall visit you when I can, but it won't be every month. However, I will know when our son's birth is imminent and will come when he is born."

"Ha, you think you know so much, that I'm suddenly pregnant after a few passionate kisses, that we'll have a son, that Box is interested in me, even though I supposedly carry your child. . . ." Na'om gasped as Tz' grabbed her by the forearm.

"This is not some game I'm playing, Na'om," Tz' said. "I've made my choices to protect you and the others I love; can't you see that?"

"So, you love this were-jaguar, that's it, isn't it?" Na'om said. "You love her more than you love me."

"Yes, no, Itzamná, don't twist my words, Na'om. I must stay here in Xibalba to protect you and her," he said. Then he placed his hand gently on Na'om's belly. "And our child."

Na'om's anger surged through her again and she backed away from Tz'. "If this is truly what you wish, then so be it. I'll leave you here to live your life with those . . . those creatures you're so fond of and return to the land of the sun and the living." She gasped as Tz' clutched her arm.

"Don't be angry, I beg you. Remember the love you've always held for me and use it when you most need it. I must stay here in order to protect our child."

"So be it. If I'm pregnant, as you claim, then I will raise our child in Pa nimá, and when he's old enough, I will have him trained as a shaman. As to whether Box takes your place in my heart, that remains to be seen." She stopped walking and looked into Tz's eyes. They had lost some of their redness and she could see her childhood friend in his face. "Will I ever see you again?" She gasped as she felt her heart cramp, and a pair of tears ran down her face.

Tz' nodded. "I shall follow your scent wherever it may take me and call on you when the moon is full." He stepped in closer and embraced Na'om before gently placing his lips against hers.

Na'om responded by kissing him back, then stepped away as she felt more tears welling in the corners of her eyes. "Then this is good-bye," she said and let out a little sob.

"Only for now; we'll meet again, I promise." Tz' hugged Na'om one more time, then stepped away. "There is one last thing I must ask you to do for me," he said. He shook his head and waved his hand from his head toward his torso. "I can't remain down here in my human form. Stay with me while I shapeshift." He opened up the leather satchel and removed one of the red-and-black jequirity beans. "I wasn't able to shapeshift with these before; hopefully it works this time."

Na'om sighed. "Bite it and let the toxin flow through you." Then she reached into her pocket and removed another piece of charcoal, which she set on a small outcropping of rock in the cave wall. "Use this charcoal to shapeshift back to your human form if you should ever change your mind."

"Give me some of your strength while I concentrate on shifting," Tz' said. "It worked with Camazotz, so maybe it'll work with you." He bit into the jequirity bean and grimaced at the bitter taste.

Na'om stepped forward and put her arms lightly around Tz's shoulders. "All right, I'm going to give you some energy now." She closed her eyes and imagined the white light of love she carried within extending from her arms and encircling Tz'. As she embraced him, she felt heat building between them, a heat that quickly grew uncomfortably hot, but she refused to stop. Just when she felt her arms and body really begin to burn, she sensed Tz' shifting and stepped back. She opened her eyes and watched as he quickly transformed back into a were-jaguar.

Thank you, Na'om, she heard him say in her mind. *I do still love you,* he said and then he took off running, disappearing into one of the many tunnels that stretched away from the cave.

She stood in the darkness alone and yearned to run after Tz'. Then she felt Ek' Balam nudge her physical body with his head and she was finally released from the dream state she'd been in. She blinked multiple times, took a deep breath, and let it out in a sob. She clutched at the ground around her, grabbing fistfuls of dirt and lime blossoms that she crushed between her fingers. With tears streaming down her face, she looked around and saw Ek' Balam patiently waiting a few steps away on the path among the trees in the orchard. The black jaguar padded over again and placed his big head against Na'om's cheek.

She wiped off her hands, then wrapped her arms around his neck and buried her face in his thick fur. "I don't know if any of that will come true or not, but for now, it's just us, boy," she whispered and felt another sob escape between her lips. The thought that Tz' wanted to stay in Xibalba was too heavy a weight to bear, and she needed to move to release the tension she felt throughout her body. She drew in another deep breath and squeezed the jaguar before standing upright. Glancing back toward the city, she saw that the guard had remained at a respectful distance all this time. She hurriedly wiped the tears from her eyes and headed deeper into the orchard.

She inhaled the sweet scent of the lime flowers, anything to distract her mind from the daydream that still floated behind her eyes. *Better to imagine I'm back in Pa nimá*, she thought as she closed her eyes. She needed to dissipate the odd mixture of love and fear that she felt toward Tz'. She slowly visualized walking on the path to her home in the circle of mahogany trees across the river from the village, a walk she had taken hundreds of times, and the effect finally calmed her nerves. *It's been so long since I've been there, though. I wonder if the jungle has reclaimed the spot. I pray to the gods that someday we'll get back there.*

She was tired and followed Ek' Balam without question on the narrow path. The night air was cool, and she wrapped her shawl tighter against her chest. Suddenly, Ek' Balam stopped directly in front of her and began to growl. She touched his tail and whispered, "What is it, boy, what do you see?" She couldn't see anything out of the ordinary. Na'om glanced behind her and saw the yellow glow of the torch the guard carried slowly approaching.

She placed her palm on Ek' Balam's back and imagined a circle of white light extending out from them, stretching in all directions through the trees. A hundred paces away, in the projected light, she saw a man sitting quietly on the ground, his back resting against the trunk of a lime tree. He appeared to be asleep.

"Come on, we'll go a different direction," Na'om said, and she began to turn around.

"Don't go, child, I've been waiting for you," the old man said. He patted the ground beside him. "Come, Na'om, we have much to discuss."

Startled, Na'om turned back around. "How do you know my name?" she asked as she hurried forward.

The old man chortled and then began to cough as spittle dribbled out of the corner of his mouth. He wiped it with the edge of his sleeve. When he had caught his breath, he looked up and said, "Who else would be wandering out here in the dark with a black jaguar as a companion?" He carefully extended one bony and arthritic hand and let Ek' Balam sniff his fingers and palm before tentatively touching Ek' Balam's muzzle.

The cat began to purr and lay down on the ground next to the old man. "Who are you?" Na'om asked while she sat down on the other side of the man. She glanced up the path and saw the guard still advancing. "It's all right," she called out. "Make yourself comfortable; we'll be here for a while." The guard nodded, retreated a few paces, and then sat cross-legged on the cool dirt.

She turned back to the man next to her. In the moonlight that filtered through the tree branches, she could see the wrinkles around his eyes and mouth, marking his age, and noticed he was quite thin.

"I'm Najtir, the shaman who was training your young friend. Chiman said you wanted to see me."

Na'om's heart skipped a beat. She decided not to tell Najtir of her dream. "I wondered if you knew why Tz' left," she said.

"Ahh," Najtir said. "Do any of us truly know what motivates another to act the way they do? I suspect Tz' left to study the dark arts with Satal. But to what end? I don't know."

"You said you were training him, though. So, why would he need Satal?"

"He wanted to shapeshift into a were-jaguar, and he wasn't able to accomplish the task, despite my best efforts to help him." Najtir sighed and shifted his legs on the ground.

Na'om once again envisioned Tz' as that animal from her dream. She shivered as she pictured his reddish glowing eyes, sharp fangs, and muscular body almost twice the size of a real jaguar.

"He told me he enjoyed the feeling of power he had the one time he had become one."

Na'om shook her head. So many of her dreams over the years had come true; would this one as well? She hoped not. She couldn't believe Tz' had really wanted to join forces with Satal; it didn't sound like the boy she'd had grown up with. *Even though they're related by blood, I can't believe Satal's lust for power or her evilness flow through Tz's veins.* The thought made her ill. *Would Tz' really turn to Satal for help and change into someone I could never love?* Sudden panic gripped her stomach as she imagined having to battle with both of them. She knew she could never bring harm to her lifelong friend; despite the ways he might have changed since she had fallen into the cenote. She drew in a deep breath and felt a shiver race across her shoulders. "Do you really think he went to Chichén Itzá to study with Satal?"

"From what little I know of him, yes, I do. The desire for power and strength does curious things, especially to those who are young and inexperienced in so many ways." Najtir coughed slightly, then leaned toward Na'om. "Tz' has much to learn still. He foolishly craves control and authority and is willing to risk much in order to achieve them. And yet, I sense he still believes all people are good at heart, a situation that is definitely not true with Satal. The combination is not a good one."

Na'om's smile faded, replaced with a deep frown. She sat in silence while her dream raced through her mind. "Even if he did meet with Satal, I can't believe he'd want to become like her." But as she spoke, Na'om felt a cold lump begin to form in the pit of her belly. How well did she really know her friend? *Whether the dream comes true or not, if Tz' went to learn from Satal, then he's already changed in many ways.* A sudden gust of wind blew quickly through the trees, rocking Na'om where she sat, and she reached out her hand to steady herself as lime blossoms rained down on the threesome.

The shaman reached over and patted her gently on the knee. "All will be well in the end, my dear, never fear. Come now, you must help an old man to his feet."

White petals drifted to the ground as Na'om stood and reached out her hands to gently pull Najtir to a stand. He leaned heavily on her offered arm, and they began to make their way back through the orchard toward the city, with Ek' Balam a few paces behind them. They were followed by the guard, who hurried in front of them as soon as he saw the gates to the city.

"Come see me later today," Najtir said. "I'm staying in Satal's old palace. It's where I was training Tz' when he left."

Na'om nodded. She remembered the place all too well since it was where she'd battled Satal for the first time. She wondered if the ropes Satal had used to tie her to the wall were still attached to the stucco. Then she shook her head. *No, Tz' would have removed those long ago,* she surmised. She looked up at the stars overhead and drew in a deep breath of cool night air. She could still smell the flowers that lingered in her long, black hair. She didn't want to think about the past anymore. She needed to concentrate on the here and now and figure out how she was going to defeat Satal for good.

The sentry rapped on one of the closed doors, and they listened as the bar was withdrawn on the inside, allowing them all to enter through the door opening. Naʼom turned her head quickly and had one last look at the openness outside before the large copper door was closed and bolted shut again. She looked at Najtir. "So, you'll help train me, develop the power to get rid of Satal?"

Najtir smiled. "I still have a few tricks I can share, but the power you need is already deep inside you, my dear."

Naʼom looked at the shaman and frowned. "I don't understand."

"When the time is ready, you'll know it."

Naʼom wanted Najtir to explain, but movement behind the shaman caught her eye. Several new guards, dressed in cotton loincloths and leather breastplates etched with the pyramid, the emblem of the city, had arrived to take over the watch. Daylight was only a few hours away. The group of men gazed at Naʼom, but they remained at a respectful distance.

The shaman held a hand up to his mouth and yawned. "Excuse me, I'm weary. Come see me this afternoon; I have a special place I'd like to take you for lunch."

All right," Naʼom replied. She beckoned to one of the men standing near the guardhouse. "See that he gets back to his home safely."

"Of course, Lady Naʼom." The guard quickly approached and offered the shaman an arm to lean on. Together, they walked at a slow pace into the darkness, which was broken only by the circle of light cast by the guard's torch.

When they had disappeared into the distance, Naʼom patted Ek' Balam on the head. "Come on, boy, we'd best get a couple of hours of sleep too." She waved away the offer of a torch by one of the sentries and headed in the opposite direction of Najtir and his escort. She sighed when she heard footsteps behind her and turned to see two of the guards following at a discreet distance.

Back at the hut she was using, she crawled into her hammock and snuggled under two woolen blankets, but sleep evaded her. She listened as Ek' Balam circled and circled in one spot on the floor before lying down with a deep moan. A baby wailed in the distance, and a pauraque bird whistled and was answered by another. Naʼom drew the blankets up over her head to block out the sounds of the city coming to life, but the more she tried not to hear, the more she heard. Someone in a courtyard nearby began chopping at a tree branch, and Na'om soon heard the crackle of a fire. The spicy scent of burning eucalyptus leaves filtered through the doorway, and Na'om rolled over in the hammock to face the wall. The swaying movement gradually eased the tension from her body, and she thankfully slipped into a deep, dreamless sleep.

It felt like only a few moments had passed when she woke up to find the late morning sun streaming into the hut through the small window opening on the opposite side of the room. She heard a *tap, tap, tap* on the side of the hut and smiled. She knew it was a red-vented woodpecker. She'd seen the red-crested bird with the yellow markings around his bill every morning for the past week. *He must be catching more bugs in the thatching*, she mused as she swung gently from side to side in the hammock. Then, there was another knock, this time on the doorframe.

Na'om sat up abruptly and placed her bare feet on the floor. "Who's there?" she called.

"It's me, Na'om, Chiman," a man's voice said.

"Come in, *Mam*," Na'om replied. She loved to be able to call this man, who had always been a helpful and protective presence in her life, grandfather. She hurried to greet him with a large hug as the older man stepped into the room.

"I've come to take you to meet Najtir," he said.

Na'om smiled and was just about to tell her grandfather she'd already met him when she changed her mind. *He'll worry if he knows I've been outside the gates alone.* "Let me fix my hair," Na'om replied.

"I'll wait outside."

Na'om quickly ran a brush through her long hair and braided it before slipping on her leather sandals. She approached the small wooden table tucked into the far corner of the room, picked up a packet made from a folded banana leaf, and tucked it into her skirt pocket. She glanced around the small room to see if she needed anything else. But there was nothing there that would help her. Najtir had said her power was deep inside. She sighed. She felt empty inside, not powerful. She knew if she ever hoped to see Tz' again, she was the one who needed to find him. Was he really in the Underworld? How would she ever get there again? She glanced at Ek' Balam, looking for answers, but the jaguar stood up and walked outside. Na'om shook her head, brushed a wisp of hair from her eyes, and pushed aside the cloth over the doorway.

Chiman turned from facing the sun when Na'om appeared. Flanked front and back by sentries, they walked side by side through the crowded streets of the city toward Satal's palace, with Ek' Balam just behind them. The people they met stood silently to one side as they passed, heads bowed in deference to Na'om. A few women fell to their knees, pulling their children down beside them. One young boy began to cry at the rough and unexpected treatment by his mother, so Na'om stopped walking and turned back.

She crouched in front of the child and lifted his tear-streaked face with her fingertips. "Come now, there's no reason to cry," she said as she searched in her skirt pocket with her other hand. She pulled out the banana leaf and unfolded the edges, exposing several pieces of honeycomb dripping with honey. "Go on, take one," she said and dipped her head toward the treats.

He glanced at his mother, who nodded; then he picked the smallest piece and popped it into his mouth.

"Oh, that was a tiny piece, take another," Na'om said. She turned to the other children who stood nearby, their eyes trained on the leaf in her hand. "Come on, all of you, take a chunk, and then we'll be on our way." The group of five clustered around her, snatching the bits of comb, leaving only the sticky leaf in her hand. She folded it up and tucked it back into her pocket before turning to the mothers nearby. "Please don't kneel if you should see me in the streets and don't force your children to do it, either. I'm just a girl like any other." The women nodded, but remained silent, their eyes cast down to the ground.

Chiman chuckled at Na'om as she rejoined him. "I'll make sure to pick up another packet of honeycomb for you at the market today."

Na'om laughed. "As soon as those children tell their friends, I'll need more than one packet, I'm afraid. It's good to have something to give them, though, as so many are still afraid of me." Na'om sighed and held up her arm to the light. The brown rosettes traced into her skin gleamed in the sun. "I suppose some will never grow used to these spots, but I forget I have them at this point."

When they reached the large house, Chiman went to step through the doorway into the inner courtyard, but Na'om placed her hand on his forearm to stop him. "I think it might be best if I talk to him alone."

"Oh, all right, yes, of course," Chiman replied and he stepped to one side. "I can wait for you here, if you like."

"No, Mam, please, we'll be fine." Na'om touched Ek' Balam on the head, and the jaguar walked forward. "The guards will protect us from any harm." She nodded, and the four sentries took up spots on either side of the entranceway. She quickly kissed Chiman on the cheek and stepped through the doorway.

Ek' Balam began to growl as he padded across the tiled floor. "Come on, it's all right," she said. Yet, she felt a shiver go up and down her spine as she crossed the courtyard and headed toward the wide steps that led to the wooden front door. She turned and looked back at the jaguar. He still waited by the entrance. "You're not coming?" she asked. In response, the cat lay down in the shade created by the thick bougainvillea vines filled with magenta flowers that climbed the high wall. Na'om frowned, then ascended the steps and knocked rapidly on the ornate carved door. She waited, but nothing happened. She was about to knock again but thought better of it and placed her ear against the door instead. She could faintly hear the *slip, slip, slip* of someone's shoes moving slowly across the floor.

The door opened, and Najtir peered out. He was dressed in a long-sleeved, deep red, linen shirt that fell to mid-thigh with a pair of matching pants. A marigold-orange cotton bag was tied by a thin cord around his waist. He stepped to one side and gestured for Na'om to come inside.

"I have dried fish," he called out through the open doorway.

Na'om laughed when she heard Ek' Balam's large feet quickly cross the courtyard. She watched as the cat took the stairs in one leap, and then he brushed against Na'om's leg as he entered the room. He paced around, sniffing the few pieces of furniture before sitting down in front of a small leather-topped table to stare intently at a brown leather pouch located in the center of the table. Beside the bag was an earthenware jug and a lacquered black wooden tray with several blue-and green-striped ceramic mugs on it.

"He has a good nose and good eyes, far better than my own, I'm afraid," Najtir said as he closed the heavy wooden door with a bit of difficulty. "Please, sit anywhere you like, while I give your friend his treats." Najtir shuffled across the room and sat down in one of the vacant leather chairs around the table. He reached over to the pouch, extracted a large, dried and salted dogfish, and laid it gently on the floor in front of Ek' Balam.

While Ek' Balam chewed on it, Na'om settled onto a wooden chair on the opposite side of the table from Najtir. She looked about the room. She only had vague memories of it as she'd been heavily drugged by Satal the last time she'd been in the house. The whole space looked and felt fresher than she remembered, though.

"Tz' and I did quite a thorough cleansing of this place many moons ago," Najtir said. He picked up the jug and poured some papaya juice into two of the cups. "I'm afraid I can't offer you much else," he said as he held a mug out to Na'om.

She took the proffered cup and sniffed the contents but didn't drink.

The shaman took a large swallow of the liquid. "It's quite safe, I assure you." He motioned for Na'om to drink.

Embarrassed, Na'om took a sip and smiled. The papaya juice was cool and sweet and soothing to her dry throat. "Thank you, it's delicious," she added. She took another sip.

"I hope you're hungry; I have a little place I like to go to for lunch in the market. But it's quite a distance for me to walk on my own, so I haven't been of late."

Na'om nodded her head. "Of course, I'd be happy to go with you." She pointed toward Ek' Balam. "That is, if you're all right with him staying here. I don't usually go into the marketplace with him as it tends to shut business down for a bit."

Najtir laughed, a dry chortle that almost set him to coughing. "I don't mind at all." Using the tabletop as support, he pushed himself up from his chair, and Na'om saw how the veins in his old, deep brown hands popped out as he pushed down. "I'll just get him a bowl of water, and then we can be on our way." He straightened the sleeve of one arm, pulling it down over the back of his hand, but not before Na'om could see the skin on his forearm didn't look normal, more scales than skin. Najtir shuffled back toward the heavy front door, which he left partially open, and Na'om watched as he disappeared into the outdoor kitchen.

Restless, Na'om stood up and patted Ek' Balam on the head. She wanted to learn more about Tz' and ask Najtir for ideas on how to defeat Satal, not go out for lunch, but she knew she needed to be patient with the elderly man. She looked about the room, noticing the mural of a battle scene painted on the wall, and the long hallway that led into the rest of the building. Her curiosity got the better of her, and throwing a quick glance back at the open doorway, she scurried down the hallway.

She glanced quickly into the first room. *Najtir must be living in here*, she thought as she looked at the several stacks of ledgers piled on the floor. A dark gray, woolen cloak and a matching linen loincloth hung from pegs driven into the stucco walls and a deep green hammock hung from one corner of the room to the other.

Na'om hurried the few feet to the next doorway and skidded to a stop. This was the room she'd battled Satal in, but it looked vastly different from the vague memories she had of it. The large cage in the corner was gone as well as the ropes that had tied her to the wall. A new blue-green hammock, doubled up on itself, hung from one hook in the center of one wall, and an old wooden wardrobe stood in the far corner. She approached it and opened the door on its copper hinges. Inside, she saw a pair of worn leather sandals and a chocolate-brown woolen blanket neatly folded on a shelf. Some paintbrushes and a few ceramic bowls of dried ink sat on another shelf. There was no sign of anything that might have belonged to Satal. *Of course, Tz' would have turned this room into his own place*, Na'om thought, and she smiled. She leaned in and buried her nose into the fabric of the blanket and felt a rush through her body as the semi-salty, sweaty scent of her childhood friend filled her head.

"Ahh, I see you've found Tz's room," Najtir said from the open doorway.

Na'om turned with a start, embarrassed to have been found poking about where she hadn't been invited.

"Not to worry, my dear. After all, these few possessions belong to your friend, not to me. Why, I'm only still here because he left without saying a word as to where I should go while he was gone. I surmise he thought I was dead, though, which probably is the reason for his hasty departure." Najtir laughed at his own words, but Na'om didn't see anything amusing in them.

The old man shuffled into the room and approached a small niche in the wall. He scooped up a statuette and handed it to Na'om.

"He made this in your likeness," he said, pressing the pottery statue into her open hand.

Na'om looked at the six-inch tall sculpture and was startled to see such a close resemblance to her own reflection in the sculpture. She turned the statue over in her hand, amazed at the amount of details Tz' had worked into it, right down to tiny leather sandals on her feet and a flower blossom tucked behind her one ear. "Box mentioned Tz' had made this." The thought of Box made her smile, and she wondered what he was doing. *Perhaps I'll go see him later today*, she thought. Suddenly, she heard a rumbling noise and looked up to see Najtir gripping his stomach with one hand. "Are you all right?" she asked and hurried to his side.

"Yes, just hungry," Najtir replied and laughed. He reached out and gripped her left wrist, motioning they should return to the front room. When they got back to the table, Na'om set the sculpture down. She didn't want to risk carrying it in her pocket while they made their way through the crowded marketplace. She looked down at Ek' Balam and smiled. "We'll be back soon." The cat yawned and laid his big head on his front paws while thumping the tip of his tail on the floor.

As they made their way out the door, Najtir grabbed a wooden staff leaning against the wall. He gripped it tightly in his left hand, while still holding on to Na'om's arm. "I shouldn't have any trouble walking now," Najtir said, but he stumbled down the three steps to the tiled courtyard.

As soon as they stepped into the street outside Satal's house, Na'om knew the slow walk to the market would test her patience. All activities and conversations in the street stopped when anyone saw them with their guards, creating an eerie, silent gauntlet for the two to pass through. Tens upon tens of eyes followed them, and then the noise resumed after they had passed. Na'om wanted to turn back and wait until nightfall to venture forth, but Najtir was determined to take her to his special eatery.

"Don't pay them any attention, Na'om," Najtir advised. "You have too many other things to consider than the likes of what the average man or woman might be thinking about you."

The marketplace was a hub of activity, so busy that many didn't see the couple with their attendant guards as they made their way through the crowd. They paused near the meat section so Najtir could rest a moment. While she waited, Na'om gazed at several dozen ocellated turkeys gobbling and pecking at the dirt inside small wooden pens, and the flies buzzing around a blood-covered wooden chopping block. A small basket filled with turkey heads was on the ground near the stump, and close by, a fire blazed under a large ceramic pot filled with water. Na'om watched as a woman dunked a plucked turkey carcass into the boiling water to rid it of its pin feathers. In another booth, men with long, black obsidian knives sliced at two deer carcasses hanging from wooden posts. They cut off strips of the lean meat and packaged them in banana leaves for the women waiting in line at the wooden counter at the front of the booth. Two young boys batted at each other with the tips of pink flamingo feathers while their mother haggled with the meat merchant over the cost of the venison. Nearby, another vendor hacked open a watermelon, showing the lush, red insides to any who passed while another man grabbed a large papaya from the mound of them at his feet and peeled the skin back, exposing the yellow interior. He thrust it at Na'om, and then, as soon as he saw who she was, he dropped the fruit in his haste to bow to her. Na'om bent down, picked up the papaya, and handed it back to the man before resuming her slow walk with Najtir.

"It's good to see some sense of normalcy has returned to the city," Na'om said as she followed Najtir into an interior aisle of the market.

"People still need to eat regardless of what's happened in the past."

They passed an older trader sitting cross-legged on a sky-blue blanket surrounded by bowls and baskets of dried herbs and spices. He held a grinding stone and bowl in his lap and was busy crushing a blend of berries. The pungent smell wafted in the air, mixing with the redolent scents from the bunches of drying plants hanging from hemp lines strung behind him. In the stall next to him, an older woman sat on a small stool in front of several large canvas bags filled with pink and white salt. Across the aisle, three booths in a row were filled with ceramic pots and jars filled with honey, and beeswax candles made in half-round coconut shells. The air hummed with bees, and Na'om ducked as one flew near her face.

The couple rounded a corner, entered a narrower aisle, and found themselves behind a muscular man dressed only in an indigo-dyed linen loincloth that hung to below his knees. He was several inches taller than Na'om, and his back and arms were covered with deep blue tattoos in geometric designs. As Na'om drew closer, she could see the patterns were made up of interlaced squares, rectangles, and triangles. She looked to either side, but there wasn't enough space to go around him, and he seemed oblivious to their presence. He balanced a large earthenware jug on one shoulder, and Na'om could see the taut muscles in the man's back and arm flex as he walked.

Suddenly, Najtir reached out and poked the man's backside with his wooden staff. The man muttered a complaint and turned around, but instantly stopped when he saw who it was who had prodded him. He bowed quickly, and liquid sloshed over the wide, open lip of the ceramic container he carried. Na'om yelped and jumped to avoid getting splattered as the liquid landed with a splash on the hardened ground underfoot. The sweet smell of papaya juice permeated the air, and people in the crowd turned to see what was going on, creating a clot in the alleyway.

"Are you all right, my lady?"

Na'om nodded and looked up at the man. *Why, he's not much older than me*, she thought as she studied his lean face and looked into his dark brown eyes. He smiled and she felt her heart beat a little quicker, so she dropped her gaze to study the crisscross of blue tattoos that stretched across his well-defined chest.

The brawny man quickly set his jug on the ground and began to push the onlookers to either side. "Make way, you fools, Lady Na'om is trying to get through. Make way for Lady Na'om and her friend," he bellowed. He gripped a young man by the shoulder and practically tossed him into the nearest booth full of woven blankets. He pushed another couple out of the way before returning to stand in front of Na'om. He bowed deeply. "My lady, please, I beg you, don't come to the market again unless you have a better escort," he said as he looked at the four guards standing nearby.

"You're quite right, it was foolish of me to venture here during the day without a full regiment," she joked.

Najtir spoke up. "I'm to blame, I'm afraid. I do so crave old T'ot's cooking."

"If my lady will allow me, I'll lead you to the place."

Na'om stared at the man's midsection as his stomach muscles rippled when he bowed again.

She shook her head slightly. "What of your wares, your jug of juice?" Na'om asked. "You must be headed someplace with it? We'll be all right on our own, I'm sure."

"The juice can wait here out of the way," the young man said. "My only wish is to serve you, my lady, in any manner that I may."

Na'om looked ahead at the people waiting for them to pass and felt a sense of safety in the stranger's presence. "What's your name?" she asked.

"Biribik, my lady," the man replied. He turned and began to walk ahead of Na'om, Najtir, and the two forward guards. "Go on, now, all of you, back to your work," he shouted. He used his arms to force his way through the throngs of people still milling about. "Let them through, I say." He led the couple straight to the section of the market filled with food booths and found old T'ot's seafood shop without any trouble.

Using his big hand, Biribik wiped off the seats of two of the three leather stools standing in front of the eatery. Then he rapped on the nearest wooden upright with his big fist, causing the whole wooden booth to shake. "T'ot," he shouted, "you've got customers!" He bowed to Na'om. "Enjoy your meal, my lady," he said and started to move away.

"Wait," Na'om said, and she touched him lightly on the forearm. Her fingers tingled at the connection, and she hastily withdrew her hand. She reached into her skirt pocket and extracted a cacao bean, which she held out to Biribik.

"No, my lady, thank you, but I won't take it. I only wanted to make sure you arrived safely at your destination."

"Well, if you won't take any payment, then I insist you join us for lunch, and then provide us with safe passage back out of this maze of stalls." Na'om pointed to the third stool on the other side of Najtir, and with a shy grin, Biribik sat down on it.

Old T'ot poked her head out from behind a thin curtain at the back of the booth and smiled when she saw them. She shuffled forward, and when she reached the counter, she leaned over and patted Najtir's arthritic hands, then hobbled to the side of the booth and leaned in to give Biribik a peck on the cheek.

"Where's my papaya juice?" she yelled at him.

Biribik jumped up from his stool, bowed to T'ot, and pointed to Na'om. "I needed to make sure they arrived here safely, Nim-ati't," he roared. "I'll bring it at once." With another bow, this time to Na'om, the youth dashed off into the crowd.

Na'om stared after him for a moment and then nudged Najtir. "Did you know he was her great-grandson?"

"Perhaps," Najtir replied, with a slight grin. He turned to face T'ot who was back behind the counter. "Two large plates of your salted crab cakes, T'ot, dear!" he shouted.

T'ot smiled, nodded her head, and shuffled back behind the curtain.

"I hope you don't mind me ordering for both of us," Najtir said. He shifted his weight on the stool, and Na'om heard the creak and pop of the old man's spine as he moved. "If you'd prefer something else," he waved his hand at the painted banner hanging over their heads that showed the various seafood dishes available, "I can order it."

"No, no, whatever you like is fine," Na'om replied. She scanned the crowds around them and wondered when Biribik would return. She wanted to ask him about his elaborate tattoos.

"Your young friend, Tz', enjoyed them for a time," Najtir said.

At the mention of Tz's name, she felt a shiver go down her spine. For a few moments, she'd forgotten about him.

Just then, Biribik reappeared near her with the large jug of papaya juice balanced carefully on his shoulder. Na'om couldn't help but stare. *I don't think I've ever seen someone so strong*, she thought as she watched Biribik step behind the wooden counter and place the ceramic container on it. He then reached underneath the board and pulled out a tray with several earthenware mugs on it. He carefully poured the liquid into the cups and set the jug on the ground, out of the way.

Na'om felt him looking at her as he handed her a mug, and she looked up into his deep brown eyes. "To your health, Lady Na'om," he said, with a twinkle in his eyes. He took a deep gulp of the juice before coming around to sit at the counter beside Najtir.

"Oh no, you forgot to order for Biribik," Na'om whispered to Najtir.

Just then, T'ot reappeared from behind the tattered cloth curtain with a tray full of food. In the center was a large platter piled high with steaming hot crab cakes and on either side were small bowls filled with a variety of different colored sauces. The spicy, rich scents of peppers and tomatoes emanated from the deep red, green, and brown mixtures, and Na'om felt her mouth water. T'ot set the heavy tray down on the counter with a thud, then reached underneath and pulled out a mug full of wooden spoons, then a stack of black-and-white-striped ceramic plates. She handed a plate to Na'om and one to Najtir and was going to return the extras when Biribik spoke up.

"Nim-ati't, what about me?" he cried. He pointed to the jug on the ground behind her. "I brought your juice!"

"Bah," T'ot replied. "You drink and eat all my profits today!" But she gave him a mischievous smile and finally handed him a plate.

Najtir used a large, carved wooden spoon to flip several of the hot crab cakes onto Na'om's plate and then did the same to his own. Then he ladled some of the deep green sauce over them, cut a piece, and popped it into his mouth. A smile of contentment spread across his face.

Na'om took a small mahogany spoon from the cup, cut the first crab cake into pieces, and blew on a piece before putting it into her mouth. Her first impression was one of salt, but as she chewed, she tasted sweet corn and fish. The texture was slightly stringy and chewy with lumps of gritty cornmeal and not at all what she had expected. She took another bite, though, savoring the complex blend of crab and corn and salt. By the third bite, she was hooked, and she smiled at Najtir. "They're good."

The trio quickly ate the entire platter of crab cakes, washing down the salty food with swigs of the papaya juice. When they were done, Biribik hopped up, stacked the dirty dishes on the tray, and took them behind the curtain.

Na'om furtively watched him as he moved, noticing the swell of his strong calves and the sinewy strength of his arms. *He looks as strong as a jaguar*, she thought. *I doubt anyone could hurt him.*

"He'd be a good bodyguard for you, my dear," Najtir said. He gently placed his hand on her forearm.

Startled out of her thoughts, Na'om jumped at the shaman's touch. "But I have Ek' Balam to protect me. And the city guards."

"Ah, but where is your cat right now?" Najtir gestured toward the people milling about. "There are certain situations where a man by your side is more helpful than the largest jaguar. As for the guards," he motioned to the men lolling against the counter of a nearby booth and watched as one man yawned. "I suspect they'd rather be guarding the walls of the city."

T'ot and Biribik reappeared and approached the counter. Najtir dipped his hand into his purse and pulled out several cacao beans. With surprising agility, he leaned forward and grabbed T'ot by one wrist and squeezed, forcing the old woman to open her hand. He dropped the beans onto her palm, then carefully folded her fingers back over them, and patted her hand with his fingers. "We'll be back tomorrow," he said loudly and slid off the stool. He picked up his staff, nodded to Na'om and Biribik, and began to move into the nearby crowd.

Biribik bent down and kissed T'ot on the cheek, then motioned to Na'om, who smiled at the old woman before hurrying after Najtir. Biribik's presence in the small alleyways forced the other patrons to one side and the other, giving Na'om and Najtir clear passage to the outer edge of the marketplace.

Na'om tapped Biribik on the shoulder, forcing him to stop in mid-stride. "We should be all right on our own now," Na'om said as she paused under the last awning. The plaza in front of them was overly bright, and her eyes watered from the glare of the sun. She hastened to wipe the tears away. She heard noises coming from the left, turned in that direction, and watched as a young turkey half walked, half flew into the mix of people in front of them. A young boy dove into the group, attempting to catch the bird, which gobbled and squawked before flying up to perch on the edge of the nearest building. An older man chased the young boy and caught him by his bare shoulder, gripping it with such strength that Na'om could see the pain on the boy's face. The crowd of people swiftly moved away from them as the man yelled at the boy and dragged him back the way they had come. The man looked up at the turkey as they passed underneath it and shouted at the bird as well.

"With all due respect, my lady, I believe it wiser to accompany you back to your own home," Biribik said.

Na'om nodded. "All right," she replied. She smiled and admitted to herself that she liked the way Biribik made it that much easier to walk through the city during the day.

As the group stepped out into the plaza, another noise forced them to stop. A dozen city guards, dressed in their leather battle gear, trotted forward and began to fan out into the market.

"Look everywhere," a male voice called out.

Na'om stepped forward and peered over Biribik's shoulder. "Yakal," she shouted and saw the man turn at the sound of his voice. She still had trouble calling him Father and preferred to use his name.

Yakal hurried forward and bowed, then grabbed the nearest guard by the arm. "Tell the others we've found her," he said. The man nodded and picked up a bone whistle that hung from a cord around his neck. He blew three short times, and the shrill notes pierced the air.

Yakal nodded to Najtir and scanned Biribik, who still stood to one side, from head to toe. "We've been searching the city for you, Na'om. You mustn't wander about all alone like this."

Na'om felt a wave of annoyance flow through her at Yakal's words. "I'm not alone," she replied. She felt Najtir grip her forearm. "Between my powers and those of Najtir's, plus Biribik's obvious physical strength, I doubt there's anyone or anything that can harm me." She pointed to the four men nearby. "And I have my guards with me as well."

Yakal shuffled his feet and looked down at the ground. "Yes, yes, of course, my apologies, I meant no disrespect. It's only that the council members wanted to meet again, and when guards were sent to Satal's palace, they found Ek' Balam, but no sign of you. . . ."

He looked up, and Na'om saw the lines of worry etched into his deeply tanned skin. Her irritation dissipated. "I'm sorry, *Ajaw*, I should have left word with someone."

"I'm to blame, if anyone is," Najtir said. "I craved some more crab cakes. But I should think we're allowed to walk *inside* the city walls without too much fuss."

"Yes, yes, of course," Yakal replied. "We'll not make the same mistake twice." He motioned for the group to begin walking again and fell into step beside Na'om. "Who is this youth, Biribik?" he whispered.

Na'om smiled and stopped walking. "The newest member of my guard detail. I'll need you to outfit him with a proper leather breastplate, shield, and whatever else he might need."

"As you wish, Lady Na'om." Yakal snapped his fingers and one of the guards stepped forward. "Take this boy to Nimal and tell him that Lady Na'om wants him properly supplied with all the gear needed as a guard."

Biribik bowed low to both Yakal and Na'om. "You honor me, my lady. I promise you'll not regret this fortuitous day." He turned and followed the guard into the nearby crowd.

Yakal leaned in close to Na'om. "The shamans have some more details they'd like to discuss with you about the counterattack," he said in a low voice.

"We'll walk Najtir back to his house and then Ek' Balam and I will meet you at the Temple of the Warriors."

Yakal bowed and prepared to leave the group. "I'll inform the others."

Na'om reached out and touched her father's arm. "Please, can we be a bit less formal with each other in the future?"

Yakal smiled, and Na'om was surprised to see how much younger he looked when he did so. "I would like that very much," he replied. And then he bowed again and left.

Na'om shook her head as she began walking beside Najtir again. "So much for dropping the formalities."

"He loves you very much, my dear," Najtir said.

Na'om turned sideways and looked at the old shaman. "Really, bowing to me and calling me 'Lady Na'om' tells you that he loves me?"

"No, not that. It's in his eyes and the way he was so worried looking when he couldn't find you. He loves you deeply."

"Hmm, I find that a bit difficult to believe considering he doesn't even know me." Na'om felt her old anger at being abandoned as a newborn child rising inside her, and she focused her attention to keep it contained.

"You mustn't let the past bother you so, Na'om. Yakal has done much to prove his loyalty to this city and to you, including risking his own life to defeat Satal in the battle here. Why, if he hadn't thrown salt water on her, the city might have fallen that night. But instead, he wounded Satal, and she and her horde fled the region instantly." Najtir patted her arm. "Let him into your heart, my child. Replace the anger with love."

Na'om nodded, but she knew it wasn't that simple. Yakal was her father, but he had never been there for her while she was growing up and never seen her until just a few weeks ago. How could he possibly love her when she was a complete stranger to him? She shook her head to clear it. *Now is not the time to be thinking about all of this*, she mused as they continued to Najtir's home.

Ek' Balam was waiting by the front door when they arrived. Na'om hurried inside and got the small statue that she'd left on the table while Najtir made himself comfortable in a nearby chair.

"Come back tomorrow, Na'om; you have much to do before the Wayeb," Najtir said.

Na'om turned with a start and was going to ask the old shaman how he knew about the counterattack, then thought better of it. "Maltiox, Najtir, I will be back in the morning," Na'om replied. She and Ek' Balam, with their guards, quickly made their way back into the street, headed to the Temple of the Warriors. She wondered what the council members wanted to discuss that hadn't been covered in their previous meeting.

Tz'

The need for meat woke Tz' from an uneasy sleep filled with vague dreams about a human, a young girl, someone he thought he might have known at some point. He struggled to remember his life before his encounter with Hun-Kamé, but it was all a blur. Frustrated and hungry, he joined Xojol in poking around in the massive bone pile.

Try under there, she said, pointing to an extra-large set of deer ribs balanced precariously on top of some peccary skulls.

Tz' pulled with his front paws and managed to snag a few bites of half-rotten meat that lay under the pile of bones. *Maltiox*, he replied as he licked his lips. *I'll be glad when we can go hunt. I'm ready for fresh meat.*

Xojol smiled, exposing her fangs. *We go in a few hours. Then we'll feast for days and days, and the other males will be happy again.* She pranced a few steps on her large paws. *I'll dance in the light of the moon and remember. . . .* She paused.

You'll remember? Tz' prompted.

Oh, nothing, it doesn't matter. What's important is that you are the pack leader, and we can exit Xibalba tonight, together. She grinned, exposing her yellowed teeth, and then turned and waved her tail in Tz's face.

Tz' smiled. He was ready to take his place and command the others to do his bidding. He was eager to see something new and different from the cave and tunnels he'd been in. And he was ready to mate with Xojol.

Xojol rubbed against him. *Later tonight, you shall feel one of the most joyous moments in an animal's life,* she purred.

Why wait? Let's go now, Tz' cried and he moved toward a tunnel entrance.

Xojol leaped and landed in front of him. *We'll have more energy once we've feasted. For now, we must rest and prepare for the night.*

Reluctantly, Tz' allowed Xojol to lead him back to his place. The other were-jaguars watched as he settled down, and then they went back to grooming and sleeping.

A nudge on his shoulder woke Tz' hours later, and he was surprised to find Xojol standing over him. *It's time. Let's go.*

Tz' arched his back and stretched but was dismayed to see several of the others, including Bajbik, had already left the cave. He quickly loped after them and angrily pushed his way to the head of the pack. Reluctantly, Bajbik stepped in behind him, and the others followed. As they moved farther away from the cave, the air smelled cleaner, fresher, and Tz' sucked it in deeply, savoring the delicate scents. Images and memories flooded his mind, and he put names to the smells: flower blossoms, cooked foods, and the myriad smells of humans. Each scent grew stronger as they approached the surface, and Tz' realized he'd never noticed there were so many different odors in the world. His nostrils flared wide when he finally stepped out of the long tunnel and into the moonlight on the surface.

The other were-jaguars flowed out around him and rapidly dispersed into the countryside, beginning their search for food, but Tz' abruptly sat down, too stunned by the beauty of the world before him to move. The dark silhouettes of ceiba trees, bunches of grasses and sedges, and small creosote bushes stood in sharp contrast to the bright light cast by the full moon, and he felt he had never seen anything so lovely. The air was warm and caressed him like a hand stroking his fur. He breathed in the tang of limes, the sweet perfume of jacaranda blossoms, and an elusive scent that filled him with yearning. Lifting his large head, he looked up into the inky sky and sucked in his breath, amazed by the millions of twinkling lights of the stars and planets. His eyes watered, and he hastily swiped at them with one paw when he caught movement out of the corner of his eye. He twisted his head to see Xojol had returned.

The first time is always a bit overpowering, she thought as she stood patiently beside Tz'. *But you mustn't forget the main reason we're here, to hunt. Come, I know a good place where you can catch a deer to bring back to the lair.*

Tz' nodded and silently followed Xojol as she led him through the creosote bushes and lime trees to a small gully. Several deer had bedded down among a thicket of ceiba trees, and with Xojol's help, Tz' brought down a large, older male. Together, they fed on the warm carcass until they couldn't eat another bite, then Tz' dragged the remains back to the entrance to the Underworld. He lay down, tired from his effort. He was still overcome by the strange sounds of night birds and nocturnal animals and the plethora of smells that drifted by on the light breeze.

Full of food, Xojol frolicked in the darkness under the nearby lime trees, chasing her own shadow as she wound in and around the tree trunks. With his eyes only half-open, Tz' watched her, amazed at her agility, and then caught his breath as a shaft of moonlight illuminated her. The shift in light transformed her into a naked, young woman, with long, strong arms and legs, rounded hips, and perky breasts that bobbed on her chest as she moved to some inner rhythm. He sat up, purring deeply, and Xojol turned to smile at him. As the shadows played back and forth across her face, she shifted in and out of human form so rapidly that Tz' had to close his eyes. He only opened them when he felt hot breath on his cheek and found Xojol panting beside him. She was a were-jaguar once again, and Tz' dropped his eyes to study the ground.

What's wrong? Xojol asked.

Nothing. Tz' refused to look at her. His desire for her ran hot through his body. *I . . . I think I ate too much, that's all.*

Ha, you're not very good at lying, are you, Xojol replied. *You saw me, the real me, didn't you? It doesn't happen very often, but I sensed it did this time.*

Tz' nodded his head. *You're so beautiful.* He lifted his head and stared into Xojol's deep orange eyes. He felt himself being drawn closer and closer to Xojol until their muzzles touched, and she purred as she rubbed her soft cheek against his.

Follow me, she whispered in his ear and began to head back into the thicket of lime trees.

Tz' hesitated, unsure of what to do or what was about to happen. He continued to watch as Xojol sauntered a few more paces toward the trees.

Then she turned her head and caught his gaze.

Come on, we have plenty of time before the others return. Come dance with me in the moonlight. She stepped into the shadows, and once again, the strange light shifted her image into that of a young woman, stretching her arms toward the sky. She beckoned toward the stars and then to Tz' to come forward and join her.

As her naked appearance drifted in and out of the light, Tz' felt more and more aroused and quickly hurried to join Xojol. Occasionally, he thought he could see his own human form, but whenever he looked directly at his limbs, they were still in the shape of a jaguar. He kept staring at Xojol as she moved lithely among the tree limbs where the bittersweet scent of lime blossoms was the strongest.

Forget your past, your former self, and just enjoy the moment, Xojol purred as she increased the tempo of her dancing. Her paws tapped a beat into the dry dirt, and Tz' found himself moving in step with her. Their tails were high on their backs as they advanced and receded, creating a duet to a tune only Xojol could hear. Then she arched her back, dropped her head, and slid onto her belly before rolling over with all four paws in the air.

She suddenly looked so silly that Tz' stopped in mid-stride and purred, a deep growling rumble that filled his chest. He flopped down beside Xojol, and they rolled together on the ground, their limbs entwined in a pleasing embrace. Without warning, Tz' felt Xojol flatten herself onto the ground underneath him, with her front paws braced against the dirt. He bit her gently in the back of the neck and began to rise up over her when a shift in the wind brought a waft of scent so tantalizing that Tz' had to turn his head. The smell was too overwhelming; he jumped up and began to run, leaping over creosote bushes and dodging around small ceiba trees, his nose constantly twitching as he followed the elusive smell.

Tz', wait, come back! Xojol cried. *You'll never make it back to the cave before the moon sets; you must come back!*

Tz' heard Xojol's words in his head and knew he should turn back, but he had to find the source of the perfume that filled his body with a depth of longing he'd never experienced before. Then, suddenly the wind shifted, and he lost track of the aroma. He loped along, searching and sniffing right and left, but the smell was gone. He stopped and looked around him. Nothing looked familiar and he had no idea where the entrance to the cave was. Fortunately, Xojol was only a hundred paces or so away, and he walked slowly toward her, his tail dragging on the ground.

When he was a foot away from Xojol, she reached out with her front paw and smacked him across the muzzle.

Hey, what was that for? he cried while he swiped at the area with his paw.

For taking off like that, she said, and then Xojol came to him and licked the spot with her raspy tongue. *We don't have much time; we must return to the cave before the moon sets.*

Tz' lifted his heavy head and saw the moon was low on the horizon. *I'm sorry, I smelled something so irresistible that I had to find out what it was.*

Un hunh, Xojol replied. *Come on; we have to hurry.* Xojol began to run and Tz' followed her. In a few minutes, they could see the cave entrance, and they slowed to a walk. *If you're nice to me, perhaps during the next full moon, I'll show you how you can visit her,* Xojol said.

Tz' leaped forward, landing directly in front of Xojol. He grabbed her head between his large front paws and bared his fangs inches from her muzzle. *What did you just say?* he demanded. *Visit who?*

The one whose scent you followed just now.

Images flooded Tz' head, and he backed away from Xojol. There *was* a girl, someone he loved. He could see her face, but he couldn't remember her name.

There's a chance to see this person, even when I'm like this?

Mmm, hmm, Xojol replied. *But we've run out of time now, so you'll have to wait.*

Tz' felt anger building inside, and he wanted nothing more than to bite Xojol's thick skull, to feel it crush beneath his fangs. He growled and forced himself to take several steps away from the young female. He lifted his nose toward the sky, concentrating on the blackness between the stars. *I could have seen her, whoever she is.* A deep, rumbling snarl started in the digits of his feet, poured up and through his body, and exploded out of his mouth, silencing the small chittering of the nocturnal animals that were hidden in the creosote bushes. He howled and yelped, spewing his frustration and pain into the night until his throat was sore.

Exhausted, he sank to the ground and didn't have the energy to move when Xojol came and knelt beside him. She ran her rough tongue up and over his face and ears, licking away the tiny flecks of spittle on his fur. She continued to groom him even when the other were-jaguars returned to the cave entrance, each male dragging the carcass of an animal.

Tz' was the last to enter the tunnel with his partially eaten deer carcass. He lingered in the shadows long after the others had disappeared into the warren of tunnels, watching the darkness, moon, and stars revolving overhead. It was only when the sky began to really lighten on the eastern horizon that he turned his back on the living. Choking back a sob, he bit into the haunch of the deer and began the arduous task of dragging it back to the main cave. He needed food to eat if he was to survive the next month, and then he would find this person and be with her, if only for a few hours.

SATAL

When Satal woke, the inside of her skin crawled as if a thousand ants marched inside her body. It was the cloud of noxious, mustard-yellow gas inside her. It pulsed and throbbed with her heartbeat, pushing against her interior, creating an itching that was impossible to scratch. She felt bloated by the thick haze and knew she needed to release it. But she didn't want the fog to settle over Chichén Itzá; no, she wanted to send this cloud to Mayapán where it could drift over her enemies. She just needed someone to deliver it.

"Tewichinel, come here," she called. Within minutes she heard the man's sandals slapping against the tile floor as he hurried down the hallway to her bedroom. He bowed as he entered the room.

"Lady Satal, how may I be of service?"

"Of all the shamans, who do you most trust?"

"Pataninel, my lady."

"And who is the least helpful?"

Tewichinel looked up and stared at Satal's face. "I don't like to speak ill of my brothers, my lady, but I would have to say Yuxba' is the least useful of all."

"Good, summon the two of them. I have a job for them to do."

"At once, my lady," Tewichinel replied and he left the room.

While Satal waited for the men to return, she struggled to remove her night shift. She didn't want to wait for Tewichinel to dress her. It was time she assumed control of her own body once again. She grimaced as a sharp twinge of pain shot down her damaged left arm to the tips of her fingers as she pulled on a dark blue shirt. Beads of sweat formed on her brow as she tugged up the waistband of her skirt. *Itzamná, I can't wait to destroy Yakal and all the people he cares about.*

She was seated at the large wooden dining table when the three shamans knocked and entered the palace.

"You summoned us, my lady?" Pataninel asked. He bowed so deeply that his black monkey skin cape touched the floor.

"Yes, yes, enough of the bowing, all of you. I have a special mission for the two of you," Satal said as she pointed at the chairs nearby. "Make yourselves comfortable."

Yuxba' and Pataninel hurried to take their seats, but Tewichinel remained standing.

"Shall I bring some refreshments, my lady?" he asked.

Satal shook her head. "It's not necessary; this won't take long." She leaned forward in her chair and looked from Yuxba' to Pataninel. "Neither of you participated directly in the attack on Mayapán, a misfortunate circumstance, but one that couldn't be avoided. Therefore, I have a special task for both of you to perform now." She reached out and touched Yuxba's hand. "Especially you, my friend."

The older, thin shaman flinched, and Satal could feel him fighting the urge to withdraw his hand.

"It's all right, Yuxba', don't be afraid. It won't require you to shapeshift. I just need you to carry a special package to Mayapán." She turned to Pataninel. "It's your task to make sure he delivers it. And if he should fail, then you are to continue, is that understood?"

"Yes, Lady Satal, of course." Pataninel smiled. "It will be an honor to serve you in any way that I can."

Satal nodded to Tewichinel who still stood near the table. "Hold him," she said as she pointed at Yuxba'. The elder shaman quickly stepped behind Yuxba' and grasped him firmly by the shoulders. Yuxba' struggled.

"Lady Satal, please, I beg you, let me go," he cried. He thrashed in his seat and Pataninel quickly jumped up and helped Tewichinel hold him fast to his seat.

Satal approached. "Open your mouth," she commanded.

"My lady, I don't understand. . . ." Yuxba' stammered.

"Quiet, just open your mouth," Satal said as she leaned in toward the shaman.

Yuxba' shook his head and wrestled against the other men. Pataninel reached out one hand and grabbed him by the chin. "Open your mouth, fool," he whispered in Yuxba's ear as he applied pressure to his jaw bone.

Yuxba' shrieked from the pain and his mouth popped open.

Satal opened her own mouth and closed her eyes. She envisioned the cloud of venomous pollen swirling inside her, rising from her belly into her throat and then her mouth before it spilled forth in a current that flowed directly into Yuxba's body. The shaman gagged and squirmed in his chair, but Pataninel continued to hold his mouth open.

As the fog flowed out of her body, Satal felt the itchiness and unease inside her abate. A sense of emptiness and peace overtook her, and she closed her mouth.

"Be still, Yuxba', wriggling about won't make it any more pleasant," Satal said. She sat down and looked at the shaman. "When you reach the outskirts of Mayapán, you must release the toxic gases inside you into the air. The sooner you do this, the better, so I urge you to leave at once." She turned to look at Pataninel. "If he should falter, you must suck the poison out of him and deliver it yourself." She stared directly into the shaman's eyes. "You understand what I'm saying?"

"Yes, Lady Satal, have no fear, we shall not fail." The shaman adjusted his cape and tapped Yuxba' on the shoulder. "Come on, no sense loitering here." Yuxba' continued to sit. His face muscles twitched, and he blinked his eyes rapidly in succession, but otherwise did nothing. Pataninel moved in front of Yuxba' and grabbed him under the armpits, lifting him from the chair. "Come on, the sooner we get going, the better you'll feel."

"May the gods grant you speed," Satal said as the two men quickly left the room.

She laughed once the men were gone. "Itzamná, I'm starved. Bring me my breakfast, Tewichinel."

"Of course, Lady Satal," the shaman said, and he hurried from the room.

That was a good day's work and the morning's not even over, Satal thought. *I wonder what else I can do to thwart the efforts of Na'om and her friends before they enter the city?*

NA'OM

When Na'om and Ek Balam arrived at the temple, Yakal was waiting outside the entrance. Na'om nodded to her father and headed straight to the meeting room, and Yakal followed. Chiman and Ajkun were seated at the large table, and Nimal and one of his guards stood near the doorway.

Ajkun stood up and hurried over to her. "Thank the gods you're all right," Ajkun said as she embraced Na'om.

"Yes, I'm fine, why wouldn't I be?" Na'om asked as she sat down in a vacant chair.

"No one knew where you were; we were worried something might have happened to you," Chiman said.

"Is this why you called another meeting?" Na'om tried to keep the irritation she felt out of her voice, but she failed.

Nimal interrupted. "Is this the person you saw last night?" he asked the guard.

"Yes, the Lady Na'om, Ajaw," the guard replied.

Na'om frowned. "What's going on?" she asked.

Nimal motioned to the guard. "All right, you may go." The man quickly left the room. "You have your answer, so I'll let you sort this out, Chiman,"

Nimal said and quickly followed the sentry down the hallway.

Na'om looked at her father and grandparents. "What is this all about?"

"That guard reported to Nimal that you went outside the gates last night without a full escort," Yakal said.

"Yes, I did, but Ek' Balam was with me. We were perfectly safe."

"No, you're not safe," Ajkun cried. "Satal is extremely powerful, and we don't know exactly what she's planning to do. You can't just leave the city, in the middle of the night, with no one to protect you."

Na'om could feel the frustration rising inside her chest. "I'm not a child, so please stop treating me like one. I'm capable of taking care of myself."

Ajkun sighed and looked to Chiman. He reached out and patted Na'om's hand. "We know that, dear, but all of us are dependent on you to defeat Satal. You're the only one in the land who can get rid of her, and that makes you even more valuable to us than before all of this mess started."

Yakal added, "Nothing matters right now except your continued safety, and we can't ensure that if you're out wandering beyond the city walls in the deepest part of the night."

"So, I'm to never be alone except inside my hut? I always have to have an escort and tell you where I'll be?" Na'om knocked her chair over as she stood up abruptly. "Where were any of you when I wandered alone through the Underworld? Why weren't you there for me then? Why did I have to come all the way to Mayapán to rescue you and then, when I needed help, you couldn't rescue me? Everyone expects me to kill Satal. You all think that by doing so, your life will go back to normal, the way it was before she attacked this city, but what about me and my life? Will anything ever be normal for me again? I've always been the outcast, the unwanted one," she paused and looked directly at Yakal before continuing. "I learned to live my life on the fringes of the village with no one but Tz' as my friend, and now, I'm suddenly thrust into this leadership role. I'm supposed to take care of everything for everyone, people I don't even know. What about me, what about Tz'? What about my life with him? None of you are thinking of what I want or need!" Angry tears rolled down Na'om's face, and she ran from the room.

"Na'om! Wait!" Ajkun cried. She ran after her granddaughter and caught up with Na'om before she could leave the building. "I realize all of this is difficult for you. Life hasn't been easy for you, and we are all asking for so much right now. But you can't imagine the torment we went through when we thought you'd died. My heart broke the day Chiman told me." Ajkun's voice quavered. She took a deep breath and smiled at Na'om. "Can you please just promise me one thing?"

Na'om felt her anger subside. She sighed and nodded.

"Please, if you must go outside the city, during the day or at night, please, just take some guards with you. We need to know that you're safe. That's all we ask."

Na'om wiped the tears from her face and leaned into her grandmother's outstretched arms. "I just want to go home, Ati't. I know everyone expects me to fight Satal, but to be honest, I don't know if I can defeat her." She drew in a deep breath and savored the spicy scents of herbs and plants that always clung to Ajkun's clothes. "I just want to find Tz' and go home and have life go back to the way it was before the raiders attacked our village." She drew in another big breath and then straightened up.

"We all want to go home, my dear." Ajkun's voice wobbled a little as she spoke. "I miss the children so much; you have no idea. . . ." She coughed, cleared her throat, and straightened her shoulders. "But we must put our emotions aside for the time being and perform the duties the gods have set before us. Life can't go back to the way it was, but we can make it as normal as possible once we return to the village." She hugged Na'om. "Will it be all right if I tell Chiman and the others that you've agreed to take guards with you if you should go outside the gates, but that in the city's walls, you're free to move about as you wish, with or without an escort."

Na'om smiled weakly and nodded. "With Ek' Balam and Biribik by my side, I doubt I'll need anyone else to protect me."

Ajkun nodded. "Tell me about this man, Biribik. Yakal says you've made him a guard."

Na'om blushed. "He came to my rescue earlier in the marketplace, and I believe I can trust him." She stopped walking as she didn't want to reenter the council room and face Chiman and Yakal again. "I'm tired, Ati't. I'm going back to my hut to lie down for a bit." She kissed her grandmother on the cheek. "Come on, boy, let's go," she said to Ek' Balam, and together, they hurried back down the empty hallway and into the bright sunlight. Two guards stepped forward to accompany Na'om, and she was too weary to protest.

The group made its way toward her hut, and when the guards left, Na'om lay down, thinking she'd take a nap. But within minutes, she knew sleep was not going to come easily, so she decided to go for a walk. She put on a long-sleeved shirt and wrapped a shawl around her head, then told Ek' Balam to stay in the hut. "I won't be in disguise with you by my side," Na'om said to the jaguar as he waited patiently by the door. "Stay here; I'll be fine on my own." Ek' Balam yawned and curled up on the floor.

Na'om went outside and stood in the small courtyard for a few minutes, trying to decide where to go, and finally chose the market. She was able to walk through the narrow streets without anyone recognizing her, and she felt a small thrill go through her body at being unseen. The market area was very busy and she almost turned away, but the sight of some brightly painted pottery bowls attracted her. She made her way past several groups of women haggling over some fresh deer meat and stopped to look at all the pretty bowls. She'd never seen so many in one place, each one painted with a different design. There were ruby-throated hummingbirds, bright green sea turtles, black crows, geometric shapes and swirls, and flowers of all kinds on the small dishes. Na'om finally found three that she especially liked and stood for a moment, trying to decide which one to buy. She settled on one painted with a bouquet of orange flowers in a small blue vase on a green background. It reminded her of the paintings she'd begun on the walls of her small hut in Pa nimá. She reached into her pocket and extracted a cacao bean, then stretched out her hand to give it to the vendor. In the process, her shirtsleeve pulled up, and she heard the man gasp as he realized who was standing in front of him.

"You honor me with your presence, Lady Na'om," the vendor said. "I cannot charge you for the bowl. Please accept it as a small gift."

"Maltiox," Na'om said. She smiled and began to turn away.

Just then, she heard the man shout, "Look, my friends, Lady Na'om is here, getting her dishes at my stall. Come shop where Lady Na'om shops."

At the mention of her name, the humming of voices slowly ceased as people in all directions turned around to stare at her.

Na'om pulled her shawl over her face, but the jaguar markings on her hands and lower legs gave her away. The crowd began to push in on all sides to see her more closely, and a few men and women reached out to touch her.

Na'om felt a wave of panic rise in her belly as she realized there was no way to escape the crowd. More hands grabbed her, tugging on her shirt and shawl, which slipped from her head, exposing her face. Some in the group gasped and stepped back, while others continued to push forward, creating a crush of bodies that forced Na'om back toward the pottery vendor's stall. She tried to keep her distance from the stacks of plates and bowls that filled the front of the booth, but the throng kept advancing, and she bumped into a pile, sending it tumbling to the ground with a loud crash.

"Get back, get back," the vendor cried as more dishes fell and broke.

"I'm sorry," Na'om said to the man. She closed her eyes as more hands poked and prodded her. *I could send out a beam of light and force everyone back, but I'm afraid I might hurt someone,* she thought.

She could hear the vendor muttering to himself as he began to pick up the broken shards of pottery.

"All right, everyone, back away," a familiar voice said.

Na'om opened her eyes and smiled.

"That means you," Box said as he gently pushed an older woman to one side. "Are you all right, my lady?" he asked as he stepped in front of Na'om, shielding her from the crowd.

"Yes, maltiox, you arrived just in time. But I'm afraid I've created quite a bit of damage in this man's booth," Na'om said.

"Hmm, I saw the whole thing, and it serves him right for thinking he could gain more business by saying your name."

"Nevertheless, I should pay him for the damage," Na'om said as she placed a few cacao beans on the ground next to the broken dishes and near the older man where he crouched in the dirt.

He looked up from his task and smiled. "Maltiox, Lady Na'om. I meant no harm to you," he said, and he ducked his head until it almost touched the ground.

Box stepped to the side of Na'om and placed his hand gently on her back. "Let's get you out of here and back to the safety of your hut, shall we?"

The light placement of his fingers sent a shiver of excitement up Na'om's spine, and she smiled again as they moved away from the groups who continued to stare at the couple. "What were you doing in the market?" she asked.

"Getting a gourd full of papaya juice to drink," Box said and held up the container. "Working the kilns is hot work, and I needed something cool to drink."

They quickly made their way back to Na'om's hut where Box smiled and hurried off before Puk'pik noticed he was gone.

Na'om put her little bowl on the one table in the room and squatted down next to Ek' Balam. "All right, I learned my lesson. Next time, we go together." She sat on the edge of the hammock and rocked back and forth. She could still feel a slight pulse of energy in the spots where Box's fingertips had touched her. And she decided she needed to see him again.

She picked up the small statue Tz' had made of her and wrapped it in a cloth, slipped on her leather sandals, and headed to the doorway. "Well, come on, I'm not going through that again," she said and laughed as Ek' Balam made a show of stretching his body before coming to stand by her side. With Ek' Balam beside her, the crowds stayed at a respectful distance, and the two made their way to Puk'pik's workshop in a few minutes.

Several potters were busy making plates, vases, and cups at small tables arranged under a large cotton tarp that kept out the hot afternoon sun. Nearby, Na'om could see several of the large kilns had been fired up and were in use. She searched the area, looking for Box, and finally saw him at the most distant kiln, carefully placing objects inside the hot domed area that would bake the soft clay into hardened objects. She walked toward him, but he was so busy that he had yet to notice her. However, the eyes of all the other potters followed her as she and Ek' Balam moved across the courtyard.

Sweat dripped down Box's bare shoulders and back, and Na'om stepped away from the heat that radiated from the open kiln. When Box had placed the final mug inside the kiln, he covered the opening with dirt and mud, sealing the heat in. Only when he was done, did he turn around and notice Na'om watching him.

"Itzamná, Lady Na'om, I had no idea you were there," Box said as he bowed to her. He wiped his sweaty hands on a small rag and stepped farther from the row of kilns. "Come, away from this heat," and he gestured that she should follow him into the shade of the nearest awning. He reached for his gourd and offered it to Na'om, but she shook her head, so Box drank, long and loudly, draining the gourd dry.

"Is there something I can help you with?" Box asked as he wiped his mouth with the back of his hand.

Na'om nodded as she pulled the likeness of herself out of her pocket and unwrapped it from the cloth she'd rolled around it. "Is this the statue Tz' made?" she asked as she handed it to Box.

He turned the small sculpture around in his hands. "Yes, yes, it is. I'm surprised he didn't take it with him," Box said. "It's a good portrait of you," he added as he handed it back.

Na'om nodded and quickly wrapped the object back up before slipping it into her pocket. She didn't know what else to say to continue the conversation, but she didn't want to leave, either.

"Is there anything else on your mind?" Box asked.

"No, no, I should let you get back to work," Na'om stammered. "I, I just didn't feel like being in my hut, that's all."

"I'm finished in a few hours. Would you like to meet at the marketplace and have something to eat together?"

Na'om smiled and blushed. "Yes, I'd like that, I'd like that very much. I'll see you in a few hours."

Box bowed. "I'll meet you at the salt sellers, Lady Na'om."

"Please, call me Na'om."

"Until then, Na'om," Box said, and he hurried back to tending the kilns.

SATAL

Satal waited impatiently for Tewichinel to unwrap the bandages from her left arm. Moons had passed since Yakal had thrown the salty water on her, and she wanted to be rid of the dressings and the sling that Tewichinel insisted she wear during the day. She looked down at her bare skin as the last wrapping fell away. Her brown flesh was scarred and puckered, pockmarked where the splashes and droplets of salt water had burned into her. Tentatively, she bent her arm at the elbow, then moved her wrist up and down and flexed her fingers. The motions were stiff and painful, but she could move her arm, for which she was grateful.

"The skin has finally healed, my lady," Tewichinel said as he bent to inspect her arm. "I don't think we'll need to apply any more calendula salve to the area." He gathered up the pile of bandages and placed them in a basket to burn later.

"Good. Now that it has, I want to see if I can still shapeshift. Fetch me a jequirity bean, a piece of charcoal, a knife, and a mug of water. Then you'll stay with me while I transform. I'll need you to feed me the charcoal once I command it."

Silently, the shaman nodded and left the room.

He doesn't think you're ready, Sachoj said in Satal's mind.

Of course, he doesn't, which is why I must prove to him and all the others that I am. The sooner I show that I am back at my full strength, the more they'll fear me and be ready to do as I command. I need to make sure Camazotz and the other gods know I've regained my abilities too. Otherwise, they'll never come when I call them to aid us during the counterattack.

Satal took off her clothes and laid them on top of several pillows stuffed in the leather and bamboo chair beside her. Tewichinel had seen her undressed so often of late that she had no qualms about being naked in front of him one more time. She smiled when he entered the room with the necessary supplies on a wooden tray. He set it on the table and handed Satal the red-and-black bean she'd requested. She picked up the sharp obsidian knife and nicked the tip of the jequirity bean, exposing the fleshy, whitish interior. Then she placed the cut end of the bean against her tongue and felt the familiar rush of numbing and burning that meant the toxin was working. She concentrated on shifting into her favorite form, the black wasp, and felt her body begin to expand and contract as it transformed into the six-foot, hairy, black insect. Her arms lengthened and divided, each one turning into three separate limbs, each of which sprouted thick black hairs. Her face warped and stretched, and she grimaced as the scarred skin around her mouth pulled tight. She closed her eyes as they divided and compounded, and when she opened them again, the room appeared in a hundred views. Her back split open and two iridescent greenish-black wings began to unfold. The right one unfurled and moved with ease, but Satal was dismayed to find her left wing was severely damaged along the outer edge. She flexed her shoulder muscles and flapped it, but the movement caused shooting pains to race up the membranes to her brain. Gritting her mouthparts, she tried to lift off the ground, but was unable to raise the left side of her body off the tiled floor. She buzzed with anger and began hopping about the room, jabbing repeatedly with her stinger at everything around her until she hit the chair that held her clothes, spilling them and the pillows underneath them onto the floor.

"My lady, perhaps it's time to return to your human shape and rest," Tewichinel said. He bent and picked up her shirt and skirt. Then he reached over to the tray, scooped up the charcoal, and held the lump in the palm of his hand.

Satal turned on the man and thrust her stinger at him. She saw the fear in Tewichinel's eyes as he jumped backward, dropping the charcoal in his haste to avoid being punctured, and she lowered herself into a chair. "Give me the antidote," she commanded.

The shaman crawled around on his bony knees for a few moments before he finally located the clump of charcoal. He brushed it off and handed it to Satal who grasped the piece in one of her many pincers. She bit a large chunk of it off and chewed it noisily and gradually felt herself turn back into her human form.

Sweat dried on her brow and she shivered. Tewichinel quickly wrapped a deep red, woolen blanket around her shoulders and helped her into a more comfortable position in the chair.

"How will I ever defeat that horrid girl if I can't fly?" Satal said. She pointed to a mug of water, and Tewichinel held the cup to her lips so she could rinse the remaining gritty charcoal from her mouth. She swished the water around and around, then spit into the empty bowl Tewichinel held to her lips.

"Perhaps a poultice made from batwing passion flowers will enhance the energy in your arm," Tewichinel said. He held up Satal's shirt, and she stood and let the man slip the cloth over her head.

She winced as she eased her left arm through the armhole and extended it into the sleeve. "There must be more we can do than just that." She stepped into the skirt Tewichinel held open and then pulled the fabric up around her waist. She sat back down and leaned into the chair as Tewichinel ran a brush through her long, gray hair and quickly braided it.

"I can consult my brother shamans and see if they have any other ideas," Tewichinel said as he prepared to leave with the tray.

Satal grabbed his arm, stopping the shaman from moving. "You'll do no such thing and not speak a word of this to anyone, is that understood?"

Tewichinel bowed deeply. "Of course, Lady Satal, it will be as you command."

Satal let go of his arm, and the shaman quickly left the room.

Well, now, isn't this a mess you're in, Sachoj said and laughed. *You need to defeat the girl to enhance your ebbing strength, yet you can't fight her because you have no strength!* The old woman's voice echoed in Satal's head, her laughter turning into the sharp hisses of a hundred snakes.

"Silence, all of you!" Satal shouted. Her voice reverberated around the large room, and she picked up and threw a pillow in her frustration.

It bounced off the wall and landed with a plop on the floor. She leaned forward, putting her elbows on her knees, then placed the palms of her hands over her eyes. She sat this way for several minutes, hoping for inspiration. *There has to be something I can do*, she thought. Finally, an idea popped into her head, but she instantly rejected it. *I'm already in his debt; I won't be beholden to him for anything more.*

He's your only chance, Satal, Sachoj hissed in her mind. *Don't be a fool. Use his energy this one last time and then you can repay him a hundredfold once you've defeated Na'om. We both know it's the only way to regain sufficient power.*

Satal nodded. She knew her great-grandmother was right, as always. She picked up the knife still lying on the table and quickly made her way to her bedroom. She opened her wooden cupboard, pulled out a fig-bark ledger, and cut off the last page of the folding book.

She went back to the front room, with the knife and paper clasped firmly in her right hand. She placed them on the table in the middle of the room, then lit a candle before pulling out her tongue and jabbing it with the point of the knife. Blood quickly welled in her mouth and she let the drops fall onto the piece of paper before her. When the paper was saturated, she held it over the flames until it finally caught fire. She held onto the piece for as long as she could, letting the smoke of her burning blood rise into the air around her. She closed her eyes and envisioned Camazotz, the bat god. "My lord, I need your help," she prayed. "Lend me the power of your wings, and I shall repay you a thousandfold once the jaguar girl has been sacrificed." She sat and waited, holding her breath for a count of one thousand before letting it out in a rush.

But there was no response from Camazotz.

She was still sitting, waiting, when Tewichinel entered the room with another tray full of items. In silence, she let the shaman smear a paste made from the batwing passion flowers on her left arm from her wrist to just above her elbow. He then covered the mixture with a clean white cloth that he secured with a piece of hemp twine.

"I'll return in an hour's time to replace the mixture, my lady," Tewichinel said.

Satal nodded but didn't reply as the shaman silently left the room again. She drummed the fingers of her right hand on the tabletop, trying to figure out why Camazotz had not responded to her blood sacrifice and plea for help.

Perhaps you owe him too much already, Sachoj hissed.

"Shush, old woman, you're not helping me think," Satal said. She hated being dependent on anyone, even a god, but she knew she had no choice. She closed her eyes and began to pray. "Camazotz, my lord, please, I need your help."

Within minutes, she felt the air stir in the room and quickly turned around. Camazotz hovered a few feet off the floor in the corner of the room.

"It's about time," she exclaimed. She stood up and strode over to the bat.

"Lady Satal, is that any way to speak to someone you so desperately need help from?" Camazotz said. "I can certainly be on my way as there is much to do in Xibalba." He flapped his wings and began to disappear from sight.

"No, no, wait," Satal said. She stopped in her tracks and bowed low to the bat god. "My lord, I apologize, I am an old and impatient woman, please, forgive me."

Camazotz laughed as his image reappeared. "My, my, I do think I like this humbler version of you. But enough of the chatter, I am a busy god. What do you want?"

Satal looked into the bat's blood-red eyes. "When I shapeshift, I find my wing remains damaged, despite my shaman's best efforts to heal it. I need the strength of your bloodline in order to fly." She pointed to the poultice on her arm. "The passion flowers will help, but we both know the real power is in you." She bowed again.

Camazotz fluffed his wings, lifting off the floor by several inches, and a waft of musty air filled the room. "I will aid you this one last time, my lady, but then you are on your own. In return, you will pay homage to me and my progeny from this day forth until your last day. I shall expect a temple built in my honor, and my kin and I will be allowed to fly wherever we like, eating whatever we like. And on the day of the big battle, we shall be given free rein over the battlefield."

Satal nodded and bowed again. "It shall be as you request, my lord. I shall tell the stonemasons to begin building your temple at once, and I'll make sure it is designed so your offspring can roost there."

"Very good, Lady Satal. I shall hold you to your word." The bat god lowered himself to the floor and folded his wings. "You must drink some of my blood, my lady. Bring the knife and make a small incision just below my collarbone."

Satal did as the god commanded, and as soon as droplets of blood appeared on his fur, she leaned in and licked them off. She tasted copper and the strangely sweet taste of death. She wanted to vomit, but she forced herself to swallow instead. She felt Camazotz brush her with his wingtip, pushing her away.

"I believe that's enough of a good thing," he said. He leaned down and spit on the area where she had jabbed him with the knife. The spot sizzled and bubbled and quickly healed over. "You must wait seven nights before you attempt to shapeshift again. This will allow my blood to circulate throughout your body, healing those parts that are damaged. You may experience some peculiarities as your body adjusts, but the symptoms will quickly fade."

Satal wanted to know more, but the bat god disappeared before she had time to ask.

Does it even matter? Sachoj asked. *It's a little late to be worried about any of that.*

Satal nodded. Sachoj was right; she couldn't undo what had just happened. She just had to wait and hope she was healed.

Na'om

Biribik was waiting for Na'om when she stepped outside her hut. It was still early in the morning, and most people were not awake yet, so the two walked in companionable silence with Ek' Balam through the mostly deserted streets. As she had done for the past several days, Na'om deliberately walked just behind Biribik, allowing him to move the few people they did encounter to one side so she could pass with ease. And the position also gave her a view of him from behind. Which, she had to admit, was a pleasurable sight. The guard uniform of leather plates covered much of Biribik's chest and back, but she could still see the muscles in his tattooed arms, shoulders, and neck. *Perhaps his overall physical strength is why I feel so safe when I'm near him*, Na'om mused. *After all, I don't really know anything about him, not his age, where he lives, or what he does for work other than to help old T'ot with her food stall.* She stopped for a minute and let him move farther away, watching him closely as he did so. *He moves like an animal, with no wasted motions.* The idea sent a shiver up her back as they continued and turned onto the street in front of Najtir's residence.

"Shall I wait here for you, Lady Na'om?" Biribik asked as they entered the inner courtyard.

"Please, I've told you before, just call me Na'om," she replied. "And no, there's no need to wait; I expect I'll be here several hours just like all the other days this week."

"Then I'll return in time to escort you both to the market for lunch." Biribik smiled and left.

Again, Na'om watched him as he moved quickly through the gate and entered the street beyond. *I wonder what kind of animal spirit he's connected to,* she thought and her mind was quickly flooded with images of a tapir as it moved about the countryside looking for food.

"He already has a wife and young child," Najtir said, interrupting Na'om's thoughts.

Startled, Na'om turned around to find the shaman in the doorway, watching her. She shook her head and hurried up the steps just behind Ek' Balam. "I don't understand; I'm not interested in him in that way," she said. "Besides, you know I'm devoted to Tz'."

"Devoted, yes, but do you truly love him?" Najtir asked as he shut the door. "Have you truly thought about the possibility that Tz' has chosen to side with Satal? What if you meet him on the battlefield? Will you be able to fight him if he's defending your one true enemy?"

"I don't believe Tz' would ever do that," Na'om said crossly as she took a seat in one of the chairs at the table. It creaked as she settled into the worn leather. A small flame flickered in a coconut shell filled with beeswax, and odd pieces of bones lay strewn about on the tabletop. Next to them was a piece of fig-bark paper covered with glyphs. A turkey feather quill had left a splotch of black ink in one corner.

Na'om wondered yet again whether she should tell Najtir of the dream she'd had about Tz'. *If any of it has a chance of being real, how do I enter the Underworld so I can find Tz'?*

"It's quite possible it *was* real," Najtir said as he pushed his divining tools to one side. "You must travel to the island where the shamans live. From there, you can easily enter Xibalba and go in search of your friend," Najtir replied as he settled himself into another of the old chairs.

"How did you know that's where I needed to find Tz'?" Na'om asked. She sat up straight and placed her arms on the table, looking directly into Najtir's eyes.

"I can hear your thoughts, my dear, and I know this dream you've had has been weighing heavily on your mind. The thought of Tz' in the

Underworld has covered you like a cloak, pressing you down, making you forget everything around you except that one thought." He reached out with his arthritic hand and placed it gently on top of Naʼom's forearm. "You must unburden yourself to me and then you'll be free to carry through with your plans, now that you know where to go." Najtir chortled and leaned back. "If I were younger, I'd venture with you, as I'd dearly love to see my brother shamans. But I am too old and will be going nowhere soon except perhaps to be with the ancestors."

"No, don't say that," Naʼom replied. She looked around the room, half expecting to see something from the Underworld waiting in the dark corners to take Najtir away.

"When the time comes, I will willingly join them, my dear, for I am very old and tired," Najtir said. "It will be a pleasure to be among my friends," and he patted her arm again. "But I have no plans to leave just yet. We must see this ordeal with Satal through to the end. Now tell me about your dream."

Naʼom nodded and quickly began to recount the tale, but she grew shy when she reached the moment when she slipped from the dream into her fantasy of swimming with Tzʼ in the cenote. She was embarrassed to mention they had been kissing each other. She stopped talking and waited.

"Such purity and innocence, a rare thing to behold," Najtir mused, and he cupped his chin with his hand. "You've never lain with a man, which explains why the dream doesn't continue."

Naʼom felt her face flush and she dropped her eyes. She had been taught by Atiʼt what it meant to be with a man, and she knew that's where babies came from, but she'd never discussed the idea with anyone else. She knew it was something girls talked about among themselves, but since she'd never had any friends, there'd been no one to chat with about the intimacies of a relationship. She certainly didn't feel comfortable speaking to Najtir about it.

"Quite all right, my dear, I do understand. I think it best you have this conversation with Ajkun later today. There are issues we must discuss, though, no matter how painful they may be. Your friend was definitely interested in dark magic long before he left here." Najtir remained standing and pointed to a book lying on the table. "I've been waiting for the appropriate time to show you this, and I believe today is the day." He reached over and flipped open the first page.

Na'om peered at the fig-bark paper and was startled to see enormous jaguar-like creatures drawn on the page in black ink. She quickly read the first lines of hieroglyphs that filled the top portion of the page. "Were-jaguars, like those I encountered in the Underworld?"

"Yes, this is the creature Tz' was so anxious to shapeshift into and the reason he left here in search of Satal. She could easily have helped him learn how to become one of these animals." Najtir continued to unfold pages and pointed to another drawing. "The were-creatures are known to mate with humans, forcing them to become one of their own. Even if Satal didn't help Tz' transform, she could have influenced a female to entice Tz' to join with her, thus securing his demise."

Na'om shifted in her chair. All this talk made her extremely uncomfortable. Tz' had always been her friend, the only person in the village willing to be one, and for that she had loved him with all her heart. But she'd never really imagined what life on a daily basis with him would be like. And she suddenly realized this would include being intimate with him if he were her husband. The idea of them lying together on a regular basis hadn't ever crossed her mind. The one time Tz' had tried to have sex with her had been before his river trip so long ago. She'd been so young, so unaware of anything back then that the whole idea had been scary. That moment surged through her mind, and she felt the same anger flare up that she'd experienced back then. *We may make love, but only on my terms, not his.* She shook her head to clear it of the past. Then she realized she'd never thought about Tz' being interested in some other girl. That thought made her fidget in her chair again. "So, you think Tz' has definitely turned into one of these animals. . . ."

"Yes. You must accept the possibility that Tz' is no longer the boy you grew up with. If he's a were-jaguar, he'll be forced to do Satal's bidding. Which is why you must let go of your feelings for him; you may come to harm if you can't defend yourself against him."

"All right, let's say he has changed. That doesn't mean I can't still love him. And more importantly, there's still a battle ahead, one I may not survive. Even if Tz' has changed toward me, it would be ridiculous for me to be looking for someone else to take Tz's place in my heart." Na'om looked at Najtir's lined face, waiting for some kind of reaction. But as usual, the shaman kept his emotions and thoughts veiled.

"I'm only suggesting that if you should suddenly find you're attracted to someone else, then you should let those emotions out to see where they might take you." Najtir finally took the seat opposite Na'om. "Love is the strongest weapon you have to use against Satal, so you must embrace those emotions when you feel them."

Na'om quickly shut the book in front of her. She didn't want to think about Tz' as any kind of animal. "I thought the purified salt we've been practicing with was the best defense against Satal."

"It's one of many, but connecting with the love you feel will be your most powerful deterrent. Only when you can embrace it fully will you have its full strength at your disposal. Now, was there anything else about your dream you wish to tell me?"

Na'om nodded. "Tz' was a were-jaguar, and in my mind, I heard him say he still loved me, but then he left to join his pack. Why would he do that? Why couldn't he leave with me?"

"If he's been fed by Hun-Kamé, then he has his own complex path to follow now. That doesn't mean you should give up hope, though. He still has an important role to play in your destiny." Najtir fussed with some of the bones on the table. "We can talk about this more after we've had some crab cakes and gone to the council meeting."

Na'om nodded. She felt relief flow through her. She knew the shaman was right. "Wait, there's another meeting? What do they want to discuss now?"

"They don't want anything; you'll be the one to gather everyone, my dear. To tell them of your intent to go to the island of the shamans in search of Tz'. You and Ek' Balam will be accompanied by Biribik and Box. The four of you will be able to travel quickly to the coast where you'll procure a canoe and proceed to the island. My dear friend, Tatá, leader of the group, will be expecting you and will show you the entrance to Xibalba."

Na'om laughed. "I mean no disrespect, but I doubt they'll approve of your plan."

Najtir suddenly gripped Na'om's forearm with a strength she didn't expect. He pointed to the pile of bones with his other hand. "The gods have shown me that there is no other path for you to follow at the moment. It is imperative that you go without delay. You must insist they let you leave. Otherwise, the future will be vastly different from the one that's been foretold."

"If what you say is true, then you must know that in my dream Tz' doesn't leave the Underworld. I don't understand why I need to go there if he's going to stay."

"It's what the gods have planned for all of us. Now, enough of talking. I'm already hungry and want some crab cakes. I'll make sure T'ot makes some extra ones tomorrow so you can take them with you on your journey."

Najtir reached for a small cotton bag on the table and opened it. He pulled out three small pieces of salted red snapper and placed them carefully on the tiled floor near Ek' Balam. "We must get your friend here some more to eat when we go to the market today," Najtir said. He wiped his hands together and bits of salt fell onto the leather tabletop. "Shall we head to T'ot's for those crab cakes?"

Frustration surged through Na'om. "If I'm leaving tomorrow, then surely there must be more for me to do than eat old T'ot's salty food?" Even as the words flew from her lips, she regretted saying them. "I'm sorry, Najtir, that was rude of me." She stood up and went over to help the old shaman from his chair. "We'll go at once, if that's what you desire."

"Not everything needs to be about work, my dear. One must learn to enjoy the little things in life and take what pleasures when you can for you never know what tomorrow will bring." Najtir stood up and with Na'om's help, moved toward the door. "I believe today will prove to be an auspicious day for you."

"If you say so," Na'om replied. When they entered the inner courtyard, she paused. "It's early still; Biribik won't be here to help us through the crowds. Should I summon some guards to accompany us?"

"Biribik is on his way; we shall meet him in the streets before we reach the marketplace."

Na'om nodded, but didn't bother to ask the shaman how he knew this. She had found that he knew many things without having received any outside information. And as he had predicted, Biribik found them before they entered the crowded marketplace. He cleared the narrow alleyways between the vendors and got them safely to T'ot's stall. Na'om helped Najtir on to a stool and sat down on the one beside him. When she looked into the food booth for signs of T'ot, she was surprised to see a girl with her back to them chopping vegetables at a small table near the far end of the enclosure. She was even more surprised when Biribik went around the front counter, walked over to the woman, and kissed her on the cheek. When she turned around, Na'om let out a small gasp.

"Mok'onel?" she asked.

The young woman nodded and hurriedly wiped her hands on the apron around her waist. "Lady Na'om, it is a pleasant surprise to see you again." Then Mok'onel dropped her head and refused to look Na'om in the eye.

"All this time, I assumed you were back in the village with the others."

"I never left the city after your father released us from the slave market. I found life here interesting, and then I met Biribik and didn't want to return." Mok'onel raised her head and finally did look at Na'om. "There was nothing for me back there, just bad memories." She reached out and grasped Biribik's hand. "The gods brought me here so I could be with Biribik and bear his children."

Biribik laughed. "Well, one child any way." He turned to Na'om. "We have a two-year-old son we named Tze'm to honor Mok's brother who was killed."

Na'om nodded. She instantly remembered the infant, of catching him as he arrived into the world, and the beautiful brown eyes he'd had. A sharp pang caught her in the throat, and she felt tears welling up. She took a deep breath and slowly let it out, easing the unspoken love from her body.

Mok'onel took Biribik's big hand and placed it on her belly. "And another child on the way, according to the midwives."

Biribik grabbed Mok'onel in his brawny arms and twirled her around the small enclosure. "Woo-hoo!" he yelled as he placed her gently back on the ground.

Na'om had to look away as the couple embraced and kissed. A deep desire to connect with someone surged through her body, and she broke out in a mild sweat. *And to hold a child and know that he or she is mine, to love and care for . . .* the thought made Na'om tense and rigid. It was only when Najtir gently placed his hand on top of hers that she began to relax.

"Come, let's eat and celebrate the good news," Najtir said.

Mok'onel nodded and hurried behind the curtain separating the two parts of the booth. She quickly returned with a platter piled high with steaming crab cakes. She placed a stack of black-and-white ceramic plates on the counter and gave everyone a wooden spoon to eat with. Biribik went behind the curtain and returned with a pitcher.

"Fresh mango juice," he said while he poured the liquid into several pottery mugs.

Na'om bit into a crab cake and sighed. Even though she'd eaten the same thing for several days in a row, she still loved the taste of salty crab mixed with sweet corn. "Where is T'ot?" she asked as she ate another bite.

"Taking care of Tze'm today," Mok'onel replied. "She's finding it harder and harder to work all day here and prefers to stay at home with him. She wants me to take over the stall for her so she can finally rest."

Biribik laughed. "As if chasing little Tze'm is any kind of rest."

"I'd like to meet him, if that's all right," Na'om said.

"It would be an honor, Na'om," Mok'onel replied. She suddenly grasped Na'om's hand. "I do hope we can become friends now that everything has changed." Then she quickly let go and stepped back from the counter.

The pressure of Mok'onel's touch tingled on Na'om's skin, and she smiled as she looked at the young woman. "I would like that, I would like that very much," she said.

After they had eaten and Biribik had safely conducted Na'om and Najtir to the Temple of the Warriors, Na'om sent him to the guard house with orders to have sentries summon Ajkun, Chiman, Yakal, and the other council members to the temple. She also told Biribik to fetch Box from the pottery workshop. She helped Najtir into one of the wooden chairs at the table and then paced back and forth in the room, impatiently waiting until everyone had gathered.

"Na'om, what's wrong?" Ajkun said as she entered the room. She nodded to Najtir and to Kubal Joron and Matz' who had already taken seats and were quietly talking to each other.

"Please, Ati't, just take a seat. Once the others are here, I'll tell you."

Bitol, Nimal, Yakal, and Chiman all entered together and quickly sat down. Box and Biribik came into the room just behind the group of men and stood against the wall on one side of the room.

"Na'om, what has happened?" Chiman said.

Na'om looked at her grandfather and could see the worry he had written all over his face.

"I must go to the island of the shamans off the coast," she said. "Ek' Balam, Box, and Biribik will accompany me for protection. Once there, I'll enter the Underworld in search of Tz'."

"No!" Ajkun exclaimed. "It's far too dangerous." She gripped Chiman's arm. "Tell her, Chiman."

"I must agree with Ajkun," Chiman said. "It's much too risky."

"Lady Na'om, we need you here to prepare for the upcoming battle,"

Nimal said. The men around the table all murmured in agreement.

¨But I must go and find Tz',¨ Na'om replied.

"There's no guarantee that you'll find Tz' or even return. The gods of Xibalba will not let you escape their grasp a second time," Chiman said.

"But I know Tz' is there, and if I find him, I can persuade him to come back with me. Then the battle with Satal will be the only difficult task ahead."

"The journey will take too long," Ajkun said. "You won't have the energy to fight Satal, which is what you must be focused on right now."

"Ati't, if we leave right away, we'll be back long before the trek to Chichén Itzá."

"But to enter the Underworld again?" Ajkun said. "I don't like the idea at all." She looked again at Chiman. "Please, tell her it's not possible."

Chiman looked at everyone seated at the table and the two youths standing nearby. "Let's take a quick vote. All in favor of Na'om leaving, raise your hands."

Na'om, Box, and Biribik raised their hands.

"All those who insist Na'om stay here to ensure her safety, raise your hands." Everyone in the room except Na'om, Box, Biribik and Najtir raised their hands. "Na'om, we all agree. It is far too dangerous and we therefore forbid you to go."

Na'om looked at Najtir. "Tell them it's important, tell them you've seen it prophesied that I should go there now."

"It is as Na'om has said; she must travel to the island of my brothers and reenter Xibalba in search of her friend. To do otherwise will jeopardize her ability to defeat Satal." Najtir shifted in his chair. "There is no other option."

A long silence hovered over the room after Najtir had given his advice.

Finally, Box stepped forward. "It will be an honor to accompany you, Na'om," he said. "I promise to defend you with my life."

"As do I," Biribik said as he joined Box.

Na'om smiled at the two youths. It would be good to be in their company and away from all the fussiness of the elders.

"If this journey must be taken, then I will lead a group of soldiers and go as well," Yakal said as he stood up.

"No," Na'om said. "We can take care of ourselves. We can travel much more quickly and be less conspicuous if it's just the four of us."

"Na'om, let your father. . . ." Ajkun cleared her throat. "Let Yakal accompany you with a few soldiers. You don't know who you might meet along the way; it would be good to have some extra protection."

Na'om could feel the tension in the room constricting her. She desperately wanted to lash out and say no, but as she looked around the room, she could see the fear and anxiety etched onto each person' face. "All right, Yakal, you shall go too, but only bring four sentries with us. Any more than that and the group will draw too much attention. The last thing I want is for Satal to learn what we are doing. She must continue to believe that Tz' is trapped and under her control."

She turned to Box and Biribik. "Gather your things; we leave in the morning."

The two men nodded and smiled. "We'll be ready."

She looked around the council room at everyone. "Maltiox, everyone, that's all." She nodded to Ek' Balam who stood up from the tile floor and stretched from head to tail. "Come on, boy, I need to pack a satchel." Then she left before anyone else could change her mind.

Satal

It was nighttime and Satal was flying, with a thousand bats around her, their sharp squeaks and pings ringing in her ears. They flew low, skimming over the countryside, searching en masse in the dim moonlight for prey. Movement caught her eye, and the group turned as one, homing in on a small peccary resting on the uneven ground. The bats swooped down and began to feed, biting with their razor-sharp fangs. The pig squirmed and squealed but was quickly silenced as more bats attacked. Satal bit and chewed, relishing the fresh, bloody meat in her mouth. She licked her lips and reached out for more, but a larger bat nipped her, and she withdrew, sucking on the bite to stop the stinging. The coppery taste of blood fascinated her; she wanted more and tried again to reach the carcass, but there were too many bats in her way. She beat her wings and lifted away from the crowd, searching the surrounding area for anything else she might feed upon. She spied an iguana perched on a large boulder and sped toward it, but misjudged the distance and banged her nose on the rock as the lizard scuttled away. Pain raced through her head, and Satal woke up.

She was in her own bed, in her room in the palace, the bed linens twisted all around her, and her stomach grumbled in hungry protest.

"Tewichinel!" she cried. She threw off the blankets. She waited in the darkness, but there was no reassuring sound of the old shaman's leather sandals slipping across the tile floor. "Tewichinel!" she called again, louder than before. Her voice echoed in the large room, bouncing off the high ceiling and reverberating down the long hallway that led to the main room.

Satal got up and slowly made her way out into the hallway. With one hand on the wall, she guided herself to the small bath room at the opposite end of the hallway and found the ceramic pot she used to relieve herself. The scent of warm piss filled the windowless room, and she hurriedly washed her hands in the turtle shell basin before leaving.

A small light appeared at the other end of the hallway, and she walked toward it, knowing the shaman had finally arrived.

"Lady Satal, how may I be of service?" Tewichinel said as he bowed low to her.

"Bring me some fresh meat; I need to eat again," Satal replied. This was the third night in a row she had awoken from dreams of feeding with a cloud of bats. She knew it was a result of sucking Camazotz's blood, but she was tired of eating in the middle of the night.

"Of course, my lady. Do you wish it cooked or prefer it raw as you've requested before?"

"Raw. No wait, bring me both. I must learn to control these cravings." Satal sat down at the table and nodded to the shaman who silently left the room.

I wonder what else I'll experience as Camazotz's blood mingles with mine, Satal mused. She stared at the small candle flame in front of her and waved her hand near it. The light danced and flickered, casting large shadows on the opposite wall. She stared at the light, seeing deep into its center, and she imagined it was Na'om's heart, beating with the strength and energy of a young woman on the threshold of greatness. She wanted that energy, needed that strength in order to continue to rule. Without it, she was nothing more than an old woman, ready to meet the gods.

She wondered what Na'om was doing at that very moment and tried to picture the jaguar girl asleep in a hammock. *What tricks will you use to stop me, I wonder? If only there were a way to know before you and your friends arrive in the city.* Satal leaned forward in her chair, peering even more deeply into the candle, wondering if she could see answers in the light. But all she did was burn the image onto her eyes so wherever she looked, she could only see the flame. She closed them, willing the impression to fade as she contemplated ideas and drummed the fingers of one hand on the wooden table. She looked up when she heard Tewichinel reappear and was glad to see the candle imprint had faded to a shadow in her vision.

Tewichinel carried a platter filled with thinly sliced, rare venison, which he placed on the table in front of her. Satal speared a piece with the tip of the knife Tewichinel provided and popped it into her mouth. She slowly chewed, savoring the bloody flavor. She stabbed another piece and held it up, letting the blood drain back onto the plate. "Want some?"

"No, my lady, but maltiox for asking," Tewichinel replied. He continued to stand near the table.

"Sit with me then while I eat," Satal ordered and motioned to the chair beside her. The shaman nodded and quickly sat down. Satal chewed and swallowed, concentrating on the mere act of eating each slice of meat in the hopes an idea would pop into her head. And finally, it did. She smiled as she put down the knife and sat back in her chair.

"We need to know what the citizens of Mayapán plan to do when they arrive here. Find Kux and send him to their city. Have him find out everything he can about Na'om and her army."

Tewichinel looked at Satal. "Kux is no longer here, my lady. He left Chichén Itzá after the defeat and hasn't been seen for weeks."

"Well, then we must send someone else. I must know what they are preparing to do." Satal chewed and swallowed another piece of meat before wiping bloody droplets of saliva from her mouth with the back of her hand. "I should have told Pataninel to stay awhile and observe things. In the morning, find Kämisanel and tell him to send a runner with the message. Pataninel is not to return until he knows what Na'om and Yakal are planning." Satal pushed the platter away from her. Her appetite was satiated for the moment, and she was ready to go back to bed.

Tewichinel hurried to stand and offered his left arm as support while carrying the lit candle in his right. Together, they walked in silence back to Satal's sleeping quarters where the shaman helped her back into bed. He turned to leave, but Satal grabbed his arm.

"Stay with me until I fall asleep," she commanded. "Perhaps with you nearby, I won't dream of being a bat again this night."

The shaman bowed and sat cross-legged by the door while Satal pulled the covers up to her chin and closed her eyes. Within minutes, despite the shaman's presence, she was dreaming again, flying with the bats and observing everything around her. The vast cloud flew low across the countryside for hours, following the large limestone sacbe that connected Chichén Itzá to Mayapán. When they approached that city's walls, several of the bats broke from the group and zoomed over the fortifications. Instantly, arrows whizzed into the air, bringing them to the ground. Another wave attempted to breach the walls, and again they were brought down by archers. Satal honed in her eyesight and could just see the silhouettes of the men perching on the stones. They were aiming to shoot yet again, so she flew higher into the air, out of reach of the arrows, and skimmed over the soldiers' heads. Far below, she knew the citizens of Mayapán lay sleeping in a multitude of huts and buildings. As she fluttered above the city streets, she could sense the presence of Na'om and her jaguar, but she was too far away to pinpoint exactly where they were. She circled back and forth in great looping arcs, trying to find them, but was unsuccessful.

When the blush of first light brushed the horizon, the group of bats turned back toward home, and Satal felt a tug deep within her chest that forced her to twist away and follow them. She lingered as long as she could, spying on the city as sunlight illuminated the streets, marketplace, and open courtyards of the many palaces and temples. She hoped for a glimpse of Na'om someplace among the huts and houses. But when several shamans appeared in the doorway of the observatory and pointed in her direction, she hurried to catch up with the rest of the bats.

When she woke up a short time later, she lay in bed, relishing the comfort of the soft mattress underneath her. She was tired from soaring through the night sky, yet triumphant as she realized she'd found her own method to spy on her enemies.

Just then, she heard a snort and brief cough, and when she looked, she was surprised to see Tewichinel asleep by the doorway. The old man had his head back against the wall, and his mouth was wide open. Satal had the impulse to drop something onto his tongue, but then thought better of the idea. *I still need him for too many things*, she thought as she clapped her hands together.

Tewichinel shook his head and rubbed his eyes, then saw Satal looking at him, and pushed himself to his feet. He adjusted his leather loincloth and began to back out of the room.

"Wait," Satal commanded and the shaman stopped.

"My lady?" he asked.

"There's no need to send someone to find Pataninel. I've discovered a way to spy on Mayapán thanks to Camazotz."

"As you wish, Lady Satal." Tewichinel bowed. "If you'll excuse me, I shall prepare your breakfast now."

"Yes, very good, go, and bring more of that passion flower poultice as well. I must strengthen my arm even more."

"Of course, my lady," the shaman said and left the room.

Satal leaned back against the pillows propped up against the limestone wall and thought more about what she had seen that night. The shamans pointing into the sky caused a shudder to race through her body. *Surely there's no way they could know it was me*, she mused.

Tz'

Tz' poked around the cave, searching for food. Once again, the piles of bones were just that, bones, with no flesh of any kind to be found. He was glad when Xojol told him that the full moon would rise that night as he felt a deep ache in his empty belly and wanted to gorge on fresh meat. But the hours passed slowly as the pack waited for the moon to rise, and eventually Tz' drifted into a hungry stupor. He shook his head when Xojol nipped him lightly on the ear, forcing himself to open his eyes.

Come on, the others have left already, Xojol said as she bounded toward the tunnel leading to the surface.

Tz' leaped after Xojol and followed her through the dark to the entrance to the cave. Once again, he was awestruck at the sight of the stars overhead and of the multitude of scents that permeated the warm night air. It was so delicious to inhale the plethora of aromas after being cooped up in the cave with its rancid and fetid scents.

Look, the males have already brought you food, Xojol said as she pointed to a large peccary that lay nearby.

Tz' hurried over to the fresh carcass and ripped into the still warm body with his large fangs. The taste of fresh meat engulfed him and he tore and grabbed at the peccary, chewing and swallowing large chunks until his stomach bulged. Only then did he look up to see Xojol standing nearby, watching him. He looked at the carcass in front of him, then back at Xojol. *Sorry, I didn't leave you much*, he said as he moved slowly away from the remains.

It's okay, Xojol said, and she took a few bites. *I'm not very hungry I guess*, she added as she moved away from the bones. She looked across the open ground in front of them and spied a large grove of ceiba trees nearby. *Come on*, she said as she headed in that direction.

As soon as she stepped into the direct moonlight, Tz' saw her transform into her womanly form. Xojol began to weave in and around the trunks of the ceiba trees, and Tz' felt a heat build inside his body. He stood up and stepped under the trees too, and in the light of that full moon, he saw himself as a man once again. He marveled at the smoothness of his own skin and felt a great yearning for something or someone, but he couldn't identify what he longed for. Xojol was several yards away and he followed her, and she began to move faster and faster among the low-hanging branches. Twice Tz' banged his head as he hurried after her until he remembered to crouch lower as he ran. Then he twisted around a tree trunk and found Xojol waiting for him in the moonlight. Her body was soft and warm and she was breathing rapidly from their game of chase. He leaned in and could smell the fresh peccary blood on her lips, and he kissed her. He felt her arms go around his neck and they both pulled toward one another, breathing in each other's ragged breaths. They kissed again and again; then Xojol pulled Tz' toward the ground, and before he knew it, they were moving together in unison, making love in the light of the full moon.

It was over in a matter of minutes, and Tz' lay on his back, watching clouds scud quickly across the sky. Suddenly, one of them crossed in front of the moon, and when he caught a glimpse of Xojol, who lay next to him, she had returned to her were-jaguar form. And he could see that he was a were-jaguar as well. *Did we really change shape or was that just an illusion?*

Xojol purred. *Is that what you're thinking after your first time?* She growled a tiny bit and then added, *We don't actually shapeshift back into our human forms. In the direct moonlight, you look like a man. But in the shadows, you remain in your were-jaguar form. But the real question is, did you enjoy it?*

Tz' barred his teeth, which glinted in the bright light. *All the tension is gone from my body*, he purred back. *I never knew something could feel so good.*

The two nuzzled each other and remained relaxed and happy as the moon made its way slowly across the sky. Xojol rolled onto her back, away from Tz', and pointed with one paw at the heavens. *Look at the light falling from the sky. And there's another and another! What does it mean?*

Tz' rolled over to look and grinned, exposing his yellowing fangs. Then his smile faded. *I don't know.* He concentrated, but couldn't conjure up the words or the reason why the stars were falling through the darkness.

Xojol turned to him. *Soon the others will return with more meat*, she said. *We shall be well fed until the next full moon now that you're leader of the pack.*

Tz' rolled onto his side again, groaning a little as his stomach was quite full. And he was still sore as he hadn't fully healed from fighting the old were-jaguar. But he felt complete and happy. Then, a sudden gust of wind raced across the open ground, and Tz' sat bolt upright as an irresistible, sweet, and spicy scent filled his nostrils.

What's wrong, Xojol asked as she stood up.

Tz's lifted and twisted his head, sniffing and searching for the source of the seductive smell. *I must find out what that is*, he said, and he began to run, following the compelling scent.

Wait, come back, there isn't time, Xojol howled, but Tz' ignored her.

He ran and ran, saliva dripping from his jaws as he pursued the odor. His shadow skimmed across the landscape as he easily flowed in and out of dry gullies, across newly planted cornfields, and through lime, avocado, and mango orchards. Tz's body felt sleek and powerful as he pushed forward. He loved stretching his front paws as far as they could reach, then pushing off with his strong hind legs to leap over short bushes and trees that stood in his way. Then without warning, he saw the distinct shapes of various huts, and in the distance, a great stone wall. It looked vaguely familiar, but he couldn't remember why. Tz' paused and sucked in great breaths as he let his long tongue, sticky with thick saliva, loll outside his mouth. The air was redolent with a hundred different smells, most of them related to humans, which made Tz' wary of getting any closer. But he could still identify that one enticing scent, and he knew he had to find its source, even though it was coming from inside the great wall.

He hurried forward, hidden by deep shadows, and slunk alongside the limestone and stucco barrier, searching for an entry point. The wall ended and then continued in a different direction, so he continued following it, still determined to get inside. All of a sudden, he heard noises above him and smelled something burning. Tz' looked up and saw bright spots of light and the shadows of two men as they moved about above him. He quickly turned around and ran the other direction, still looking for a way to get inside. Finally, he came to a large ceiba tree growing within a few feet of the enclosure. Careful of the spines that covered the tree's trunk, Tz' climbed into it, scampering up until he was many feet in the air. He searched for a branch that extended toward the wall and carefully walked the length of it. It bent precariously under his weight as he edged closer and closer to the end of it, and with a great leap, he sprang from the tree, caught the edge of the wall with his claws, and pulled himself up onto the stones. He glanced around, but no one had seen him, and he quickly dropped to the ground on the other side.

He drew in another deep breath and set off in a fast lope toward the seductive smell. It tickled his nostrils, and he huffed as he ran. He had never smelled something so intoxicating, and excitement raced through him like a fast-moving fever, leaving him cold inside while his skin burned with heat. As he moved deeper into the city, the scent grew even stronger, so he slowed his pace, padding gently and quietly through the shadows toward one hut among many.

He hesitated outside the small structure, approached the doorway, and using his head, he pushed aside the covering. A small patch of moonlight illuminated a corner of the room from a window opening in the stucco wall, and he could see a person lying in a hammock stretched across the room. Saliva dripped from his jaws and on to the ground. His skin tingled with energy, and he quivered all over. Silently, he padded inside.

He gazed down at the woman lying curled on her side, her fingers wrapped tightly in the edge of the blue woven blanket that covered her body. Tz' breathed in deeply and felt a rush as her scent flowed through his entire body. His tail trembled, and his ears twitched as he leaned in closer. He wanted to lick her, taste her, ever so gently bite her, and he pushed at the edge of the blanket, just grazing her arm with his wide, wet nose. A jolt of energy shocked him, and he whimpered as he jerked backward. Still asleep, the woman rolled onto her back, tossing off the blanket as she moved. Tz' growled softly when he saw the numerous jaguar spots on her mocha skin. *What happened to you?* he thought. His mouth watered as he looked at the woman in her white night dress. He could see the outline of her small breasts and wide hips, and his whole body shook with desire. He crouched down, the tip of his tail twitched rapidly, and he wiggled his hind legs as he prepared to pounce.

Instantly, he was knocked off his feet as something charged him. With his head down and hackles raised, he turned around and could see the yellow eyes of a black jaguar staring at him.

Leave, now, before it's too late, Tz' heard the black jaguar say in his head.

Tz' lowered his head and uttered a low growl. *How dare you stop me! I'm the leader of the were-jaguars and will go where I please.* He took a step forward, but the smaller cat stood in his way.

You must leave, Tz', now, before the moon sets.

Tz' stopped at the sound of his name. *Who are you?*

An old friend, the black jaguar responded. *You must return to your cave before the moon sets, or you'll die and never see Na'om again.*

Na'om. The name rang like a bell in the back of Tz's head, and a dizzying barrage of images from his human life flooded his mind, causing him to stagger. *I must speak to her,* he said. He took a step toward the hammock, but the black jaguar blocked him.

No. You must leave! She cannot see you the way you are right now.

Tz' knew the black jaguar was right, but he couldn't make himself leave. Then he heard the creak of the hammock ropes as Na'om shifted her weight in the bed.

"Ek' Balam, what's wrong? Why are you growling?" Na'om said while she sat up and rubbed her eyes.

Tz' knew he had only seconds to escape before Na'om saw him, and he turned and bolted back through the doorway. He raced through the silent city streets, looking for a way out, and he saw one of the smaller gates stood slightly ajar. He hit the copper door with his broad shoulder, forcing it back on its leather hinges, and fled into the countryside before the sleepy guard on duty could chase after him. He glanced skyward and saw the first tinges of pink and orange on the horizon and knew he had only a matter of moments to return to the Underworld or he would perish. So, he ran and ran, following the contours of the land back to the cave, gasping for breath as the darkness continued to lift. He had to make it back safely or he would never see Na'om again. The thought of her name gave him a burst of speed, and he crested a small gully and was grateful to see the cave entrance just ahead of him. He ran several hundred yards into the tunnel until he could barely see the outside, and only then did he sink to the tunnel floor in exhaustion.

I was such a fool to have gone so far, he thought. *And an even bigger fool to have ignored my mother's warning. I forgot I am a man and that my life is meant to be spent with Na'om. Why did I eat the food the skeleton gods offered me? Itzamná, I even agreed to their offer and became the leader of the were-jaguars!* Just then, Tz' heard a noise in the distance and instantly sat up, his ears perked toward the darkness. He growled, but was met with silence. He slumped a bit as weariness washed over him. *How will I ever be with Na'om now?* In the darkness, he heard another sound and concentrated; something was purring. *Who's there?* he growled.

Two yellow-orange eyes appeared in the gloom. *It's me, Xojol*, the were-jaguar said as she stepped forward. *I'm happy to see you made it back before the sunrise.*

At the sight of Xojol, Tz' instantly knew he had made another terrible mistake in mating with her. *Get away from me*, he yowled. He wanted to crush Xojol's head between his jaws and then run out into the sun where the light of day would burn the blackness from his heart and the skin from his bones.

Xojol continued to purr as she walked toward Tz'. *Come now, it's not so bad*, she said. *You're the leader of the pack. You'll have all the meat you can eat and can mate with me whenever you want. Surely that's worth something.*

It's not the life I was destined to have! Tz' yelped.

Are you sure about that? Xojol asked as she advanced within a few feet of Tz'. *You wanted to be a powerful were-jaguar so you went to see Satal. And she sent you here, into Xibalba, where you've become the creature you so desired to be. You've gained the respect and admiration of those around you. Perhaps that girl is not the destiny the gods have set before you.* Xojol stepped forward until she was right next to Tz'. *Come*, she purred in his ear, *it's time to feast and enjoy life.* She gently licked Tz' behind the ear, sending a buzz of energy through his body.

Tz' felt some of his anger and frustration dissipate as Xojol continued to groom him. Reluctantly, he turned away from the small patch of daylight and agreed to follow Xojol back to the cave.

And with every step deeper into the darkness, Tz' forgot more and more of Na'om. By the time they reached the cave, he had a hearty appetite and eagerly tore into the paunch of a small deer that the males had set aside especially for him, with Xojol happily by his side.

YAKAL

Yakal walked slowly toward his home. He needed to tell Uskab about Na'om's decision to go to the island of the shamans and that he would be going as well. But he knew his young wife all too well; she would not be happy with the news. She was playing with Mayibal when he approached their small courtyard, and after a brief hug, he got right to the point.

"Why do you have to be the one to go with her? Surely you can send some trusted guards to watch over her," Uskab pouted as she bounced Mayibal on her hip.

"You know why, my love. I'm her father and must stand beside her. I'll only be gone seven days, and if we're successful and can bring Tz' home, then we'll have an advantage when we go into battle with Satal. Right now, that old witch believes she has the upper hand by controlling Tz', but if Na'om is right and he's trapped in the Underworld and there's a chance to rescue him, then we must go."

"Well, I don't like the idea at all," Uskab said and a tear escaped and ran down her cheek. "What if something happens to you?" she sobbed. Mayibal began to wail as well.

"Shh, my loves," Yakal said as he hurried to wrap the two of them in a big hug. "I'll be fine, I promise. We're taking four trusted guards with us; we'll travel quickly and be back before you know it."

"Promise me you won't go anywhere near Xibalba," Uskab begged. "If Na'om believes she can return there without harm, let her go, but you must remain in the land of the living."

Yakal kissed Uskab on the forehead and then tickled Mayibal on his bare belly to get him to laugh instead of cry. "I'll be fine, I promise you," he said.

Before dawn the next day, Yakal and the guards were already waiting at the main gates to the city when Na'om, Ek' Balam, Box, and Biribik appeared. The three youths each carried a pack basket full of supplies. Yakal picked up his own basket and nodded to the guards, who were already laden down with more food and bedding.

"All right, let's go," Yakal said, and the sentries at the gate opened the copper doors to let the group through.

"Wait," a woman shouted.

Yakal turned to look. "Kärinik, what are you doing here?" he asked as the older woman ran to join the group.

"I know the route to the coast as well as anyone and can take a path that will keep us hidden from most people so we don't draw any untoward attention," she said. "If we travel to my hut, you can use my canoe to reach the island; it will be faster to travel by sea from there than walking overland for two days before procuring a canoe."

Na'om smiled as the older woman gave her a hug. "I'm glad you're coming with us," she whispered as she gave the woman a small kiss on the cheek. "I was feeling outnumbered," she added.

"Right then, let's go," Kärinik said and took the lead on the sacbe, heading due north toward the ocean.

The group walked for hours, with little said. Yakal noted with some dismay that Na'om kept company much of the time with Box and Biribik or with Kärinik. He had hoped this trip might entice her to speak to him. Instead, he walked in the company of the guards. It was only when they had stopped for the night, and the guards, Box, and Biribik set about making camp that Yakal sat down with Na'om and Kärinik.

"Are you both all right?" Yakal said. He feared they might have walked too long and quickly, especially for Kärinik. He could certainly feel the day's march in his own legs.

Kärinik smiled and patted him on the shoulder. "I'm in good shape, never you fear. I walk the sand dunes all day long, so this trodden path is easy to traverse."

"I'm fine, Yakal," Na'om said.

Yakal winced at hearing his name. He longed to tell Na'om to call him Tat, but he knew that if his daughter was anything like him, insisting that she call him Father would only make it less likely she would do so.

Yakal didn't know what to say, and in the silence, Na'om got up and went in search of Box and Biribik. Yakal sighed.

"Give it time," Kärinik advised as she patted the man on the knee. "You'll need to earn her trust if you expect her to embrace you as her father."

"It's that obvious?" Yakal asked.

"Hmm, to me, yes," the older woman responded. Then she smiled. "Let's make something to eat, eh? I'm starved."

The evening passed quietly, with the guards taking turns protecting the group. At one point, Na'om went off into the dark to relieve herself with only Ek' Balam by her side. Yakal almost followed to make sure no harm came to her, but Box got up quickly and headed in the same direction, so Yakal sat back down. Several minutes passed and there was no sign of any of them, which made him anxious.

"I'm going to see what's going on," he muttered to the closest guard. He could hear laughter and voices in the distance and headed in that direction. The moon gave off barely enough light to see by, and Yakal stumbled more than once over unseen rocks and plants. He reached a small gully and lurched down the rocky embankment. The voices were louder now and he hurried forward, eager to make sure everyone was all right. He followed the winding gulch, passing a cluster of several small ceiba trees, and stopped in his tracks when he saw Ek' Balam, who was eating something, and then Na'om and Box.

The youth had his arms around Na'om, and as Yakal watched, he drew her in for a kiss. It was brief, but when their lips touched, sparks of bluish white light shot out in multiple directions.

"Did you see that?" Box exclaimed as he stepped away from Na'om.

Just then, Ek' Balam looked up from the lizard he was eating and growled. Na'om turned and saw Yakal. "What are you doing here?" she asked.

Yakal stepped forward. "What's going on?" he demanded. "Na'om, are you all right?"

Box walked toward Yakal. "Nothing's the matter," he said.

"I wasn't speaking to you."

"I'm fine, Yakal," Na'om said.

Yakal could hear the exasperation in his daughter's voice.

"Lord Yakal," Box said, "we've discovered that whenever we touch, Na'om experiences a tingling feeling in that place, so *I* wondered what would happen if we kissed."

"I'm sure you did!" Yakal replied. He glared at Box, who took a step backward.

By now Na'om and Ek' Balam had walked to Yakal, and she stood defiantly in front of him. "I *asked* him to kiss me; I've never been kissed, not that you would know. I wanted to experience what it feels like since I'm about to go into the Underworld again, and only the gods know what might happen down there."

"It meant nothing, Lord Yakal, I swear," Box said.

But Yakal doubted that was true for Box and he wondered what the encounter really meant for Na'om.

"We are on a mission to rescue Tz'; let's not forget that," Yakal replied.

Even in the dark, Yakal could feel the look that Na'om gave him like a stab wound to his chest.

"I have never forgotten the true reason we're here," Na'om said. "Nor would I dream of abandoning Tz' in any way. He is my oldest and dearest friend, and I'm willing to risk my life to bring him back to the land of the living. That's far more than anyone's ever done for me." And with that last comment, Na'om and Ek' Balam strode back toward the camp fire, leaving Yakal and Box on their own.

"My lord," Box began to speak, but Yakal held up his hand.

"No, don't say anything, I deserved that comment." He sighed. "I should tell you what happened in the past so you'll have a better understanding of my relationship with Na'om. Her mother died right after birthing Na'om. I was young, impetuous, and not thinking clearly in my grief. I fled the village where Na'om was born, leaving her to be raised by Ajkun, her grandmother. I thought I was doing it to protect her. I knew Satal might learn of Na'om's existence since she'd been born at the very end of the Wayeb, giving her powers that Satal would undoubtedly crave. So, I left and never looked back. I married Uskab and started a new family and never once mentioned to anyone that I had a daughter in Pa nimá. And then the village was attacked when Satal learned Naʼom lived there. Many villagers, including Chiman and Ajkun and Tzʼ, were brought to Mayapán to be sold as slaves. I released them, but I couldn't save Naʼom when she arrived in the region, hoping to rescue them. Satal had captured her, there was a skirmish at the cenote, and then they both fell in. At that point, we all thought Naʼom and Satal had perished. Little did any of us know that both of them would survive in their own ways." Yakal fell silent.

"Tzʼ told me some of this story, but I didn't know why you had left Naʼom as an infant," Box said. "I can understand her anger at you, and I can also understand your desire to make amends."

"Maltiox," Yakal replied. "I'm sorry for lashing out at you. I think we should get back to the others."

Box nodded and the two men stumbled their way back through the dark, arid landscape. "It was much easier walking with Naʼom," Box said and laughed. "She can project a light all around her; it's amazing."

"*She's* amazing, you mean," Yakal chided. "And gives a good kiss from what I saw." He laughed as he sensed Box's embarrassment. "Your secret is safe with me, never fear."

The next day, Kärinik took a path through the scrubby brush, creosote bushes, and ceiba trees that avoided the many small villages in the area. She eventually led them past murky lagoons full of stagnant sea water that smelled of dead fish but were a haven for all sorts of birds Yakal had never seen. Every now and then, Yakal walked near Naʼom, hoping she would speak to him, but she refused to even look in his direction. He knew she was mad at him for interfering the night before, but he didn't know how to make amends. By dusk, the group had arrived at the many salt-drying pools made of stones. Dozens of workers cut the reddish pink salt that had dried on the edges of the ponds into great chunks that they loaded into pack baskets. A steady stream of men marched off with the heavy loads on their backs, their tumplines digging into their foreheads with the weight.

"That's your salt, Naʼom," Yakal said. "We should have plenty for the battle ahead."

The group waited in the brush nearby until the workers had left for the day, and the late afternoon sun had turned the pools a deep blood red. Then Kärinik led them around the ponds and onward into the sand dunes.

It was dark by the time they reached her hut. In the scant moonlight, Yakal was amazed to see the curling white froth of the deep blue waves as they crashed onto the sand.

"It's even more beautiful in the daylight," Kärinik said as she hurried toward the hut. She entered and lit some candles. "Oh, it's so good to be home," she exclaimed as she stood in the doorway.

Na'om smiled, then ran forward to the top of a dune, and drew in a deep breath of the salty air. "I missed this place," she said as she held out her arms and spun in place. She leaned her head backward and looked up at the dark sky where a million stars had appeared. "Isn't it lovely," she asked Box as he came to stand beside her.

"Yes, it most certainly is," he replied. "I've never seen the ocean before."

"It's beautiful; you'll see in the morning," Na'om said.

She and Kärinik worked together to make a meal for everyone, and soon the guards had settled in for the night. Yakal, Box, and Biribik laid out blankets in the hardened sand in front of the hut, while Kärinik and Na'om agreed to share the hammock inside. After a feast of dried fish, Ek' Balam lay down across the doorway, effectively protecting the women inside.

Tucked into his blankets, Yakal could hear the murmur of the women's voices. He desperately wanted to know what they were talking about and hoped Na'om was not telling Kärinik about Box's kiss.

Daylight had not yet made an appearance when Kärinik roused everyone from their slumber. She shook Yakal and forced him to get up. "You must take Na'om and the boys and go. I only have one canoe, so leave the guards here with me. They won't be welcome on the island anyway."

Yakal nodded. "Yes, I had wondered about that." He turned to Box and Biribik, but frowned when he looked more closely at the second youth. "Are you all right?" he asked.

Biribik shook his head and pointed toward the ocean. "That terrifies me," he confessed.

The slightest hint of light showed the immensity of the ocean in front of them, and as he listened to the waves crashing on the sand, Yakal also felt a shiver of fear run through his body. He had never ventured onto such an open amount of water, but he knew he needed to control his distress in order to take Na'om where she needed to go. "Would you prefer to stay here with Kärinik?" he asked Biribik.

"My lord, I will give my right hand to the gods if I don't have to set foot in a canoe on that," he replied as he pointed to the sea.

"Now, now, nothing so drastic is needed," Yakal reassured him. "I doubt there'd be room for you in the canoe anyway," he added. He turned to Kärinik. "You can put him to use for a day or two, can't you?" he asked.

Kärinik smiled and pointed toward the roof of the hut. "I think it's high time I replace the palm frond thatching, and that will go much easier with the help of Biribik and the guards."

"Then that's settled. Biribik will stay and help you, and Box and I will take Na'om and Ek' Balam to the island."

Na'om

In the predawn darkness, Na'om couldn't see the waves that surged in and out against the shoreline close to where she stood. But she sensed the energy they held, and she shivered. She was anxious about embarking on this journey across such a large body of water. Traveling by canoe on a river was one thing; she knew she could swim to shore if anything should happen, but now they needed to go beyond the shoreline to avoid the breaking waves, a distance too far for her to comfortably swim. And if they were to reach the island of the shamans in one day, they needed to journey as far as possible before the sun broke above the horizon line. But Na'om was afraid to leave before they could truly see the water.

The stars still twinkled brightly in the night sky, a sight that normally filled her with awe. But looking into the blackness, unable to discern where the darkness of the sky met the blue-black water, she'd never felt so small or vulnerable. And she didn't know what she'd discover once she reached the island. What if the shamans didn't allow her to pass? And even if they did, what if she entered the Underworld and couldn't find Tz'? And worse still, what if she became trapped again, wandering the passageways until she simply gave up hope and stopped moving? She shivered again, wrapped her shawl tighter around her body, and looked at the land behind her, hoping for a better glimpse of the sun. She could barely see Kärinik's small hut where the group had spent the night.

Too tense to eat, Na'om picked at her corn porridge and eventually gave her bowl to Ek' Balam who lapped up the mush in two swipes of his tongue. Then Kärinik showed the men where her dugout canoe was hidden in the brush near the brackish waters below the hut. The four guards easily carried the heavy wooden canoe up the sand dunes, past the house, and down to the beach, where they deposited it near the crashing waves. Kärinik handed paddles to Yakal and Box and gave one to Na'om as well. It was lighter and smaller than the other two. "This is my own paddle; I want you to have it," she said.

Na'om felt her heart fill with love for the older woman. "Maltiox, I promise to return it," she said as she gave Kärinik a hug.

"Go straight out until you're beyond the waves," Kärinik told Yakal and Box. "Then turn west, away from the rising sun and follow the shoreline. If you paddle all day, you should be able to see the island before the sun sets."

"See you in a few days," Na'om said. She was reluctant to let go of the older woman.

"Na'om, we're ready when you are," Box said. He was holding the canoe steady on the beach.

Na'om nodded to him and then stepped into the middle of the dugout. She gently folded her skirt around her legs and sat down. She motioned for Ek' Balam to join her, and the jaguar leapt into the middle and stood with his large head pointed toward the open water.

Box and Yakal nodded to each other, and with the help of the guards, the men gently shoved the dugout across the wet sand and into the oncoming waves. Na'om picked up her paddle and held the boat steady while Box nimbly climbed into the stern. They waited while Yakal climbed aboard, and then they all paddled into the oncoming surf.

Ek' Balam growled as an unseen wave broke on his side of the dugout, splashing him with cool water, and Na'om petted him gently on his back. "It's all right," she said, but she didn't feel confident as another wave slapped her side of the canoe and soaked her legs.

Na'om felt the canoe rock from side to side as Box continued to sweep the blade of his paddle through the water. She instantly grabbed the gunwale to steady herself, but then let go and thrust her own paddle into the water again. But she had difficulty maneuvering her paddle through the waves, so she quickly laid it on the bottom of the canoe and clutched the gunwale with her hand.

With the two men paddling, the canoe continued forward slowly. Whitewater crashed down on them, and spray quickly soaked Na'om's clothes. Finally, they passed through the breakers and settled into a rhythm of cresting one wave and then another. The up and down motion bothered Na'om's stomach, and she closed her eyes. Then she clutched the gunwale and leaned over the side, emptying her stomach of the little food she'd eaten that morning. She groaned and silently prayed to Xaman Ek, the travelers' god, to provide them with a safe passage. She kept her eyes closed and continued to whisper to Xaman Ek as they pushed farther out into the sea.

Soon, Box turned the canoe so they were headed west, and the canoe rocked from side to side as they rose and fell with the swells. The motion was more soothing, and Na'om relaxed. She felt the warmth of the ascending sun's rays on the side of her face, and despite her still queasy stomach, she opened her eyes to look around. Directly in front of her and off to her right, the blue-green water stretched away as far as she could see, with nothing visible in either direction.

She twisted her head and looked over her left shoulder, and she gasped when she saw the land was just a small strip of sand dunes and scrubby trees in the distance. She knew she could never swim that far if they should capsize, and she gripped the gunwale more tightly. She didn't want to let go until they had reached the island. She glanced behind her and gave Box a weak smile. His face was pale, his mouth set in a straight line. *He looks terrible*, Na'om thought, *but he's still paddling. I must do the same,* she admonished, and she picked up her blade and dipped it into the water once again.

Ek' Balam let out a sigh and leaned forward, draping his head over the wooden thwart in front of him, and Na'om quickly ran her fingertips lightly down his spine. She felt a tingling in her hand and arm and sent the energy toward her upset stomach, hoping that she could quell the discomfort she still felt. *I hope Box has us headed in the right direction. I'd hate to be out here for days and days.*

She twisted around and gave Box a smile. "You do know where we're going?"

Box nodded. "I believe so. Based on what Kärinik said before we left and what the shamans in Mayapán told us, we should be able to see the island before nightfall. It will take all day, though." He smiled again, exposing his white teeth in his dark face. "Take a break when you must, but we will make better time if we all paddle."

Na'om nodded, Box resumed paddling, and she did the same, even though she already felt weary. At that moment, she wanted nothing more than to drop into a deep sleep, lulled there by the steady rocking of the canoe as it pushed its way through the water. But there was more work to be done before any of them could sleep, so she forced herself to concentrate on the task at hand. *We must reach the island, and I must rescue Tz'. Then, perhaps, there will be time to rest before the inevitable confrontation with Satal.* She closed her eyes and leaned deeper into each pull of her paddle through the water, forcing the weariness from her bones through the sheer effort of movement.

She only opened her eyes when she heard Yakal's voice.

"Look there, I think I see something."

Na'om opened her eyes and strained to see anything. The sun was much higher now and reflected off the surface of the water, causing her to squint against the glare. But in the distance, she could just see an outline of something darker against the blue water. As the canoe continued forward, the shape slowly gained definition. It was the island. Na'om let out a sigh and felt some of the tension lift from her shoulders. Although she had known this trip by sea was shorter than going overland, it had still bothered her; she just didn't realize until that moment how much.

Although the island grew larger with every stroke they made, it still remained far in the distance. Na'om grew impatient. She needed to stand up and stretch and to empty her bladder. She looked to her right. The shore was closer now, and she turned around to speak to Box. "Can we go inland just for a few minutes? My legs have gone numb from sitting for so long."

"Yes, of course," Box replied. His stomach grumbled and he laughed. "I need to eat something and take a break."

Na'om felt Box turn the canoe, and they headed toward land. As they drew closer, Na'om realized the area looked almost identical to where they had left that morning, and she had the strange sensation that they hadn't really traveled along the coastline at all, but had been paddling all day in a large circle.

The canoe was swept to shore by several large breakers, and Yakal hopped out into the frothy, white, knee-deep water and pulled on the bow, helping to bring the boat up onto drier sand. Box held out his hand to Na'om and helped her over the side while Ek' Balam nimbly leaped over the gunwale and headed straight for the scruffy bushes growing from the sand dunes several yards away.

Na'om's legs were all tingly, and she stomped her feet on the hard-packed sand to bring the blood back into circulation. "I'll be right back," Na'om said to the men and quickly followed the jaguar into the trees and grasses. As soon as she was out of sight, she squatted down and relieved her very full bladder. She watched through the branches of a small ceiba tree as Box and Yakal also headed toward a patch of trees off to her right and smiled. *I guess I wasn't the only one in need of a break,* she thought as she stood back up and straightened her clothes.

Everyone gathered back at the canoe, and Box pulled out a basket filled with food. "We'll eat as quickly as possible and then be on our way," he said as he handed everyone a tamale. He looked at Ek' Balam, then peeled the corn husk off another tamale and tossed the steamed corn pastry to the jaguar. Ek' Balam caught the food in his mouth and swallowed it in a couple of bites.

Na'om broke her tamale into two parts and gave Ek' Balam the smaller piece. He made it disappear in one bite and looked expectantly at the other piece. "Oh no, this part is mine, you've had enough for now," Na'om said as she took a big bite of the turkey-filled pastry. Ek' Balam let out a sigh and lay down on the sand, his big head nestled across the top of his front paws.

Na'om smiled as Box handed her one of their three water gourds, but she only drank a few sips as she didn't want to reexperience the sensation of an overly full bladder two times in one day.

Both men quickly finished their meal and looked at Na'om, who was still eating. "Oh, I can finish this in the canoe," she said. She stuffed the remaining pastry in her pocket and hurried toward the boat. Yakal nodded, but didn't speak to her. *He's still upset; I must apologize for the harsh words I said earlier.* But she still didn't say anything. Once she was seated, the men launched the canoe, and she resumed the tiring task of paddling. Her hands were blistered, and her shoulders and arms ached, but she continued to thrust her paddle into the water, knowing that each stroke brought them closer to their destination.

Once they were past the breakers, Box and Yakal intensified their efforts, and they surged forward. *They must be as eager to reach the island as I am*, she thought. But the combination of the food in her belly and the hot afternoon sun made her drowsy, and before she knew it, the paddle had slipped from her hands. She yawned multiple times and then she curled up in the bottom of the canoe and quickly drifted off into a dreamless sleep.

She only woke when she heard Yakal and Box conversing. Still lethargic, she half sat up in the canoe and peered over the gunwale. The sun was much lower in the sky, and she could see a variety of huts and buildings on the island as well as discern that a giant ceiba tree was growing in the middle of it. Lit torches ringed the clearing where the tree stood, even though the sun had yet to set.

"That must be the largest ceiba tree ever," Na'om said. In the increasing dusk, she noticed several men working near the base of the tree.

Box skillfully ran the canoe up onto the sandy shore, but before Yakal could disembark, several of the shamans came running toward them.

"You can't land here; this is a sacred island, go back to wherever you came from," the men shouted.

Undisturbed by their demands, Yakal calmly stepped onto the shore.

A shaman ran right up to him and poked him in the chest with his fingertip. "Didn't you hear what we said? This is a sacred place; go back to your fishing village."

"We're not fishermen, and we're not going anywhere."

Na'om smiled as she sat up and stepped out of the canoe. Ek' Balam hopped onto the sand and stood beside her.

"Lady Na'om, my apologies," the shaman said. "We had no idea you were onboard."

Na'om was surprised. "How do you know who I am?"

He smiled, flashing several gold teeth. "News travels rapidly to us through a variety of channels. We heard of your powers and knew that one day soon you'd be joining us. You've come to find the quickest route to Xibalba and to your friend, Tz', yes?"

At that point, Na'om noticed an elderly shaman slowing making his way toward them. By the light of the torch he carried, Na'om could see he was dressed in a long-sleeved blue tunic that extended below his knees, with a matching pair of linen trousers, and a jaguar skin cape draped across his shoulders.

The other shamans fell back a step and bowed to this man, and she knew he had to be their leader.

"Ajaw," she said. "Your brother, Najtir, sends his greetings from Mayapán. I must enter Xibalba and understand that this is the best place to do so."

"Lady Naom, welcome. My name is Tatá, and I, all of us, are at your service." He turned to the younger shaman who had forbidden them to land. "Eqomal, you shall work directly with Lady Naom's escorts and provide them with whatever they need while I attend to Lady Naom myself."

The younger man bowed. "As you command, Ajaw," he said.

Naom saw a flash of anger cross the man's face at the reprimand.

"Lord Tatá, my friends will be no burden to you as we brought our own food, water, and bedding. They'll be fine here on the beach until I return," Naom said.

"There's no need to sleep on the sand. We have lodging for them and will provide them with whatever they may need if we can supply it," Tatá replied.

Naom smiled and then remembered the scroll Najtir had given her. She turned back to the canoe and rummaged in one of the baskets. She handed the rolled paper to Tatá. "From Najtir, who sends his greetings to you all."

"Maltiox, my lady, please come and refresh yourself and tell me of your journey." Tatá clapped his hands. "Food and beverages for our guests, and some salted fish for your jaguar friend as well." The group began to walk toward the base of the tree.

"Maltiox," Naom said. "But first, can you help me?"

"But of course," Tatá replied. He waved his hand toward the gigantic ceiba tree in the clearing. "*Yax che*, the tree of life and death. Through it, we can draw upon the power of all the gods, for it is the center of our universe. Enter near its roots and you can descend into the nine levels of Xibalba. Step into the hollow of its trunk and you can ascend into the thirteen realms of heaven."

Naom took several steps closer to the huge tree and looked upward into its branches. She had never seen anything so big. The limbs towered over a hundred feet above her head. The trunk was massive, far larger in girth than any tree she had ever seen, too large to encircle even if several people linked their arms together around the base. The trunk and branches were covered with hundreds of sharp, pointed spines, and she shivered, imagining for a moment being pinned against such a spot.

"Well, it seems I came to the right place," Na'om said. Suddenly, she felt a tugging on her skirt and looked down, expecting to see a child standing next to her, but no one was there. She glanced toward the other shamans standing behind Tatá, and the sensation stopped as soon as she looked their way. She turned to face Tatá again and the tugging resumed. She snapped her head toward the men nearby and the feeling stopped again.

Oh, you won't drain my energy so easily, she thought as she quickly imagined a white light enveloping her body. She touched Ek' Balam on the head and pushed the bubble around him as well. One of the shamans dipped his head in acknowledgment, and the group of men took a few steps back.

"Do you wish to rest tonight and begin your journey tomorrow?" Tatá asked.

"No, I need to go now," Na'om replied. "There have been far too many delays already. I won't wait any longer." She turned to Box. "Get me my pack basket," she said.

Box turned and trotted down to the canoe, grabbed one of several baskets, and hurried back to Na'om. He held the basket steady while Na'om slipped the leather straps over her shoulders. "We've enough food and water for several days, and I'm confident we'll be back before it runs out."

Box leaned in toward Na'om. "You're sure you don't want me to come with you?" he whispered.

Na'om gave him a weak smile as she placed her hand on his forearm. Her fingers tingled where they touched his skin. "I told you before, I have to do this on my own."

"No one is permitted into Xibalba without proper preparations," Tatá said sternly. Then he bowed his head to Na'om. "With the exception of Lady Na'om."

Na'om patted the knife she carried on her hip. "This will keep me safe." Box nodded and Na'om turned to Yakal.

"Yakal," she paused, "I'm sorry for my words the other night. I know you only have my best interests at heart."

Yakal smiled and nodded and then reached into the pouch he carried at his waist. He pulled out a simple beaded necklace and slipped it over

Na'om's head. "It's been blessed by the shamans in Mayapán and will bring you safety in your travels," he said as he placed the tiniest kiss on Na'om's cheek.

Na'om smiled and then turned to Tatá. "I'm ready."

Her male companions remained silent as Na'om and Ek' Balam followed Tatá to the other side of the ceiba tree. In the glow of the torches, she could see the top three rungs of a wooden ladder sticking out of a large hole in the ground near the base of the tree.

"The ladder will take you to the cenote below. Tunnels into Xibalba radiate outward from the pool of water, but only you can decide which one to enter to find your friend," Tatá said. "And, Lady Na'om, remember that this is just one way to enter and leave the Underworld. Your journey may take you far from here, in which case you may return to the land of the living by a different route. Nonetheless, my fellow shamans and I will know when you've surfaced again regardless of where it takes place." He pointed to one of the lit torches. "Do you wish to take a light with you?"

"No, we'll be fine," Na'om said. She looked at the ladder and then at Ek' Balam. "I'm more concerned about how he'll get down there."

As if in answer, Ek' Balam went over to the opening and leapt into the darkness, disappearing into the void without a glance back at Na'om.

"Ek' Balam!" Na'om shouted. But it was too late; the jaguar was gone. "I'd better hurry and catch up to him," she said as she ran over to the ladder. As she was about to descend below the level of the ground, she glanced back up at the shamans who had gathered around the opening. "Wish me luck," she said.

"You don't need luck, you have all the power you'll need inside you," Tatá said. "May the gods be on your side, Na'om."

Na'om nodded and continued to climb down the ladder. As she descended, it got progressively darker, and she worried she'd miss Ek' Balam in the blackness. But within minutes, her hand brushed against something soft as she reached for the rung below her, and she smiled. "Ek' Balam, is that you?" she asked. She extended a pulse of white light in that direction.

Wings fluttered in the sudden light, and a dozen small bats took off into the air around Na'om. She shivered in revulsion and repeatedly wiped her hand on her skirt, but she could feel the warmth of their soft, furry bodies on her skin. Fearful of what else she might encounter in the dark, she cast out a ball of white light, and was startled to see numerous clay figurines tucked into the cracks and crevices of the cave wall. *These must be the funeral statues Box told me about*, she thought. The air grew warmer and more humid the farther she penetrated the depths, and she looked anxiously for any sign of an opening in the cave walls and for Ek' Balam, but he was nowhere to be seen. And then her foot suddenly touched the ground. She stepped off the ladder and arched her head back to see the surface, but it was lost in the blackness.

"Ek' Balam?" she called and her voice echoed around her. She felt movement and heard the distinctive squeaking of bats and the brush of their wings as they flitted past. A large gray rat scurried out from a dark corner, and Na'om stepped back onto the ladder as the creature ran under her feet. "Enough of this," she admonished herself as she placed her feet on solid ground once again. "Ek' Balam, where are you?"

Na'om heard a purring in the darkness and extended her light in that direction. The light reflected off the deep blue water of the cenote and then she smiled when she saw her friend sitting in the opening to a tunnel. "I knew you'd know where to go down here," she said while she walked over to him. She rubbed behind the jaguar's tattered ear. "Come on, boy, let's find Tz' and bring him back to the light," she said, and together they entered the darkness.

SATAL

As soon as she felt herself shift into a bat, Satal waited until most of the others had flown on ahead, and then she zoomed down closer to the sacbe that gleamed white in the moonlight. The limestone causeway was empty of people, but she hoped to find something that would signal Pataninel and Yuxba' had traveled this section of the road on their way to Mayapán. She sniffed the air and caught a faint whiff of something unpleasant, like the scent of the dead mouse she'd recently found in the food cupboard in her outdoor kitchen. She fluttered closer, taking care not to use her left wing too much, and she noticed tiny droplets of blood spattered on the limestone. The trail led off the causeway and into the nearby creosote bushes and she followed, fearful and excited at what she might find.

A pattern of footprints in the dry dirt, then more blood, some sputum, and finally a large pile of undigested food, but there was no sign of either shaman. She circled the area, flying just above the ceiba and nance trees growing in the area, but she couldn't see anything that resembled a body.

Yuxba' must be holding on, she thought. She flew upward again and began to follow the sacbe once more.

For several hours, she fluttered on by herself, ignoring the increasing pain in her left wing and the constant rumbling of her empty belly that demanded meat. She had to know if the two men had arrived and delivered their package. And then finally, she spied a glistening puddle of blackness and smelled the sharp, coppery scent of a large amount of blood. She flew in close and followed the spots, which were easy to see even in the darkness. They led her away from the sacbe once again and into a grove of avocado trees.

As she drew closer, she spied the two shamans. She could see Pataninel had taken off his pack basket and was standing near the trunk of one of the larger trees, and Yuxba' was propped up against the base of it. Yuxba's normally dark brown face was pale, and he reeked of the sweet scent of death. Satal smiled and continued to flutter just out of the men's line of sight.

"Open your mouth, Yuxba', and let it all out," Pataninel said. "We're close enough to Mayapán that whatever you carry within you will do its intended harm."

Yuxba' shook his head. "Not close . . . enough," he said. He drew in a ragged breath. "You must take . . . it closer," he said and gulped in a bit of air. A line of spittle dribbled out of the corner of his mouth.

"Ha, if you think I'm going through with that, you're wrong," Pataninel said. He leaned in close and whispered into Yuxba's ear.

Satal was too far away to hear what he said, but she noticed Yuxba's attempt to smile. More drool ran down his cheek, and he made a weak attempt to wipe it away.

"I can carry you closer, but you'll surely die if you hold on to whatever it is you have inside you, or you can let it go now and hope that you recover," Pataninel said. He reached up into the tree branches and grabbed a ripe avocado. He reached for the knife he carried at his waist and sliced the fruit open. He held the green half without the seed in front of Yuxba's face. "Smell that? Don't you want to eat it and feel better again?"

Yuxba' coughed and blood splattered the avocado. Pataninel threw it away in disgust. "Must get . . . closer," Yuxba' sputtered. "Satal . . . is watching."

"At this time of night, the old witch is asleep in her bed. We're days away and have nothing to fear from her."

"Nooo," Yuxba' gasped. "There. . . ." he said and made a feeble attempt to point into the night sky. "Must get closer."

Satal flew behind several branches so she was less visible.

"All right, if that's your choice, then I'll make the decision for you," Pataninel said, and he thrust his knife into Yuxba's heart.

Yuxba's eyes went wide and then his head dropped to one side. His mouth gaped open, and instantly the cloud of noxious yellow that Satal had placed within him began to filter out from between his teeth. Pataninel stepped several paces away, avoiding the tendrils of smoke that filled the air. He wiped his blade on several leaves, which he threw into the nearby bushes, then he plucked several ripe avocados, placed them in the pack basket, and swung it up onto his back.

"Sorry, old friend, but I must leave you here and return to the city, to my family and friends," he said, and he hurried back the way they had come.

Satal flew down and perched on a tree limb several feet from Yuxba'. She watched as the yellow toxins steadily flowed from his body and were lifted up into the night sky by a light breeze. As it mixed with the air, the cloud grew larger, like a tiny flame that grows when fed bits of twigs and dried coconut husk. *What's done is done*, she thought. The spreading haze moved higher and drifted west toward Mayapán and its inhabitants.

Even though the sky was beginning to grow lighter, Satal continued to follow the haze. She was just able to see the distant walls of the city turn a mustard-yellow before she had to turn back and return to her real body, still asleep in her bed in Chichén Itzá.

When she awoke, she grinned, despite the deep ache that stretched from her left shoulder to her fingertips. She knew she had taxed her arm's strength, but she didn't care. *The poisons have been delivered*, she thought. *Now I just need to decide what to do with Pataninel when he returns.* And she smirked at the thought.

AJKUN

Ajkun slowly eased herself out of the hammock and dressed quietly. She didn't want to wake Chiman. She smiled as she looked as his weathered, wrinkled face. He was still handsome despite the years. He had a few white hairs, but most of it was still thick and black, and he had stayed in good physical shape. Not like many men his age who developed a paunch and had skinny arms and legs. It was good to be his partner after all the years without him. She smiled again. *I'll let him sleep and not wake him until the porridge is hot.*

The first thing Ajkun noticed when she stepped outside was the strange yellowish-green color of the sky. And then she realized it wasn't the sky, but some type of dust in the air. She swiped her hand across the wooden counter where she kept her cooking utensils and her palm came away covered with the fine powder. Everything she touched had the same coating on it. She didn't know what it was and didn't like the gritty feeling it left on her skin, so she hurried to wash her hands. But the pottery pot by the turtle shell basin was empty. Again.

"Why can't he ever leave me some water?" Ajkun muttered as she reached under the counter and found the spare water gourd. She shook it and was grateful it was full. She poured some water into the shell before emptying the rest of it into the pottery container. She quickly washed her hands and then gathered together the empty water gourds. She'd have to go get them filled at the cenote before she could make porridge for breakfast. She peeked into the hut she shared with Chiman. He was still sound asleep in the hammock.

"Of course, he sleeps like a baby through anything," Ajkun said under her breath. "I have to go get water," she stated loudly, hoping she'd wake up Chiman. She really wanted him to get up and start the fire so it would be ready when she returned, but he only grunted and rolled over onto his side.

Irritated that she hadn't been able to rouse him, Ajkun grabbed the gourds by their leather cords and hurried toward the cenote. The air was clearer now as most of the silty powder had drifted to the ground, but Ajkun was dismayed to see her sandals quickly became coated in the yellowish-green substance. Only a few other people were out in the streets, and no one bothered to say hello or good morning. It was just as well as Ajkun only wanted to get the water and get back to the hut. She had plenty to do and didn't want to waste any more time.

When she arrived at the cenote, a few other older women were standing near the watering hole with their own pile of gourds to fill. Their feet were also covered in the fine dust, along with a layer on their shoulders and hair. However, there was no sign of the boys who tended the ropes and dropped the wooden buckets into the water several feet below the surface. Ajkun nodded to the other women but made no move to engage in any conversations. She didn't know any of them and had no interest in being friendly. But after several minutes had passed, with still no sign of any of the boys, Ajkun grew impatient.

"This is ridiculous," she said as she marched over to the rope. "How difficult can this be?" She picked up the bucket, threw it over the edge, and was satisfied to hear it splash into the water. She grabbed the end of the rope and began to pull, bringing the water to the surface. "Come on," she said to the other women. "Who was first? Let's get these gourds filled and get back to work."

The women made a quick line and Ajkun helped one after another fill their gourds. Her arms began to ache from throwing and lifting the heavy wooden bucket, but none of the women offered to take a turn. And suddenly, Ajkun was left alone, with her own gourds to fill and no one to help hold them while she poured the water. Annoyance washed through her body in a wave, and she grabbed a gourd and jammed it between her feet to steady it. She lifted the heavy bucket and poured the water, but the gourd wobbled and the water splashed all over her.

"Itzamná, why?" she muttered. "I just need my water and then I can get back to the hut and make Chiman his breakfast." She put the gourd down, stepped a few paces away, and shook her feet. Droplets of yellow water flew through the air, and as her skin was cleansed of the yellow dust, Ajkun felt her mood shift. She no longer felt cross at the other women or at Chiman for not helping. She hurried to the bucket, filled it again with water, and deliberately poured the liquid over her feet, scrubbing away the remains of the dust and dirt.

She filled her gourds and returned home, noticing with each step that a layer of the sickly yellow dust reappeared, and with it her irritation. There was no sign of Chiman outside, so she thoroughly washed her feet and again noticed the change in her mood.

"Chiman, wake up," she cried as she entered the hut. "Something's wrong!"

"My love, what's the matter?" Chiman asked as he sat up and rubbed his eyes.

"A yellow coating on everything outside that came from the sky and makes me angry every time I come in contact with it."

Chiman laughed. "Perhaps it's just pollen from the many orchards around the city."

"No, don't laugh, I tell you, it's different. Come see," Ajkun said, and she tugged on Chiman's arm. "And none of the boys were at the cenote; I had to draw my own water and did so for several other women who were waiting."

"Hmm, that is unusual. I will speak to Bitol and find out what happened."

As she waited for Chiman to dress and brush his hair, Ajkun closed her eyes and listened. By now she should have been hearing lively chatter as the neighbors got ready for their own work days, children laughing and playing in the alley between the houses, and the cooing, chirping, and twittering of the flocks of doves, flycatchers, and the occasional green jay that came to perch in the trees in the area. Instead, she heard raised voices, a child wailing, and someone retching. Another person cried out in pain, followed by more children crying.

"Something's wrong, Chiman," Ajkun said. "I just know it."

Chiman didn't answer, just leaned over and gave her a quick kiss on the cheek before stepping outside. Ajkun followed, but she as soon as she came in contact with the yellow dust, she felt her impatience rising. "Don't you feel it?" she questioned Chiman.

"No, my dear, I don't feel anything different." He looked around at the layers of silt covering everything and brushed some aside with his hands before sitting on his favorite wooden stump by the fire pit. "Come now, how about some breakfast before I go to work?"

"You'll have to make do with leftover tamales," Ajkun said as she reached into a covered basket and pulled out some tamales wrapped in banana leaves. "I haven't had time to cook this morning."

"I see; well, I think I'll pick something up at the market," Chiman replied. He walked to the counter and picked up one of the many water gourds. "I'll be back later," he said as he kissed Ajkun again.

Her frustration grew as she watched him leave. *Something is wrong, I know it. Oh, how I wish Na'om were here. I pray to the gods that she's safe.*

Unhappy and unable to focus, Ajkun washed her hands and feet and stepped back inside the hut. She immediately began to feel better and decided to do some weaving to calm her nerves. She tied one end of the loom to a small hook in the wall, wrapped the strap around her waist, and then sat down at just the right distance from the wall to create a good tension on the warp. The repetitive motion of sending the shuttle full of blue cotton from one side of the backstrap loom to the other helped her concentrate. She needed to finish this piece of fabric, which would become one sleeve of the outfit she was making for Na'om. *Every time I come in contact with that dust, I'm not myself,* she mused as she beat the weft into place. *But I can't stay inside all day; there are chores to do and food to cook. I shall have to give the outside a thorough cleaning and maybe then it won't bother me so.* She worked a while longer on her weaving and, pleased with the results, she left the loom and went outside. She swept the counter, wiped off the stumps, swept the ground, and then used much of the water she had gathered that morning to thoroughly wash everything. As the last bits of yellow flowed away from the hut, she took a deep breath. She felt better, despite the residue clinging to her hands and feet.

She had just finished washing up and was going to eat a late lunch when she saw Alom approaching in a hurry.

"Ajkun, you must come quickly," Alom said.

"What's the matter?" Ajkun asked.

"It's little Mayibal. He won't stop crying. Uskab and I have tried everything. He keeps saying something is biting him, but we can see nothing on his body. Uskab even gave him a bath, which quieted him for a time, so she set him down to play. But within minutes, he was back to crying again and complaining of having little bugs all over him."

"And you, how do you feel?" Ajkun asked.

"Me, I'm all right, except for a terrible pain in my head, behind my eyes. The higher the sun gets in the sky, the more it hurts."

Ajkun nodded. "I'll be right with you. Let me just grab a few things that might help Mayibal." Ajkun returned to the tent and picked up her pack basket full of salves and ointments. Perhaps one of them would help the little boy. She also grabbed her shawl, which she handed to Alom when she went back outside. "Wrap this around your head and pull it forward to shield your eyes from the direct sun," she told her friend. "That should help your headache."

"I wish Yakal were here," Alom said. "He can always quiet the child, no matter what ails him."

Together, the two women moved quickly through the streets of the city. As they walked, Ajkun looked around at the people they met. No one smiled, no one offered them a greeting. Men and women argued inside some of the huts they passed while other couples sat silently in their courtyards, oblivious to the children crying at their feet. Ajkun stopped walking and looked more closely. Each child was covered with a fine layer of the odd silt.

She grabbed Alom's arm. "When did your headache start?"

"Oh, I don't know, sometime this morning. Why?"

"Was it before or after you went outside?"

"I don't know; I don't remember. After, I guess."

"Hmm, all right." They continued walking.

Uskab was pacing up and down the tiny courtyard inside the fence when the women approached. Mayibal was held tightly in her arms, his crying filling the air all around. His skin had patches of dust on it.

"You must bathe him again, Uskab," Ajkun commanded. "Wash away that yellow dirt on him and then take him inside while we clean the area."

Uskab nodded and set about giving Mayibal a bath. As soon as the dust was rinsed off his skin, Mayibal stopped crying and splashed happily in the tepid water. Uskab took a towel off a hook to dry her son, and a cloud of dust arose from it.

"Stop!" Ajkun commanded. "You mustn't touch him with anything that's been in contact with this yellow powder."

"I don't understand," Uskab said.

"I believe there's something in this dust that's affecting everyone. I've been irritated with everything this morning. Alom has a bad headache. Your son won't stop crying. People are unfriendly; none of this is normal."

"I haven't felt like eating today," Uskab admitted.

"It's causing different problems for different people."

"So, what do we do?" Alom asked. "It's everywhere!"

"I cleaned everything covered in this silt at our hut and we must do the same here," Ajkun instructed Alom. Uskab nodded, picked up her wet son, and took him inside.

Together, the two older women wiped down as much as they could, then they swept the ground, and rinsed the area with water. They used what little water remained to wash their faces, hands, and feet, but their clothes still had the dust on them. By then, it was mid-afternoon and Ajkun was tired. She hadn't eaten anything all day and could feel her stomach grumble.

"We'll need to wash all our clothes and everything out there!" Alom stated as she pointed to the city at large. Abruptly, she sat down on a wooden stump near the fire. She rested her elbows on her knees and put her head in her hands, massaging her temples.

"I'll speak to Chiman. We must have the shamans give offerings to Chaac. Perhaps if the rain god is listening, he'll provide us with a heavy downpour that will wash all this away." She patted Alom on the shoulder. "Stay here with Uskab; I'll find Chiman and speak to him."

Ajkun looked out at the street. Enough people had passed by the house so the dirt had mixed with the dust; it was no longer a visible layer and she hoped that would mean she wouldn't be as affected by it.

As she walked toward the round observatory building of the shamans, she passed groups of men finishing their daily work on the much-needed leather shields and vest plates for the warriors. Farther on, other men gathered the piles of arrow shafts they'd carved and carried the bundles on their shoulders to the fletchers. She smiled when she saw Lintat and

Memetik sitting with the other boys among the baskets of feathers in every hue imaginable. But none of the youths looked up. Ajkun sighed. All the boys worked long hours for the master fletchers, sorting and organizing the feathers by color and length. They set aside the best for the fine headdresses worn by the elite and the shamans while other piles were specifically saved for arrows. Each fletcher had his favorite feathers he liked to use on his arrows, and one could tell who had made the arrow by the color combination on it. She continued onward and saw the stonemasons were still fixing buildings damaged in the battle. *None of the men seem bothered by this dust. It's the women and children who are distressed. I wonder why?* Ajkun mused. Then she laughed. *Of course, we're often more perceptive to subtle changes in our environment.* She hurried onward. She needed to find Chiman and tell him what she thought had to be done.

At the observatory, one of the older shamans sat cross-legged on a woven reed mat in the shade provided by the overhanging roof.

"Ajaw," Ajkun asked as she approached the man. "Is Chiman inside?"

"No, my lady, he went home early as he said he didn't feel well." The man turned his hands palm-side up. "He had strange spots on his hands and welts on his feet."

"Has anyone else had such symptoms?"

"Some of my brother shamans also have marks on their skin."

"Did they come in contact with the yellow powder that fell from the sky early this morning?"

"Perhaps," the shaman mused. "They arise much earlier than me to study the morning stars."

"Maltiox," Ajkun said. She looked up as she turned to leave. The sun had traveled across the sky and was headed toward the western horizon. A small cloud of bats swooped through the air, searching for insects, and Ajkun shivered. The streets were filled with people headed home from the market and from their respective jobs, but they didn't chatter happily as they normally would. Most walked with their eyes focused on the ground, lost in their own thoughts, as if a heavy weight were felt by each and every one of them. Ajkun pushed her way through the throngs, eager to return to the hut she shared with Chiman. He was sitting by the fire, poking at the embers with a long stick. His deep chocolate skin had a pale sheen to it, and Ajkun could see how carefully he held the stick in one hand.

"Chiman!" Ajkun said as she went to him. "Let me see your hands."

He obediently turned his hands, and Ajkun gasped as she saw the blisters that had formed on his palms.

"I don't know what I did," Chiman muttered.

"You did nothing," Ajkun replied. "It's the dust you came in contact with this morning." She tugged on her lower lip, deep in thought, and the image of bats flittered through her mind. Suddenly she knew who was behind this pervasive sickness. "Satal has done something to poison us all through this fine silt. We must give tribute to Chac and pray he sends us a healing, cleansing rain to wash the dust away."

"I should have listened to you this morning. I'm sorry, my love." Chiman said.

Ajkun leaned down and kissed his cheek. His skin was hot to the touch. "Come, you must bathe and get inside where it is clean."

"No, first, I must tell the shamans of your idea. Then and only then will I be able to rest and heal from this."

"You're too ill to go back to the temple. Write them a note and I'll find someone to deliver it. And then you must rest." Ajkun went inside the hut and returned with Chiman's turkey feather quill, ink bowl, and a piece of fig-bark. He quickly wrote a note to the shamans, and when the ink was dry, he folded the paper and sealed it with a blob of beeswax from the candle Ajkun provided. He pressed the ring he wore into the soft wax, leaving the impression of a quetzal bird. He handed the parcel to Ajkun and smiled weakly. "Maltiox, my dear."

Ajkun nodded and headed to the street. Several young boys were kicking a leather ball around, pretending they were warriors playing the great ball game. Ajkun approached the group.

"Which of you is the fastest runner?" she asked.

A lean, young boy of about ten stepped forward and thrust his chest on proudly. "My lady, I am," he said.

Ajkun smiled. "Do you know your way to the round temple?"

The boy nodded. Ajkun held up the paper in her hand. "Deliver this safely, come back with an answer, and there shall be a cacao bean for you when you return."

"Lucky," a younger boy murmured as the older youth snatched the paper and set off running.

Ajkun turned to the rest of the group, who had begun to disperse. "How about some fresh papaya for all of you?"

The remaining five boys all nodded and followed Ajkun back to the yard where she quickly peeled and cut a large ripe papaya into multiple strips of the sweet flesh. She handed each child a piece and then wiped her sticky hands on a clean towel. "Off you go now, that's right," Ajkun said. She shooed the boys back into the street.

"Maltiox, my lady," the boys said, and they quickly ate the fruit before running away.

Chiman had watched from his place by the fire. "Is there any left for me?"

Ajkun nodded and placed the last piece of papaya on a pottery plate, which she handed to Chiman. She had hoped to eat it herself. "I'll heat some water for you." It was only as she turned to the water gourds to fill the ceramic pot on the fire that she realized she'd used up all the water cleaning the area. "Itzamná, this day has been one of the most vexing," she cried. "I need more water; stay here and I'll return as quickly as I can."

Chiman nodded and Ajkun once again gathered up the gourds. She hurried through the crowded streets, hoping she'd return in time to pay the young boy for his troubles. There was a line of women waiting for water at the cenote, but three youths were there with ropes and buckets, so the wait was far shorter than earlier in the day.

"Maltiox," Ajkun said as the young man quickly filled her gourds. Laden down with the water, Ajkun walked more slowly back to the hut. Chiman was reading a piece of fig-bark when she arrived. "Is that from the other shamans?" she asked as she set the heavy gourds on the outside counter. She dumped the contents of two gourds into the pot on the hearth and turned to Chiman.

"Yes, but I'm afraid they don't feel this dust was created by Satal. They won't perform any special ceremonies."

"Fools," Ajkun muttered as she assisted Chiman to the turtle shell basin. "I shall go speak to them in person as soon as you're resting," she said.

Chiman smiled. "My love, these men won't pay attention to you. They only heed their fellow shamans and the council members who pay them tribute."

"You mean Matz' and Kubal Joron," Ajkun said, and she imagined the men in their fine clothes and jewelry. She looked down at her huipil and skirt. Both were stained from all the cleaning she'd done that day.

"Well, *I* am a member of the council, so they *will* listen to me, I just need to change my clothes, so they recognize me for who I am." She stood up a little straighter. "After all, I am the ati't of Na'om, the one who will save us all on from Satal. They must honor that." She helped Chiman indoors and got him settled into the hammock they shared, then she changed her clothes, brushed her hair, and tied it up with a colorful headscarf. She put on her turquoise earrings and matching necklace and turned to ask Chiman's opinion. But he was fast asleep.

"Of course," Ajkun muttered. She slipped back outside and headed once again to the temple of the shamans. Fortunately, the streets were almost empty now, and she arrived quickly. She climbed the stairs to the building's entrance and knocked on the ornately carved wooden door. But there was no answer. "Hello, is anyone there?" she cried as she rapped on the door again. No one responded.

Weary from all her exertions of the day, Ajkun almost sat down on the steps for a good cry, but she mustered up some last reserves of strength and headed back to her hut. She had to do something; she couldn't let Satal defeat them like this.

As she passed one of the many stone platforms where ceremonial dances and sacrifices were performed, she got an idea. She turned and headed to the market, praying some of the vendors were still at their stalls. Fortunately, one potter still sat among his stacks of wares and Ajkun approached with a smile. She looked about, hoping he had what she needed among the plates, bowls, and urns. Several small statues stood on a piece of cloth in one corner of the stall.

"I need an effigy of Chac," she said.

The man stood up, leaned over a pile of black-and-white plates, and grabbed a small figurine. "This is the only one I have," he said as he handed it to her. "It's got a broken piece on the headdress," he added as he pointed out the chip in the pottery.

"That's all right; I'll take it," Ajkun said and she gave the man a cacao bean.

"Oh, that's too much," the vendor said. "I have no change."

"That's all right," Ajkun replied.

"Maltiox, my lady," the man said and bowed. "You can return at any time and get things you need for your home, free of charge."

Ajkun nodded and quickly returned to the hut. She went inside, saw that Chiman was still asleep, and quietly gathered some things before returning to the counter outside. She placed a short piece of dark blue cloth on the wooden slab, then set down the statue of Chac, and added a bowl, a piece of fig-bark, and one of her stingray needles. She lit a candle from the embers in the firepit and placed that nearby. She stood back and studied the small statue. The rain god held a stone ax in one hand, the skin on his long, curled nose was covered with fish scales, and his bulging eyes seemed to look back at her. She shivered, hoping she was doing the right thing. She had seen Chiman perform ceremonies before and thought she had everything she needed. As she held the tip of the needle in the flames, she prayed. "Lord Chac, please hear me, I beg you. Send us your lifeblood, your life-giving rain, to cleanse us of this dust that has fallen upon the land. We need you to help us and I give you this offering, my lifeblood, in return." Ajkun quickly poked the sharp stingray spine into a couple of the fingertips of her left hand and let the blood drip onto the paper in the bowl. She held it to the flame and when it had caught fire, she set it in the bowl to burn. Once it had turned to ash, she nodded to the statue, then wiped it clean and wrapped it in a cloth. She looked around the area for a safe place to place the statue and finally settled on putting it in the bottom of the basket where she stored corn. *Chiman will never find it there.* Her fingertips throbbed, so she washed away the remaining dried blood and applied some calendula salve to speed the healing. Then she went to sit by the fire, but as she poked at the embers, she realized she was suddenly too tired to do anything except go to sleep. "May the rains come in the night and wash us clean," she muttered as she blew out the candle and went to bed.

But the next morning dawned bright and clear. Ajkun fussed over Chiman, who was still too ill to get up. As the hours passed slowly, Ajkun kept looking at the sky, hoping for a glimpse of dark clouds on the horizon, but there were none. When she went to the market for some papayas and mangoes, she noticed the women vendors were sullen or silent. Gone was their usual banter and free offerings to entice customers to purchase from them instead of their neighbors. And as she passed an area where the stonemasons should have been at work, none of the men were there. Chiman ate little that day and although Ajkun applied more calendula salve to his hands and feet, Ajkun worried he was getting worse. She went to bed that night praying once again for rain. And woke to clear skies.

Frustrated that her blood offering to Chac had not been heard, she once again dressed in her best outfit and jewelry and went to see the shamans.

She knocked on the heavy door and a young shaman with fresh tattoos of howler monkeys inked onto both shoulders opened it. She noticed that his thumb and first two fingers on his left hand were stained a deep blue.

"My lady, how may we help you?" the youth asked as he bowed low.

"I am the Lady Ajkun, ati't to Naòm, and I must speak to the shamans."

The young man stepped aside, allowing Ajkun into the round building. She had never been inside and was curious to see the interior. She looked up and could see the domed ceiling covered in stucco high above her head. Various slits in the roof let sunlight in. Underneath each of these openings was a wooden platform attached to the stone walls, accessed by a variety of wooden ladders and walkways.

The young shaman noticed her interest. "My brothers watch the stars in the sky each night from those openings, and I record what they see in the ledgers we keep." He held up his left hand. "Those of us who are scribes all carry the stain of our profession." He pointed to a small chair next to a wooden table. "Please, take a seat and I'll see if anyone is awake yet who may speak to you." He hurried through a doorway and into a small courtyard surrounded on all sides by stone buildings where the shamans slept, cooked, and went about their daily lives.

The young man soon returned with the same older shaman Ajkun had spoken to days before. He wore a jaguar skin cape over his bony shoulders and walked with a slight limp. She stood up and bowed as they approached, and the younger man helped the shaman into the chair Ajkun had vacated.

"Lady Ajkun, it is a pleasure to meet you. My name is Nima Winaq, and I am the oldest of the brothers here. How may we be of service today?"

Ajkun decided to come straight to the point. "The yellow pollen that fell from the sky the other day has affected everyone who comes in contact with it. Children no longer laugh and play, women are silent or angry, and the men are despondent about their work. I believe Satal is behind this dust that is affecting us all, and I ask that the shamans present offerings to Chac so that he might send us rain, which will cleanse the area."

Nima Winaq nodded his head. "We've noticed the disturbances in the city and in the surrounding villages but did not equate the issues with this dust that fell. It's almost time for the rainy season to begin; perhaps it would be beneficial to present Chac with some offerings and entice him to send us an early rain. Honoring the gods is always a good idea regardless of the reasons behind it." The old shaman struggled to his feet and bowed to Ajkun. "I will tell my brothers to conduct a ritual this afternoon, and perhaps we shall be blessed with rain later this night." He bowed again and motioned for the young scribe to help him back to his room.

"Maltiox, Ajaw," Ajkun said as she bowed too. "Maltiox."

Elated that her idea had been so readily accepted, by the eldest shaman no less, Ajkun felt better than she had in days. *I shall present Chac with another blood offering as well, and then we have to hope that he answers our prayers*, she thought as she hurried back to Chiman. She knew that as soon as the rains came, Chiman and all the others who had been afflicted would begin to heal. *We must all regain our strength if we are to march in less than two moons' time to defeat Satal.*

When Chiman was asleep, Ajkun once again offered Chac a blood offering. She went to bed that night convinced the god would hear her prayers along with those of the shamans.

The next day, she heard the distant rumble of thunder for many hours. The air was thick with humidity, which made Ajkun feel sluggish and irritated. Then in the late afternoon, the sky turned a deep gray-green, and gentle drops of rain came down. People came outside and laughed and danced in the streets as the air turned cooler. Rivulets of yellowish water streamed from the edges of roofs and swirled away down the streets, leaving little trace of the odd pollen. Young boys chased each other around the main plaza, stomping in the muddy puddles that formed, covering themselves from head to toe with grit, but no one stopped them. The rain was an early blessing for the growing season from Chac, and many offered food items and blood-saturated bark to the god to thank him.

That night, Ajkun snuggled close to Chiman, content to listen to his soft breathing and the patter of the rain on the thatched roof. *All will be well now*, she thought as she drifted off to sleep.

SATAL

Satal was weary and thoroughly soaked from her latest flight with Camazotz's bats. She'd traveled as far as Mayapán again and discovered it was raining there. As she dried herself off with a towel, Satal muttered, "So, they think they can wash away my poison with a dose of rain? We'll see about that." She dropped the wet towel on the tile floor and put on a clean shirt and skirt. Once she felt presentable, she called out, "Tewichinel!"

Within minutes, the shaman was at the door of her bedroom. "My lady?" he asked as he bowed.

"Tell your brother shamans to make blood sacrifices and offer the gifts to Chac. He has blessed the citizens of Mayapán with an early, beneficial rain, but I want him to make it pour."

"At once, Lady Satal," Tewichinel said and bowed before leaving.

Satal listened to the *slip, slip, slip* of the old shaman's leather sandals on the tiles until she couldn't hear them any longer. "There must be something else I can do," she muttered.

There's something else you must *do, my dear,* Sachoj whispered.

Startled out of her thoughts, Satal looked around, half expecting to see the head of Sachoj floating in the air nearby. But the room was empty. "Speak up, woman, I can barely hear you," Satal said.

You were so dismayed to discover it was raining in Mayapán that you neglected to notice an even more serious situation, Sachoj said loudly.

"Well, go on, don't leave me waiting," Satal replied as she stood up and began to pace back and forth. "What did I miss?"

Na'om and some of her friends weren't there; they've journeyed to the island of the shamans where Tatá has provided Na'om and that pet jaguar of hers the means to enter Xibalba. She's going to bring Tz' back with her. Your powers are definitely slipping, my dear. In the past you would have noticed this instantly.

"Enough!" Satal roared. Her blood grew hot, and she threw off the shawl she'd wrapped around her shoulders. "So, the girl thinks she can get her beloved to come home. We'll see about that."

Satal scurried about, collecting the items she needed from the wooden cupboard in the corner of the room. She placed a pillow on the floor and sat down, packed the bowl of her pipe with mushroom dust, lit it, and took a deep breath of the smoke. "I shall summon Xojol and tell her to attack Na'om as soon as she enters the first tunnel." The mushrooms moved Satal into a deep meditative state, and she quickly sent her spirit in search of the female were-jaguar.

When her life-force manifested in the Underworld as a yellowish-green glow, she raced through the labyrinth of tunnels until she reached the House of the Jaguars. But Tz' and Xojol were both gone. *Where could they be?* The other were-jaguars looked at her wavering light with wariness, but they made no move to show reverence or fear. Even Bajbik had forgotten who she was. *I must remember to punish them for that*, Satal thought as she looked around frantically. *Get up, all of you*, she commanded. *Go find the intruder at once!* She sent a flash of light in the direction of Bajbik, who leapt up with a yelp. He snarled at her, then growled at the others, and took off running, with the pack in tow.

Satal left the empty cave and headed in the opposite direction. She knew that at any moment, Na'om might find Tz' and entice him to return to the land of the living. *Not if I can get to her first!* Satal pushed her life-force harder and faster, surging through the dark tunnels until her physical body ached, and she knew she could only last a few more minutes in her spiritual state.

She rounded a corner in the blackness and sensed movement nearby. With little energy left, she charged forward and discovered Hun-Kamé and Vucub-Kamé squabbling over a pile of bones.

When Vucub-Kamé saw the eerie light of Satal's life form hovering nearby, he grabbed his brother, Hun-Kamé, by the ulna. "It's Lady Satal," he hissed as he bowed so deeply that his skull grazed the dirt and rocks on the shaft's floor.

Hun-Kamé turned and bowed too. "Lady Satal, it's a pleasure to see you." The skeleton waved his bony hand at the rubble around them. "We enjoyed your latest sacrifices, my lady, and hope you'll be sending us some more soon?"

"Yes, yes, but I don't have time for chitchat, my lord," Satal gasped. "I'm looking for a were-jaguar; I must send her to attack Na'om who has entered Xibalba in search of her friend, Tz'."

Hun-Kamé grinned, exposing the rotten teeth still left in his skeletal jaws. "Lady Na'om is here, now? We must find her ourselves; she defeated us too many times on her last visit to our lovely realm." He pointed his finger toward the opposite direction. "You'll find the were-jaguar you seek is in that direction, my lady, but she's far away." He peered more closely at Satal's ethereal form. "I don't believe you'll have time to meet her, unless you plan to remain here."

"Yes, Lady Satal, do stay; we'd so enjoy having a new friend in this place, wouldn't we Hun-Kamé?" Vucub-Kamé said as he rubbed his bony hands together.

"No, I have important business in the realm above. You must find the were-jaguars and have them attack Na'om. Under no circumstances must she leave Xibalba," Satal commanded. She could feel her energy slipping away. "Please, my lords, take care of Na'om, and I shall offer multiple sacrifices to you both."

Hun-Kamé grabbed Vucub-Kamé by his humerus. "Come, Brother, let's help Lady Satal and find Na'om. Surely this time we can conceive of some trick to keep the girl down here."

Satal nodded to the two skeletons, and they whizzed off in the direction Hun-Kamé had said led to Xojol. At that point, Satal felt her spirit's vigor dissipating, and she hurried to return to her body.

Her physical form had slumped to the hard tile floor, and she had difficulty pushing herself upright. She sat in the deepening shadows, resting for several minutes. Finally, she called out for Tewichinel. But the shaman didn't appear. "Sachoj, can *you* hear me?" she said.

Yes, of course.

"Keep me informed of what happens with Naʼom," she said. Just then Tewichinel appeared in the doorway to her room.

"My lady, are you all right?" the shaman asked as he hurried to her side. He knelt to gently lift Satal in his arms and carry her to the bed. "Rest here and I'll bring you some hot cacao to drink to restore your energy." He bowed and ran from the room.

"Maltiox, my friend," Satal said weakly. It felt good to lie on the soft mattress and stare at the discolored spots on the ceiling where moisture had leaked through the tile roof. She had expended far more energy than she should have, but she knew it wasn't a waste. *With the were-jaguars and the skeleton gods after Naʼom, she hasn't any chance of escaping this time. And then there will be no need for a battle, for I shall already have won!*

Tz'

From his new, dominant spot in the large cave, Tz' watched Xojol playing with the other female were-jaguars. Using their front paws, they were batting an old deer skull back and forth in an open area between the piles of skeletons, trying not to let the skull touch the ground. Xojol leapt and jumped about, by far the most graceful of the females as she swatted again and again at the old bone. Tz' grinned and stretched forward, then arched his back before wiggling his tail. He felt good; he had fed well the night before and slept peacefully despite the snores of some of the older males. He nuzzled around among his private stash, found a piece of peccary, and lay back down. Gripping the meat between his front paws, he turned his head sideways and gnawed at the tough, dry piece, ripping off snippets that he let soften in his mouth before swallowing. He followed Xojol's movements with his eyes, enjoying the sight of her twisting and turning her lithe body as she pranced and moved about the small space to whack the skull back to her friends.

Suddenly, Xojol missed, and the skull crashed to the ground, breaking into multiple pieces. Instantly, the females growled and hissed at her, but Xojol just sat on her haunches and grinned, exposing her yellowish fangs. As quickly as the group had formed, it separated, each female going off to her own private space, leaving Xojol sitting by herself. She turned her head and caught Tz' gaping at her.

She sprang over the rubble and balanced on a pile of gnawed bones, looking directly at Tz'. *You don't have much room.*

Tz' sat up and looked around. He had cleared just enough space between the cave wall and the mounds of old skeletons so he could lie down, but there was no space for two.

Xojol bent down, picked up a rib in her teeth, and flung it to one side. Then she scrabbled with her big paws, pulling a heap of bones, broken fragments, and dirt into a pile until there was enough exposed dirt for her to squeeze in next to Tz'. She snatched the last bite of dried peccary from Tz' and swallowed it whole before lying down. *That's better,* she mused as she nibbled gently on Tz's ear.

Her touch aroused him, and Tz' desperately wanted to mate with her again.

What's on your mind? Xojol whispered.

You, us, Tz' replied as he rolled onto his side and faced her. *I want to.* He didn't know how to tell Xojol what he needed.

Fortunately, Xojol immediately knew what he had in mind as she jumped to her feet and beckoned to him. *Follow me,* she said as she swished her tail about.

Together, they headed to one of the closest tunnels and entered the darkness, Xojol rapidly leading the way away from the cave. After several minutes, she took a turn to the right and ran the length of another tunnel, finally stopping when she reached a spot where the night sky was visible through a hole in the ceiling high overhead. The fresh air was invigorating and intoxicating, and Tz' drew in deep breaths to clear the stale smells of the cave from his mind.

Come here, Xojol whispered.

Tz' quickly made his way to her side and began to purr. The tension in him was strong, and he could feel Xojol's desire emanating from her like a blanket of heat. They nuzzled each other, and Xojol began to groom Tz', forcing him to lie down while she licked him from head to tail. With each stroke of her raspy tongue, his longing intensified. Her scent dazzled him as she moved about him. The only thing on his mind was mating with this female, so he jumped to his feet and pushed Xojol to the ground.

He stood over her back, feeling strong and powerful, and bent down to grip the nape of her neck with his front teeth. He felt her energy radiating outward and lowered his belly toward her back. Then suddenly, Xojol whipped her head to one side and hissed.

Get off me, she snarled as she stood up, easily pushing Tz's smaller body to one side.

Wait, what's wrong? Tz' growled.

They're here, Xojol snapped and jerked her head to the right.

Tz' looked, but could see nothing in the darkness. *Who, who's here?* He peered closer into the blackness, and he could just barely see two skeletal bodies in the dark.

Xojol hissed at the spot, and Tz' watched as the hair on her nape rose to its full length. And then, without a word, she turned away from Tz' and began to run.

Wait, what's the matter? Tz' cried as he raced after her.

Xojol twisted her head over her shoulder. *An intruder*, she snarled and she pushed forward, moving much faster than Tz'.

He quickly lost sight of her in the labyrinth of tunnels. Panting, he stopped to catch his breath, letting his tongue loll out of his mouth. He breathed quickly and deeply, all the while listening for sounds. He tilted his head and could just hear the tromping of multiple paws far ahead. He ran and ran, twisting and turning through the dark, catching his fur on the roots and rocks that protruded from the walls and ceiling of the tunnel, but he ignored the pain. He had to locate the pack and find out who the intruder could be.

He careened around a corner and heard growls, snarls, and the yelping of the pack as they battled something ahead in the darkness. Tz' raced forward, turned another corner, and slid to a halt. He had found them.

They were attacking a girl, tearing at her with their claws and snipping at her with their teeth. A large black jaguar stood by her side, swatting at two of the younger male were-jaguars. The girl held a knife in one hand, which she slashed about in the air, but she was unable to keep the were-jaguars at bay. The smell coming from her made him salivate and he wanted to rip into her skin and drink her fresh blood. Tz' saw Xojol swipe her big paw across the air, knocking the knife from the girl's hand. She quickly dropped to the ground, covering her head with her arms. And then she screamed.

"*Tz! Tz*, if you're here, help me, I beg you! *Tzzzz!*"

She knows my name; she knows me! Without thinking, Tz' leaped into the fray, landing on the back of the nearest were-jaguar. He bit into his neck, drawing thick blood, then jumped to the next creature, which he slashed across the nose with his claws. He advanced toward the girl, who lay sobbing on the ground. He growled, hissed, and spit at the other were-jaguars, forcing them to back away.

I am your leader, he snarled. *Leave this girl and go back to the cave.*

Slowly, the were-jaguars began to disappear one by one into the darkness until Xojol and Bajbik were the last two were-jaguars in the tunnel. They spit and hissed at Tz', and Xojol made another swipe with her paw at the girl, but the black jaguar leapt toward her, forcing her to flee.

You're no longer leader of the pack, Bajbik snarled, and he turned and squirted urine in the girl's direction.

Tz' leapt forward, getting the brunt of the noxious spray in his face and chest, but he was able to keep it from landing on the girl. He rubbed his muzzle in the dirt and swiped at his eyes before leaning down to check on her. *She's still breathing*, he thought, and he slowly paced around the limp form. He had seen the girl before, but he couldn't remember where. Despite the lingering rancid scent of Bajbik's urine, the air was redolent with the girl's sweet, succulent smell, and a line of drool dangled from his lower jaw as he sucked it in. He wanted to taste that deliciousness and stepped forward, but a deep, warning growl from the black jaguar forced Tz' to stop. He looked up at the cat's yellow eyes and knew he was no match for the creature. Reluctantly, he turned and put his nose to the ground, searching for Xojol's scent. Once he found it, he took one step and then another away from the prone body, although his every fiber longed to remain by her side. He turned the corner and walked a few more paces, until he was out of sight. He paused with his head tilted, listening with every fiber of his body. Suddenly, he heard the black jaguar utter a low moan and then heavy paws struck the dry dirt as the jaguar raced away.

Cautiously and quietly, Tz' returned to the girl. She was all alone and hadn't moved. He lay down next to her, wiggling inch by inch until his body was almost pressed against hers. With the tip of his tongue, he licked her arm, and an electric shock jolted him.

I have seen you before, he thought as his tongue burned with pain. But no matter how hard he tried, he couldn't place where he'd been with the girl before. He moved a few inches away. *All right, I won't touch you, but*

I'll stay here until you wake up or that black jaguar returns. Tz' nestled his head on his paws, alert to any danger, and settled in to wait.

He drifted off to sleep once, waking when he thought he heard noises nearby. He stood up and rushed around the corner to hide. Peering back, he saw Hun-Kamé and Vucub-Kamé scuttle up to the prone girl and drop something onto her before they scurried into the dark in the opposite direction. He could hear them chortling for the longest time and wondered what kind of mischief the gods had been up to. He hurried back to the girl and sniffed her all over. Thankfully, she was still breathing. Other than a handful of blue corn kernels on her belly, she appeared no different than before, so after urinating several paces away, he lay back down.

His stomach growled, and he fought the deep desire to tear into the warm body next to him. But the tip of his tongue still burned, and he had no desire to experience that again. *How did she know my name?* Tz' wondered for the hundredth time. *I must know her, but who is she?* Ever so slowly, his eyes closed and eventually, he slept.

The vibration of pounding feet woke Tz' and he leapt to his feet, teeth bared and claws at the ready to fight whatever was approaching. Then a sudden light in the far distance broke through the darkness, and Tz's turned and fled, leaving the girl on her own.

Yakal

Yakal sat in the dappled shade cast by the ceiba tree and watched as Box walked around and around its large trunk. He wasn't surprised to see that each time Box drew close to the large hole at the tree's base, he stepped backward, away from the darkness that seemed to hover at ground level. *I never should have allowed Na'om to go through with this plan*, Yakal thought as he stood up. He stretched skyward, but still couldn't touch any of the lower branches of the sacred tree.

"She's been gone two days," Box said as he approached Yakal. "When do we stop waiting and go find her?" He bent over and picked up a small stick, which he began to break into tiny pieces.

"You know what Tatá said: no one is allowed into Xibalba unless they're willing to die. Many have tried and never returned."

"So, why did the shamans let Na'om go?"

Yakal laughed. "I doubt they had any choice but to say yes. Besides, she's been there before, which gives her special powers, we hope." Yakal walked slowly to the ladder and peered over its rungs into the shadows below. A slight shimmer of sunlight reflected off the water in the cenote near the bottom of the ladder, but otherwise, it was dark. He shuddered at the thought of descending into that blackness. He knew if he was forced to, he could collect fresh water from the pool at the roots of the giant tree, but to go any farther underground would be oppressive. He was fearful of being trapped underground, far away from the sunlight, with the weight of the land pressing down on him. And he was terrified of what might lurk in the multitude of tunnels and passageways that the shamans said radiated away from the cenote. Yakal opened his mouth to shout into the abyss and then thought better of it. "She'll only come back when she's found Tz'," he said to Box who had come to stand by him.

"And if she doesn't find him? Then what?" Box said.

Yakal turned to look at the youth. "You really care about her, don't you?" he said. "That kiss wasn't just you doing what Na'om requested."

Box nodded. "You're right. I can see why Tz' was in love with her and why he was so upset when he thought he had lost her." He tossed some pieces of wood over the edge.

"And if they reappear together, where does that leave you?" Yakal asked.

"Itzamná, I don't know. Tz' is my friend, so if he's able to be with her, I have to be happy for him."

"But on the other hand, you'd just as soon Na'om reappear alone?"

Box hung his head. "It's that obvious?"

"Only if you pay close attention," Yakal laughed. He briefly put his arm around Box's shoulder. "I like you, Box, and would be honored to welcome you into my family, if the gods deem it part of your destiny."

"Maltiox, Yakal, I appreciate that. But I don't know if Na'om has any feelings for me at all. She's been so focused on finding Tz' that I don't know if she's even really noticed me."

"Ha, ha, ha, never fear, my friend. If I'm correct, she's taken note, and on more than one occasion, I might add."

Box grinned but didn't say anything.

As the men turned away from the hole, they heard footsteps. Several of the shamans were headed in their direction. Each man carried a large wooden bucket in each hand.

"We must get our drinking water for the day," Eqomal said. He pushed between Yakal and Box on his way to the ladder.

"Yes, yes, of course, Ajaw, we'll move out of your way," Yakal said as he bowed and backed away from the tree. He reached out a hand and yanked on Box's arm, pulling him backward.

"He really doesn't like us, does he?" Box whispered.

"I'm afraid we're upsetting his daily routine by being here," Yakal replied. "Probably attending to us is some kind of punishment for not letting our canoe onshore the other day." Yakal looked at the line of shamans and knew he had to do something. He nodded to Box. "We can't just stand here, doing nothing. In fact, we've waited long enough; I'm going to talk to Tatá and persuade him to let one of the shamans go look for her."

Box nodded. He threw the remainder of the stick on the ground and wiped his hands on his loincloth. "I'll go with you."

Together, the two men approached the largest hut where Tatá lived. Yakal knocked on the bamboo pole that formed part of the doorway.

"Come in."

The two men entered and bowed deeply before the senior shaman who sat on an array of cushions on the floor. He placed a scroll on the ground next to him and looked up.

"Ajaw," Yakal said, "we have been waiting for two days for Lady Na'om to return. I fear some harm has come to her, and I humbly ask that you send one of your shamans into Xibalba to find her."

"No, I'm sorry, that is not possible," Tatá said.

"But Ajaw, we cannot just sit here and do nothing. She might be in some kind of danger and need help."

"The Lady Na'om knew the risks when she agreed to enter the Underworld. And she chose to go anyway in order to find the one she believes she loves." Tatá looked directly at Box when he said this. "She's been blessed by the balams and bears their markings upon her skin; she will know how to protect herself." He turned to pick up the scroll and began to read, ignoring Yakal and Box who still stood before him.

Yakal put his hand on Box's forearm and tugged slightly. "Come on, we might as well wait in our hut and return to the tree when the others are done with their chores."

Reluctantly, Yakal entered the small enclosure the shamans had allowed them to use. But he was still too anxious to lie down in the hammock he'd been given and proceeded to pace back and forth in the hut until Box begged him to stop. Every now and then, Yakal looked out from behind the deerskin covering the doorway to see if the shamans had left the tree, but they still continued to haul water up from the depths. Once they reached ground level, they hurried to empty the buckets into a series of large earthenware jugs lined up against the wall of the largest hut.

"Itzamná, how much water do they need?" he mumbled to himself. Finally, he sat down and crossed his legs in the doorway, holding the deerskin to one side with his hand so he could see the goings on in the immediate area. Soon, the sultry afternoon air made him sleepy, and he briefly leaned his head against the wooden door support. Box gently snored in his hammock, and Yakal closed his eyes against the bright glare outside. It felt good to rest, to let his mind wander and his body relax. He imagined what Uskab might be doing at that moment, perhaps bathing Mayibal in his turtle shell bath, and he smiled and relaxed even more. *Perhaps it is time for another child, a brother or sister for little Mayibal. I know it would make Uskab happy.* Then his thoughts turned to Na'om, and his mind raced back in time to when *she* had been the newborn and how he had fled the village before he had known the joys of being a father. *I was such a young fool*, he thought and then he slept, slumped against the doorway.

When he heard someone shout, Yakal startled awake. He struggled to stand upright as more shamans shouted and called to one another. He watched as several of the men quickly appeared on the ladder and almost leapt onto the ground in their haste to move away from it.

A few moments passed before there was a growl, and Ek' Balam's head suddenly appeared. "Box, wake up, they're back," Yakal said. He kicked at the sleeping youth. Yakal hurried toward the tree and quickly went to Ek' Balam, who was growling softly.

"Hey, boy, where's Na'om?" Yakal asked as he knelt down in front of the jaguar. Ek' Balam snarled and snapped his head toward the ladder. "She's on her way; all right, we'll wait for her." Yakal nodded to the shamans who hovered nearby. "We'll be done here very soon."

Box joined Yakal. "Where is she?" He looked down the ladder. "There's nobody in sight."

Ek' Balam growled again and stepped toward the ladder. He flicked his head around to Yakal and Box and then faced the hole.

"What is it, Ek' Balam?" Yakal asked. "Where is Na'om?"

Ek' Balam placed his paw on the ladder.

"Itzamná, is she hurt?" Box cried. He moved toward the ladder.

"Stop!" shouted Eqomal. "You're not allowed into Xibalba. We thought Tatá made that very clear."

"Na'om needs our help, and I'm willing to risk my life to save her," Box said, and he placed his hand on the bamboo rail closest to him.

"Even so, you can't just descend into the Underworld without proper protection, which only Tatá can provide," Eqomal replied.

Without thinking, Yakal stepped forward and placed his hand on Box's forearm. "Box, you're young and have a full life ahead of you. If anyone goes, it will be me. I'm her father, and I vowed when we left Mayapán that I'd let no harm come to her." *And I must amend the wrong I did when she was an infant*, he thought.

Box nodded and slowly stepped out of the way.

"Ask Tatá to come and prepare me. There is no time to lose," Yakal demanded.

"As you wish, Lord Yakal," Eqomal replied. He snapped his fingers and two of the youngest men went running off. They quickly returned with Tatá, who carried a large turtle shell covered with a cotton cloth.

"So, you wish to enter Xibalba . . . my friend, do you understand the dangers you may encounter?" Tatá asked as he placed the large shell on the ground.

"I do, and I'm willing to accept the risk. Besides, I won't be alone, I'll have Ek' Balam with me, isn't that right, boy?" Yakal replied. He certainly hoped the jaguar would accompany him; otherwise, how would he know where to find Na'om?

"Normally, before entering the Underworld, we would do a cleansing ceremony, giving you the opportunity to purify your body and your mind, but I can see there is no time for that," Tatá said. "There is only one way I may provide some protection to you while you search for Lady Na'om." He motioned for one of the younger shamans to pick up the turtle shell. Tatá removed the cloth and Yakal could see the bowl was filled with a blood-red paste. "Remove all your clothes," he ordered.

Yakal nodded and quickly slipped off his shirt, loincloth, and sandals. He stood naked in front of the other men.

"You must smear this paste over every inch of your body," Tatá instructed. "Leave no part exposed and those areas where you cannot reach, we shall assist you."

Yakal drew in a quick breath and let it out, then scooped up a handful of the paste. "What is this?" he asked as he quickly wiped it all over his face, neck, and arms.

"Red salt from the salt pools nearby that I have blessed, cinnabar, coconut oil, and beeswax. The salt and cinnabar will ward off evil, and the coconut oil and beeswax allow the mixture to stick to your body. It is the only combination we know that will protect you against those who may wish to do you harm."

Yakal grimaced as he felt one of the shamans rub blobs of the grainy mixture into his hair. Bits and pieces fell into his eyes, and they burned momentarily. When he was fully covered from his head to the tops of his feet, he turned to look at Tatá. "Well, will this be sufficient?" he asked.

Tatá nodded. "You may get dressed again, but before you put your sandals on, smear some on the soles of your feet. One can never be too careful when entering the Underworld. We will remain near the ladder and await your return. When you reach the surface again, go directly to the ocean. You must remove this mixture as quickly as possible or suffer for it. Once you're in the water, we'll provide further instructions at that point. May the gods be with you," Tatá said.

Yakal looked at Box. "I hope to see you soon."

Box nodded. "Stay safe." Both men watched as Ek' Balam took a flying leap over the edge of the hole and disappeared.

Now that Yakal was actually about to enter the Underworld, his fears resurfaced, and he felt his heart begin to pound in his chest. He drew in a deep breath, looked at the dappled sunlight all around him, took the torch Eqomal gave him, and quickly descended the ladder. A minute later, Ek' Balam appeared at his side.

"All right, boy, show me where she is," Yakal said. Ek' Balam took off running and Yakal hurried to follow him.

The light Yakal carried barely illuminated the various tunnels they ran through. The air was humid, and his mouth quickly grew dry. He wished he'd thought to bring a gourd full of water. Sweat beaded on his brow, which he wiped away with the back of his hand, and salty water leaked into the corner of his eye. As he continued to jog after Ek' Balam, he caught glimpses of roots protruding from the low roof, and he had to swerve around sticks and rocks that stuck out from the limestone walls. Every now and then, he thought he saw piles of bones, but whether human or animal he didn't know and didn't care. *My only concern is finding Naóm,* he thought as he narrowly avoided yet another stick jutting from the wall. Deeper and deeper into the Underground the two companions went, and soon Yakal had no idea which direction to take to return to the surface.

The tunnel grew smaller, and Yakal had to crouch to keep from banging his head. The lack of space pressed in on him, and his anxiety of being trapped returned. "Itzamná, please help me," he prayed.

"He'll be of little help down here," a voice said.

Yakal halted in mid-stride in the soft sand underfoot. He swung the torch around, searching for the owner of the voice. Ek' Balam growled and moved closer to Yakal. "Who's there, what do you want?" Yakal cried. He swung the torch again and gasped.

A skeleton was standing a few feet away, pointing its bony finger at Yakal. "You, my friend," and the skeleton cackled.

Suddenly, a second, smaller skeleton appeared. "Look, Hun-Kamé, look at his forehead," it said.

"Shush, Vucub-Kamé," the first skeleton replied. He motioned again with his bony finger, pointing it directly at Yakal's head.

Yakal winced as he felt a sharp pain in between his temples. He reached up with one hand and felt bare skin. "No," he cried. He quickly searched his hair and found a glob of the paste left by the shamans. He smeared it over his exposed skin and the pain faded to a dull ache.

The skeletons both sighed. "He's smart, that one," Vucub-Kamé said.

"Quiet," Hun-Kamé replied, and he swung his fist to hit Vucub-Kamé, but the skeleton ducked and Hun-Kamé's arm sailed through empty air.

Ek' Balam growled and stepped toward the skeleton gods. Feeling emboldened, Yakal swung the torch and also threw the remaining paste in his hands in the gods' direction. They both shrieked with pain and fright and scurried into the darkness.

Instantly, Ek' Balam began to run again and Yakal hurried to keep up.

"How much farther, Ek' Balam?" Yakal cried as he felt a pain start in his side. He was not used to so much running and knew he needed a break soon.

Fortunately, Ek' Balam stopped only a few hundred paces ahead and Yakal rushed forward. "Na'om," he cried. She was curled on her side on the ground, her arms wrapped over the top of her head. Scratches and scrapes covered her arms and legs, and her clothes were torn in multiple places. "Na'om!" Yakal cried again, but there was no answer. He quickly knelt beside her and placed his fingertips gently on her throat. The tiniest heartbeat was palpable in his fingers. "Thank the gods you're still alive," Yakal said. He leaned the torch against the wall of the tunnel and scooped

Na'om into his arms, but quickly realized he would have to leave the light behind.

"All right, Ek' Balam, lead the way and get us out of here before we encounter any more creatures."

Ek' Balam growled and began to walk at a rapid pace back through the tunnels to the surface. Yakal hurried beside the jaguar, keeping his body close enough to the cat to feel his fur. *Itzamná, if I lose touch with Ek' Balam, I'll never find my way out as I can't see anything.* He cried out in pain as an unseen stick protruding from the tunnel wall raked his arm. Then he banged his toes on a rock and hobbled forward, desperate to keep up with Ek' Balam. But he had to stop multiple times and readjust Na'om in his arms, which made Ek' Balam growl. "Sorry, boy, I can't help it." He finally swung Na'om's upper body over his shoulder and was able to walk more quickly. He was sweating with his exertions and knew much of the protective salve he'd been covered with had slowly melted away. He felt exposed and vulnerable. "Itzamná, I beg you, help me reach the land of the living with Na'om, and I promise to offer you blood sacrifices in return for your help." He ran more quickly and soon was scratched by more unseen roots and sticks, but he ignored the pain and continued behind Ek' Balam.

Finally, as his legs and arms burned with the effort of walking and carrying Na'om, he saw Ek' Balam duck through one low archway, and as he followed, he sighed with deep relief. The cenote was in front of him and on the opposite side was the ladder. Torch light spilled down from above and Ek' Balam scrabbled up the rungs.

"They're back," Box shouted, and Yakal was overjoyed to hear his voice.

Three of the shamans quickly descended into the cavern, while those at the top lowered a large basket on a hemp rope. The men helped Yakal gently place Na'om in the basket and then they tugged on the rope. The basket slowly was raised up while the shamans steadied it from the ladder. When the way was clear, Yakal took one last look back toward the darkness before scrabbling up the rungs. When he reached the surface, he could see Tatá and the others clustered around Na'om, who was slowly being helped to her feet.

"Itzamná, I'm so glad to see you," Box said. He moved toward Yakal to give him a hug, but Yakal waved him away.

"I must go to the ocean straightaway. Tell the shamans I need their help too."

Box nodded and hurried to get Eqomal while Yakal ran to the ocean in the light of the new moon. He waded and crashed through the small waves until he was chest deep in the water and then dove underneath, staying under as long as he could hold his breath. When he surfaced, the water around him frothed and bubbled.

Eqomal waded out to meet him. He carried a pottery bowl in his hand, which he handed to Yakal. "Drink this, all of it. It will flush the toxins from your body."

Yakal nodded. The liquid was bitter and salty, but Yakal forced himself to swallow it. He handed the empty bowl back to Eqomal and almost instantly felt his stomach churn. He hurried several feet away and vomited into the water, again and again until he was heaving up nothing but air.

Weak and achy, Yakal plodded back through the water to Eqomal, who handed him a thick piece of cloth. "Good, you've emptied your insides, now you must scrub the darkness from the rest of your body. Remove your clothes and your sandals here in the water; let the water take them away from you."

Wearily, Yakal nodded, undressed, and began to scour his body with the cloth. His exposed skin burned as the remaining paste fell off and the dark waters bubbled and foamed all around him. When he felt he had attacked every spot, he turned to Eqomal. "Is there anything else I must do?" he said.

"Leave the cloth here in the water and come to shore. We have fresh hot water for you to bathe in and clean clothes for you to wear. And a feast of chocolate to fill your empty belly." He reached out and gave Yakal his arm, who took it with gratitude.

"I'm amazed you survived. Truthfully, I never expected to see you again," Eqomal said as they stepped on the small rocky beach. "I have never ventured into Xibalba and pray that I only go there when I am called by the ancestors." He bowed to Yakal. "You are either a fool or a brave man, but if there is anything I can do to help you, don't hesitate to ask."

"Maltiox," Yakal replied. "My only concern for the moment is that Naʼom is all right."

"The Lady Naʼom has regained consciousness and is now speaking to Tatá. She's suffered several injuries, but none that are life-threatening. After a day or two of rest, she should have recovered sufficiently for you all to return to Mayapán and continue with the paths the gods have placed you on." Just then, a young shaman ran up to the two men and handed Yakal a towel, which he wrapped around his waist. "Come, let's get you bathed, dressed, and fed, and then you shall be able to see Lady Na'om yourself."

Yakal nodded and let the two shamans help him across the sharp rocks and sand to the warm fires and welcoming torches that flooded the area near the huts with light. It was only when he entered the first circles of light that he could see shadowy patches on his arms and legs.

He gripped Eqomal's arm. "Look; what has happened?"

Eqomal peered at the spots. "You've been touched by the darkness anywhere the salve fell off your body."

"Will they heal?"

"Given time and the proper salve, possibly. Some of our shamans have had the same thing happen to them. You may feel ill at times, so you must consume sufficient salt. That will help purge the blackness from your body."

Box appeared and looked at Yakal. "Are you all right?

"I think so; I hope so. How is Na'om?"

"She's resting, but has asked to speak to you once you've been attended to." He motioned to Eqomal that he could help Yakal and the shaman moved away. "Where is Tz'?"

"I don't know. The only person I found was Na'om. Has she said anything to you?"

"Nothing. And I'm afraid to ask."

Yakal gave Box a weak smile. "Rest easy, my friend, we'll find out in good time. But right now, I need something to eat and some of that salve Eqomal mentioned; these spots are burning with pain."

Box nodded and helped Yakal to the nearby hut where the shamans waited to tend to his needs.

Tz'

After leaving the girl, Tz' followed Xojol's scent for many hours before finally seeing areas that looked familiar. When he entered the cave, the other were-jaguars were licking their wounds or sleeping. Those that were awake stopped and watched him as he skirted the various groups, making his way over to Xojol. Several of the males hissed as he passed, and old Bajbik spat in his direction, but Tz' ignored them all and lay down beside Xojol. He hoped she would turn and groom him as he had several scratches and cuts on his body that needed attention, but the female cat jumped up and left, joining the group of other females who had lain down together. Irritated by her actions, he stood up and followed her. He loomed large over the females and growled, and the unit stood up, including Xojol. One by one the females slunk away until only Xojol remained in that area of the cave. She lay back down with her back to Tz'.

What's wrong? he asked as he stood over Xojol. She ignored him. He put his right paw on her back. *I asked you a question,* he said.

She snapped her head around and snarled, *Get your paw off me, now.*

Tz' lifted his foot, but remained where he was standing, effectively blocking Xojol from leaving. *I don't understand,* he finally admitted.

Xojol twisted her body around until she faced Tz'. *You, you came to the aid of that intruder! We were ordered by our supreme leader to hurt her and you stood over her, protecting her, instead of attacking. You hurt your brothers and sisters with your claws. I thought you were one of us, but you're really still a human at heart.*

Tz' lay down in the rocky dirt and sighed. *I don't know why I did that. There was something about that girl that made me want to help her, not hurt her. I don't know who she is or why she was here in Xibalba, but she knew my name as I heard her call it several times. I felt I had to help her, but Itzamná knows why.*

You don't know her? Xojol asked.

I may have, but I don't remember her now, Tz' replied. *Her scent drives me crazy, and I want to mate with her, but I don't know why.* He put his big head on his front paws and sighed. *I'm sorry; I should have listened to you when you told me to attack, but I just couldn't.*

He sensed Xojol scooting closer to him in the dirt.

You're sure you don't know who she was? she asked.

No, Tz' said. *I wish I did, as it might explain so many things, but at this point, I've forgotten.*

The others won't ignore what you did, you realize that, Xojol said as she began to gently lick the wound on Tz' left ear. *You probably won't be the leader of the pack now, at least not until you do something to prove you're worthy again,* she added.

As long as you forgive me, I don't care, Tz' said and sighed. The need to be in control of the pack was no longer a priority, but he didn't want to lose Xojol's friendship. And he had to find out who this girl was and why she had such an effect on him. There was a connection between them, he was sure of it, and he was determined to find out what that link was. But for now, all he wanted to do was relax into the calming space Xojol was creating with her tongue as she continued to lick his various wounds.

NA'OM

When there was a rap on the door to the hut, Na'om pushed herself up as best she could on the pile of pillows the shamans had placed around her. "Come in," she said and smiled weakly when Yakal entered the room.

She motioned for him to sit down near her. "Are you all right?" she asked as she looked at the red, rough splotches on his arms and legs.

"I'll be fine, with time and the liberal use of a salve made from the yellow flowers of the senna plant, or at least that's what Eqomal and the other shamans tell me," Yakal replied. "But I'm not here to talk about me; tell me what happened in the Underworld. Where is Tz'? Why didn't he return with you?"

Na'om nodded. She had told Tatá the truth, and Yakal needed to know as well. *Perhaps by telling yet another person, the situation will begin to make sense because to be honest, I'm still confused by it all.* "Ek' Balam and I headed to the House of the Jaguars and it was all as it had appeared in my dream. We found the tunnel full of bones outside the cave and we waited a bit, hoping that Tz' would appear. I knew that once he did, I would be able to persuade him to eat the charcoal I had brought, and then we would all be able to return. After quite some time, a were-jaguar did appear, and

I attempted to communicate with it, but it never spoke to me like I had envisioned Tz' would do. Then another were-jaguar arrived and another, and suddenly the whole pack was around me. That's when I knew things had taken a drastic turn from the dream I'd had." She stopped and took a sip of the hot cacao the shamans had brought her. She pointed to the earthenware pot still half full of the bitter liquid. "Would you like some?"

"No, maltiox, I drank several mugs of it before coming to see you. Eqomal insisted it would help me recover."

"Hmm, the food of the gods," Naòm said. She set the cup down and wiped her mouth with the edge of her sleeve. "Anyway, I wasn't able to tell if Tz' was among the pack or not. The next thing I knew, the were-jaguars had attacked. Ek' Balam fought bravely and managed to keep some of them at bay, but there were just too many of them. I hesitated to use my knife for fear of harming Tz' if he was there, but ultimately, I had no choice but to slash at them in the hopes they'd go away. But they didn't; they just kept swiping at me with their big claws and tearing at my clothes. I finally curled up in a ball, shouting to Tz' that if he could hear me, he would get the others away from me. I think he did arrive; I vaguely remember one were-jaguar racing into the middle of the pack and fighting with some of them before I lost consciousness."

"So, none of it was the way you saw it in your dream, the one you told Najtir about?" Yakal asked.

"No, nothing of the sort. Tz' was supposed to shapeshift back into a human, and we were to find the cenote and go swimming." Naòm sighed, and a tear dripped down her cheek. "I've failed to bring him back to the light, Yakal, and now he's lost to us forever."

Yakal reached over and patted Naòm on the leg. "Perhaps not forever; we still have the battle with Satal. Maybe he can only be released from his imprisonment when she's dead."

"I don't know. I've never had my dreams not come true; I don't understand why this one didn't. I was so sure this trip was the right thing to do, especially after Najtir insisted it was the best course of action."

"We'll have to get back to the city and ask him." Yakal said. "Do you remember anything else?"

"No, nothing, but I did find some blue corn in the pocket of my skirt that wasn't there when I entered Xibalba. When I showed it to Tatá, he wrapped it up carefully in some fig-bark paper and took it away. I asked him why, but he refused to say."

"That's odd," Yakal said as he stood up. "Well, for now, you should rest. We can stay here as long as you need to regain your strength."

Na'om nodded. "You must get better too, Yakal, for the Underworld has left its marks on you." She smiled and watched as Yakal slipped back outside. She could hear him speaking to someone and then heard Box's voice. She was glad he was nearby. And then she realized she had forgotten to thank Yakal for coming to her aid. *He risked his life to save mine, and I'm grateful for that. I should have told him that.* Then the old anger of being left as an infant flooded her mind. *But what he did still doesn't wipe away all the years he was never a part of my life.*

She leaned back against the pillows and closed her eyes. *Itzamná, why didn't Tz' come with me?* she pondered. *What really happened down there after I blacked out?* She had a vague sense that one were-jaguar had remained by her side and even licked her arm, but after that, she couldn't remember anything. *Why does everything have to be so complicated? My whole life I've felt drawn to Tz', but that was before I met Box. . . Why did I ever ask him to kiss me? And now Yakal suspects there's something going on between us. Is that kiss the reason Tz' never responded to me? But it was just a peck, and I so wanted to experience something of life in case I died down there.* Frustrated with everything, Na'om shifted her weight, easing the pressure from some of the scratches along her back and thighs.

She felt different everywhere, not just on her skin where the were-jaguars had clawed and bitten her, but in her core as well. It was as if the marks they'd created had traveled into her being, tarnishing her on the inside as well as the outside. The shamans had applied salves to her open wounds, but could they do anything about the damage on the inside? She opened her eyes when she remembered that Kärinik had insisted she bathe in the ocean when she'd found her on the beach so many moons ago. *The shamans never suggested I do such a thing,* she thought as she hurried to stand up. *Maybe because they're afraid to see me naked*, she surmised. *But it may be the only way to stop the darkness of Xibalba from penetrating any deeper.*

With Ek' Balam by her side, Na'om stepped from the hut and was instantly greeted by one of the younger shamans. "I must bathe in the ocean," she said as she stepped around the young man and headed toward the beach.

"But, my lady," the shaman started to say, then thought better of it and ran the opposite direction.

He's probably gone to find Tatá to tell him what I'm doing. Na'om continued walking and was pleased to see Box appear.

The youth ran over to her. "Na'om, is everything all right?" he asked.

"Yes, but I must bathe in the salt water to purify myself," she said as she continued forward.

"Is that allowed, I mean, shouldn't you wait and speak to the shamans?" Box asked. He looked behind him to see if anyone was around, but the men had all vanished. He hurried to catch up to Na'om, who was at the water's edge.

"If you don't want to see me naked, I suggest you look the other way," she said as she dropped the simple shift she'd been wearing on the sand and stepped into the ocean. She quickly dove into the next oncoming wave and swam into the froth, hoping the seawater was deep enough to hide her nakedness from Box. She surfaced, spluttering water right and left as the salt water burned in the open wounds on her body. She bit her lip, forcing herself not to scream as the pain intensified with a heat she had never known before. *And now I know why the shamans didn't suggest I enter the ocean.* She fought against the throbbing and stinging, willing herself to remain in the water. As her tears mingled with the spray kicked up by the breaking waves, she was grateful to see the water all around her had turned a dark black. She knew that the darkness was slowly leaving her body, and she moved to the side, into clean water, which quickly turned dark as well. Gradually, as the waters cleared, the pain subsided until only a dull ache remained near her stomach. When she could see through the blue waters to the sand below, she turned to face the island. Box was standing with his back to the sea, holding her clothes in his hands.

She swam and splashed forward until the water was only a few inches deep. "Box," she called, "toss me my things so I may dress." She quickly stood up as her shift came flying over Box's shoulder. "Maltiox," she said as she pulled the fabric over her wet body. She stepped forward and appeared by Box's side.

"Do you feel better now?" he asked.

Na'om smiled. "Yes, I believe the salt water worked its magic yet again. It feels good to be alive." She reached out and gave his right hand a squeeze. "I'm glad you're here." Then she ran up the beach, back to her hut, before Box could respond.

She spent a restless night tossing on the bed of pillows, and more than once she felt Ek' Balam nuzzle her hand, which woke her up. Her dreams were vague and unsettling, filled with imagery of the were-jaguars, bones, and blood. Her heart was filled with grief when she thought of Tz' still imprisoned among them, and she couldn't help but feel she had failed in her quest. Finally, in the predawn light, she went outside, drawn back toward the entrance to the Underworld. She circled the giant ceiba tree multiple times, and each time she passed the ladder, she had to fight the urge to climb down the bamboo rungs to the darkness below and go back to searching for Tz'. She knew any attempts were futile, though. He was trapped as a were-jaguar and would be until Satal was defeated. In Na'om's mind, it didn't matter how he'd become one, either through trickery or by choice; the fact remained that he was there, in the darkness with the dead, while she was among the light and the living. She headed to the beach and stood in the first rays of the rising sun where she closed her eyes and prayed. *Maltiox, Itzamná, for this day and for all the days ahead. May I be worthy of the life-force you've given me yet again. And may Tz' and I meet again, in the land of the living.* She only turned when she heard footsteps approaching. It was Tatá. He wore a simple green loincloth and a jaguar cape over his shoulders.

"Lady Na'om, what a pleasure to see you looking so healthy this morning," Tatá said. "I trust you slept well?"

"Actually, no, bad dreams, I'm afraid. Ones that I don't think will go away until we are away from the entrance to the Underworld, so we'll be leaving the island today."

"As you wish, my lady," Tatá said as he bowed. "I will tell my brother shamans to prepare a meal for you to take on your voyage."

"Maltiox, Tatá, for everything," Na'om said. She hesitated, wondering if she should mention her sense of failure to this man.

"You have not failed, my lady," Tatá said. He noticed the look of surprise on Na'om's face. "Yes, I can hear your thoughts, just as my brother Najtir can hear them. It is a useful ability at times like this. I cannot erase the grief you feel at the loss of your friend, but I can tell you that your trip into the Underworld was eventful. Perhaps even successful, although not in ways you might expect." Tatá turned back to the group of huts. "Come now, let's have a hearty breakfast and send you on your way."

Na'om quickly informed Box and Yakal that she wanted to leave, so the men gathered together their belongings and stashed them in the canoe. After they had eaten breakfast of papaya slices and bowls of thick corn porridge with honey, she took the package of turtle-filled tamales and coconuts offered by Eqomal and bowed to all the shamans, who bowed in return.

"Our prayers will be with all of you during the battle," Tatá said. "Remember, Na'om, the power you need to defeat Satal resides in you. Draw on that strength and you shall be victorious."

Ek' Balam jumped into the dugout, and Na'om settled beside him while Box, Yakal, and some of the younger shamans heaved the heavy canoe off the wet sand and into the oncoming surf. Even though she knew they faced a hard day of paddling before they reached the safety and comfort of Kärinik's hut, Na'om was glad to see the island grow smaller as the men paddled into the rising sun.

AJKUN

W hen Ajkun woke, a deluge was coming down. Lightning flashed and thunder roared while the water came down in sheets, obscuring her view out the doorway and turning the streets to rivers of mud. She sighed and turned her back on the outside. Days ago, Chac had blessed them with light showers that fed the soil, filled the cenotes, and made everyone dance with joy as they knew the growing season was upon them. Then the rain had continued, and with each passing day, the storms had intensified. Everything indoors was damp to the touch, and anything outside was thoroughly soaked. In the brief lulls between downpours, Ajkun had tried several times to start a fire but had had no luck; she and Chiman had been forced to eat cold food. On this morning, she knew they needed something hot to eat; she had a chill that penetrated deep into her bones. It reminded her of the deep cold she'd experienced when she was connected to Na'om during her time trapped in the Underworld. *That was a coldness I thought I'd never recover from and one I don't care to revisit.*

Ajkun looked at Chiman who still slept wrapped in the two woolen blankets they owned. She decided not to wake him. *He needs his rest*, she thought. The downpour slowed to a steadier rain, so she covered herself in her thick woolen shawl and made her way to the market, praying that some of the vendors were selling hot food. Fortunately, several women were there with large pottery basins full of steaming stews and soups, so she held out her earthenware jug and had a woman give her several ladles of iguana and manioc stew. On the way back to the hut, she did her best to avoid the fast rivulets that ran through the streets, but her sandaled feet were quickly covered in thick, red mud. She avoided the large puddles that had formed and noticed the children no longer played with fig-bark boats in the water. They huddled silently in their doorways, peering out at her as she passed with her basket.

The damp had settled deeper into her bones by the time she returned to the hut, but she stood with her feet under the steady drip coming off the eaves to wash away the mud. Then she quickly changed her wet clothes for a drier set.

"Did I do something wrong when I appealed to Chac to send us rain?" Ajkun murmured as she watched the torrent continue to pelt the ground.

"What did you say, my dear?" Chiman asked. He yawned and came to stand beside her in the doorway. His body radiated warmth, and Ajkun moved closer, snuggling up under the blanket Chiman still had wrapped around his shoulders.

"Did the shamans do something wrong when they appealed to the rain god? Why else would it rain with such intensity?" She let the deer hide fall back over the doorway and turned to offer Chiman a bowl of soup.

"Lord Chac is a fickle and tricky god who is easily persuaded to shift his loyalties, depending upon the number of sacrifices he's been given. He'll soon grow weary of tormenting us, and the storms will let up, you'll see," Chiman said. He adjusted his blanket and continued to eat his bowl of stew.

"Well, I can only hope that Naom and the others are far enough away that these rains aren't affecting them. They've been gone a full week, though, so I pray they aren't traveling in it."

"I'm sure they're fine; perhaps they're waiting at Kärinik's hut until this weather passes. In any case, I'll give an offering to Xaman Ek to ensure their safe return," Chiman said as he handed Ajkun his empty pottery bowl. "Maltiox, I needed something warm." He held up his hands. "My blisters are disappearing as you predicted now that the pollen has disappeared, but I must admit, I've never seen it rain with such force for so many days in a row."

"Nor I," Ajkun said. "But maybe it's normal for here? I shall have to ask Alom when I see her. I long for it to stop, though, so we may resume our preparations for the counterattack."

"Fortunately, I listened to your advice, and we moved all the salt-filled vests into the Temple of the Warriors before this all started." Chiman moved his wooden stool closer to Ajkun. "For now, all we can do is sit and wait."

Ajkun laughed as she stood up and stretched out the hammock. "That's not all we can do," she said as she took Chiman by the hand and helped him lie down.

Later in the afternoon, the rains lessened once again, and Chiman left to consult with the shamans of the city and to give a blood offering to Xaman Ek. Ajkun hurried over to see Alom and was happy to see Uskab and Mayibal were visiting.

"Come in, Ajkun, come in," Alom said as she held back the peccary hide covering the doorway to her thatched hut. "How are you faring with all this weather?"

"Well enough; I had to purchase cooked food this morning just so Chiman and I would have something hot to eat. Is this amount of rain normal for you?"

"No, my dear, usually it rains gently day after day, with the occasional thunder and lightning. If I didn't know better, I'd say Satal had something to do with this. The viciousness of the rain, the way it almost hisses as it comes down, reminds me of her and her evil ways," Alom said.

Ajkun looked at Alom with surprise. "Itzamná, of course, that's it," she exclaimed. "Chiman said just this morning how erratic Lord Chac can be; perhaps Satal offered the rain god better sacrifices, and he moved his alliances to her. I shall speak to Chiman; maybe there is something that can be done to persuade Lord Chac to halt these downpours."

Suddenly, there was a bright flash of light, instantly followed by a horrific crack of thunder that made the women jump and set Mayibal crying.

"Shh, little one, everything's all right," Uskab said, but Ajkun could see the fear on the young woman's face.

"It's as if Lord Chac heard you speak," Alom said.

Ajkun looked nervously at the thatching overhead as the rain drummed down once again. "I meant no offense, my lord."

Ajkun conversed with the two women and played with Mayibal, but she was distracted by the idea that Satal might have somehow caused the torrential rains, and she left after a short time. When she returned to her hut, she looked around nervously for Chiman before she pulled out her statue of Chac from the corn basket. *This time I shall make a greater offering, and perhaps that will persuade him to ease the rains.* She searched around the hut and found a small piece of copal that Chiman had set to one side. She placed that in a pottery bowl and set it afire, letting the smoke circle the statue and fill the small hut. The she used the tip of her obsidian knife to make a slash across the palm of her left hand. She winced as the blood welled up and dripped onto the sheet of fig-bark she had at the ready. She bowed in front of the effigy and prayed, "Lord Chac, I am a humble woman, and yet I beg you to listen to my pleas. We need the rains to lessen so we may go about our daily lives again. I present you with this simple offering in the hopes you'll take pity on us." She set the bark on fire and stepped back as the smoke billowed upward. Then she concentrated on sending her prayers to the rain god and watched in amazement as a reddish glow appeared around her hands. Her fingers tingled and she stretched them, watching as the light extended farther from her body. But as soon as the paper turned to ash, the light disappeared. She smeared some *ch'om* leaf resin on her wound, then wrapped her hand in a clean piece of cloth. *If Chiman should ask what happened, I'll tell him my knife slipped when I was cutting open an avocado,* she thought. But she didn't have a chance to find the avocado before Chiman appeared in the doorway.

"What's going on here?" he asked as he stepped into the smoke-filled room. He looked at the effigy, the piles of ash, and Ajkun's bandaged hand.

Ajkun felt her face redden. "I'm sorry, Chiman, I had to do something to counteract Satal's efforts. I thought my offering might persuade the rain god to take pity on us; a foolish notion, I know."

Chiman walked forward and wrapped Ajkun in his arms. "Not foolish, my dear, but it probably won't be heard. Lord Chac is picky about who he accepts offerings from and how they are presented. Never fear, though, I've spoken to the other shamans, and they shall perform a ritual later today to appease him."

Ajkun nodded and hurried to remove all the objects. She was embarrassed to have thought her efforts would make a difference. But as she carefully placed the statue of Chac on one of the shelves in the room, she realized it had grown quiet outside. After days of rain drumming on the thatching, the silence was loud in comparison. She hurried to the doorway and stepped outside. The roof eaves still dripped and everything was soaked, but the rain had stopped.

"Chiman, come quickly, look," Ajkun said. She pointed up where the clouds had parted and the sun shone through. A rainbow quickly arched across the sky, neither end visible from those who viewed it from below.

"Itzamná," Chiman said as he wrapped his arms around Ajkun and gave her an embrace from behind. "You're more powerful than I realized; it appears Lord Chac has accepted your offering!"

Ajkun smiled. *Maltiox, my lord*, she thought. It felt good to know she had thwarted Satal.

NA'OM

Once they had left the full protection of the island, a strong wind turned the water into whitecaps, which sloshed over the gunwales, instantly soaking all of them. Na'om felt her stomach churn and leaned over the side of the dugout to heave. She got slapped in the face with a wave and clutched the gunwale as the water took her breath away.

"Maybe we should turn back!" Box yelled from his position in the stern. "Try to leave when the wind's not so strong."

Na'om shook her head. "No, we've delayed long enough." Then she pointed to the sky where dark clouds had formed on the horizon. "We could be trapped on the island for days if that storm blows in."

"Well, it's going to be difficult to paddle into the wind," Yakal yelled over his shoulder. "We may need to find a different route back to Kärinik's hut."

"I spoke to Eqomal while all of you were in the Underworld!" Box shouted. "He said they get their supplies from a small fishing village directly across from the island. I say we go there and then travel along the coastline."

Na'om and Yakal both nodded in agreement, and Box maneuvered the canoe through the heavy chop so it now rolled from side to side as the waves slapped the dugout. Na'om felt her stomach twist and churn, and she threw up what little remained of breakfast. Then she heard Box vomit too. Ek' Balam flattened himself against the bottom of the canoe and Na'om could see the whites of his claws where he dug them into the soft wood. "It's all right, boy," Na'om whispered as she patted him on his wet head.

She shivered as yet another wave slopped over the gunwale and added several more inches of water to the bottom of the canoe. "Give me something to bail with, or we'll swamp with the amount of water we're taking on!" Na'om yelled. Their movement stopped as Box dug through one of the baskets near him.

"All I have is this stupid shell I found!" he said as he tossed the large seashell toward Na'om. It hit her in the arm, slicing it open, and she winced as the salt water splashed into the cut. But there wasn't time to complain. She took the large shell and scooped up a tiny bit of water and threw it over the gunwale. She did it again, and again, and again, but her attempts were futile. Each wave that hit them added more water than she'd been able to bail out.

She looked up from her work and groaned. The dark clouds that had been so far away were closer, much closer. She could see flashes of lightning flicker downward and thought she could hear the distant rumble of thunder. Sheets of gray-green rain slanted from the clouds to the waves below, turning the whole area black. *Maybe we should go back.* She looked behind her. Box looked pale in the waning light; his black hair was plastered to his forehead from the salt spray. And she couldn't see the island. She turned around and looked past Yakal, but she couldn't see land in that direction either.

"How much farther?" she cried. Another large wave hit them broadside, and the canoe rocked to the right, throwing her against the edge of the craft. Ek' Balam lost his grip and slid toward her, adding his weight to that side, which dipped the gunwale under the waves.

Sea water poured into the canoe, flipping it over, tossing all of them and their gear into the churning ocean. Na'om sank under the waves and quickly began kicking with her feet, pushing toward the surface. She reached out, found Ek' Balam, and grabbed his fur, willing him to get them to safety. She broke the plane of water and gulped in deep breaths of air, gasping as the waves continued to smack her in the face. She strained to see if Yakal and Box were nearby. The overturned canoe floated several feet away and she swam in its direction, hoping she'd spy the men in the water. The thought of losing them filled her heart with dread, and she choked on sea water when she drew in a deep breath. *Please let them be all right,* she prayed as she fought the wind and waves and drew closer to the canoe.

"Na'om, Na'om!" Box shouted.

When she heard Box's voice, Na'om felt giddy with joy. She grabbed the edge of the canoe and yelled, "I'm here at the canoe. Where are you?"

She heard Box laugh. "On the other side," he said.

Na'om held onto the edge of the rocking canoe with one hand and awkwardly made her way around the dugout to the opposite side. She had never been so happy to see someone. She swam up to Box. "Are you all right?" she said.

"Yes, a little bruised, but I'll be fine," Box said. "We have to find Yakal."

"Do you think we can tip the canoe back over?" Na'om asked as she treaded water in the chop. The boat swayed and bobbed up and down.

"Maybe on the next wave," Box said. "Ready, set, now."

Together, the two heaved and the canoe flipped over, but water filled it halfway to its gunwales. "Move back a bit, and I'll try to get rid of some of this water," Box said.

Na'om swam with Ek' Balam away from the canoe and watched as Box got in and began to rock the dugout from side to side, sloshing out more water with each move than came in from the waves that continued to slap the boat. When only a few inches remained in the bottom, he motioned for Na'om and Ek' Balam to join him. He pulled Na'om into the canoe first and together they managed to get the wet jaguar in as well.

Na'om stood up and scanned the nearby water, looking for Yakal. But she had to sit down quickly when another large wave threatened to flip them over again. "Where is Yakal?" she said.

Just then, lightning flashed, filling the sky with light, followed by the long, low rumble of thunder. And then it began to pour.

"Yakal, Yakal! Where are you?" she screamed. *Itzamná, I never thanked him for saving me, and now I may never get the chance,* Na'om thought as she peered into the gloom. The dark rain filled the sky and she couldn't see where it ended and the ocean began.

"Yakal!" Box yelled. "Yakal!"

Ek' Balam sat up and jumped to the bow of the canoe. He stood on the gunwale, pushing the edge of the dugout to one side again.

"Ek' Balam, sit down," Na'om commanded. The cat stepped off the gunwale and the canoe slowly righted itself, but the jaguar refused to sit. He flicked his head and began to growl.

"I think he sees something," Box said. He leaned over the edge of the canoe and began to paddle with his hands. "Come on, we have to see if that's Yakal."

Na'om nodded, bent over her side of the dugout, and scooped the water with her cupped hands. Ek' Balam sat down in the bow and slowly, the canoe began to zig-zag its way through the storm. After several minutes, Ek' Balam stood up again and then without warning, he leaped over the bow and into the oncoming waves.

"Ek' Balam!" Na'om shouted.

"Look, over there," Box said and pointed.

Na'om followed his outstretched arm and could just barely see the black jaguar's head as it poked through the water. The cat was swimming away from them, and he disappeared from view when the next wave crested. "Come on, we have to go after him," Na'om said as she began to scoop water again. She was cold through, and through and her arms ached with a weariness she had never known before, but two lives depended on them, so she ignored the pain and continued to propel the canoe forward.

Finally, she looked up and could see Ek' Balam swimming in a circle through the rough water and the head of Yakal just behind the cat.

"Over there," she cried, and she and Box renewed their efforts to get to them.

Box leaned over the edge of the canoe and grabbed Yakal by the arm. "Come on, you can't give up on us now," he said as he pulled on Yakal. He reached lower and grabbed the older man by his loincloth and tugged with all his might. Finally, Yakal's weak body flipped into the canoe. "All right, now for Ek' Balam," Box panted. "Hold onto my waist while I get him," he said to Na'om.

Na'om wrapped her arms around Box's waist and felt a shiver of energy zip through her body as her wet arms touched his bare skin. Box held open his arms and Ek' Balam swam into them, then Box squeezed the cat and lurched backward at the same time, dragging the heavy jaguar half into the canoe.

Ek' Balam scrabbled with his hind paws and clawed the nearby wood with his front claws, accidentally scratching Box across the arms in the process. Bloody and exhausted, the three of them tumbled into the bottom of the dugout. Yakal pushed himself partially upright and coughed up a mouthful of salt water.

"Maltiox, Ek' Balam, I don't believe I would have lasted much longer," Yakal said hoarsely.

The four of them sat motionless in the canoe, exhausted from their exertions. The rain pounded them, and the wind and waves rocked the boat, but none of them had the energy to bail out the water that continued to accumulate all around them.

"Even if we had a way to paddle, I don't know which way to go," Box said. He shifted his body in the cold water filling the canoe.

"Let's rest a bit and pray the storm blows through quickly," Na'om said. She was so tired that she wanted to fall asleep, but she feared if she did, she would never wake up.

Dejected, they sat in silence. And waited. And waited. Twice Na'om had to nudge Box and Yakal to prevent them from falling asleep. The boat continued to rock and drift, and then, suddenly, both men slipped into slumber and so did she, out on the open sea.

It was Ek' Balam's roar that forced Na'om to open her eyes. The jaguar was once again standing in the bow, and as Na'om watched, he leapt from the canoe.

"No!" Na'om shouted and she struggled to sit up, but fell over onto her elbow when the canoe ran aground. "Ow," Na'om cried as she pushed up with her arms. She looked over the gunwale and the canoe swayed from side to side. "Thank the gods, we've reached land," she cried. She pushed on Yakal's arm and tapped Box on the head. "We've run aground," she cried as she stepped over the gunwale and into the shallow water.

She looked around as she waded toward shore or what there was of it. Most of the tiny beach was covered with seaweed, pieces of dried wood, and thick clumps of trees. Their roots twisted and turned and seemed to grow right out of the ocean.

"What is this place?" she cried as she stepped onto the base of a tree. She reached for a branch over her head and hoisted herself higher. Despite the rain that still fell, she could see they had entered calmer waters that stretched all around them. Beyond was the open ocean, covered with whitecaps. The flat water nearby was intersected everywhere with more of these strange trees. Their green leaves and interlocked branches formed an impenetrable jungle in places, and Na'om sighed. "We won't get anywhere going in that direction."

Yakal and Box joined her on the tiny island that was only three paces across and six paces long.

"What kind of trees are these?" she asked.

"Mangroves," Box replied. "They grow so thick that no one can get through them."

"Which means we're nowhere near the village Eqomal told you about," Yakal said as he sat down with a sigh on a twisted root.

Just then, Ek' Balam bounded out of the thick underbrush with an iguana in his mouth. He sloshed through several feet of water, placed the creature in front of Na'om, and stood waiting. "Go on, boy, you eat it," she said. "You certainly deserve it after today."

The jaguar lay down on the spot and happily ate the small lizard in three bites.

"I think we can use some of these dead roots as poles to propel us through the shallow water. We'll eventually come across somebody or someplace," Box said. He quickly began to wriggle one of the longer pieces of driftwood out from one of the piles and eventually worked it free. He then got two more, handing one to Yakal and the other to Na'om.

"Come on, then, we need to get moving before we all catch a chill," Box said as he waded back to the canoe. He held it steady while Yakal, Na'om, and Ek' Balam jumped in. Then he heaved with all his strength and got the boat to float. But the water inside the canoe still sloshed about, covering their ankles.

"Wait, let me find something to use to bail out the canoe," Na'om said as she leaped back into the shallows. She hurried back to the beach and marched all the way around the tiny island, peering into all the jumbled piles of wood and intertwined tree roots in the hopes of finding a shell or empty coconut husk to use as a scoop. Luck was on her side when she spied an empty turtle shell, which she grabbed.

She splashed back to the canoe, waving the carapace over her head. "This may take some time," she said as she climbed back aboard and began emptying the dugout.

"At least the rain is letting up," Yakal said as he pointed to the sky.

The clouds broke apart and a ray of sunlight hit the area, dazzling the three of them with its brilliance. Steam rose from their clothes as the heat rapidly increased, but Na'om was grateful for the warmth. She was so chilled she didn't think she'd ever feel warm again.

Box stepped into the stern of the canoe and pushed with his long pole while Yakal did the same from the bow. Slowly, the dugout lurched forward through the shallow waters, and the group inched their way up the coastline in search of people. Hours passed, and the sun's heat thoroughly dried their clothes, but then they fell prey to another problem. They had no food or water and the lagoon they poled through was too brackish to drink.

"Maybe we can find a coconut palm someplace?" Na'om suggested.

Box turned the canoe closer to shore, but the only living trees they saw were the endless mangroves. Na'om felt her energy desert her as her mouth grew drier and drier. She sat down in the canoe and watched the shoreline drift by, searching for something that might help them.

The sun sank lower toward the horizon. "Wait, stop, go back," she cried. "I think I saw a coconut over there," she said. She pointed to a tangle of tree roots. Sure enough, lodged in their embrace was a yellowish-green coconut. When Box had angled the canoe up to it, Na'om reached out and plucked the coconut from its location. She shook it and was happy to hear the water slosh around inside.

"How do we open it?" she said as she handed it to Box.

"I wish I had a knife," he replied. "Yakal, hold the canoe steady while I attempt to split it open on this rock." He bent over the side of the canoe and repeatedly banged the husk against the rock, but he had no luck in penetrating the tough exterior.

"Give it to me," Na'om said. "Maybe I can use this shell to open it while you two continue to pole us forward." Using the rough edge of the small turtle shell, Na'om sawed away at the fibrous husk, extracting minuscule pieces at a time. When she had cut into the exterior an inch or so, she was able to grasp a handful of the rough fibers and pull on them, exposing the coconut's hard interior shell. "Look, I did it," she exclaimed as she held the fruit up. She braced the coconut between her knees and then took the pole Box had given her and repeatedly jabbed at the hard fruit. Finally, she heard a slight pop and saw liquid begin to leak out from the slit she'd created. She grabbed the coconut and held it to her lips, slurping the tiny drops of water that leaked from the hole. She passed the husk to Box.

"Here, drink," she said.

Box took a few tiny sips and handed the coconut back. "Here, Yakal, drink," Na'om said. She watched as her father tilted the coconut back and took a long swig. He handed it back to her. "Now you, Ek' Balam," she said as she held the husk above the jaguar's head and let the precious drops drip into his open muzzle. She shook the coconut and heard only the tiniest bit of noise, so she held the crack to her lips and sucked the last bits of fluid from the area. "All right, now to crack this open so we can eat something," she said. After much effort, she was finally able to break the hard coconut and peel off some of the white flesh. She handed jagged pieces to Yakal and Box and set to chewing the dense nut meat. The little bit of nutrients revived them all, and they were able to keep the canoe moving forward. But night quickly fell, and there was still no sign of a village anywhere along the coastline.

When it had grown too dark for Box to tell where sky and sea met, he stopped poling. "I think we have to find someplace safe and sleep," he said as he yawned.

Na'om nodded. "I agree; we can't go on until daybreak."

Box turned the canoe toward the nearest mangrove clump and shoved the bow of the dugout deep into the root jumble. "Hopefully, that will keep us lodged here for the night," he said as he laid down his pole. He put his hands close to his face and grimaced.

"Let me see," Na'om said as she scrambled over to him. She peered at Box's hands, which were bleeding from blisters that had popped. "I'm sorry; I wish I had some salve to give you," she said as she stepped away. She sat down with her back to the gunwale, with Ek' Balam curled at her feet. "This is all my fault," she cried. "We should have stayed on the island for another few days; then we wouldn't have been caught in this storm."

"It's too late to lament wrong decisions," Yakal said. He made himself comfortable on the bottom of the canoe, and within minutes, he and Box were sound asleep.

But despite the gentle rocking of the canoe and her exhaustion, Na'om was suddenly wide awake and all too aware that her impatience to leave the island had placed all their lives at stake. *I was such a fool to even make this trip at all*, Na'om thought as she looked at the scratches and cuts on her arms and legs. *I risked my life and the lives of others to save Tz', and yet, he didn't appear. Or if he did, he was one of those horrible creatures.*

Why did I ever think he'd leave with me? He's not the boy I remember, and I don't know if he'll ever be the same. Tears welled in Na'om's eyes, and she used the edge of the shift she wore to wipe them away. *But then, I'm not the same girl who lived in the village with him.* She shivered in the damp night air. *So, do we even belong together?* The thought made Na'om's heart cramp, and she gasped at the pain.

"Na'om, what's wrong?" Box murmured.

"Nothing, go back to sleep," she whispered. She edged closer to Ek' Balam, whose soft, furry body gave off a nice radiant heat, and laid her head on her arm on the gunwale. She stared into the blackness, listening to the crash of the waves in the distance and was just about to close her eyes when she spotted a light in the darkness. But then it disappeared. She rubbed her eyes and sat up again, straining to see in the inky night. Yes, there was a light and behind it another and yet another.

"Box, Yakal, wake up, there are lights in the distance," Na'om said as she jostled the men.

"Hmm, what?" Yakal said.

"Lights, in the distance. And I can hear men's voices. Come on," Na'om said.

Box hopped into the dark water and pushed the bow out from among the tree roots. Then he cried out in pain and clutched the gunwale while he held his left foot above the water. A large crab dangled from his big toe. He grabbed the creature and yanked it off, flinging it far into the distance, then hopped back into the boat. "Those must be crabbers," he said as he picked up his pole and began moving the canoe across the still waters.

"Hello, can you hear us?" Na'om shouted. "We're here, hello!"

The lights continued to grow larger, and the group was surprised to see multiple canoes in the water. Some of the men were fishing for crabs, but three of the dugouts made a straight path toward Na'om's voice. "Keep shouting," a man said. "We're coming to get you."

"That sounded like Eqomal," Yakal remarked as he thrust his pole deep into the sandy bottom and pushed off. The canoe lurched forward yet again.

Once the canoes were close enough so that the torches the men carried illuminated the area, Na'om could see several of the shamans from the island were in the dugouts.

"Lady Na'om, we give thanks that you're all right," Eqomal said as the canoe he was in drew alongside their boat. "When we saw the storm approaching, we expected you to turn back, but when you didn't, we knew we needed to come find you."

"I thank you for searching for us," Na'om replied. She gestured around the canoe. "As you can see, we lost everything."

Eqomal nodded and hurried to pass over a large basket covered with a blanket. "Food and water, my lady, and a blanket to keep you warm." He nodded to one of his brother shamans who took two black monkey skin capes from the basket by his feet. He handed one to Yakal and the other to Box. "You must be exhausted. If you and Box will each move to one of our canoes, my brothers and I will deliver you safely up the coast."

Na'om nodded and watched as the two men awkwardly moved about until Yakal was in the center of one canoe and Box was the passenger in another. Then Eqomal stepped into her canoe. "Wait, they need food," she said.

Eqomal smiled. "We have plenty of provisions, my lady," he replied and snapped his fingers. More baskets appeared in the other two canoes, and Yakal and Box smiled as they held up gourds of sweet water and packets of steaming tamales.

Satisfied that they were taken care of, Na'om watched as the shamans in the two other canoes began to swiftly paddle back the way they had come. Eqomal picked up his own paddle and they followed, the canoe moving rapidly through the black waters.

Gradually, as the horizon turned from black to deep purple to pinkish red, Na'om was able to discern more of the coastline and could see they'd left the mangrove trees behind and had moved closer to the open sea.

"We'll need to go out past the breakers so we can continue up the coast," Eqomal said.

Na'om nodded, even though the thought of being on the rough waves made her nervous. She gripped the gunwale with both hands as the canoe broke through the oncoming surge and crashed down into the approaching waves. Fortunately, Eqomal was an expert at leveraging the canoe through the water, so the rolling of the canoe was kept to a minimum.

By the time the sun was high overhead, Na'om recognized the area they were traveling past. She felt a thrill go through her body when she saw Kärinik and Biribik walking the beach in the distance. Eqomal quickly brought them to shore, and Na'om didn't wait for him to steady the canoe. She and Ek' Balam jumped into the shallows and waded through the surging tide where Kärinik and Biribik waited for them.

"Thank the gods you're back," Kärinik said as she gave Na'om a hug. "We've been so worried, especially with the storm we just had." She stood back and looked more closely at Na'om and the marks all over her body visible through the threadbare shift she wore. "Come on, let's get you back to the hut, where I have some spare clothes you can wear."

"Wait, I must thank Eqomal and the others for helping us," Na'om said. She turned to the group of shamans who were listening to Yakal and Box describe what had happened.

"Lady Na'om, is there anything else we can do for you?" Eqomal said as he bowed.

"No, no, I just wanted to thank you all," Na'om stammered. She held up her empty hands. "I only wish I had something to give you for your efforts."

"To serve is our purpose and our reward," Eqomal replied. He reached over, lifted Na'om's hand, and placed a gentle kiss on the back of it. "We shall answer your call for help whenever you should need us." He looked to the sky. "Now, we must be off if we hope to return to the island before nightfall."

Na'om nodded and stepped back. "Maltiox, all of you." She watched as Yakal, Box, and Eqomal embraced. And then the shamans went back to their canoes and headed out to sea.

The group walked together up the beach until they reached the sand dunes where Kärinik's hut was built. Na'om stopped to look around and noticed there was new thatching on the roof and a new ring of stones for a firepit, with long logs placed around it for seating. She smiled. The skies had cleared, and the sea had calmed, and the blueness of it all stretched as far as she could see. *This spot always makes me happy.* Then she hurried ahead into the hut with Kärinik and Ek' Balam while the men reunited with the guards who had remained at a respectful distance. Exhausted, Na'om was grateful to sink into one of the wooden chairs at the small table. She watched as Kärinik dragged a wooden chest out from the wall and opened the heavy lid. The older woman pulled out a skirt and shirt, which she handed to Na'om. "We've done this before," she laughed as she pushed the trunk back.

Na'om quickly changed her outfit and sat back down. She took a deep breath and let it out as Kärinik sat down opposite her. "I failed to bring

Tz' back." And the tears that she'd held at bay for so long cascaded down her face.

Kärinik reached out and grasped Na'om's hands in her own. "Shh, it will be all right. Tell me what happened."

Na'om nodded, sniffled a few times, and then proceeded to tell her about entering the Underworld, being attacked by the were-jaguars, and the storm at sea when they'd almost lost their lives. "I don't know what to do at this point," Na'om said as she hiccuped.

"We go back to Mayapán and fight Satal when the time comes. I believe that her death will release your friend from his bonds. Only then will you know how to continue."

"I'm not sure if I'm meant to be with him or not," Na'om said.

Kärinik squeezed her hands again. "Is there someone else who might have caught your eye? There is no dishonor in loving another."

Na'om hung her head and nodded. She looked up as she whispered, "Box." She sat up straighter in her chair and looked directly at her friend. "He's been so good to me, never wavering, always standing by my side and helping in any way that he can. The few times we've touched, there's been an energy connection with him that I've never experienced with another person." Na'om hung her head again. "I even asked him to kiss me on the way here, which was quick and sweet." She looked up again. "Do you think that's why Tz' didn't return? He knew I was interested in someone else?" Na'om got up and began to pace about the small room. "Oh, what have I done?" she cried.

Kärinik hurried to Na'om's side and wrapped her in a big hug. "Shh, you mustn't fret so; you've done nothing wrong. All will be well, you'll see. Right now, you need to rest for a bit after your long ordeal, and later, after you're refreshed, things will be better." She quickly hung the large hammock across the room and helped Na'om lie down. "Sleep now while I check on the men," she said as she kissed Na'om on the forehead.

Na'om was so tired that she didn't even hear Kärinik leave the room. She went into a deep, dark sleep and only woke hours later, when the only light in the room came from a small candle set on the wooden table. She lay in the hammock, listening to the *shush, shush* of the waves as they surged in and out on the beach and then the murmur of multiple voices outside. *This hut and this spot are so special*, Na'om thought. *I feel at home here, like I do when I'm in the house Tz' and I built in Pa nimá.*

One day, I'll come back here and visit Kärinik for several days. She sighed.
*But tomorrow, we must leave and head back to Mayapán. Everyone will be
worried since we've been gone so long.*

Reluctantly, Na'om got up and straightened her clothes and hair. She
didn't want to spoil the moment of peace she felt, but she was hungry and
could smell something cooking on the fire outside. Ek' Balam got up from
his spot across the doorway when Na'om appeared. Yakal, Box, Biribik,
Kärinik, and the guards were all seated on logs around the fire ring and
turned at the sound of her footsteps.

"Come, sit by the fire and have some roasted peccary," Yakal said as
he and Box moved to one side so Na'om could sit down on the log.

"Maltiox," Na'om replied as she accepted the plate of grilled meat from
Biribik. She bit into a greasy slice and sighed. "Hmm, this is so good," she
said as she took another bite. She started to hand the plate to Box, but he
refused it.

"No, no, we've all eaten, so have as much as you like. Even Ek' Balam
has had his fill," Box said and laughed. "Look."

They all turned and saw that the jaguar was sound asleep. "He's stayed
awake all this time; he deserves a good rest," Yakal said. "I am forever in
that jaguar's debt."

Na'om nodded. "As am I."

"So, when we do we return to the city?" Biribik said.

Na'om looked at the young man's face and could sense he'd had enough
leisure time on the beach. But she could easily stay a few more days to
relax and recuperate.

"We should leave tomorrow since we've been gone too long as it is,"
Yakal said.

Na'om looked at her father and knew he was anxious to get back to
Uskab and Mayibal. But she really didn't want to return to the crowded city
and the tension surrounding the impending attack. Fortunately, Kärinik
came to her rescue before she had to say anything.

"I think Na'om might need a day or two to rest here," the older woman
said. She held up her hand to stop Yakal before he could protest. "I know
you want to get back to your family and Biribik needs to return as well. So,
this is what I suggest. You both go tomorrow and take two of the guards
with you. Na'om and I will follow in a few days' time with the other two
guards. They will be able to protect us, if we should need it."

"What about me?" Box said.

Kärinik laughed. "That's up to you."

"Well, I wouldn't mind staying a day or two here since I've never been to the coast before," Box admitted. "That is, if it's all right with everyone."

"Then it's settled," Naʼom said. "Yakal and Biribik shall return to the city and tell everyone we're all right, and we shall return after a much-needed rest." Satisfied that everyone was happy with the decision, Naʼom felt some of the tension in her body dissipate. And she spent the next few hours enjoying herself as she listened to Yakal and the other men tell stories about adventures they'd had in the past.

Later, when the two women had retired to the hut and had settled into the hammock together, Naʼom turned to Kärinik. "Maltiox for suggesting that we stay here while Yakal and Biribik return to Mayapán."

"I knew you needed some extra time here to think about things. Being near the ocean can be a salve to the soul, which is why I've always chosen to live here." Kärinik propped herself up on one elbow in the swaying hammock. "By the way, I've been meaning to tell you that if anything should happen to me during the attack, I want you to have this land and this house. Of all the people who've come here, you're the one who appreciates the beauty of it the most, so I want you to have it."

Naʼom was stunned. "But what about your daughter, Alixel? Won't she want this home? Or Mial and Ukabal? Surely, they should be the ones to inherit this land from their grandmother?"

Kärinik patted Naʼom on the arm. "Long ago Alixel told me she wanted nothing to do with this place as it only ever reminds her of the loss of her father. And Ukabal and Mial are too young. No, if something should happen so that I am forced to meet my ancestors, then I want this property to go to you, Naʼom, so you have a place of your own that brings you as much joy as it does me."

Naʼom reached over and embraced the older woman. "Maltiox, Kärinik, this means so much to me. I truly love this place and often think I could live here until the end of my days. I would never tire of watching where the sea meets the sky. But nothing will happen to you, so I'll just have to come visit when I can."

The two women went to sleep and were up at first light to say good-bye to Yakal and Biribik.

"You're sure this is what you want to do?" Yakal asked.

"Yes. You need to return to your families before they worry any longer. Tell Chiman and Ajkun that we're fine, and we'll be back in no time." Na'om gave Yakal an awkward hug and waved them off. It was only later, when she was sitting by the fire, eating breakfast with Box, Kärinik, and the two guards that she realized she'd still not thanked Yakal for rescuing her. It was a heavy weight she felt in her chest, and she vowed to say something as soon as they returned to the city.

The next few days passed quickly. Na'om spent a lot of time alone, wandering the shoreline with Ek' Balam. She looked like she was searching for seashells and interesting rocks, but she was trying to still the whirlwind of recollections and considerations that filled her mind. One minute she was reminiscing about her childhood with Tz', and the next she pondered what another kiss from Box would feel like. She craved answers to the variety of questions that plagued her, but the sea and the sand refused to divulge any solutions. Meanwhile, Kärinik took Box out in the canoe and showed him how to bait carved obsidian hooks and cast them out into the water. At every meal, they feasted on fresh killifish, dogfish, or tarpon. At one point, Box landed a barracuda, and as Na'om watched it being cooked over the fire, she shuddered to think creatures with so many teeth lived in the depths of the ocean, a place where she'd been swimming a few days before.

When Box wasn't fishing, he occasionally joined Na'om on her walks or splashed in the shallows with her. She was grateful that he never asked her for more details about her time in the Underworld and never mentioned Tz'.

Late one afternoon, they wandered far from Kärinik's hut, chatting about simple things, and when Na'om finally really looked around, she realized they were near the entrance to the cave where she had escaped Xibalba the first time she'd been there. She hurried forward, eager to see the darkness, but when the black hole appeared in the sand dunes high up the beach, Ek' Balam and Box both hesitated to go near it.

Na'om marched steadily through the shifting sands toward the entrance and only stopped when she was a few feet from it. She could feel cool air radiating out from the spot and was tempted to step inside, but stopped when Box called out to her.

"Wait, Na'om, what is this place?" he cried as he scrambled to her.

"The cave where I left the Underworld the first time." She turned back toward the hole.

"Don't go in there. Aren't you afraid of dying?" Box said as he took a few steps back toward the water. "I was terrified when we were in that storm the other day."

Na'om turned to face him. "Of dying, no; I've been close to it several times. And this cave doesn't frighten me."

"So, is there anything that does scare you?"

"Itzamná, yes, of course." Na'om hesitated.

"I'm sorry; that was rude of me to ask."

"No, no, it's all right. You'll laugh, though and think me silly." Na'om smiled quickly. "I'm afraid of not living life to the fullest. I've always been the outsider, looking on as others have fun, start families, and go about their daily lives with purpose and intention. *If* I defeat Satal, then what do I do with my life? Everything leads to that one moment in time, but what comes after that? I used to think I'd spend my days in Pa nimá, with Tz', but now I don't know. He didn't appear like I thought he would, and now that I've seen other parts of the country, this place for instance, I'm not sure where I belong or what I should do."

She didn't add that she was torn by her devotion to her old friend and confused about her feelings toward Box. For the hundredth time, she wondered if her affection toward Box were the reason Tz' hadn't appeared. *Why else would he stay hidden from me?* she thought as she picked up a rock and threw it into the cave. She listened for it to hit something, but there was no sound.

"Perhaps Kärinik or Ajkun can help you find some answers," Box said. "For what it's worth, when we return to Mayapán, I can help you have some fun before we leave for Chichén Itzá, starting with taking you to dinner at the marketplace."

"Maltiox, I'd like that."

That evening, Box and Kärinik went out on the glassy sea in the dugout with a torch and used bits and pieces of fish to catch a basket of crabs while Na'om paced back and forth on the top of the sand dunes, watching their light as it bobbed about in the dark. She felt anxious, knowing if anything happened to either of them while out on the water, she'd never forgive herself. *Why did I agree to stay all this time?* she fretted. *I have more questions than answers, and nothing can be resolved until Satal is dead.* She didn't relax until the canoe had beached and the two were safely back at the hut. Kärinik quickly brought a pot of water to boil and made salted crab, but she had no corn or eggs to make fried cakes. While eating the plain salted crabmeat, Na'om decided they needed to return to Mayapán. She missed the variety of foods available from the marketplace, she needed to see Ajkun and Chiman once again, and she had to resume her responsibilities. *Maybe if my mind is forced to think about Satal and how to defeat her, I won't have time to think about Box or Tz'.* That thought brought a halt to the endless reflections that had swirled for so long in her mind.

"We'll start our return to the city tomorrow," Na'om said as she put her empty plate on the ground. "Be ready to leave at first light." Now that her decision had been made, Na'om was eager for daybreak and the start of her trek back to the city.

Yakal

Yakal had to admit it; he was exhausted. The march to Kärinik's hut had been difficult, but the return trip to Mayapán was even more strenuous. He could only assume it had something to do with having been in the Underworld, a fact he wanted to keep from Uskab. *But with all these spots on my body, there's no way to hide what happened,* he mused.

He was glad when he heard the clamor of the thousands who called Mayapán home; the noise meant they were almost there, and then he could rest. He wanted to sleep for a week, but he knew there was too much work ahead to dally any longer. Only when the actual gates of the city were in sight did Yakal fully realize that they had failed in their mission. And now he had to explain that to Ajkun, Chiman, and the other council members.

"No rest for the weary," Yakal muttered.

Biribik looked at him and nodded. "Back to work for all of us," he said.

Yakal's work began before he had even passed the gates into the city as Chiman and Nimal were standing guard.

"Yakal, Biribik," Chiman said as he stepped forward. He scanned the crowd of people still entering the gates. "Where are the others? Where's Na'om and Tz'?"

Yakal sighed and touched the older man's arm. "Gather everyone at the Temple of the Warriors and I'll explain," he said wearily.

"No! I demand an answer, here, now. Where is Naòm?" Chiman cried.

Several people looked in his direction at the sound of his raised voice and Nimal came to stand beside Chiman. "It might be best if you have this discussion someplace more private, eh?" he said, and he began to lead the way toward the guardhouse. He motioned for the four guards on duty to vacate the building and ushered Chiman, Yakal, and Biribik inside.

Yakal held up his hand to stop Chiman from speaking. "Naòm, Box, and Kärinik are fine; they stayed at Kärinik's hut to rest and will return with the guards in a few days." He pointed to Biribik. "We needed to get back to our families so they wouldn't worry."

"But where is Tz'?" Chiman demanded. "You haven't mentioned my son!"

"I'm sorry to tell you, my friend, that he is still trapped in Xibalba. Naòm never found him, or if she did, he remained a were-jaguar, and so she was unable to communicate with him and convince him to leave the Underworld and return to the land of the living."

Yakal watched as the anger on Chiman's face was replaced with a wave of anguish and grief. "I'm sorry, Chiman, truly I am."

"Maltiox, Yakal. I know Naòm did the best she could."

"She risked her life," Yakal said, but he didn't elaborate. *Better Chiman and the others hear Naòm's tale from her own lips than mine.*

"You both must be weary and eager to see your wives," Nimal said. "I'll post extra guards at the gate, and the minute we see the others returning, I'll make sure you all know."

"Maltiox, Nimal," Chiman said. He stepped back outside. "I think I'd better go tell Ajkun the news on my own."

Yakal nodded. Then he stepped forward and hugged Biribik. "Keep the details of the trip to yourself for now," he whispered in the youth's ear. "Best no one knows Naòm was attacked by the were-jaguars until she tells them the story."

Biribik nodded and stepped back. He turned to Nimal. "I'll be ready for guard duty the minute Naòm returns. Until then, I must make sure my family is safe." He quickly left the area and disappeared into the throng that moved into the city as night approached.

"Take one of the guards with you, Yakal," Nimal said, "so you make it home safely."

Yakal agreed, and the young guard with his obsidian knife at his side stepped into the thinning crowds. By the time they were past the marketplace, they could easily maneuver the almost empty streets. Yakal had never felt so humbled and happy as when they rounded the street corner and he saw Uskab sitting by the fire with Mayibal on her lap. "You can go now," he told the guard. "I'll be fine."

At the sound of his voice, Uskab looked up and shrieked. She ran to the gate and held it open so Yakal could enter the small courtyard. "I was so worried," Uskab said. "I thought you'd never return." Tears of happiness filled her eyes.

"Shh, my love, I'm here now," Yakal said as he sat down on the wooden stool Uskab had just vacated. He held out his arms and Mayibal squirmed down from Uskab's grasp and toddled into Yakal's arms. He sniffed his son's sweet scent and hugged him as the tears ran down.

"Yakal, is everything all right?" Uskab asked as she knelt by his side. She touched the spots still visible on Yakal's arms. "What happened?"

"I'd rather not talk about it tonight," Yakal said. "Tomorrow, I promise."

"Well, I'll speak to Ajkun and have her make you a special salve," Uskab said as she prepared to get up.

Yakal placed his hand on her arm, preventing her from moving. "Not tonight, my love. Besides, the shamans gave me one of their concoctions. First, I must eat and bathe and then, once this little one is sound asleep, I only wish to lie in your arms . . . and perhaps, we can make him a little brother or sister?"

Uskab squealed with delight and hurried to kiss Yakal soundly on the lips. "Tonight would be a perfect night," she said. Then she set about preparing a meal while Yakal felt the weight of the past weeks gently slip from his shoulders. *It's good to be home and surrounded by family*, he thought.

NA'OM

At first light, Na'om left the small hut and looked at the ocean one last time. She felt a heaviness in her body and really just wanted to go back to sleep, but she had made her decision. They needed to return to Mayapán. The night before, she had discussed the idea of detouring to the village of Xiat with Kärinik so she could visit her daughter and grandchildren, but the older woman felt it was safer if they stayed away from the area. Na'om sighed and tried to shake off the feeling that something was wrong. *The past few days here have been so enjoyable,* she thought. *I don't understand why I feel so apprehensive now.*

She gazed at the pink-and-blue horizon, then turned her back on the sea and joined the others as they headed over the sand dunes and down to the nearest small lagoon. Kärinik took the lead, following narrow footpaths that meandered past the stagnant pools of algae-covered water. The smell of dead fish hung in the humid air, and Na'om felt sick to her stomach. She drank a small amount of water from the gourd she carried, but that did little to ease her nausea. Her pace slowed and Box hurried to her side.

"Are you all right?"

"My stomach, that's all," Na'om said and she gave him a weak smile. "Something I ate, I guess. I'll be fine soon." But she knew that wasn't true, and the rising heat, the smells, and the glare of the sun off the pools of water made it all worse.

After several hours of walking, they had finally moved far inland and were on drier land where small shrubs and trees offered pockets of shade. Kärinik found a large group of young ceiba trees and suggested they rest for a bit. Na'om sank to the ground, exhausted, and refused any of the food Box offered her.

"Why didn't you tell me you were ill? Kärinik demanded, seating herself next to Na'om. "We could have delayed traveling for another day until you felt better."

"I'm not sure that would have made any difference," Na'om replied. "It might be something I ate or nervousness; I'm not sure. No, the best thing is to return to Mayapán and see how preparations are going. I can rest then."

Kärinik searched the area nearby and found some small piñuela fruits to eat. "Try to eat these; they should help," she said as she handed them to Na'om.

As the afternoon progressed, Na'om's stomachache did disappear, and by the time they made camp for the night in the brush on the outskirts of a small village, she was truly hungry and eagerly ate the tamales Kärinik had purchased from a local vendor.

The group sat around a small fire that kept the evening chill at bay, but they were all weary from the day's march and curled up to sleep soon after the sun set for the evening. Na'om lay down on a wool blanket, with Ek' Balam on one side for comfort and warmth. Kärinik lay on her other side, and Box was near the guards. Na'om quickly fell asleep, but woke when she heard Ek' Balam get up and begin to growl. The fire had gone out, but the stars and moon cast a bit of light on the area. Na'om saw Ek' Balam's black shape move toward the surrounding brush.

"Hey, boy, what is it?" she whispered. She sat up and watched as he pounced on something in the bushes and then heard a thud as he flung it into the dirt. She quickly got up and went to him. When she was several feet from the others, she cast out a small bit of light in order to see. Ek' Balam was standing near the creosote bushes and balché trees and growling at the underbrush.

Na'om pushed her light forward and gasped. Several large moccasin snakes lay curled up and ready to strike, their tails rattling in rhythm with each other. "Come, boy, leave them alone, and perhaps they'll go away,"

Na'om said as she laid her hand on Ek' Balam's back. Then she heard a rustling noise to her right and glimpsed movement so she concentrated and spread her light in that direction. Several gray and brown spearhead snakes were slithering through the dusty dirt, headed toward her. Just behind them were more rattlesnakes. She turned again and could see even more snakes in the distance.

"Ek' Balam, come away now, back to the fire," she ordered. She turned and ran. "Wake up, wake up, get the fire going," she cried as she bent down and shook Box.

"What's the matter?" Box said as he stood up.

"Snakes, a dozen or more snakes, and headed toward us."

Box roused the guards, ordering them to stand ready with their knives, and then he bent and blew on the embers until a bright fire was burning. Kärinik shivered as she hastily picked up each blanket on the ground and shook it out. She staggered under the weight of them, but didn't dare set them down again.

"Here, stuff them into the pack baskets," Na'om said as she hastily folded one of the blankets. She looked around and noticed Ek' Balam was still several feet away. "Ek' Balam, get back here," she cried. She touched a piece of dry wood into the flames, creating a burning torch, and swept it back and forth in front of her as she marched over to the jaguar. He continued to growl and stare into the brush. The dozen or more snakes had not retreated and flicked their tongues in and out as they seemed to study the big cat.

Na'om swung the torch near them and one struck at the flames. Startled, Na'om jerked backward and dropped the branch, which promptly went out. The snake struck again, narrowly missing Na'om's arm as she reached for the stick. She leapt back just as all the rattlers and moccasins attacked, leaping, striking, and hissing in full force. Na'om screamed as one viper almost bit her leg. Ek' Balam leapt into the air as a moccasin snake bit his front leg. He grabbed it by the body and crunched down on it with his powerful jaws, but the snake continued to whip its tail around, hitting Ek' Balam in the shoulder with more venom.

Box and the guards ran forward with torches, which they dropped on the ground, creating a circle of fire, but it didn't force the snakes to retreat. They squirmed and writhed around the torches, still headed toward Ek' Balam and Na'om. The two guards hacked at the closest snakes with their obsidian knives, but as soon as they killed one, another appeared. Box grabbed Naʼom by the hand and dragged her toward the main fire.

"Ek' Balam, get back here," Naʼom cried as she jumped.

"It's just a stick," Box said as he picked up the piece of wood and threw it away.

Naʼom watched in horror as Ek' Balam bent down and snatched up two more snakes, which he tossed with his head into the dirt nearby. They squirmed and wriggled about, hissing and striking at everything within range. Then he snarled as another snake struck him in the front paw.

"Ek' Balam!" Naʼom screamed. She pulled away from Box, ran forward, and closed her eyes. She felt energy surging from deep inside her and she pushed it outward in a wave of brilliant light that caught the nearest creosote bushes on fire. Snapping and crackling in the dry undergrowth, the fire quickly spread to more dense brush. Dozens of snakes jerked and twisted in random spasms as the flames consumed their hiding places and cooked them to a blackened crisp.

The guards continued to slash at the remaining snakes and then they each grabbed a blanket and began to beat down the flames. "We can't set the whole countryside on fire," one guard muttered as he repeatedly whacked at a creosote bush.

Naʼom hurried to Ek' Balam, who was having trouble standing. "Quickly, help me with him," she cried. "He's been bitten multiple times." Kärinik and Box grabbed the last two blankets, ran to Naʼom, and laid them on the ground near the big jaguar.

"Lie down, boy, you'll be okay," Naʼom said as she gently pushed Ek' Balam on his side. He half-fell onto the soft blankets and lay there, breathing heavily. Naʼom nodded to Kärinik and Box. "Let's carry him to the fire where I can see him better." Each woman grabbed a front corner and Box picked up the back of the blankets and they hauled the heavy cat to the makeshift firepit. Naʼom knelt down and peered at Ek' Balam's front paw and leg. "He's been bitten multiple times in this front leg." She paused as she continued to scan the jaguar's body, "But I think that's the only place he's been bitten."

Ek' Balam began to struggle to sit up and Kärinik spoke. "You must keep him lying still until we can draw the poison from his body. The more he moves, the quicker the toxins will spread." She held up a small obsidian knife. "The best thing is to cut the areas and force them to bleed, squeezing as much of the poison out as you can."

Na'om nodded as she took the knife from the woman. Tears filled her eyes as she leaned down to kiss Ek' Balam on the muzzle. "I'm sorry I have to hurt you like this," she said as she held the blade near the flames to sterilize it. She rubbed Ek' Balam behind the ear, took a deep breath, and sliced into his shoulder. The cat jerked his head and growled at her, snapping with his large teeth just inches from Na'om's hand. "I'm sorry, I'm sorry," Na'om said as she dropped the knife and began to squeeze the cut area. Green pus welled up and mingled with the blood that matted into the cat's fur. Ek' Balam snarled again and Na'om looked up at Box and Kärinik. "I don't know if I can do this," she cried.

"You have to, Na'om. Otherwise, he'll die. The toxins are already working their way into his system," Box said. He squatted near the jaguar's head and looked into the cat's eyes. "Hey, boy, we must hurt you to help you, all right?" He reached out and tentatively touched the cat on the muzzle between his eyes, forcing Ek' Balam to close them. "That's right, boy, just close your eyes, and this will all be over soon," he said in a soothing voice. He kept running his finger down the cat's nose, over and over again. He nodded at Na'om. "Keep going, cut the other bites and squeeze out the pus. I will try to keep him from biting you."

"Be careful, Box," Kärinik advised. She knelt on the ground near Ek' Balam's back and began to stroke his fur gently right behind his head. Then she began to hum a soft tune that seemed to relax the cat.

"All right, I think he has two, maybe three bites on his foreleg," Na'om said. She slashed one, two, three times with the knife, and each time, Ek' Balam jerked his head toward the pain, but then fell back, too exhausted now to even growl.

"Shh, almost done, boy," Na'om said as she pinched and pressed on the thin skin and muscle on the front of his shin bone. Droplets of yellow pus oozed out, and she wiped the bloody mess away with a cloth. "I think that's all of them," she said as she looked up. Dirt, tears, and sweat mingled on her face and she swiped at it with the cuff of her one sleeve. "Will he be all right now?" she asked Kärinik.

"Honestly, I don't know. I think it's best if we get him to Mayapán as quickly as possible. The shamans there will have remedies for snake bites, I'm sure."

"If they don't, Ati't will know what to do," Na'om said. "She has a cure for everything." She petted Ek' Balam in his favorite spot behind his ear and was grateful to hear the softest of purrs. She leaned down and kissed him on the cheek. "I love you," she whispered in his ear. "I don't think we should stay here any longer; we can walk through the rest of the night and be at Mayapán before the sun is high overhead," she said as she slowly stood up. She looked at Ek' Balam, who panted softly. She filled a coconut bowl with a bit of water and helped the cat drink a bit. "We'll have to carry him the rest of the way."

Box nodded and hurried over to help the guards stamp out the last remaining flames nearby. Dead snake carcasses lay about everywhere. "Help me gather some branches to make a framework for the blankets. We need to carry Ek' Balam to safety."

The men quickly tied four long branches into a frame, which they then attached to the blankets underneath Ek' Balam. Everyone shouldered their pack baskets, Na'om and Kärinik each grabbed a flaming stick for a torch, and Box kicked dirt onto the firepit, extinguishing the flames. One guard knelt in front of Ek' Balam and the other in the back, and together they were able to lift the jaguar into the air. Na'om and Kärinik took the lead, picking their way through the dark landscape while Box brought up the rear. It was slow going in the dark, and every now and then, Na'om made everyone stop while she checked on Ek' Balam. Bits of white froth bubbled at the corner of his mouth and she dipped a cloth into some water, squeezing the drops onto his swollen tongue. When the guards needed a break, Na'om refused to stop. She and Kärinik grabbed the front and Box carried the rear of the makeshift carrier and eventually they reached the edge of the sacbe that ran from Mayapán to the outlying villages.

"It'll be much faster if we use the roadway rather than following trails through the brush," Box said.

Na'om nodded and together, they hoisted Ek' Balam up on the wide limestone road. Daylight was just arriving, so the sacbe was empty, but Na'om knew that soon the causeway would be teeming with people headed to and from the city. "Keep the crowds back as best you can," she advised the guards. She bent down and looked at Ek' Balam in the growing light and lifted one eyelid. All she could see was the white of his eye. "We don't have time to waste."

They set off at a brisk pace, with the guards once again carrying the jaguar. As Na'om had anticipated, the higher the sun rose in the east, the more people appeared on the sacbe. But they took one look at the group traveling together and stopped, moving respectfully and silently to one side. Then one young man came forward, caught a glimpse of Ek' Balam, and without a word, turned and ran.

"Where's he going?" Kärinik asked as she hurried to keep up.

"Hopefully to get help," Box replied. He walked up to the rear guard. "Do you want to switch again?" he asked.

"No, my lord, but if you could carry my pack basket, that would be a help," the guard said.

"I'll take it for you," a young woman said as she appeared near the men. "I'm going to Mayapán and want to help."

"Maltiox," the guard said as Box helped slip the heavy basket from his shoulders.

The woman hefted it onto her back and continued to walk beside the group. "What happened?"

"We were camped for the night and were attacked by snakes," Na'om said. "He defended us and was bitten several times." She waved a hand over the prone jaguar's body, and several flies buzzed up into the air and then resettled near the jaguar's wounds.

They continued to walk as quickly as possible, but the sacbe continued to fill with people, and it became more and more difficult to push their way through. The guards stopped and Box went to talk to them.

"I think we'll have to carry Ek' Balam so you can create a path for us to get through," he told the men. Sweat ran down their bare backs, and each man drained the last of the water they had in their gourds.

As the group began to reposition themselves so Na'om, Box, and Kärinik could carry Ek' Balam, a cry went up in the crowd ahead of them. The helpful young woman hurried ahead and returned with a smile on her face.

"What's happening?" Na'om asked.

"It's the runners, Be Anim and Tik Anim, and their cousins Jumumik and Jututik."

She stepped aside and Na'om could see the four men racing toward them. Each set of twins carried a litter between them. They hurried to Na'om and bowed and she smiled. "Maltiox," she replied as she stepped onto the one wooden platform. "How did you know we needed help?" she asked Jumumik.

"News traveled from person to person along the sacbe to where we were training for some races, so we stopped what we were doing and came at once."

Naʼom watched as Box helped Be Anim and Tik Anim place Ekʼ Balam on his blankets onto the other litter.

"Weʼll see you later today in Mayapán," Kärinik said as she grasped Naʼomʼs hand. "Now go."

Naʼom nodded, and the men hoisted her to their shoulders and set off on a fast trot. She grabbed the edges of the platform and held on as best she could. The swaying motion brought on a wave of nausea and she swallowed multiple times to keep what little food sheʼd eaten down. *Now is not the time to be sick*, she thought. *I must get Ekʼ Balam to the shamans.*

The four men ran and ran, putting the distance they needed to travel behind them at a rapid pace. Naʼom looked up at the sky and silently prayed. *Itzamná, thank you for sending these men to help me. I beg you, save my dear Ekʼ Balamʼs life.* She watched as the men carried them past fields of chaya, beans, and squash, and orchards of mamey, star apple, mango, and papaya.

In a few hoursʼ time, she could see the top of the pyramid above the nearby mahogany trees and knew they had almost made it. The group pushed through the crowds, reaching the wide city gates.

"Make way, make way, for Lady Naʼom," Be Anim cried. He and Tik Anim carried Ekʼ Balam through the copper doors and their cousins followed with Naʼom.

Suddenly, Nimal appeared at Naʼomʼs right side. "Itzamná, whatʼs happened?"

"Ekʼ Balam is hurt; I must get him to the shamans," Naʼom said.

Nimal motioned to several guards who hurried over. "Clear the streets immediately and take Lady Naʼom and Ekʼ Balam to the Temple of the Shamans. And you," he said as he pointed his finger at one young man. "Go find Chiman and Ajkun and tell them Lady Naʼom has returned."

"Maltiox," Naʼom shouted over her shoulder as the twins whisked her away.

Within minutes, the men arrived at the temple, and Naʼom hurried up the steep steps to the door. She rapped on it and waited impatiently for someone to appear. "Hello, is anyone there?" she cried. "I must speak to someone at once."

After several minutes, the door finally opened and Nima Winaq peered out. When he saw Na'om, he instantly bowed and stepped back to allow her to enter the courtyard. "My lady, what can we do for you?" he said as he peered at Na'om.

Na'om motioned for the twins to bring Ek' Balam up the stairs and into the temple. "He's been struck multiple times by snakes, mainly in his front leg," Na'om said as she stepped to Ek' Balam's side. His breathing was shallow, and more spittle had collected in the corner of his muzzle.

Nima Winaq took one look at the jaguar and bowed again to Na'om. "Bring him into this room where he'll be out of the direct sun," he said to Jumumik and Jututik as he shuffled toward the nearest doorway. "I must gather some herbs and remedies and will return with my brother shamans who will assist me. Please, make yourself comfortable, my lady," the shaman said as he hurried outside again.

Na'om turned to the four cousins and reached into the pouch she carried at her waist. She extracted a handful of cacao beans. "Here, for your hard work," Na'om said as she tried to give them to Be Anim.

"No, my lady, we'll accept no payment from you. It is an honor to serve you and Ek' Balam."

"Maltiox," Na'om replied. "I don't know how long I'll be here, so you should get some rest."

As soon as the men had left, Na'om knelt on the floor next to Ek' Balam and began to pet him, hoping to hear his soft purr. But the big jaguar was unresponsive. Na'om took a cloth from her pouch and wiped away the globs of white froth from his mouth and laid her head against his chest. She could feel the slight rise and fall of his body as he drew in quick, short breaths. *Itzamná, where are the shamans*, she fretted.

Several more minutes passed before she heard multiple footsteps approaching. Nima Winaq and three other shamans swarmed into the room. One carried a censor shaped like a seated coatimundi, with its ringed tail wrapped around its fat body. Its outstretched paws were filled with smoldering copal. Another shaman carried a black pottery bowl of red salt, the third man had several bundles of leaves in a basket, while Nima Winaq had a collection of green, orange, and yellow feathers in his hand. Na'om stepped to one side so the men could help Ek' Balam. The burning copal quickly filled the room with pungent smoke and the shaman placed the pottery effigy in the doorway where it continued to billow into the room. Nima Winaq hurriedly placed a ring of red salt around Ek' Balam's body and then took the various bundles of leaves from the basket. He handed one to each shaman and they began to rapidly chew the dark-green, smooth leaves. Once they'd formed a thick paste in their mouths, they spit the mixture into the empty pottery bowl.

He looked up at Na'om. "Please, come sit beside him and talk to him softly. Let him know we mean him no harm."

"What is that? Na'om asked, pointing to the dark-green muddle in the bowl. She squatted on the floor next to Ek' Balam and began to pet him.

"Leaves from the chacah and xabalam trees; they are both good for drawing out snakebite venom," Nima Winaq said. "But I'm afraid the salve will cause pain, which is why I need you to keep him calm." He quickly dipped his fingers into the slimy dark mixture and spread it on Ek' Balam's shoulder.

The jaguar jerked his leg, but didn't open his eyes. The shaman found the other snake bites and placed the leaf mixture on each of them and each time, Ek' Balam twitched and spasmed, but he didn't wake.

Na'om continued to stroke Ek' Balam's soft fur while Nima Winaq began to mutter under his breath and wave the collection of feathers up and down Ek' Balam's leg. The other shamans took up the chant as they slowly circled the group. By now, the copal smoke was dense in the room and Na'om felt her eyes burn as the air stirred all around her. She coughed into her shirt sleeve and kept waiting for Ek' Balam to open his eyes. "How long before he wakes up?"

"The poison is deep into his system," Nima Winaq replied. "We'll change the poultices in an hour's time and hope that helps. In the meantime, we shall continue to pray that your friend finds his way out of Xibalba and returns to us."

Na'om nodded, but she felt her heart constrict at the thought Ek' Balam was in the Underworld yet again and this time all alone. Tears slipped down her cheeks, and she stumbled from the room before the men could see. The bright sunlight blinded her, forcing her to squeeze her eyes shut, and the instant heat made her dizzy and nauseous. She swayed back and forth, then dropped to her knees on the hard tiles underfoot. She bent double and coughed up a bit of sour-tasting spittle. *Itzamná, please help Ek' Balam*, she prayed. *I don't know if I can defeat Satal without him.* That thought sat like a rock in her stomach, and Na'om scrabbled to the nearest corner of the courtyard and threw up. She looked around for some water to wash the mess away, but before she could find any, a young apprentice appeared with a bucket and rags and motioned that he would clean it up.

"Maltiox," Na'om said. She was embarrassed about the mess she'd made and headed back into the room to sit by Ek' Balam.

The shamans were still chanting, but Nima Winaq had stopped fluttering his bundle of feathers over Ek' Balam's leg and body.

"Is he all right?" Na'om asked as she knelt by the jaguar.

"He's in a deep trance at this point; we must give him time to heal." Nima Winaq slowly got to his feet and motioned for Na'om to come with him outside. He noticed Na'om's reluctance to leave the room. "My brothers will come at once if there's any change in his condition," the shaman said as he held out his arm to Na'om. "Come; we have much to discuss."

Na'om petted Ek' Balam one more time, then hurried after the old man. He slowly walked down the tile pathway to another room and motioned for Na'om to enter. "We can talk privately in here," he said as he pointed to the two leather chairs and the small table. A round platter of pastries, a pitcher of tamarind juice, and two pottery mugs sat waiting for them. Nima Winaq poured Na'om a glass of juice and handed it to her. "Drink; you need to keep up your strength, for the battle and the baby."

Na'om spit out the juice she had in her mouth in a spray that splattered the leather tabletop. "Baby, what baby?" she cried as she used the edge of her sleeve and hastily wiped at the droplets staining the leather. She felt her face grow red with the mere thought.

"You're with child; that's why you feel nauseated at times and want to sleep more than normal. Najtir told me this might happen, and we're pleased to see that it has."

"But, my lord, I, I . . . I've never lain with a man," Na'om finally stated.

"Even so, you carry a child, a child conceived when you were in Xibalba."

"But I don't understand how this is possible," Na'om said. She put her hands on her stomach, and instantly knew in her heart that the shaman was right; she was pregnant.

"The gods have given you this gift, one you must protect and cherish at all costs." Nima Winaq picked up a corn pastry covered with raspberries and took a big bite. "The power of a woman with child is as vast as the heavens above; Najtir and I believe this strength will aid you in your fight against Satal. But only if you use the energy at the right time and in the right way."

"My lord, I don't understand." Na'om could feel her frustration rising at the enigmatic way the shaman spoke to her.

Nima Winaq put his pastry down and leaned toward Na'om. "At some point in the battle, you'll have to make a choice. Only you will know when to make it and which option is the correct one to pick." He leaned back and picked up his pastry again.

Na'om sat watching him, hoping for some more information, but the shaman remained silent. The two sat without speaking for several minutes, the only sounds that of the shaman chewing his food and slurping from his mug. Finally, he sighed and stood up. "I'll check on Ek' Balam and replace the poultices with new ones. You may rest here as long as you need."

Na'om nodded and let the old man leave the room. She had been so startled by the idea that she was pregnant that she'd momentarily forgotten Ek' Balam was sick. She knew there was little she could do for the jaguar, so she remained seated. She put her hands on her belly again and slowly rubbed them in a small circle. She thought back to the recent events in the Underworld and vaguely remembered seeing Hun-Kamé and Vucub-Kamé. *Could the skeleton gods have done this to me after I blacked out?* She took a small sip of the tart tamarind juice and found it more refreshing than she remembered. She eagerly drank more and then reached for a pastry. *I must talk to Ajkun and find out what I need to do to ensure the health of this baby.* She leaned back in her chair and closed her eyes, trying to remember the slightest detail that might help her know more about how this child had come to be.

But a loud growl and a cry of pain snapped her out of her reverie, and Na'om hurried outside, down the walkway, and reentered the smoke-filled room. Ek' Balam still lay on his side on the floor, and one of the young shamans was holding a white cloth to his hand. Na'om could see it was stained with blood. "Are you all right?" she asked.

"Yes, my lady, just a slight nip on my little finger," the man said as he bowed.

She knelt down next to Ek' Balam, but the cat still appeared unresponsive. "What happened?" she asked Nima Winaq.

"We attempted to give him some water to help flush the snake poison from his body, but he snapped at my brother."

Na'om noticed a small pottery bowl on the floor, with a wet rag floating in it. "I'll give him some," she said as she picked up the cloth and then gently parted Ek' Balam's lips. She let the water drip onto his teeth and sighed when he swallowed. She continued to give the jaguar water for several minutes until it began to run down his cheek. "I want to stay here with him until he improves."

Nima Winaq nodded as he stood up. "We'll bring you a hammock, blankets, and later some more food. And I shall send a message to Chiman to let him know you're here."

"Maltiox, my lord," Na'om said as she stroked Ek' Balam's soft fur.

One of the shamans hurried away and came back within a few minutes with the hammock and several blankets, which he quickly set up for Na'om.

"Come, my brothers, we must let Lady Na'om rest," Nima Winaq said. He bowed, and the men left the room, leaving Na'om alone with Ek' Balam. She took the pile of blankets and spread them on the floor, then lay down close to the jaguar so she could easily keep her hand on his side. "I'm here, boy," she whispered. "Come back to me now, all right? I need you, more than ever." With one hand on Ek' Balam and the other on her belly, she fell asleep. But she woke within minutes when she heard Chiman's voice outside in the courtyard. She stood up and still half-asleep, she staggered outside into the heat and sunlight.

"Mam, I'm here," she said as she rubbed her eyes and blinked several times.

"Na'om, thank the gods you're all right," Chiman said as he gave her a long hug. He finally let go and stood back to look at her. "How is Ek' Balam? Nima Winaq briefly told me about the snake attack."

"The shamans are doing everything they can for him," Na'om said. She felt tears welling in her eyes and hastily swiped at them. "I'm going to stay here until he's well enough to be moved."

"Yes, yes, of course. I'll tell Ajkun that you're all right; she's been so worried these past few days."

Na'om gave him a half-smile. "I'll come see her as soon as I can, I promise. Right now, though, I need to be with Ek' Balam." She gave Chiman a hug and turned to leave.

"Would you like me to sit with you?"

Na'om looked at her grandfather's lined face and saw the worry he carried written all over it. She wanted nothing more than to talk to someone who loved her about everything that had happened from the moment they'd left Mayapán to the time they'd returned. But as much as she loved her grandfather, he was a man, and deep in her heart, she knew that some things would only be understood by Ajkun, another woman. So, she forced a bright smile on her own face. "Maltiox, Mam, but I think it's best if I just sit quietly with him for now. When he wakes up and I can have him moved to my hut, I'll send for you." Then she hurried back into the dark room before she could change her mind.

SATAL

Satal sat in one of the many worn leather chairs in her darkened dining room and brooded over the upcoming battle. *I don't believe I shall have the shamans shapeshift this time unless it's absolutely necessary*, she mused. *I don't trust that they'll be able to control themselves. No, I shall transform and attack Na'om, and that should suffice.* She tapped her fingers on the arm of the chair. *I must remember to tell Tewichinel to bring Pataninel to me once he enters the city. He will pay for his insubordination!* Minutes passed as her thoughts swirled about. *That damn jaguar should be dead by now; I don't understand what went wrong!*

Suddenly, Sachoj's shrunken head appeared in the air directly in front of Satal and she jerked backward in her chair, upsetting the small wooden table beside her, which crashed to the floor.

How is it possible that your relatives failed? she questioned Sachoj. *You have such command over the whole snake realm, so why is that jaguar still alive?*

They bit him multiple times, my dear, but the shamans of Mayapán wield potent energy bestowed upon them by Itzamná himself, which is a power far greater than I can summon from the depths of Xibalba.

Is there no way to destroy that animal or the girl?!

I think only in direct combat will you be able to defeat her. Fortunately, Na'om will have no chance against your army and those you summon from Xibalba. Sachoj chortled and hissed. *Especially now that she knows her beloved Tz' is a were-jaguar, more animal than human, and more interested in destroying her than having a life with her.*

Satal stood up and rapidly moved away from the hovering head. She paced back and forth, knowing Sachoj's eyes were following her the whole time. "But is that enough?" she cried.

"My lady, did you call for me?" Tewichinel asked as he appeared in the doorway, carrying a lit candle in a small pottery dish. "I thought I heard a loud noise," he said, then he bent down and righted the table before placing the candle on it. Using a piece of straw, he hurried to light the other candles in the room, banishing the shadows to the corners and high ceiling.

Satal watched as Sachoj moved deeper into the corner. "Go away!" Satal mumbled and watched as the shaman bowed and turned to leave. "No, not you . . . her," she said and waved her hand in the air. "You stay. Everything's fine; I just, I just, oh, never mind." She slumped in the chair and put her head in her hands. "I don't know how she did it," she muttered.

"My lady," Tewichinel said as he moved closer. He held up a scroll in one hand. "I've received word from one of my brother shamans that Lady Na'om went to the island and entered Xibalba."

"Yes, yes, I know, and she survived because her father, Yakal, rescued her! I should have killed him when he was a child and still under my power, but his father, Q'alel, always kept a watchful eye on me when I was near the boy."

Tewichinel cleared his throat and unrolled more of the scroll. "My brother writes that he believes Na'om was touched by the gods while in Xibalba. He says she bears the markings of their work in her body."

"Yes, yes, we know all this. The girl is covered with jaguar spots from the last time she was down there." Satal turned to face Tewichinel. "Does that scroll say anything we *don't* know?"

"It appears she has grown fond of a young man named Box, which might be useful. If this relationship blossoms, then perhaps Na'om's loyalties will be divided. If both Tz' and this boy, Box, are in harm's way, she'll need to choose one over the other, giving you a potential advantage."

"Hmm, yes, you're right. Find out everything that you can about Box and report back to me. And make more sacrifices to the gods. I want them all on my side before we enter the Wayeb."

"As you wish, my lady. I will have the guards bring the last of the prisoners from Mayapán to the sacred cenote in the early evening."

"And tell the guards to keep a watch out for Pataninel. I want him brought to me the moment he returns."

Tewichinel bowed and left the room.

Satal sat and listened to the *slip, slip, slip* of his leather sandals on the tile floor and finally heard the creak of the copper hinges on the heavy wooden door as he left the building. *There must be something else I can do*, Satal thought as she plucked at the threads on the blanket next to her. *That girl has survived visiting Xibalba twice and a storm at sea, but she's still human and therefore vulnerable.* But no new ideas came to her.

She dozed where she sat and only woke when she heard voices approaching. Tewichinel and Kämisanel firmly gripped the arms of Pataninel who struggled between them.

"My lady," Kämisanel said, "we found your shaman only a few moments ago, skulking about the marketplace, en route to his home where his wife and children eagerly await his return."

Pataninel shrugged off the other men and knelt on the floor. "My lady, I have no idea why you have summoned me thus. Yuxba' and I delivered your 'package' to the outskirts of Mayapán as you requested. Unfortunately, Yuxba' did not survive the journey."

"Ha, you take me for a fool. You should have listened to Yuxba' when he said I was nearby. I know Yuxba' begged you to carry the 'package' closer, but instead, you drove that dagger you carry at your waist straight into Yuxba's heart and then left him to the vultures." Satal watched with pleasure as the shaman's face turned a chalky gray.

"Take him to the temple built in honor of Camazotz and tie him to the walls of the inner chamber. I believe Camazotz's relatives will enjoy a bit of fresh meat to feast upon."

"No, my lady, I implore you, let me make amends to you. I'll do anything, anything at all. Please, what about my wife and children?"

"If you continue to beg, I shall tell my guards to bring them to the temple as well." She nodded and flicked her hand in dismissal.

Pataninel slumped to the floor so Tewichinel and Kämisanel grabbed him under each armpit and half-carried, half-dragged him to the door.

Satal sat back in her chair and imagined the hundreds of bats that now roosted in the roof of the new temple descending upon the man and eating him one tiny bite at a time. The thought of blood made her mouth water and she grinned. She'd tell Tewichinel she needed some fresh raw venison for dinner.

AJKUN

Ajkun nodded to the guards outside Naʼomʼs hut. "You may leave us for the next few hours," she said. The guards smiled and promptly left the courtyard. Ajkun sighed. *The less people know, the better*, she thought. Then she tapped lightly on the doorframe and waited for a response.

Naʼom appeared in the doorway and held the blanket to one side to let Ajkun enter. "Atiʼt, I'm so glad you're here." She gave Ajkun a hug before offering her the one chair in the room.

Ajkun set the basket she carried on the floor. "How is he doing?" Ajkun said as she knelt next to Ekʼ Balam. She stroked him gently on his head and was pleased to hear him give a little purr.

"Better, which is why I brought him home. The shamans were ever so helpful, but after a week, I just needed to be alone with him. Nima Winaq thinks he'll be strong enough to travel by the time we have to leave for Chichén Itzá. But I'm going to request that he be carried on a litter much of the way, even though I know he won't like it. He has to conserve his strength for the battle, not expend it on the trip there."

"Quite right," Ajkun said as she took a seat. She waved to Naʼom to sit in the hammock, which she did. "And how are you doing, my dear? It's been quite a whirlwind of events from what little Chiman has told me."

"I don't even know where to begin," Na'om said. She hung her head and tears dripped down onto her hands in her lap. "I tried to find Tz', but I failed, and then we almost all drowned in that horrible storm. I was so grateful to Kärinik when she suggested we stay a few days longer and relax at the beach. It's such a beautiful spot, with the sky meeting the vast blue of the ocean so you can't tell where one stops and the other begins. And the warm sand on my feet and the *shush, shush, shush* of the waves as they rushed into shore . . . I needed that time to walk and think about things, but now I wonder if by delaying our return, I put Ek' Balam in harm's way. And then he got so sick and I thought he'd die. Oh, Ati't, I just don't know about anything anymore!"

"Shh, child, it will be all right," Ajkun said as she moved to sit next to Na'om. She put her arm around her shoulder and gave her a hug. "Come now, we have a lot to discuss. So, pull yourself together," she said as she handed Na'om a clean cloth to wipe her eyes and nose. "Is there anything else you can remember from your time in the Underworld? Chiman says Nima Winaq told him you're with child."

Na'om shook her head. "No, I've been through all the moments in my mind numerous times. Once the were-jaguars attacked me, I lay down and curled up tight to protect myself, and then everything went black. I don't really remember anything more than that except the odd sensation of traveling upside down through the darkness. Yakal tells me I moaned a few times when he was carrying me back through the tunnels to the ladder at the base of the ceiba tree. I did find some blue corn kernels in my skirt pocket when I came to, which was odd. I gave them to the head shaman, Tatá, right away, but he never said what they might mean."

"The gods must have placed them on you, perhaps to create this child. If you are pregnant, it would explain your upset stomach, tiredness, and general feelings of insecurity. But first, we must determine if you truly are with child. I'll just do a quick exam and then we can go from there."

Na'om nodded and lay down and let Ajkun check her body.

"Well, some of the physical signs do point in this direction. The gods must have blessed you since I know you've never lain with a man." Ajkun sighed. She knew carrying a child while trying to fight Satal would take all of Na'om's strength.

"Your body is going through a tremendous change and using up vast amounts of energy to create this new life. We must make sure you eat well, and I've brought you some *ox* leaves to brew into a potent tea that will help make and the baby strong in the months ahead." She picked up the basket and pulled out a small canvas sack that she placed on the table. "Make sure to drink this morning and night and include a few spoons of honey since the leaves can be bitter."

She sat back down in the chair and leaned forward. "You'll only be partway through your pregnancy when we travel, so you must conserve your strength. Both you and Ek' Balam should be carried to Chichén Itzá. I'll make arrangements for this with Chiman and the other council members later today. And when we can finally return to the village, then you must rest and allow the baby to fill you." She smiled. "I know you feel overwhelmed right now, but when you hold your son in your arms for the first time, it will be so worth the effort."

Na'om smiled. "And you'll be there to deliver him, won't you?"

Ajkun's heart swelled with love for her granddaughter. "If the gods allow it, I'll gladly help you bring your child, my great-grandchild, into this world with these old and arthritic hands," she said as she held them up in the air. "And now, tell me about Box. I believe you've grown fond of him, and I know he has feelings for you. He's come by the hut every day to ask Chiman about you."

Na'om looked up. "He's like no man I've ever known. He's kind and caring and makes me laugh. He's dedicated to helping me in any way that he can. But I won't let myself think of him as anything more than a friend until I know Tz' is safe and Satal is dead."

"Do you want me to tell him to leave you alone?" Ajkun asked.

"No, no, Ati't, that's not what I mean. I just . . . I just need to concentrate on the tasks ahead of me. Once I know everyone is safe, then I need to see what Tz' wants, and then I can move forward."

"And what about what you want, my dear? Have you considered a relationship with Box is what your heart is moving toward?"

Ajkun could see lines of worry spread across Na'om's face.

"I honestly don't know what I want at this point. None of my dreams are coming true, I'm experiencing things I've never felt before . . . In all honesty, I'd like to go back to the beach and just live there for the next several months and not worry about anything except what way to cook fish for dinner!"

Ajkun laughed. "This place you describe sounds wonderful. I hope

I can see it myself one day. But for now, I'll work on keeping you and your child as healthy as can be." She poked about in the basket again. "I brought some calendula salve for Ek' Balam's wounds," she said as she placed a coconut shell on the table. "And I brought you some of those corn pastries that we had at the council meeting a few weeks ago. They'll be soothing to your stomach." She placed the small bundle wrapped in banana leaf next to the other items. Then she stood up and hugged Na'om again. "Come to me whenever you have a question, all right?"

"Maltiox, Ati't, I promise I'll come see you every day."

Ajkun petted Ek' Balam gently on the head before going to the doorway. "Rest now, my dear, and I'll be back late this afternoon with some food for both of you."

"Maltiox, Ati't, I love you," Na'om said as she lay down in the hammock.

"I love you too, sweet girl. Now close your eyes and try not to worry. The gods have a path for each of us to follow, and we must trust that they know what's best."

The overhead sun cast a strong glare in Ajkun's face when she stepped out from the thatching, and she quickly squinted, but she still sneezed three times in rapid succession. She was pleased to see the guards had already returned, but had respectfully maintained their distance from the doorway.

"I shall tell Nimal that you're both doing an excellent job," she said as she motioned for the men to take their places by the door.

"Maltiox, Lady Ajkun," the men replied.

There's still so much to be done to prepare for this battle, Ajkun mused as she meandered toward her hut. *And then there's the long trek to Chichén Itzá. Satal will certainly have people watching out for the army and will know long in advance how many of us are coming and what day we'll arrive. She'll hold all the advantages in the palm of her hand unless we think of some way to surprise her.* She stopped to watch a group of children at play. The oldest child put his hands over his eyes and began to count out loud, while the younger children scurried in multiple directions, looking for someplace to hide. Ajkun laughed when she saw two young boys attempting to hide behind the same small bush. *Why, they're hiding in plain sight.* Yet the boy who had counted didn't even look in their direction as he raced around the area searching for his playmates.

"That's it!" Ajkun exclaimed aloud. She hurried down the alleyways to the hut she shared with Chiman and was happy to see him sitting near the fire when she entered the small yard.

"You look particularly happy, my dear," Chiman said as he stood and gave Ajkun a kiss on the forehead. "Everything is well with Na'om?"

"Yes, yes, she's fine, she's pregnant by the grace of the gods, but she's young and strong and should be able to travel. I do think both she and Ek' Balam should make the journey by litter so they are well rested when we arrive at the outskirts of Chichén Itzá."

"Hmm, not a bad idea, I'll suggest it to Nimal and have him make the arrangements."

Ajkun sat down on the empty stool next to Chiman and leaned forward. "I've been wondering . . . I'm no expert in the art of war, but if we all just march straight to the city, won't Satal know exactly how many men we have and how best to fight the army?"

"Well, yes, that's the way it is, I'm afraid," Chiman admitted.

"What if we did something a bit different that would throw her off her guard?" Ajkun was too excited to sit and began to pace back and forth. "What if Nimal sent small groups of warriors out every few days starting today to the north, south, and east of that city? They could disguise themselves as laborers and carry their weapons and leather armor in their pack baskets and stay with the families near the city who are loyal to our cause. The men would be well rested if they left now. Then when we arrive from the west, Satal will think our army small and easily defeated, not realizing we have men who can surge in from the other directions."

Chiman reached up and grabbed Ajkun's hand, forcing her to stop walking. "When did you become such a strategist, my love?" he asked as he stood and held her tightly to him. He stepped back a pace and looked at Ajkun. "That is probably the most brilliant idea I've ever heard."

Ajkun felt her face flush with pride. "The idea just came to me, and of course it's up to you and Bitol and Nimal to figure out the logistics of it all."

"I'm leaving right now to go talk to them. With men in place long before the Wayeb starts, Satal won't know which direction to defend. When Nimal and Bitol agree to the idea, we'll call a council meeting and tell the others."

Ajkun smiled and waved Chiman off. She was pleased that Chiman had agreed with her, and her love for him flowed through her body, making her hands tingle. She glanced down and saw they were glowing with a reddish light. *Just like when I prayed to Lord Chac*, she thought. In her mind, Ajkun pictured walking the paths in Pa nimá, working with her herbs and salves, and the children playing in the stream, and she laughed when she saw the light blossom and spread to the rest of her body. *When I think of those I love, the things I love to do, and home, the light grows. This must be how Na'om does it as well.* Then she sat down abruptly, overcome with fatigue. Working with the light had drained her of her energy. And she suddenly understood how much effort it would take for Na'om to defeat Satal. Now her biggest concern was Na'om. *I must do whatever it takes during the battle to make sure Na'om remains healthy and safe so my great-grandchild can be born in Pa nimá.*

NA'OM

N a'om woke with a start when she heard a quick *rap, rap, rap* on the wall outside.

"Na'om, are you there?" Box said. "Your grandmother has called a council meeting and sent me to escort you."

Na'om yawned and got up from the hammock. "Yes, just give me a minute and I'll be right there." She hurried around in the semi-darkness, brushing her hair and patting her cheeks to redden them. She knew without glancing into the large piece of pyrite on the nearby table that she looked pale and tired, and she didn't want Box to worry about her.

She stooped to check on Ek' Balam who was still fast asleep. "Rest, boy, I'll be back as soon as I can," she said as she gave the jaguar a kiss on the cheek.

"Hello, sorry to wake you, but Ajkun said it was important," Box said as he led the way into the alleyway.

Three guards waiting outside the small fence around Na'om's hut fell into place around the couple, their lit torches making a splash of brightness in the dusky night. The group quickly made their way through the almost deserted streets to the Temple of the Warriors.

Inside, more torches in brackets high on the walls lit the hallway to the inner council room where Na'om saw everyone had gathered.

"Na'om, good, you're here," Chiman said as he held out a chair for her to sit.

"What's going on, Mam?" she asked. "Is everything all right?"

"Yes, yes, quite all right. Ajkun has come up with an idea that I think will be quite helpful in the battle ahead. But I should let her explain." Chiman turned and smiled at Ajkun.

Ajkun stood up and dipped her head to acknowledge Nimal and Bitol, then turned to Na'om. "I've already discussed this with some of the others and they agree it's a good idea. We'll be sending many of our warriors toward Chichén Itzá now where they'll remain in hiding until the time of the attack. Then when we arrive with a small contingent of warriors, Satal will think she has an easy victory ahead of her."

"Only to be ambushed when our men come out of hiding," Na'om finished, and she grinned. "What a good idea." Then she turned to Chiman. "I also have a thought that might work. The shamans say we must attack during the Wayeb, but they didn't say which day of the Wayeb. Satal will undoubtedly be expecting us on the first day and will have all her allies at the ready. But what if we wait until the final day to attack? By then, the gods will have surely grown tired of waiting and abandoned Satal, giving us yet another advantage in this battle."

Chiman turned to Nimal and Bitol. "Well, could it work?"

"The men will be far more eager to battle their enemies when the portal to Xibalba is about to close rather than just opening," Nimal said. "We just have to time our arrival so we reach the outskirts of the city at daybreak of the last day, but that won't be difficult to calculate."

"Satal will be at her most vulnerable at that point," Yakal said. "Her anger and frustration will make her act in haste; all we need is one chance to strike and we should be able to defeat her."

"Good, then I'll leave you men to make the arrangements," Na'om said as she stood up. She looked at Box. "I think I'm actually hungry; do you mind going with me to the market for some food?"

Box grinned. "Of course, it would be my pleasure."

The two left with their guards and headed to the almost empty marketplace. A few food vendors still remained open, however, and Na'om settled on a small bowl of turkey soup while Box chose a thick piece of fried venison with chaya. After she'd eaten, Na'om purchased some fresh fish for Ek' Balam and once they were back at her hut, she thanked Box before slipping quickly inside.

Ek' Balam happily ate the fish and drank a large bowl of water, which made Na'om happy. "You're getting your strength back, eh, boy?" she said as she rubbed him behind his ears.

She knew without Ek' Balam she'd have no chance against Satal and whatever army she might be amassing. *I suppose that could mean Tz' if he's still in the form of a were-jaguar*, she thought as she got ready for bed.

The next few weeks passed in a quick blur of activities. Na'om continued to meet with Najtir, who helped her finetune her ability to disguise her thoughts. She refined her concentration and control of her energy, sending it where and when she wanted. Najtir also insisted she eat as many salted crab cakes as she could tolerate, telling her the crabmeat was good for the baby and the salt would help protect them both against any evil Satal might throw their way. Their daily walk to the market was a nice interlude in each hectic day, and Na'om enjoyed visiting with Mok'onel on the days she was helping T'ot at the stand.

At the now daily council meetings, Nimal and Bitol reported on the number of men who had left that day on their march to the villages surrounding Chichén Itzá and gave reports on the amount of salt that had been harvested and sent with the men.

In the evenings, Na'om and Box often went for a meal at the marketplace and Na'om was grateful that Ajkun and Chiman did nothing to stop her from enjoying this time with him.

It was only when she was alone in her hut at night that Na'om fretted about the upcoming battle. As each day passed, her anxiety grew, making it more and more difficult to sleep. She finally asked Ajkun for some herbs to help her relax and drank a mug each night before lying down. As she waited for sleep to arrive, she tried to envision any number of scenarios that might occur once they arrived in Chichén Itzá, but she knew that when dealing with Satal, almost anything was possible, including things she could never imagine. *We just have to wait and see when we get there*, she thought as she stroked Ek' Balam's head.

And then the day finally arrived when they needed to leave. Na'om packed a small basket of personal belongings. Since she was going to be carried, she didn't want to burden the bearers with too much weight.

She had also insisted that Chiman, Ajkun, Alom, Kärinik, and Noy be carried as well. She didn't want them too tired. At first, they had protested, but then they finally acquiesced to Na'om's demands. Lintat refused to be carried with Noy, though, insisting he was a young, healthy boy who could easily walk twice as far. Yakal, Box, and Biribik agreed to march alongside the litters to help protect Na'om and the others while Nimal and Bitol remained with the two hundred warriors who would accompany them on the journey.

The large group congregated at the Temple of the Warriors and began the march to the main gates of Mayapán. Women, children, and the elderly lined the sides of the large boulevard, shouting and waving to the warriors as they passed in rows of ten abreast. Each man was dressed in a leather breastplate and loincloth, with leather wrappings that extended from his wrists to his elbows and his ankles to his knees. Every man had an obsidian knife and wooden shield; some carried long wooden staves with obsidian points, while others had bows and quivers of arrows carefully fletched by Xik' and the other master fletchers of the city. Behind them came the slaves burdened with large pack baskets full of food, bedding, and the other items needed to feed and house an army on the march for the next several days.

Na'om, Ek' Balam, and the others walked at a respectable distance from the slaves. The crowds grew silent as Na'om passed, and many dropped to their knees. Na'om could hear their fervent prayers as she passed. When the warriors and slaves had passed through the main gates. Najtir halted the procession so he could perform a brief blessing.

Braziers of copal burned on the ground near his feet, and he carefully picked one up and walked around each of them, covering them in the thick smoke. Then he sprinkled grains of salt into each person's hair before offering them a sip of a bitter tea made from the leaves of the *dzudzuc* shrub, which would help protect them from Satal's evilness. He stopped in front of Na'om and pulled a necklace of obsidian beads out of the pouch at his waist. He carefully put it on her.

"This will also help protect you from any sorcery Satal might use," Najtir said. "Don't take it off until you know she's dead. Only then should you remove it and have it buried with her so as to keep her witchery with her body."

"Maltiox, Najtir, I won't take it off until I know it's safe to do so." Na'om glanced to her side and saw the men waiting with the litters. Four of the runners were Jumumik, Jututik, Be Anim, and Tik Anim, the cousin twins who had helped her before. She smiled at the men and was happy to see they would be the ones to carry her and Ek' Balam.

"We shall go like the wind, Lady Na'om," Be Anim said as he helped her settle onto the low stool tied to the wooden platform. "Tell us when you wish to stop and rest; we will do as you command."

"Maltiox," Na'om said as she readjusted her position. Her stomach was queasy, but she refused to get sick in front of so many watchful eyes. She glanced at Ajkun, who looked very nervous. "Hold on tight to the stool, Ati't. It helps you find your balance. All right, let's be on our way."

Najtir bowed and moved aside while the great gates swung open. "May the gods bring you safely home, all of you," he shouted as the group quickly streamed through the opening and onto the wide sacbe in front of the city.

May the gods be on our side, Na'om prayed as she took one last look at the city that she'd called home for these past several moons. *May the gods be on our side.*

SATAL

Satal blew out the flame of the candle in front of her as the first rays of the sun inched across the tile floor of the main room of her abode. She had spent the previous hour summoning her favorite creatures of the dark, and she was ready for the day to really begin. She tapped her index finger impatiently on the leather tabletop in front of her, waiting for her shamans to arrive.

Happy name day, Satal, Sachoj whispered. *The portal to the Wayeb is opening, and you will be victorious come sundown.*

Maltiox, may the blessings of the gods be with us today, Satal replied.

The gods of Xibalba, you mean, Sachoj corrected.

Hmm, yes, I suppose we can't ask all the gods to be supportive of us in our endeavors, at least for today. Satal tilted her head as she heard footsteps approaching the front door, followed by a tentative knock.

"Come in, come in," she urged as she stood up and smoothed her skirt with one hand.

One by one, her entourage of shamans, led by Tewichinel, entered the room. All the men were dressed in their ceremonial best: deep red linen shirts and matching linen pants, leather vest plates embossed with the emblem of the city's pyramid, and leather arm and calf bands that extended from wrist to elbow and ankle to knee. A thick leather cord wound around each man's waist, holding the scabbard for his long obsidian blade. And each one carried a headdress made of layers of scarlet macaw and green quetzal feathers in one hand and a sharp, obsidian-tipped wooden spear in the other.

Satal nodded to them as they gathered. "Today, we engage in the biggest battle of our lives," she said. "There is no room for error; our warriors must defeat our mortal enemies, and we must capture the girl, Na'om. Then I shall sacrifice her to the gods and rid our world of her presence."

The men remained silent. "Are there any questions?" The shamans said nothing. "I've already called upon some of our allies to join us, so let's begin." The men hastily moved toward the door, and once outside, they formed a protective unit around Satal. But she could see little in front of her as the men's headdresses blocked her view, so she elbowed the men aside and strode in the lead. Tewichinel took his place a respectable two feet behind her and motioned for the other shamans to do the same. As the group moved quickly through the deserted streets toward the central plaza, they could hear the shouts of the warriors as they took up their positions on the outskirts of the city. Underneath was another layer of sound, the rustling and shuffling of the thousands of creatures Satal had invoked to join them.

Shrieks and hoots from howler and black spider monkeys greeted Satal as she stepped onto the packed dirt of the grand plaza in front of the pyramid. She waved her hand in acknowledgment and turned to look at the ground around her. It undulated with the thousands of scorpions, centipedes, and snakes of all sorts she had called forth. The men behind her gasped at the sight, and she turned to them. "Come, they won't harm you. Look," she said, and she took several steps forward. The creatures parted and remained so, letting the shamans walk forward without harm.

The group headed to the steps of the pyramid, and with Tewichinel's help, Satal slowly ascended the steep stairs to the pyramid's second level where she had a good view of the area in front of her. *Now we wait*, she thought. She smiled as she imagined her hardened warriors engaging in battle with the army from Mayapán. *The ground shall run red with blood by nightfall.* She could almost hear the *clash* and *crack* of obsidian knives against wooden shields and the *shush* of arrows and the *whoosh* of rocks expelled from slingshots. With her army surrounding the city, she had little to fear. If anything, she worried Na'om wouldn't be able to make it into the city center and she snapped her fingers toward one of the guards.

"Make sure Kämisanel knows to let Na'om through the ranks. I must have her come to me here in order to sacrifice her." The guard nodded and took off at a run.

Suddenly, there was a loud crack of thunder and Ah-Pekku appeared high in the sky, followed by Camazotz, who swooped down to the pyramid.

"Lady Satal, happy name day," Camazotz said as he flapped his wings slowly and drifted up and down.

"Maltiox, my lord," Satal replied. "Will your relatives be joining us?"

"Of course, they wouldn't miss this chance to feast at will. And they thank you for the tasty morsel you provided the other day too."

"A small token of my gratitude for all that you've done. And I needed an appropriate way to rid myself of the traitor Pataninel." Satal squinted into the brightening sky and could see clouds of bats flying from the east. "I see your clan is approaching. They're welcome to join us or go in search of prey."

"Maltiox, my lady, I think our contribution to this battle will be the greatest if we stay here by your side."

Satal smiled and bowed low to the bat god. She had hoped he'd stay, but she also knew that each god was fickle and could not be pushed into doing something he didn't want to do.

With several more cracks of thunder, Yum Cimil and Poxlam arrived. The god of death emitted a sweet, sickly scent, and Satal was glad when he moved downwind. Buluc-Chabtan appeared next, his hands filled with pointed skewers, and Ahalgan, whose skeletal body reeked of pus. Then Hun-Batz popped into view, which set all the monkeys to shrieking and howling with such intensity that Satal had to clamp her hands over her ears. "My Lord Hun-Batz, I beg you," she cried, "bring them to order before we all go deaf."

The great lord waved his hairy arms, and the multitude of creatures quieted down, but they continued to race and jump about on the plaza with excitement.

Ahalpuh and Ah-Cun-Can arrived together and the snakes and serpents hissed and writhed in honor of their lord.

Satal smiled at the gods who hovered in the air around her. "My lords,

I thank you for coming on this wondrous day when the Wayeb stands open and evil is allowed to spill across the land. My mortal army will defeat our enemies, but your assistance is greatly appreciated. We shall remain here, awaiting the girl, Na'om, who is our biggest threat. Once she's defeated, I promise you, the Wayeb shall not be the only time when you'll be allowed to roam the land. Every day shall be open to you!"

The gods nodded and smiled as they bobbed up and down and moved about. Satal could see they were ready to engage in battle, so she bowed low to them.

"My lords, each of you has a special gift. Please, feel free to use it as you wish on our enemies near and far."

In a flash of bright light, most of the gods disappeared, leaving only Camazotz, Ah-Cun-Can, and Hun-Batz behind.

"I am honored to have your presence, my lords," Satal said as she bowed again to the three figures. "When the time is right, I will shapeshift and join you in the final destruction of Na'om and her group."

Suddenly, the sky turned an eerie dark green as Tlacolotl made his appearance. In the gloom created by the god of darkness, Satal continued to listen for the sounds of battle, but there was nothing, which surprised her. With the sun halfway to its zenith, she had expected to hear the cries and screams of men at war. She turned to watch the insects milling around on the plaza below her, presuming they'd make a concentrated push toward Na'om when she arrived, but the creatures continued to wander about without purpose.

An hour passed and then another and Satal's impatience and frustration continued to build. She wanted to sit down, but she hadn't thought she'd need to. Thankfully Tewichinel appeared with a small stool and placed it on the wide step that she stood upon.

"Where are they?" she demanded as she sat down.

"I've sent some guards to find Kämisanel, my lady, who should know how far away the army is. We should have an answer at any moment." Tewichinel bowed and respectfully moved back down the stairs.

"Shall I go and have a look, Lady Satal?" Camazotz asked as he swooped down to stand next to Satal.

"If it pleases my lord, yes, that would be most helpful," Satal said. She could feel her frustration mounting and bit her tongue so as not to say something that would annoy the god.

In a swirl of bats, Camazotz took off into the sky, and Satal watched as he became a small black speck in the deep gloom. His leaving acted as a signal for the others, and Hun-Batz, Ah-Cun-Can, and Tlacolotl also left. As soon as the god of darkness disappeared, the bright sun shone through, and Satal felt the day's heat press down on her. Within minutes, she was sweaty and tired. She was ready to get the battle and the day over with.

Camazotz quickly returned. "My lady, there is no army within a day's march of the city. I'm afraid your battle will have to wait."

And before Satal could reply, the bat god disappeared, and the multitude of bats still in the air quickly followed. Satal scanned the plaza and saw her lead shaman arriving at a jog.

"Tewichinel," Satal shouted. "What do the guards say?"

"Kämisanel reports . . . there are no signs of the enemy . . . anywhere near the city, my lady," Tewichinel said as he drew in deep breaths and bowed. "I'm afraid Lord Camazotz is correct . . . we must wait until they arrive before we can fight them."

Satal stood up, grabbed the stool, and flung it as hard as she could. It sailed through the air and landed with a crash several steps below her, breaking into several pieces. "Get me back to my palace this instant," she cried as she held out her arms for support. The last thing she needed was to fall down the steep stairs in front of her shamans. Tewichinel snapped his fingers and Ch'o ran up the stairs and helped him get Satal back down on the ground.

"I want hourly reports from the guards. The first man to see the army approaching shall receive five cacao beans," Satal said as she marched out of the central plaza.

Once in the cool interior of her palace, Satal stripped off her outer clothes and wandered about in her undergarments until she felt the sweat dry on her body. She sank into one of the leather chairs at the large table and drank the cool papaya juice that Tewichinel had left for her.

"Where is she?" she cried and her voice echoed throughout the large room. "The shamans said the attack would be during the Wayeb!"

Ah, but they didn't say which day of the Wayeb, did they? Sachoj hissed.

"Shush, old woman, I have no need of your wit today," Satal shouted, and she threw her empty mug against the wall where it smashed into multiple pottery shards.

Perhaps you'll have better luck tomorrow, Sachoj replied and quickly disappeared.

Tewichinel faithfully appeared each hour with the latest news, but no one had seen any signs of the enemy army.

"Send our fastest runners farther into the countryside. They have to be somewhere," Satal told the shaman.

By nightfall, there had been no change in the news. Satal offered the gods of Xibalba a blood offering and regretfully sent the centipedes, scorpions, snakes, and monkeys she had summoned back to their homes. Then, she went to bed, but she barely slept. Her anger was a heated poker inside her, making her stomach painful regardless of which way she tried to lie.

In the morning, she dressed hurriedly so as to be ready for Tewichinel when he arrived with the news she longed to hear. However, each hour passed and each report remained the same, and Satal's fury grew until she felt she could no longer contain the heat inside her. She repeatedly sipped cool coconut water to quench some of her fever as it threatened to burn her from the inside out. And when she went to bed that night, she was still waiting for a sighting.

On the third day of the Wayeb, Tewichinel continued to deliver the same news. Unable to sit still, Satal paced up and down the corridors in her palace. Eventually she grew tired of this and walked to the city's outskirts, looking for any sign of the gods of Xibalba, but it appeared they had all gone their separate ways. When Satal drew near the army, she could see many of the men lolling about, joking and laughing, which incensed Satal even more. She snapped her fingers and ordered Tewichinel to have some of the most disloyal men sacrificed at once to the gods.

"Perhaps some fresh blood will entice them to return to me when I call on them again," she said as she watched the nearest guards grab their own kind and haul them off in the direction of the large cenote on the other side of the city.

By day four of the Wayeb, Satal was despondent and ready to sacrifice most of her shamans who had failed to give her the proper timing of the attack. But Tewichinel wisely counseled Satal to hold steady. He was convinced Na'om and her army would arrive before the Wayeb closed. Late in the day, he appeared with a scroll in hand.

"My lady, Kämisanel says his runners have returned. Na'om, the black jaguar, and many others approach by litter, with an army of about two hundred men in the lead."

"We shall be more than ready to handle that small an army. And where are they?"

Tewichinel consulted the scroll in his hand. "They are within striking distance."

"Which means the battle will be tomorrow," Satal replied. "I shall summon my allies again and be ready to attack the moment they enter the city."

"It will be a glorious victory, Lady Satal, one well worth the wait," Tewichinel said as he bowed low. "Rest easily now and soon Na'om shall be defeated."

Tz'

Early in the morning, after a particularly large meal, Tz' began to slip into sleep, but he felt an increasing pressure in his chest. Something was pulling on him, wrapping itself ever more tightly around his torso, and he scratched at his belly, trying to loosen whatever was squeezing him. His ribs hurt, he had trouble breathing, and he scrabbled more frantically to undo the band that was crushing him. The sensation grew stronger, tighter; he couldn't breathe, and Tz' clawed at his gut, thrashing back and forth on the dirt floor of the cave, frantic to loosen whatever had hold of him. He opened his eyes, searching for Xojol, but she was across the cave with the other females and oblivious to what was happening.

Then, suddenly, Bajbik roared, his voice echoing throughout the cave. Tz' struggled, wincing with pain, and finally sat up to watch Bajbik. This was the first time since Tz' had defeated him that he'd really made his presence known. The old were-jaguar limped back and forth in a tight loop in front of a dark passageway leading from the cave. He swished his tail rapidly from side to side, and the mangy fur on his back from his hunched shoulders to his bony hips bristled upward. Tz' shivered. Despite Bajbik's obvious age, he was still a formidable creature. Grumbling in response to Bajbik's repeated growls, the other were-jaguars scrambled to form a group in the middle of the cave. *The old cat still has power over the others,* he thought. *I should let them know I'm the one in charge.* But Tz' didn't move except to swipe at the strange tightness wrapped around his belly.

Bajbik roared again, and the sound vibrated in the air, echoes overlapping echoes. Tz's body quivered in response. The others bunched together more rapidly, and suddenly, Tz' questioned whether he was still the leader of the group. Most of the were-jaguars had ignored him since the incident with the intruder, and at that moment, Tz' didn't dare push Bajbik to find out who was really in charge. Instead, he tilted his head, trying to understand what was happening. Sensing some kind of danger, he leapt over a ribcage, landed softly on the well-packed dirt, and hurried to stand near Xojol. He desperately wanted to ask her what was going on, but he was afraid one of the others might hear his thoughts. As if she knew he had questions, Xojol threw a glance in his direction, nodded her head, and moved backward a pace so they were closer together.

Tz' watched as Bajbik turned abruptly and began to run down the dark tunnel, with the other were-jaguars following just behind him.

Xojol waited, letting a short distance build, then turned to Tz'. *We've been summoned to the surface. Come on, we must go,* she cried. She loped after the others.

Tz' stood still, shaking his head from side to side. *I don't understand,* Tz' shouted as Xojol disappeared from view. He looked around the cave, wondering what to do. Then he felt that same strange tightness on his body, pulling him forward, and he too began to run.

It took several minutes before he caught up with Xojol. *It's not the full moon,* he thought as he steadied his pace to match hers.

No, it's the last day of the Wayeb, and she has ordered us to appear.

Tz' stopped as vague memories flitted through his mind. *Who?*

She who controls us. We must hurry and obey her commands, Xojol replied before loping after the rest of the group.

Tz' watched her disappear into the dark and wondered why he felt so nervous. He knew he should know who Xojol was talking about, but he couldn't remember the woman's name. He arched his back, his fur fluffed away from his body, and he growled at the emptiness to release the tension building in his body. Then he sprinted down the long tunnel, anxious to reach the others.

As he ran, the tunnel grew lighter and lighter, until Tz' could see the opening to the surface and the sun rising in the east. Tz' stopped, fearful of venturing out into the light. He didn't know what would happen if the sunlight touched him. He looked around for any of the others, but they were all gone. He closed his eyes, praying he wouldn't burst into flames, and stepped into the open. When he didn't, he lifted his head to the sky, feeling the sun's first heat warming his skin. It was strangely soothing and refreshing, and Tz' suddenly remembered he had stood with his face to the sun before. Snippets of a different life flitted through his mind. He was a young boy, standing in a river of cool water with his face turned to the sky. Nearby a young girl splashed about, and on the riverbank, a large black jaguar lay in the shade of a mahogany tree. *Na'om and Ek' Balam.* The names popped into his mind, and more images and memories flooded his thoughts. Then a wave of despair crashed over him as he remembered bits and pieces of his recent encounter in the tunnel with the girl, the girl he realized had been Na'om. He knew then that he could have left the Underworld and been with her all this time. *If only I hadn't been such a fool,* he howled. He lifted his head and closed his eyes, praying to Itzamná for guidance.

The brilliant sun drove away more of the darkness and confusion that had cloaked him during his stay with the were-jaguars. He'd been a man in the not-too-distant past. He lifted his front paw and imagined it was an arm. He lifted his hind paw and could envision it as his leg. He needed to shapeshift back into his human form while he was above ground. He knew there was a way to do it, but before he could focus on how, he was yanked back into the moment by the strange tugging on his animal body.

He lowered his head and opened his eyes, then set off running, following the acrid scent of the were-jaguars until he reached the edge of a large plaza, near a four-sided pyramid far bigger than any he'd ever seen. Troops of spider monkeys and black monkeys chattered and screeched as they jostled and pushed for space on the upper levels of the multiple sets of stairs and white limestone walls of the pyramid. Tz' felt saliva pool in his mouth at the sight of so much fresh food, but he resisted the urge to snatch a monkey off the pyramid. The ground nearby swarmed with thousands of centipedes and scorpions scrabbling over one another in a writhing, twisting river of poisonous barbs and tails while hundreds of bats swooped in vast clouds high overhead.

A bonfire burned in the center of the plaza, and dozens of men, clad in loincloths and leather vests, swayed in unison in front of the flames to the rhythm a dozen drummers beat on waist-high drums. The warriors thrust their spears high into the sky, waved their shields, and stomped their feet as the tempo increased.

Finally, Tz' saw the were-jaguars grouped together on the far side of the plaza, and he made a wide circle around the encroaching river of insects to join them. *What's happening?* he asked Xojol.

But she didn't answer. Bits of frothy saliva pooled in the corners of her mouth, and he stared into her eyes, hoping to connect with her. But at that moment, Xojol was pure were-jaguar, intent only on killing.

Suddenly, a flash of lightning streaked across the sky, followed by a loud crack of thunder that vibrated in Tz's chest. The pack of were-jaguars took off running, loping easily in quick leaps and bounds across the plaza as they followed their old leader. Tz' felt the tightness in his chest, pulling at him to pursue the others, and he almost took off. But he resisted the wrenching sensation. The daylight had given him momentary clarity on who he really was, a human, not an animal of the Underworld. He wouldn't respond like the others. He dug his claws into the packed dirt under his feet, splaying his toes out on each foot to get a firmer grip. He scrabbled and clung to the soil, fighting against the base instinct to obey. But the pressure to conform was too strong; he was still a were-jaguar, and he had to let go. He ran low and fast across the open ground until he caught up with the pack. They wove their way through the city streets, past large temple buildings, the open-air market with its provocative smells of meat, and into the districts full of huts where the citizens of the city had barred their doors against the evils of the Wayeb.

In a small section of his brain, Tz' remembered yet again that he had been human, and he dug his claws into the ground once more, coming to a screeching halt. *What's happening, why can't I fight this urge?* he howled. As he moved his head, he caught sight of his shadow cast onto a limestone wall. Outwardly, he was a were-jaguar. And he feared he had been with the creatures so long that he was one on the inside as well. He forced himself to concentrate on the one name that mattered, *Na'om*. Then the tugging on his chest began again, and he mindlessly complied, heeding the summons.

He sucked in great mouthfuls of air heavy with a thick, viscous energy that filled his bones, making him want to rip and tear at anyone who defied him. He ran and ran, following the scent of the others and eventually caught up with them once more. The pack turned a corner onto another avenue, and he saw a group of shamans dressed in deep red clothing, wearing quetzal and macaw feather headdresses. They surrounded an old woman. It was she, the one who commanded them.

And at once, Tz' remembered her name. *Satal!* In a flash, he remembered who she was and what she'd done. *You had me thrown into the cenote and made me what I am today.* Anger coursed through Tz' body, and he leaped forward, ready to rip Satal to pieces.

Satal glanced in his direction and quickly lifted her hand, stopping Tz' in mid-leap. He fell to the ground, landing awkwardly on his left hind leg. He whimpered slightly as he put weight on it, but growls from several of the were-jaguars around him silenced him.

"You've been summoned to fight for me," Satal said to the pack of were-jaguars.

Several of the group slunk closer to the shamans, who quickly turned their spears at an angle so the sharp obsidian barbs at the ends of the wooden shafts pointed directly at their throats. The were-jaguars stopped in mid-stride and hissed and spat at the shamans, who continued to thrust their spears at the cats, forcing them to step backward a pace or two.

"You shall prowl the streets on the outskirts of the city until we know the enemy is within the city limits. Then you'll push them toward the central plaza where we shall all be waiting to engage them." Satal waved her hand. "Go now and make haste, for we need to win this battle today while the Wayeb still stands open."

Snarls and growls filled the air, and the pack took off running again. But Tz' remained where he stood, watching Satal, who had turned back to her shamans. He took a step closer and then another, until he was within leaping distance of her. He got ready to spring when Satal abruptly turned around and faced him.

"Still here, I see," Satal said. "My dear grandson, surely you don't mean to attack me? Why, I believe you've done everything you set out to achieve. You've obviously learned to shapeshift and have transformed into the very creature you longed to become. You even became leader of the pack, at least for a while. What else could you want?"

My freedom from all of this, Tz' snarled. *This creature is not who I really am.*

"Oh, but it is, especially now that you've grown so close to Xojol."

Tz' felt his body flush with heat. He had no idea how Satal knew about Xojol. He felt a shiver go through him as he heard her laugh.

"Do you really think that creature was able to communicate with you all on her own?"

Tz's jaw dropped open, and his tongue lolled to one side. He couldn't believe what he was hearing.

She laughed again. "Clearly you did from the look on your face. No, I'm afraid your sweet Xojol is just a were-jaguar, a creature of Xibalba, destined to live in darkness except for the one night of the full moon. I was the one who made it so she could talk to you." Satal laughed again. "Your real destiny was to be with Na'om, to have a child with her, joining your innate powers with hers, but I've managed to thwart the gods and their plans. Na'om will soon be in my hands, and I'll take her strength and add it to my own, making me the most powerful among the living and an equal among the gods."

Tz' tensed his whole body. He would kill this old woman or die trying.

Satal raised her hand and Tz' felt as if a huge weight had landed on his back. He fell to the ground under the pressure until his belly was firm against the dirt.

"Ha, you'll do no such thing. You are a creature of Xibalba now and under my command. Go and join the others. Hunt down the one woman you once loved and bring her to me. I want you near me when I kill her." Satal dismissed Tz' with a flick of her hand.

And before he could verbally respond, his body reacted, forcing him to flee the area at a run. Nose to the ground, he searched for a trace scent of the others and finally picked up Xojol's body odor from among the thousands of smells that permeated the packed dirt streets. He followed the trail until he found the were-jaguars at the base of a raised temple on the edge of the city. Bajbik lay on the lowest step, his head down on his front paws. He looked exhausted, and the other cats paced back and forth, waiting for something to happen. Tz' approached, but didn't draw too close. He needed to think before he acted.

I must help Na'om; it's the only way she'll be able to defeat Satal. He looked again at the old leader and wondered if Bajbik would challenge him if he tried to take control of the pack. *If I can lead them away from the city, then Na'om will be safe from them at least. I must convince Xojol to follow me. Only with her support will I regain control of the whole pack.*

The younger males looked at Tz' as he approached and they hissed at him, but he ignored them and walked over to Xojol. *Xojol, will you help me?* There was no answer from the female. *Xojol?* Again, no reassuring voice answered him. That's when Tz' realized just how cleverly Satal had manipulated him so she could gain access to the one thing she desired most, Na'om's power.

Tz' knew in that instant he had to resist every urge that made him more animal-like. He had to fight to keep what shreds of humanness remained and knew that if he returned to the Underworld, he'd once again forget he'd ever been human. By the time the next full moon arrived, and he could reemerge at the surface, it might be too late to ever change back. *Somehow, I must lure the others away and still reach out to Na'om and warn her about Satal.*

He turned from Xojol and growled at the whole group, forcing them to turn toward him. *Are you going to just wait until Bajbik can stand or will you follow your true leader? I know the smell of the woman we seek. I shall find her and take her to Satal.* Tz' snarled and yapped, praying the pack understood him, and then he set off at a slow lope down the nearest street. He twisted his head back and forth in the air as he ran, searching for the slightest trace of Na'om's scent. He wanted to move in the opposite direction from where she might be until he'd successfully lured the pack a safe distance away. Then he'd return and warn Na'om. He reached the end of the block and had to decide between going left or right; he chose right and turned his head just far enough to see the other were-jaguars had finally decided to leave Bajbik and were indeed following him. He yipped at them to move faster and started to lope again. Within minutes, he caught a whiff of the sweet-spicy aroma that was uniquely Na'om. The scent was pure enticement, and he couldn't stop himself from bounding rapidly through the streets, heading directly toward the tantalizing smell, with the rest of the were-jaguars not far behind.

After several minutes, with his chest heaving from his endeavors, he rounded a corner and found himself back at the edge of the great plaza. The large four-tiered pyramid now stood at the far end of the open square, and he could see Satal and her shamans gathering at its base. The smell of Na'om filled his mind; it was so alluring that drool pooled in his mouth and he swallowed rapidly. She was close, so close, and his immediate desire was to find her and attack. *No, that's not right.* He struggled to remember. *Satal, I must warn her about Satal,* he muttered. He took a deep breath in and out, forcing himself to concentrate. But then the rest of the were-jaguars appeared, and before Tz' could block them, the whole group surged forward, snarling and hissing, pushing him to one side as they raced ahead into the great plaza.

SATAL

After her encounter with the were-jaguars, Satal continued to the great square. She was pleased to see the creatures she'd summoned had returned. She waved her hand and opened a clear path through the snakes, scorpions, and centipedes to the pyramid. A group of warriors continued to dance around the large bonfire near the base of the stone structure, but when they saw her, they immediately stopped and took up positions on all four sides of the pyramid. The stone table she'd instructed her shamans to erect was placed near the bonfire. *A perfect spot to perform the sacrifices today*, she thought. Tewichinel and the other shamans circled the platform, and Satal stood with them for a few minutes, but she quickly realized she couldn't see the plaza. So, she snapped her fingers and Tewichinel and K'oy helped her up the steep stairs of the pyramid. She took a stance on the second level where she had a clear view of the area. Her nerves tingled with excitement, and she longed for the moment when Na'om's blood would drip onto the sacrificial table.

Once the sun had crested the nearby trees, Camazotz, Hun-Batz, and Ah-Cun-Can appeared within minutes of each other.

Satal nodded to them all. "Will any of the other gods be arriving today?" she asked Camazotz.

"I fear our brothers have lost interest in this particular skirmish, Lady Satal," the bat god replied. "But the three of us should be more than enough help."

Satal nodded. If the rumors were true and Na'om only had an army of two hundred men, then she had nothing to fear. The girl would be dead before nightfall, and she'd quickly become the ruler of the entire region. Then she looked down at her shamans and snapped her fingers to summon Tewichinel. "Have your brothers ready to shapeshift if the need arises," she commanded.

"Of course, my lady," he replied. "I have the jequirity beans for them in this pouch," he said as he patted the bag dangling at his side. He returned to his position among his fellow shamans.

Satal smiled as the first sounds of battle drifted to her ears. *And now it begins.* Then she pulled out her own jequirity bean from the pocket in her skirt and held it between two fingers. The urge to shapeshift was great and she almost bit into the bean, but she forced herself to stop. *I must conserve my energy until Na'om has appeared,* she reminded herself.

She scanned the great plaza and chortled when she saw the pack of were-jaguars at the opposite end. *My grandson is a bigger fool than I ever imagined,* she thought. *He still thinks he loves the girl despite what he's been through. If only love were that powerful,* she mused. She watched as the were-jaguars sniffed the ground and then took off running, quickly vacating the plaza once again.

Time passed slowly and Satal felt the heat of the day pressing down on her head and shoulders. "Where is she?" she shouted to Tewichinel. She had expected Kämisanel to bring her the girl within minutes.

"There's been no sign of her, my lady."

Satal felt her frustration building, and she turned to Camazotz, Hun-Batz, and Ah-Cun-Can. "My lords, please, send your troops out into the city streets. Have them find the girl and bring her here."

"With pleasure, Lady Satal," Camazotz said. Instantly the bat god and the cloud of bats that had been swooping above his head spread out and flew away in multiple directions.

Hun-Batz waved his hairy arms and the troops of spider and howler monkeys climbing about the pyramid began to hoot and howl. In groups of four, five, and six, they leapt to the great mall and disappeared into the city with Hun-Batz in the lead.

Ah-Cun-Can mumbled to his offspring, and the snakes and serpents that carpeted the area slithered into a massive unit that undulated toward the opposite end of the square. Ah-Cun-Can reared up high and then burrowed down into the ground, disappearing from view.

It won't be long now, Satal thought and she smiled. She gripped the jequirty bean tighter in her fingers. *I don't want to wait any longer.* She brought the bitter bean to her lips.

Patience, Satal, my dear, you must be patient, Sachoj hissed in Satal's mind.

Satal stopped just before she bit down and she heaved a deep sigh. She knew her great-grandmother was right; she needed to wait. There was still plenty of time to shapeshift. Once Na'om was in her grasp, then she could transform and plunge her stinger deep into the girl's chest, fulfilling the destiny that was so rightly hers. She would then be the supreme leader that every mortal and even the gods feared.

But she longed to feel the strength of her wings lifting her from the pyramid steps.

Just a little while longer, my dear, Sachoj hissed. *Then you'll be invincible.*

Reluctantly, Satal returned the jequirty bean to her pocket. And she went back to scanning the plaza for any sign of the girl and her entourage.

Na'om

The distant cries and screams of wounded men and the crash of obsidian spears against wooden shields woke Na'om from the lightest sleep. She bolted upright and looked around; it was just sunrise and she could barely see the field where they had camped for the night. The ring of warriors that encircled the group had lit torches to ward off the blackness, but they did little to banish the gloom. Ek' Balam was awake and growling softly as he looked toward the east where the noises were coming from. Ajkun, Alom, Noy, Kärinik, and the other women in the group were still sleeping, but she could see them beginning to stir. She tossed off the blankets she'd slept in and hurried to the nearest bushes to relieve her full bladder. Chiman, Yakal, and Box were awake and talking nearby when she returned.

"What's happening?" she asked. "Where's Biribik?"

"He's with Nimal, who sent the warriors ahead of us, as we had planned," Chiman said. "But it sounds like they encountered Satal's army at the outskirts of the city."

Box smiled at Na'om. "We're safe here, for the time being."

Just then, Jumumik came running toward them out of the darkness. "My lady," he said as he bowed, "my lords, we ran into a contingent of Satal's warriors nearby, but Lord Nimal says he has still sent three regiments forward to secure the north, south, and east sectors of the city. My cousins are with those groups. They will alert the men in hiding that the battle has begun and instruct those loyal to us to begin circling the city's outskirts with a trail of salt. Once our warriors are in position and the path is complete, we shall return to you here."

A cool breeze ruffled Na'om's hair, and she shuddered as if someone had touched her.

Ajkun approached them and gave Na'om a quick hug. "Happy name day, Na'om." She looked more closely at her granddaughter. "Are you all right, my dear?" she asked. "You look pale."

"Yes, Ati't, under the circumstances, I'm fine." Na'om gave her grandmother a quick peck on the cheek to reassure her. But she could hear the high-pitched whine in her ears that she always linked with Satal and knew the woman was awake and waiting for her.

"The Wayeb won't close until sundown, but we must still defeat Satal today regardless of what she's summoned from Xibalba," Chiman said.

"So, we stay with our plan," Yakal said. "We wait until Nimal signals the way is clear, then we enter the city, find that old witch, and kill her, forcing her creatures to return to the Underworld."

Na'om looked at her father and could see the anger in his eyes. She gave him a half-smile. *If only it were that simple,* she thought. She was going to say something to that effect, then thought better of it and didn't speak. She turned instead to Jumumik. "Did Nimal make sure each warrior is carrying gourds full of salt water with him, not fresh water?" she asked.

Jumumik nodded. "And a bag of salt, as you requested. And each is wearing a vest of salt, my lady," he added. "They've been instructed to pour the grains of salt out in a circle and stand inside it in the event they're attacked and to throw the water at the enemy."

"Good, then we should have nothing to fear," Yakal interrupted. "Salt water brought Satal and her army crashing down when they attacked Mayapán, so there's no reason to believe it won't work again."

"Let's hope so," Ajkun said.

Several piercing screams broke the stillness, and the small group turned as one toward the sounds.

"Are you sure we're safe here, Chiman?" Ajkun asked as she linked her arm through his.

"Yes, my dear, I believe we're out of harm's way for now. The city is at least an hour from here; it's only the calm of the night that lets the sounds travel so far." He bent down and gave her a kiss on the cheek.

Na'om closed her eyes and concentrated, listening to the noises, filtering out those of the nocturnal animals scuttling about nearby. She didn't want to wait until after dawn to find Satal; the sooner the woman was dead, the better off they would all be. She opened her eyes and looked at the group of young women who were standing talking to Noy, Alom, and Kärinik. She could see the fear on all their faces. They were accustomed to remaining indoors during the Wayeb where they were safe. Yet, here they were, the twenty or so girls who had volunteered to come in order to aid the wounded with the salves and poultices they each carried in a pack basket on her back.

More screams carried across the open ground, and Na'om turned back to Chiman.

"I don't think we should wait until Nimal gives the all clear," she said.

"But it's too dangerous to go anywhere now," he replied.

"There are brave men out there who need our help with their wounds," she replied. She pointed to the group of women. "If we keep them busy tending to the wounded and dying, they won't have time to grow more scared."

Chiman looked around at the maidens. Some were crying, while others had knelt down in the dirt to pray.

"I agree with Na'om," Box said. "We can see well enough by the light of the torches to walk, and by the time we reach the city, it will be well past daybreak."

"The sooner we destroy Satal, the better, and then we can all go home again," Ajkun said.

Na'om looked at her grandmother in surprise. She wasn't used to hearing anger in her voice. "Just remember that Ek' Balam and I are the ones who will engage with Satal. I don't want any of you getting hurt." She turned to Jumumik. "Find Lord Nimal and tell him our plans have changed. We'll march to the city now and look for Satal. Once your cousins have returned and the great salt trail has been laid, come find us. Only when I know Satal and her army are inside the completed circle will I be able to defeat her."

Jumumik nodded. "We shall go like the wind, my lady, so your victory comes quickly and easily." He turned and raced away, becoming just a speck in the dark within minutes.

"Leave everything here that might slow us down," Na'om said as she walked over to the group of women who were busy stuffing blankets and bedding into pack baskets. "Bring your salves and healing herbs, your knives, and wear your salt vests, but leave everything else." The women nodded and quickly moved to obey.

Once the entire group had put on their salt vests, they received bags of salt and gourds of salt water from Lintat, who had joined the small group of warriors Nimal had left to protect them. Chiman, Yakal, and Box each had a large knife and a wooden shield. Ajkun, Alom, Noy, and Kärinik also carried obsidian knives. The unit stepped up onto the limestone sacbe and over the next hour or so made their way to the outskirts of Chichén Itzá. As soon as the fields turned to streets lined with houses, they saw the dead and wounded where they had fallen, and the younger women hurried forward to offer aid to all the men, friend and foe, who lay moaning on the ground. Na'om looked ahead, and in the increasing light, she saw the top of the large pyramid dedicated to Kukulcan rising almost one hundred feet into the air above the surrounding buildings. She had never seen such a tall structure before. Flanked by several warriors, Na'om and Ek' Balam took the lead, followed by Chiman, Yakal, Lintat, and Box, who guarded Ajkun, Alom, Noy, and Kärinik. When they turned a corner and entered yet another street, they surprised a flock of ocellated turkeys that gobbled and squawked at them before taking flight toward the roof of a nearby home.

The street widened, and the crash and thwack of fighting echoed off the walls of the houses. Na'om felt her stomach tighten with anxiety as more screams filled the air. At any moment, Na'om knew they could encounter Satal and her army from the Underworld. The group moved slowly forward, pausing at each corner to check the whereabouts of their enemies. They rounded yet another corner and discovered Biribik, Nimal, and his regiment engaged in one-to-one combat with enemy warriors.

"I feel certain Satal is at the pyramid," Chiman said. "We must turn around and find another way to get to the central plaza." He began to lead the women back the way they had come.

Na'om remained where she stood, mesmerized by the sheer brutality of the fight in front of her. Each man appeared to move in slow motion, swinging obsidian blades down to smash upon wooden shields, or thrusting spears forward to hit against leather, skin, and bones. Biribik lunged his blade forward, stabbing a man in the chest, then stepped over the body and advanced on the next enemy. An intense whining filled her ears, muffling the sound of the men's shields cracking as the sharp spear points penetrated the thick wood. Blood splattered onto the ground when obsidian blades met flesh, but Na'om heard the grunts and cries of the men as if her head were under water.

Ajkun looked over her shoulder and saw Na'om and Ek' Balam still standing only a few feet from harm's way. "Na'om!" she cried. "Come on; we can't stay here."

Box rushed forward and grabbed Na'om by the arm, yanking her out of the way as several arrows whizzed in their direction. "Let's go," he shouted as he tugged on her arm again.

Dizzy from the droning in her head, Na'om nodded and quickly touched Ek' Balam. The buzzing diminished and she rapidly pushed a thin barrier of light out around her body. Blue sparks arced from her forearm to Box's hand, and he shuddered, releasing his grip on her.

By now, the light of morning had spread across the city, turning dark shadows into daylight. The group wound its way through another few empty streets, but they stopped when they heard the rapid pounding of feet coming in their direction.

"Get ready," Yakal shouted as he drew his knife and stepped in front of Na'om.

Shrieks and howls resonated off the stucco walls as a group of six black howler monkeys rounded the corner and confronted them. They were massive, mature males and they began to screech and hoot, leaping and jumping about as they bared their teeth.

One younger male raced up the side of the nearest wall, clung to the stucco tiles on the roof's edge, then leapt back to the ground, only a few feet from Yakal. The monkey stuck out his dingy yellow teeth and yowled. Then it reached out with its massive claws and took a swipe at Yakal's arm.

Yakal jumped backward, but the monkey caught his arm with its claw and a line of blood quickly welled up. "Ahh!" Yakal shouted, and he plunged forward, skewering the howler monkey in the leg. The animal shrieked and stepped back as the other five males advanced toward the group. Then they stopped moving and stepped to one side as Hun-Batz manifested among them. The monkeys bowed low and then began shrieking again as Hun-Batz took up a stance in the middle of the alleyway. His body towered over the other monkeys and the rank stench of unwashed fur quickly filled the air.

"Hurry, lay a line of salt across the street," Na'om shouted.

Alom and Noy handed their salt bags to two of the warriors who rushed to pour the grains across the dirt.

"Get behind me, all of you," Na'om commanded. The creatures were so close to her that their hot breath fluffed her hair. One male stepped on the line of salt and Na'om knelt down, pushed out with her light of energy, and set the trail of salt on fire. The blaze raced out in both directions and the monkey caught in the wave of flames screamed as his fur on his foot and leg burned. Hun-Batz roared and bared his long yellow fangs, while the other monkeys hooted, moaned, and yowled, beating their chests with their fists. Some leapt up and down and raced back and forth in the narrow alley, but they made no attempt to get through.

"That should keep them trapped for a few minutes," Na'om said.

"Long enough for us to find another way to the pyramid," Box said.

The group turned and ran down the nearest empty street and when they were safe, they slowed to a walk to conserve their strength.

"How did you know the salt would burn like that?" Chiman asked Na'om as he walked beside her.

"It was Najtir's idea and I practiced it with him a few times," Na'om replied.

They entered another street and found it littered with bodies. The women quickly looked away, and the men were relieved to see the dead were not from Mayapán. Box stopped to see if any of the fallen were still alive, but none of them had a pulse.

"What happened to them?" Box said. He pointed to the marks on the men's arms and faces. "They look like they've been bitten."

Na'om squatted by one of the bodies and an all too familiar musty smell arose around her. "Camazotz and his bats, I think. They attacked, not knowing whether they were friend or enemy."

"If this is the work of Camazotz, then it didn't matter who they were," Chiman replied. "The bat god and his kin will take their meals from whomever they encounter."

Ajkun shuddered. "Well, I hope we don't see them."

But she had barely spoken when the group heard a whirring in the air above them and saw a great cloud of bats, with Camazotz in the lead, flying directly at them.

"Take cover," Box shouted.

"Where?" Kärinik and Noy cried as they grabbed each other. They hurried to huddle together in one of the empty doorways lining the street.

The others scattered as well, racing to other doorways, which offered hardly any defense. Alom tripped and landed on her hands and knees in the middle of the street.

"Chuch, watch out," Yakal shouted as he rushed over to help her. They both dropped to their bellies as the bats rushed in, flying low and fast, headed toward the row of bodies.

"Throw the salt water at them as they fly by," Chiman shouted. He and Ajkun held their gourds ready.

Na'om quickly uncorked her own gourd, and as the bats whizzed past, she flung her arm wide, spraying many of the creatures with the salt water. She felt them scream as the salt spray hit their wings, forcing dozens to the ground, where they lay flapping and flipping about. The remaining cloud of bats swerved and whirled around, racing straight back at Na'om and Ek' Balam.

Box ran from his spot across the street and tossed his salt water on them. Dozens more of the bats fell down, while the remainder of the group swooped up high over Box's head. Box threw more water at them, but they were too high in the air. The salty water gently sprinkled back down on top of him, soaking him lightly.

Camazotz rushed in and snatched at Box, but the bat god screamed when he touched the salt water on Box's clothes and it burned his feet.

"You shall pay for this!" the bat god roared.

But even though he and his cousins swerved and swooped up near the roofs of the buildings lining the street, they didn't fly any closer.

Ajkun looked out from her doorway. "Do we dare go on?"

"We have to give it a try," Na'om shouted as she and Ek' Balam stepped into the street. She glanced overhead and could see the top of the pyramid. "We must be close to the central plaza," she cried, and she and Ek' Balam began to run.

The others regrouped and ran as well, each one glancing back to make sure the bats remained where they were. Ek' Balam was the first to turn into the next street, and Na'om almost ran into him as she rounded the corner as he had stopped in the middle of the street. Na'om peered down the alley and saw a multitude of snakes slithering in their direction. She turned to Ek' Balam. "Come on, boy, it's the fastest way to the plaza," she said as she ran a few paces toward the snakes. But Ek' Balam remained grounded, growling and shivering from head to tail. The others caught up to them.

"What's wrong with him?" Lintat asked as he pointed to Ek' Balam. "Why is he shaking like that?"

"He's afraid of the snakes," Ajkun said as she knelt next to Lintat. "Na'om, we must find a different route."

"All right, let's go," Na'om said. And she turned around and led the way into a wider avenue that she felt sure would lead to the great plaza, the pyramid, and Satal. Suddenly, she heard the brisk beat of several drums echoing off the stucco buildings all around her and the undertone of running feet pounding the dirt street.

"Get ready," Yakal commanded the small troop of warriors. "Defend Lady Na'om at all costs," he ordered. The men quickly formed a unit in front of the men and women, their spears thrust in front of them, with their shields protecting their bodies. Yakal pulled out his obsidian blade and took up a stance in front of Na'om.

Box pulled out his own knife and stood on Na'om's left side. Ek' Balam remained at Na'om's right side.

Chiman urged the older women to fall behind him. "Brace yourselves," he warned the women.

Ajkun nodded and reached out to the other women who quickly linked hands. "We stand with you, Na'om," she cried.

A troop of enemy warriors rounded the corner and came to a stop about twenty paces in front of the group. The men held their knives and spears in front of them, ready to engage in battle. But they made no move to advance.

Ek' Balam began to growl and he turned in the opposite direction. And then Na'om heard the sounds of feet behind her and she spun around. Yet another group of warriors approached them from behind. They were trapped in the street with no place to go. An older man dressed in leather armor over his green linen shirt and loincloth advanced to stand before her. He removed his scarlet macaw headdress and bowed.

"I am Kämisanel, leader of Lady Satal's army. My lady awaits you in the great plaza, Na'om," the man said. "If you don't engage in battle, no one in your group will be harmed. Lady Satal's only interest lies in you and your jaguar friend."

Na'om twisted to look at Chiman and Yakal. "Tell the men to put down their weapons. We'll do as they say and no one will get hurt."

"Na'om, no, you mustn't let her take you like this," Ajkun whispered.

"Silence, old woman, or you shall be the first to die," Kämisanel yelled.

"Touch her and *you* shall die by my bare hands," Chiman said as he took several steps toward the warrior.

Na'om looked from person to person. "Mam, please, all of you, calm down. We'll go and willingly, if it means you all remain safe."

She turned back to the warrior. "Let them go, and Ek' Balam and I will come with you."

"I believe Lady Satal wishes that your friends and family witness your sacrifice. Now, drop your weapons." He took several steps forward as did both sets of warriors, their spears and knives drawn.

"Do as he orders," Na'om said as she pulled out her knife. She touched the water gourd and bag at her side and quickly shook her head no, then dropped the obsidian blade on the ground. The small group of men and women dropped their shields, spears, and knives.

"All of you will now come with us to the plaza where Lady Satal is waiting for you." Kämisanel bowed again, then shouted to his warriors on the other side of the group. "Let's go; back to the pyramid."

The warriors turned and began to quickly stride down the street. Kämisanel pushed past Na'om, Ek' Balam, and the others and marched just ahead of them. The remaining troop brought up the rear, making it impossible for Na'om to even think about escaping. With each step forward, the buzzing in her ears grew louder, until she had trouble hearing any of the sounds around her. She sensed Ek' Balam also felt the noise because the jaguar kept shaking and twitching his head.

It took only minutes before the entourage stepped onto the great open mall. Hundreds of scorpions and centipedes meandered about the empty plain, but Na'om took no notice of them. No, her attention was instantly drawn to the tall, four-sided pyramid at the end of the square and the small figure that stood on the pyramid's second level. She could see a group of shamans waiting at the base of the structure.

"There's Satal," Yakal said as he pointed at the pyramid. "I'd recognize her anywhere."

"Well done, my lord," Kämisanel replied as he turned to the group. "Yes, that's Lady Satal. Quickly now, we mustn't waste any more time. Head to the base of the pyramid, please." He waved his spear and forced the small group to hurry down the long plaza.

As they walked, Camazotz and his clouds of bats swirled in and out of the few clouds in the sky. Na'om was pleased to see that the men guarding them were nervous at the sight of them. And she paid attention to the men who helped Satal down the steep stairs. *She's weaker than I thought.*

Surrounded by her shamans, Satal approached the group while they were still several paces from the pyramid.

"Lady Satal, it is my honor to present you with the girl you've been seeking," Kämisanel said. His feather headdress swept the ground in front of him as he inclined his head.

"Well done, Kämisanel, well done," Satal replied. "You and your men shall be richly rewarded for your efforts." Satal smiled at the group in front of her. "Chiman, Yakal, I never expected to see either of you again. This day only gets better and better. I shall have plenty of people to sacrifice to the gods." She turned to Tewichinel and Ch'o. "Bring Na'om to the sacrificial table," she commanded.

Yakal stepped forward. "Don't you dare touch her," he shouted. He reached for his knife, but quickly dropped his hand again when he touched the empty scabbard.

"Ah, Yakal, I shall thoroughly enjoy witnessing your death after I've dealt with Na'om," Satal chortled. "You've been nothing but a problem to me ever since you were a child." She turned to several of the closest warriors. "Watch this one closely; there's no saying what he might try to do." The men nodded and thrust their long spears in Yakal's direction, forcing him to step back to the others under guard.

Being this close to Satal, the buzzing in Na'om's head was so intense that she felt sick to her stomach with the pain. She clamped her hands over her ears, hoping that would block the sound, but she knew it was a noise only she and Ek' Balam could hear.

"So, we finally meet at last," Satal said as she stepped directly in front of Na'om.

Her voice droned in Na'om's ears.

"You don't know how much I've longed for this day." Satal began to pace back and forth.

"I can't say I feel the same way," Na'om replied. "What do you want from me?" When Satal's back was turned, she tentatively reached out and was able to just barely touch Ek' Balam. His energy quickly sparked through her fingertips, and she slid her feet slowly closer to his body.

"That's close enough, my dear," Satal said, and she shook her finger in warning as she faced her again.

Na'om stopped moving, but she felt Ek' Balam sidle sideways until his flank was touching her leg. She placed her hand squarely on the top of his head and instantly felt the deep energy he possessed flow directly into her.

"You'll never get away with whatever you've planned," Na'om said and she slowly began to push her light energy outward.

"Oh, my dear, you have no idea how much I want to destroy you right now, but I'm still waiting for someone to arrive." Then she glanced down the square and chortled. "It won't be long now."

Na'om and Ek' Balam turned around and watched as the pack of were-jaguars, noses to the ground, entered the plaza. Ek' Balam's hair bristled under Na'om's fingertips, and she felt him shudder as he began to growl deep within his chest. "Easy, boy, we must wait until the moment is just right," she warned. She scanned the area, but there was no sign of any of the warriors from Mayapán. She tentatively took a step toward Chiman, Yakal, and the others who were only a few feet away. *If I can just get a little closer, I can protect them*, she thought. But she stopped when Satal stepped directly in front of her.

"Ah, my dear, I thought Najtir would have trained you to mask your thoughts a bit better than that," Satal responded. She pointed at Alom. "One more step and she'll be the first to die."

Anger coursed through Na'om and she pushed out with her energy, sending a circle of scorching heat around the group. Satal jumped backward, barely avoiding the blaze that flared up. But the quick burst of flames gave Na'om and Ek' Balam the chance to rejoin the others.

Ajkun touched Na'om on the arm. "Conserve your strength, Na'om," she warned.

Na'om looked toward the were-jaguars and saw them lift their heads and stare directly at her. *They've caught my scent*, she thought and she braced herself against Ek' Balam as the pack ran full bore toward them. But the creatures stopped when they reached the charred area and bent to sniff the burnt dirt. None of them dared cross the narrow line. Naóm stared at each one in turn, hoping she could figure out which one might be Tz'. But they all looked similar in the bright light.

Tz', are you there?

The were-jaguars turned in Naóm's direction. She could see their reddish eyes and the droplets of saliva that fell to the burnt ground and hear the low growls the male cats made as they began to pad back and forth again.

"Can't you tell which one is the boy you love?" Satal mocked. She waved her hands and her warriors stepped several paces away as the snarling, growling were-jaguars took positions a few feet from each other, enclosing the captured group on all sides.

Several of the Mayapán warriors turned to look at Naóm and she could see how terrified they were. When a large male were-jaguar roared, she glanced away when one young soldier urinated on the ground.

Bats swooped across the open air just above all their heads, and the women crouched to avoid them. A low growl emanated from a young male were-jaguar, and he leapt into the air, catching a bat on the fly. Naóm heard the crunch of bones as he ate it.

She turned in a slow circle, hoping to identify which of the creatures might be Tz'. She watched as an older male, covered in scars, limped toward the charred soil, and carefully placed one front paw onto the burned soil. He jerked it back, as if it had been burned. But he quickly did it again, and Naóm understood that he realized it was safe to touch the scorched ground. With his back lowered, his tail swishing from side to side, he stepped over the line and slunk toward the group. When he was only a few feet away, he stopped and growled, and the rest of the were-jaguars quickly crossed the singed dirt, making the circle around Naóm and the others much tighter.

Some of the warriors waved their arms in front of them and were greeted with growls.

"Steady, men, don't do anything yet," Yakal warned.

"Naóm, what shall we do?" Ajkun asked.

"You still can't tell, can you, Naóm?" Satal teased. "Surely true love will show itself, eh?"

Naóm took a deep breath and let it out. "All right, I'll play your little game," she shouted to Satal. She turned to the group around her. "I'll see if

I can connect with Tz'," she whispered. "Be ready for anything," she added. Na'om closed her eyes against the dangerous creatures standing in front of her and sent out a beam of energy. *Tz', if you can hear me, answer me now, before we fight and hurt one another.*

Satal laughed from several feet away. "I can't believe you don't recognize your young friend."

Na'om ignored Satal's taunts and concentrated on looking at the creatures just a few steps away. The males were obviously bigger than the females and some of them were much older as their fur around their muzzles had a white tinge to it. It was the were-jaguar who hung toward the back that intrigued her the most, though. He was on the small side for a male, but obviously didn't fear her or the white light that surrounded them.

The creature stared directly at Na'om, twisted its head to one side, and sniffed the air. Na'om could see drops of saliva in the corner of its mouth, and she shuddered. The cat took another step forward, and Ek' Balam moved forward as well until the two jaguars were only a few feet apart.

"Be careful, Ek' Balam," Na'om said. But she was surprised to suddenly hear purring. Yet, she couldn't tell if it was coming from Ek' Balam or the were-jaguar in front of him. She moved to stand next to Ek' Balam and realized it was the were-jaguar who was purring.

Na'om turned her head to look behind her as she heard Ajkun speak. Her grandmother had linked arms with the other women and was projecting a reddish glow, something Na'om had never seen her do before.

"Protect us, Itzamná, and send our love outward to these creatures so that they may feel your presence," Ajkun said.

The glow of light around the four women grew brighter and reached the were-jaguar in front of Na'om. It lowered its body closer to the ground and stepped forward again so that its muzzle and face were surrounded by the light. Na'om didn't understand why this cat wasn't driven away, and she wasn't sure what to do. Part of her wanted to offer her hand for it to sniff and part of her knew she needed to blast it with white light and send it and the pack running back to Satal.

Then without warning, the oldest were-jaguar rushed the group, headed straight for Ajkun. She screamed as his front paw raked her left arm before he darted away. The creature turned and Chiman jumped in front of Ajkun, blocking the cat's path, and the were-jaguar hissed and spit, then pounced on Chiman. He fell to the ground, fighting against the beast with both hands as it tore at his stomach and chest with its long claws. Instantly, the small male in front of Na'om turned and attacked the larger were-jaguar, knocking it sideways off Chiman and onto the dirt. The two cats rolled over and over in the scorched ground and their howls and snarls filled the air as Na'om and Ajkun hurried to Chiman. Na'om instantly surrounded Chiman in a glow of protection, but she felt a bit dizzy as she leaned in to look at his bloody wound. The big cat had ripped at his midsection, and Chiman was bleeding from the slashes in his side as well as multiple claw marks on his hands and forearms. Ajkun yanked on her skirt, tearing off a large piece, which she quickly pressed into Chiman's wound to stem the flow of blood and then she used more of her skirt to swiftly bind her arm. Na'om's concentration wavered as she helped Chiman into a more comfortable position, and her light around the larger group wobbled and dimmed.

Ajkun gripped Chiman's hand tightly. "Don't you dare die on me," she cried and a reddish glow quickly encircled the both of them.

Na'om stood up and hurried to Ek' Balam's side again. Her head ached, and she felt as if a tremendous weight had been placed upon her back. Her protective circle was dimmer, weaker, and she knew she had little time left.

Satal waved her hands and the rest of the were-jaguars attacked. Alom and Noy shrieked as they narrowly missed being slashed by the claws of one of the female were-jaguars. Then Camazotz sent his offspring diving in from the sky, and Yakal screamed as several creatures bit him on the shoulder, taking chunks of skin and cloth with them as they turned and flew away. Blood streamed down Yakal's arm, and he swung his bag of salt, clipping a bat in mid-flight, knocking it to the ground. Several more bats surged in, latching onto Yakal's back, where they began to chew, but Kärinik quickly tore off her salt-filled leather vest and hit them with it, forcing them to detach. The bats dropped to the ground and Yakal stomped on them.

"Quickly, Na'om, extend your light and love to Yakal before he's torn apart," Noy shouted.

Na'om placed her hand on Ek' Balam's back, and pushed outward yet again, sending forth another bright blast of heat and light. The effort left her trembling. The bubble of brilliance drove back all the animals and illuminated the space around the group as if the sun had doubled in size.

On the far side of the light, Satal clapped her hands with glee. "Ah, such beautiful power," she exclaimed. "And soon it will be mine."

"We need to get Chiman out of here," Ajkun said as she peered again at Chiman's gash. "He needs to have the wound cleaned and will need stitches."

"I'll take him," Yakal said. He nodded toward two of the warriors who hurried over to Chiman's side, waiting to lift him from the ground.

Na'om could see multiple dark red splotches of blood on Yakal's shirt where the bats had bitten him.

Yakal stepped toward Satal. "Lady Satal, let us attend to our wounded. You have the girl; let the rest of us go." Then he turned his back on her and hurried to Chiman.

Startled by his words, Na'om looked at her father. *Does he really mean that?* And then she noticed that Yakal had removed his water gourd and was lifting it to his mouth as if to take a drink. She faced Satal. "Let them go and I'll do whatever you ask."

"Oh, it's not quite that simple, Na'om. Your family and friends shall bear witness to your sacrifice." Then Satal turned to her shamans. "It's time," she said and nodded to Tewichinel. The shamans formed a group, and Satal reached into her pocket and pulled out the jequirty bean.

What is she doing now? Na'om wondered. The older woman was blocked from view by the tall men in their ceremonial headdresses. She looked at Chiman and could see by the grimace on his face that he was in terrible pain. *We must get him some help. Where is Jumumik, Jututik or one of their cousins? Where are our warriors? Surely, they must be close by now.* She looked left and right, hoping to see any of the runners coming across the plaza to let her know the giant circle of salt around the city was complete.

The buzzing in her ears intensified, and Na'om felt another wave of nausea overwhelm her, forcing her to eject the little bit she'd eaten hours before. The light around the group wavered and she felt the others press against her as the circle of protection grew smaller. Several of the Mayapán warriors were no longer shielded, and she heard one man shriek as a were-jaguar grabbed him by the arm and began to drag him away. Na'om wiped her mouth and looked up when she heard Noy and Alom scream.

She watched as Satal rose from the group of shamans as the giant wasp Yakal had described to them from his encounter with her so many moons ago. Satal's iridescent wings shimmered in the sunlight, lifting her elongated, black body high into the air. A stinger the length of a forearm protruded from the base of Satal's abdomen, a stinger that Na'om knew carried the power of death within it. Satal's warriors drew back, fearful of the creature that hovered over their heads.

Na'om swallowed hard and gripped Ek' Balam tightly by the scruff of his neck. "Don't lose touch with me, boy," she commanded. "Stay close, all of you, and men, throw out your salt," she said. The warriors ripped open the bags at their sides and broadcast the salt, but were quickly stopped when Satal's men threw their spears into the group, pinning several of the Mayapán fighters to the ground. Their screams mingled with the continued growling of the were-jaguars and the howls and hoots of the howler and spider monkeys that had arrived with Hun-Batz. The monkeys hung back, though and Na'om sensed they had learned a lesson from the first time they'd attacked. They were staying clear of her protective circle.

Na'om pushed outward with her light, and the tips of her fingers went numb from the flow of energy through her body. The circle rippled outward in waves, cremating the scorpions and centipedes that had crept forward, and driving all the animals back yet another pace. Satal flew upward to avoid the blast, and she buzzed in circles around their heads. Na'om knew she was looking for a weak spot so she could zoom in and attack.

"Itzamná, help us," Noy and Alom cried. They clutched each other and began to cry. Kärinik joined them and wrapped her arms around the two women.

"We mustn't show our fear," she whispered. "Think of anything that brings you happiness and joy and use that strength to create a wall of energy to shield yourself."

All of a sudden, shouts and cries from across the plaza drew everyone's attention. Men from both armies spilled onto the great open square from one of the large streets. They slashed and fought with knives, spears, and wooden shields. A volley of arrows whizzed through the air, striking some Mayapán warriors in their chests, but their salt-filled vests halted the obsidian arrowheads from penetrating to flesh. Na'om watched as her men ripped the arrows out and sent them back into the air, hitting Satal's men, killing them instantly. Then more Mayapán warriors appeared from other side streets, quickly filling the plaza. Nimal raised his spear and shook it in defiance as he, Biribik, and his regiment hurried toward them. Kämisanel and the warriors guarding Na'om's group turned to face their enemies, but it was easy to see they were outnumbered.

"Lady Naʾom, the circle is almost complete," a voice yelled.

Naʾom searched the crowd of fighting men and caught a glimpse of Be Anim running toward her. He carried a large sack of salt on his back and she could see the trail of reddish grains it was leaving behind him.

Then she watched in horror as Satal flew down and stabbed Be Anim in the chest with her powerful stinger. Be Anim crashed to the ground, and Satal flew up out of harm's way.

"The circle isn't finished," Kärinik cried. She ripped open her bag of salt and began to run toward Be Anim's body, trailing the blessed salt behind her.

"No, Kärinik, come back," Ajkun cried. She looked to Naʾom. "Do something before she gets hurt."

Naʾom nodded and stepped forward with Ek' Balam. She sent her energy behind her to protect the group and then held out one hand, forcing a beam of light outward toward Kärinik. But the woman was too far away. Naʾom trembled and shook, squeezing as much strength as she could muster toward those she needed to shield. *If Kärinik can make it to Be Anim, she'll be safe.* And then an enemy spear arced through the air and hit Kärinik in the chest, killing her instantly. The woman fell forward, spilling her bag of salt.

In shock, Naʾom dropped to her knees and sobbed. A whoosh of air instinctively made her duck her head as Satal rushed in to strike her, but Naʾom sent out a blast that forced Satal to swerve away. Naʾom fell to the ground, seized Ek' Balam by his tail, and curled up, cradling her belly, thinking of her unborn child who might never see the light of day. Then in her mind, she heard Najtir say, '*The power lies deep within you.*' Her love for her infant raced through her, sending shivers of heat and cold through her veins, and she closed her eyes and concentrated. *The power of love . . . love for my unborn son, love for Ati't, Chiman, Tz', and the others, love for Ek' Balam, my love of nature, of my home in Pa nimá, of the wildness of the ocean, and my love of life itself.* Then an image of the giant ceiba tree on the shamans' island popped into her mind and the words that Tatá had spoken. '*The tree of life and death. The center of our universe and through it a source of power.*' . . . Deep inside her chest, Naʾom felt a warmth bud and blossom, and then it grew in heat and intensity, pushing outward in increasing waves. *My love for my son, for Ati't, Chiman, Tz' and the others*, Naʾom repeated as she slowly stood and opened her eyes.

She looked at the continuing battle; time had slowed and everybody was moving so slowly, but she knew they only needed a few more minutes to turn the war in their favor. She only had to defeat Satal. She heard Nima Winaq's words in her mind. *'The power of a woman with child is as vast as the heavens above . . . but only if you use the energy at the right time and in the right way.' Of course, it's obvious to me now,* Na'om thought. *This is why the gods gave me this child, to use it to defeat Satal and save the others.* She reached down and removed her salt vest, dropped her water gourd, and bag of salt. Then she placed her hand on Ek' Balam and leaned down. "Stay here," she commanded as she continued to push her energy outward, sending her intense love to everyone around her. Then she walked away from the group.

"Na'om, stop, what are you doing?" Yakal cried.

Na'om ignored him and walked farther into the square. She thought of the ceiba tree roots deep beneath the soil and planted her feet, sending energy down into the ground. She stretched her arms above her head, imagining them reaching as high as the ceiba tree branches, directly into the heavens. Vulnerable and exposed, she prayed to the gods. "Lords Itzamná, Chac, Vucub-Kamé, Hun-Kamé, and all the gods who govern the heavens, our realm, and Xibalba, I beg of you, help me defeat this woman. Take me and my child and spare the lives of those I love. If Satal obtains the power she so desperately craves, she will be unstoppable. I beg you, take my life so that the others may live."

The shushing of air was her only warning as Satal rushed in, aiming straight for her chest.

Na'om stood firm but heard pounding feet and was knocked to the ground just as Satal struck. She looked aghast as the young male were-jaguar caught the poisonous stinger in his flank, dropping instantly to the hard-packed dirt. The creature writhed in pain as Satal pulled her stinger free, and Na'om scrabbled to the were-jaguar's side. Instantly, she knew it must be Tz'. She touched the were-jaguar lightly on the head and felt the creature's love for her fill her body.

Finish her, Na'om, the were-jaguar said.

Na'om nodded and threw her body across the open ground, straining to reach just one speck of salt. But she quickly curled into a ball, shielding her belly, when she felt Satal whoosh down on top of her again. Then she pushed outward with the love she felt for Tz' and the others and a spark arced from her fingertips, leaping quickly from salt grain to salt grain to salt grain until it flowed into the bag of salt Kärinik had dropped, where it flashed high and burned, setting off an explosion of blinding light that raced across the plaza, out into the streets and flared into the air. The dome of light covered the entire plaza and the streets surrounding the great pyramid where it swirled high and low, knocking everyone to the ground.

With her ears ringing, Na'om squinted and caught a glimpse of the giant wasp flapping and scrabbling on her back on the ground. Then she dimly felt feet running on the hard dirt and watched as Yakal raced forward and threw the contents of several water gourds on top of the creature as it struggled to strike at anything and everything with its toxic stinger. The salt water hit the wasp full force and it shrieked as its wings sizzled and burned. Noy and Alom hurried forward and threw their remaining bags of salt on the insect. Na'om slowly stood up and watched as the insect writhed and thrashed about, twisting and turning as the salt slowly ate through its carapace and into the soft flesh inside. At that point, she shook her head in pity. *No creature should suffer so.* She held onto Ek' Balam and sent a final blast of light straight at the creature, which stopped it dead.

In a daze, Na'om was aware that Noy and Alom held tightly to each other, their sobs filling the sudden silence. She saw Yakal hurry over to Kärinik and pull the spear from her chest, which he threw on the ground with disgust. He removed his vest and laid it over Kärinik's face. She looked back at the body of the giant wasp and was relieved to see it hadn't moved. Her ears rang, she was dizzy, and she dropped to her knees, placing her forehead against Ek' Balam's side.

"We did it, boy, we did it," she murmured.

Nimal and his regiment ran forward and quickly surrounded Kämisanel and the men who had guarded the group. The warriors put down their weapons and it was apparent the battle was over when Kämisanel laid down his obsidian blade at Nimal's feet.

"Tie them all up; we'll sacrifice them later," Nimal commanded. Then he pointed to the group of shamans who huddled together near the sacrificial altar. "Tie them up as well."

But before his warriors could comply, Tewichinel ran across the open ground and fell to his knees beside the wasp. "My lady, my lady," he wept. He quickly reached into the pouch at his side, pulled out a piece of charcoal, and crumbled it onto the mandibles of the insect. Immediately, the creature began to writhe and move, shapeshifting back into the naked and badly burned human body of Satal. Tewichinel removed his ceremonial cape and laid it gently over Satal.

Nimal marched over to the man and shoved his spear in his face. "Get up, now, no more of your witchery, old man."

"Ajaw, I beg to be allowed to bury my lady with her family."

"Only Lady Naʾom shall decide what to do with Satal."

Naʾom slowly got up and went to the were-jaguar who had saved her life. A flicker of light remained in his reddish eyes. "Give me some of that charcoal," she demanded.

Nimal nodded and Tewichinel hurried to give a piece to Naʾom. She crumbled the charcoal onto the were-jaguar's lips and then stood back as the creature also shapeshifted, back into the form of Tzʾ, but his limbs and torso remained covered with tawny fur. "Tzʾ, I knew it was you," she cried as she knelt by his side. The wound created by Satal's stinger had punched a hole through his abdomen and Naʾom knew there was nothing she could do to save him.

Nimal grabbed the cape covering Satal and draped it over Tzʾ to hide his nakedness.

Naʾom sobbed as she clutched Tzʾs hand. "Tzʾ, oh, Tzʾ, why did you do it? Why did you sacrifice yourself?"

"Because I love you and I want you to live, to raise your son, and be happy," Tzʾ whispered. "I made so many mistakes, but this was not one of them."

"But I could have saved you. You could have returned to Pa nimá and lived with Chiman and the others," Naʾom cried.

Tzʾ twitched his fingers, also covered with fur, and he drew in a ragged breath. "I spent too much time in Xibalba; I know now I could never have regained my full human shape." He heaved a great sigh.

Naʾom felt his energy slip through her fingers and dissipate into the ground. "*Nooo!*" she cried. The tears ran down her face and blended into the dirt. She only turned when she felt a gentle hand on her shoulder. It was Noy.

"Come, Naʾom, Chiman hasn't much time left, either. Come say your good-byes."

Naʾom scrabbled to her feet and ran to Chiman's side. "Mam, Mam, stay with us," she cried. She couldn't bear to lose him too.

Chiman smiled at her weakly. "Ah, Na'om, I'm so pleased to see you again," he said. "And I see Tz' is standing just behind you. So good to see you two together at last. . ."

Na'om whipped her head around, but the area behind her was empty.

"Mam, stay with us." She turned to Ajkun. "Isn't there anything you can do?" she cried.

Ajkun lifted her tear-stained face. "Out here, away from my salves and herbs, no, nothing. I'm losing the love of my life," she sobbed as she placed her head on Chiman's shoulder.

The women cried together, and Na'om braced herself as she felt Chiman's energy flow out of his body and into the dirt. She lifted her head and screamed and only moved away when Box appeared and helped lift her to her feet.

"Come away, Na'om, you must rest now," Box said. "The battle is over, so you can rest." He walked with her to the first step of the pyramid and helped her sit down. "Lean against me, and we'll just sit awhile and let the others tend to the wounded."

In a daze, Na'om did as Box instructed. She slumped against his shoulder and let the tears flow easily down her face. The weight of everything pressed down on her, and suddenly she panicked when she realized Ek' Balam wasn't by her side. She sat upright and looked around but felt relief when she spied the jaguar lying next to Tz's body. She sagged against Box again, watching as the Mayapán warriors worked to bring the wounded to Ajkun and the other women who had appeared. She sobbed when Biribik walked by with Kärinik's body and gently laid it on the ground next to Chiman. And when they had placed Tz's body beside the others, she got up and went to sit by them, the people that she loved who had sacrificed so much.

"Do you want me to stay with you?" Box asked.

"No, no, I'll be all right," Na'om replied. "Maltiox, Box. Go and help the others. I'm just going to rest here a little bit." She smiled weakly and laid her head on Tz's shoulder.

Box nodded and stepped away. And despite the noise all around her, Na'om slipped into a exhausted, dreamless sleep.

YAKAL

Yakal walked over to see Na'om, who had slumped to the ground. He nodded to Box. "She's asleep?"

"Yes, completely exhausted," Box replied. "I don't imagine she'll wake for some time." He looked around for something to use as a pillow and finally took off his leather vest, which he slid under Na'om's head.

"Are you all right?" he asked Yakal as he stood up again.

Yakal's cotton shirt was stained with splotches of dried blood. "I'll live," Yakal replied. "Which is more than I expected, actually." He turned and surveyed the great plaza littered with bodies. Thankfully, the were-jaguars, snakes, serpents, and other creatures called forth by Satal had fled. He searched the sky for signs of Camazotz or the other gods, but they had disappeared as well. "I can't believe she's dead," he said as he and Box walked over to Satal's body. Another cape had been thrown over her nakedness, leaving only her burned face exposed.

"What do we do with her now?" Box asked.

"Her head shaman insists she be buried with her family. He says he's the only one left who knows where the cave is, and if he's allowed to take her body there, he swears he'll kill himself so that no one can find her," Yakal said.

"Should we wait to find out what Na'om wants to do?" Box asked.

"Honestly, I think she's had to make enough decisions for quite some time." Yakal stepped forward and paced off the length of Satal's body. "She's small; do you think she'd fit into a large urn?"

"Probably. Why, what do you have in mind?"

"Let the old man have his ceremony, but we put the old witch in a pottery urn and pack it with salt. That way she'll never come back to life."

"Can we trust him to make his sacrifice?"

"We'll go along and make sure he does," Yakal replied. He waved to Nimal who hurried over. "Send some of your men into the marketplace and have them find the biggest pottery urn they can. I want Satal out of sight before Na'om wakes up."

Nimal pointed to several men who ran off, returning within minutes with one of the largest water containers they could find. They carried it on poles shoved through the large loops on either side of the neck of the vessel. Two men removed the heavy lid, and the four warriors lifted Satal by her limbs and dumped her in. "Bring me any salt you can find," Yakal ordered. Then he took off his own vest, ripped it open at one of the many seams, and poured the salt over Satal's head. With several men working, they were able to fill the urn to the brim. Yakal slid the lid in place and had two men tie it down to the loops with a piece of hemp cord.

"Bring the shaman here," Yakal ordered and Nimal marched away to get him.

Tewichinel, his hands tied behind his back, awkwardly bowed low to Yakal. "My lord, you asked for me?" he said.

"Yes, we've decided you can bury Satal with her family," Yakal said. "She's inside this urn." He nodded to the four warriors. "They'll carry her to the cave, and we'll go along to make sure you fulfill your promise."

"As you wish, my lord. Might I humbly request one more thing?" Tewichinel begged.

"That depends; speak your mind."

"I only wish to say farewell to my brother shamans, my lord. We have lived our whole lives together, you see."

Box stepped close to Yakal and whispered in his ear. "I don't trust this man. Something tells me it would be a bad idea to let him near the others."

Yakal nodded in acknowledgment. "Tell me, how did Satal shapeshift into the wasp? It was quite the sight."

He watched as the shaman's face lit up with pride. "Why, she only had to bite into the jequirity bean she carried."

Yakal snapped his fingers at a warrior. "Get that pouch off him." The man sliced through the woven strap holding the bag to Tewichinel and handed it to Yakal. Yakal untied the drawstring and dumped the contents on the ground. "Jequirity beans, I presume?" he asked as he turned to look at Tewichinel. He ground the beans into the dirt with his heel.

"All right, let's go," he said, and the four warriors strained to lift the heavy urn off the ground.

"Shouldn't we wait for Na'om to wake up?" Box asked.

"No, let's get this business finished," Yakal said. "Tell the others we'll be back as soon as we can," he said to Nimal. Then he bent down and picked up a blade from a fallen warrior.

Following his example, Box armed himself as well. The small entourage wove their way through the piles of bodies and groups of wounded men. No one stopped to question them, and it took over two hours to walk through the city streets and out into the countryside. The shadows were long across the ground when they finally neared an outcropping of rocks.

Yakal motioned for the warriors to put the urn down. "Are we close?" he asked Tewichinel.

"Yes, my lord."

Yakal looked at Box. "Do you think we can carry it the rest of the way ourselves? I'd like to send these men back to the city before night falls."

Box nodded. "Yes, I think so."

Yakal turned to the four warriors. "Go back now and help your brothers with the wounded and dead. Tell anyone where you've been and I shall personally cut your tongues out and offer them as sacrifices to the gods."

The men fled, leaving Tewichinel, Yakal, and Box in the deepening shadows. He turned and cut the hemp rope binding the shaman's hands. "You'll carry the front of the poles; we'll carry the back," Yakal said as he poked Tewichinel with the tip of his knife blade.

Tewichinel bent down and grasped both poles, one in either hand, and hoisted them to his bony shoulders. The urn slid backward and threatened to fall, but Yakal and Box hurried to lift their ends of the poles. Together, the three slowly made their way to the large pile of rocks and boulders.

Tewichinel inclined his head toward the left. "Just inside that crevice is the cave where Satal's ancestors have been buried for all time."

They worked their way around a large boulder, through the gap in the rocks, and within several paces, they were inside the large cave.

"I wish we had a torch with us," Box said. "I can't see anything."

"There is a torch here, my lords," Tewichinel replied. He began to set his end of the poles down and Yakal and Box followed, letting the urn land gently on the dirt underfoot.

Tewichinel moved forward, struck two rocks together, creating sparks, and instantly got the torch to bloom into flame. He handed it to Yakal and stood next to the limestone wall pitted with holes and crannies.

Yakal waved the torch about and was surprised to see multiple urns placed in various niches carved into the soft limestone. "Well, it appears there are many of Satal's ancestors here; she'll have plenty of company for all eternity."

"Only one in Lady Satal's family is missing, my lord. The great Lady Sachoj whose head, I hear, you tossed into a cenote many, many moons ago."

Yakal smiled at the memory. "Yes, and that was also the day Satal captured Na'om and dragged her into that same cenote. Thank the gods Na'om survived her ordeals in Xibalba and was able to return to us and defeat Satal." Then he heard a noise from the back of the cave and swung the light in that direction. Several snakes began to rise from their slumber.

"Snakes?" Box said. "Yakal, let's get out of here." He bent down, pulled the two wooden poles from the large loops on the neck of the urn, and held one of them at an angle, ready to hit a snake if it attacked.

"The house of Lady Satal has always been associated with snakes and serpents," Tewichinel said and he smiled. A snake had appeared by his neck and began to wind across his shoulders.

"Enough chatter," Yakal said. "Where do you wish to die?" He thrust the obsidian blade at the shaman.

"Any of these ledges will do for my lady's urn. Once she's settled, I will happily end my life so as to be at her side in Xibalba." Tewichinel bent down and began to lift the urn by one of its ceramic loops. The snake slid from his arm and wriggled on the dry dirt through the shaman's feet before curling up next to the cave wall.

Box hurried to the other side of the urn and together, the two men hoisted it level with a spot near some of the other containers. But inches from the rocky shelf, Tewichinel let go, and Yakal heard a distinctive *ping* as the pottery dropped onto the limestone.

He shoved Tewichinel, pushing him aside. Then Yakal bent down to examine the pottery. In the blazing light, he could see a hairline crack had shivered its way partially up the side of the container. "Box, you're the potter, do you think that will matter?"

"Honestly, I don't know. But we don't have a replacement anywhere near here, and I doubt I'd be able to find this place again."

"Hmm, you're right," Yakal replied. He thrust the blade at Tewichinel. "All right, old man, enough with the tricks, it's time." He glanced around and saw more snakes were arriving through all the holes in the limestone.

"With pleasure, my lords," Tewichinel replied as he grabbed the blade. He turned it so the point faced him and then he thrust the dagger deep into his own heart. He staggered three steps and fell forward onto Satal's urn, his arms draped awkwardly across the lid. Blood ran down the sides of the vessel, leaving wavy patterns of red on the dusty sides.

"Is he dead?" Box asked.

Yakal stepped forward, grabbed him by the shoulder, and yanked him backward, letting the shaman's body flop onto the dirt. "I believe so," Yakal replied. He swung the torch around and gasped at the number of snakes slithering about. "Come on, let's get out of here before any of them strike us."

The two men hurried back outside and were relieved to see there was still light in the sky despite the sun having set. Yakal set the torch down in the soft ground. "We'll need that to get back to the city, but before we leave, I want to fill in that hole so no one finds this spot." He began to throw large and small rocks into the opening and Box quickly joined him. The sharp stones tore at Yakal's hands, but he refused to stop. It was almost dark by the time they were done, and Yakal was satisfied that no one would find the entrance to the cave.

Yakal, hungry and more tired than he'd ever been, plodded with Box across the countryside back to the city. Once they arrived on the great plaza, he could see several funeral pyres were already burning. They hurried toward the group at the base of the pyramid.

Na'om rushed forward when she saw them approach. "Where have you been?" she demanded. "Nimal refused to say where you'd gone."

"We took Satal's body to a place where no one will ever find it. The only man who knew the location other than us is dead." Yakal crouched down as he felt a wave of dizziness pass through him.

"What's wrong?" Na'om cried as she knelt down next to him.

"Tired, hungry, and in need of some medical attention," Yakal said as he held out his hands.

Naòm gasped when she saw the deep cuts and scrapes.

Box grimaced. "I need some help too."

Naòm put her hand under Yakal's elbow and helped him to his feet. "Come, Tat, come and say your good-byes, and then you can rest." She linked her other arm through Box's arm and together they walked to the three pyres that remained unlit.

Yakal could see Chiman's body on one, Tz's on the next pyre, and Kärinik had been laid on the last pile of wood. He felt a deep ache in his throat as he looked at his old friend, at the boy turned man who had given his life for Naòm, and at the woman he'd barely known, but had liked from the moment he had met her. The tears slid down his dirty face, and he made no attempt to hide his pain. With his free hand, he took the torch Nimal gave him and set fire to Kärinik's pyre. Then he handed the torch to Naòm.

She leaned forward and touched the next pile of coconut husks and wooden shavings with the flame and stepped back as the fire raced upward, engulfing Tz'. She sobbed as she handed the torch to Ajkun.

Yakal saw how old and tired Ajkun looked and stepped forward to assist her. The torch wobbled as she took it from Naòm even though she grasped it with both hands. Then Yakal helped guide her to the final pyre and layer of kindling, which she ignited. The blaze flared high and Yakal felt the heat of it singing his eyebrows and face. Ajkun swayed at his side and he gently moved her back several paces. He linked arms with Naòm, who clutched onto Box. Ek' Balam padded close, and together, they all stood and watched as their loved ones joined the ancestors through the dancing sparks and flames that leapt into the dark sky.

NA'OM

Na'om reached down and felt for Ek' Balam. Ever since their return to Mayapán, she'd needed his company more than ever. He was the only thing familiar in a world turned upside down, now that Kärinik, Chiman, and Tz' were gone. She felt a hard lump form in her throat and swallowed. She knew she mustn't be so upset about their passing. They had all died in battle, a death that brought great honor to them all. But that fact did little to ease her tremendous grief. She was still alive and had to remain so without any of them, a task she didn't feel up to achieving. Then she felt the jaguar's soft fur under her fingertips and was grateful he was close by. No reassuring tingle of energy passed between them though, which worried her. Najtir had said it might take many moons before her strength returned, and even then, it might not be as robust as it had been. She knew she shouldn't worry, but she did. *Without that power, I feel so vulnerable,* she mused as she swung in the hammock. Then she touched the obsidian bead necklace still around her neck, the necklace Najtir had given her and told her to bury with Satal. *I wish I'd had a chance to put this around the old witch's neck. But Yakal and Box said they wouldn't be able to find their way back to the cave, and they swear that Satal is truly gone.* Na'om sighed. She was still very tired after the long march back to the city, which had taken almost half a moon. They had carried the wounded on litters and brought the ashes of the dead back in pottery jars to be buried by their loved ones. The victory ceremonies had lasted for many days, and Na'om and Ek' Balam had been the center of attention, which she had tried to deflect by telling anyone who would listen of how brave everyone else had been. Kubal Joron, Matz', and Memetik had been the only ones to truly believe her, though.

Finally, life was beginning to return to normal in the city, and she was glad that she and Ajkun and some of the others would be leaving for Pa nimá in two days' time. *It will be good to see the village again,* she thought.

Then she cupped her hands under her belly and smiled. Despite her willingness to sacrifice her life to the gods, they had spared her and the life of her son. The baby was growing, and soon she knew she'd feel his first kicks. She wanted to be back in Pa nimá and well rested long before her child arrived. She imagined him running to the river and splashing in the shallow water like she had done as a child, and she smiled again.

Then a quick knock on the doorway brought Na'om back to the present. "Na'om, are you there?" Box said.

Na'om slipped from the hammock. "Come in, come in," she said as she straightened her dress.

"I'm sorry; I didn't realize you were napping. I can come back later," Box said, turning to leave.

"No, no, it's all right. I mustn't sleep the whole day away," Na'om said and laughed.

Box smiled. "Najtir wants us to go get crab cakes with him. He knows it will be his last chance to see you, and he wants to send you off with a large stack of them for your journey."

Na'om smiled. "Yes, all right, let me just brush my hair for a moment."

"I'll wait outside. Take your time."

Na'om looked around the hut for the package she'd purchased the day before. It was a new censor in the shape of a black jaguar. She hoped Najtir would like it and remember her and Ek' Balam each time he used it.

Stepping outside, she saw several guards waiting to escort her through the crowded city streets. "Another thing I won't miss," she said. She touched Ek' Balam again. She wouldn't leave him in the hut.

"What's that?" Box asked.

"Oh, it's nothing," Na'om replied. She motioned for the guards to lead the way.

The group arrived at the marketplace and stopped when they found Biribik and Najtir. Na'om gave them each a hug and looped her arm through Najtir's so she could help the old shaman to T'ot's booth.

Mok'onel was working behind the counter when they arrived, and she hurried to greet them. She pulled Na'om into a strong embrace and then took her hand and placed it on her own swelling belly. "Did you feel that?" she asked.

Na'om nodded. She had felt the child move before, but she knew Mok'onel meant well by her attentions. "He's a strong one, just like his father."

Mok'onel smiled. "Strong and brave if the stories Biribik tells me are true."

"Every word, I promise," Na'om said. "I watched him fight alongside Nimal and his warriors and Biribik brought down many of our enemies. You should be very proud of him."

"I am and so grateful he came back to me, to our little family," she added as little Tze'm came running out from behind the curtain and clutched at her skirt.

"Chuch, T'ot needs your help," Tze'm said and then he dashed over to Biribik who scooped him up and swung him high into the air.

T'ot appeared with a large platter loaded with stacks of crab cakes and Mok'onel hurried over to take the heavy dish from the older woman.

"Na'om, Najtir, I'm so happy to see you again," T'ot shouted.

"This will be my last visit for a while, I'm sorry to say," Na'om said as she settled on the stool in between Box and Najtir. She handed the package she'd brought to Najtir. "A little gift for you."

"Oh, my dear, you didn't need to do that," Najtir said. He quickly unwrapped the parcel and held the black jaguar censor in his hands. "I love it and shall use it from now on for all my work," he said as he gently put the ceramic piece on the table. "Maltiox, my dear," he added as he lightly kissed Na'om's hand.

She blushed and looked away. Then, to avoid any more awkward moments, she cut into the stack of crab cakes in front of her and sighed as the rich corn and salty seafood melted in her mouth. When she'd swallowed, she turned to T'ot. She raised her voice. "These just keep getting better and better."

"Mok'onel made these, not me," T'ot said and laughed. "She's the cook now; I just play with little Tze'm!"

When they were done eating, Mok'onel handed Na'om a cotton cloth tied with hemp string. "More crab cakes for your journey."

"Maltiox, Mok'onel."

"Promise me that you'll come visit one day so our children get to know one another, eh?"

Na'om smiled. "I'd like that. Yes, I'll bring my son once I'm able to travel again." She gave Mok'onel a hug and turned to Box and Najtir. "Let's go."

Back at the edge of the marketplace, she said good-bye to Najtir and Biribik.

"Not good-bye," Biribik said. "Mok' and I expect to see you before many moons have passed."

Na'om nodded, gave Najtir another hug, and then walked away before either of them could see the tears streaming down her face.

Once back at her hut, Na'om paused at the doorway. She didn't want to be left alone.

"Should I stay with you?" Box asked.

"Would you mind?"

"Of course not."

Na'om sat down on the hammock and offered Box the stool. A deep silence filled the room, and she didn't know what to say. She'd be leaving in a day and knew Box would be staying in the city to carry on with his life.

Then Box leaned forward and took Na'om's hands in his. "How are you feeling?"

Na'om stared into Box's deep brown eyes and could see how weary he looked. "I'm tired, so incredibly tired," she admitted.

"I've been to the temple many times and prayed to Itzamná to bring you back into the light," Box said. His face flushed, and he dropped his eyes to look at the ground.

Na'om reached over and touched him gently on his knee. "Maltiox, Box." She inhaled deeply and could smell incense and wood smoke on Box's dark-green cotton shirt and loincloth. The scent tickled her nose, and she almost sneezed, but she drew in another deep breath as the mix of odors was pleasant as well.

"What will you do when you return to your village?" Box asked. He looked directly into Na'om's eyes.

"Get ready to have this child the gods have planted within me. Beyond that, I don't know."

Box stood up and walked about the small room. And then he stopped in front of the urn that held Tz's ashes. He touched it briefly and turned to her. "I know you're still grieving for Tz', but you must know I want to be with you, to share my life with you. I've never wanted any woman more," Box said. He looked at her. "I also respect your feelings toward Tz' and know that it might be too soon for you to harbor any interest in someone like me. But if you can find room in your heart for me, then I shall love you until the day the gods force me to join our ancestors."

Na'om nodded. "Maltiox, Box." She didn't know what to say. For months, her only thought had been to bring Tz' back from Xibalba, and she had assumed their lives would continue to intertwine from that moment forward. But then he had died, leaving an emptiness inside her. She did feel drawn to Box in ways that she still didn't fully understand. *Oh, my feelings are so mixed up*, she thought and let out a big sigh. She laid her head back in the hammock.

Box stopped moving and looked deep into Na'om's eyes. "You're tired, I'll go," he said. He headed toward the door.

"Box, please don't be upset with me; you've given me a lot to think about, things I never thought could be possible until now. I just haven't had enough time to understand everything that's happened." She held out her hands. "Can I get a hug before you go?"

Box smiled. "Of course." He strode across the room, leaned down to hug Na'om, and then gave her the tiniest kiss on her cheek. "I'll come back tomorrow, if that's all right."

"Yes, please, I would like that as it's my last day in the city," Na'om said. "And Box?"

"Yes?"

"Maltiox."

Box nodded. "Until tomorrow."

But as soon as he was out of sight, Na'om felt her heart cramp and she leapt from the hammock and ran outside. "*Box!*" she shouted. And she was relieved to see him turn around and hurry back.

"I can't make any promises just yet, but I won't know if I can love you if I don't get to know you better. Will you come with us to the village and stay until I can make up my mind? I know it's a lot to ask."

Box smiled and gave Na'om another hug. "Nothing would bring me greater pleasure. I'll follow you wherever you go and help you in any way that I can until you know for sure if I'm a worthy companion. I promise that if I'm not, I'll walk away and not look back. I'll go now and tell Puk'pik I'm leaving with you."

Na'om laughed. "We lost our potter in the attack on the village, so your skills will be needed by many." She squeezed Box's arm. "Maltiox, my friend." And then she scurried into her hut before she started to cry.

The next day went by quickly as Na'om visited everyone she knew in Mayapán and said her good-byes. Kubal Joron and Matz' gave her a beautiful jade necklace and a dress of the softest blue linen, and Memetik gave Lintat a new quiver full of arrows that he had fletched himself.

That evening, Alom, Yakal, and Uskab served a large meal for Ajkun, Na'om, Noy, and Lintat. The women cried as they said farewell. The departure was difficult for Na'om, but she realized it was even harder for the older women. It was a long journey between the village and the city, which might prove to be too arduous for any of them to make, so they might never see each other again.

Na'om stood to one side and let the older women leave with Box. She wanted a private moment with Yakal.

"Yakal, Tat, maltiox for everything. I wish now I'd had more time to get to know you. You and Uskab and Mayibal and the baby are all welcome to come stay us whenever you like."

Yakal smiled. "You'll have a hard time keeping me away, Na'om, when I know I'll be a grandfather after several moons. When Uskab is able to travel, we'll come visit. And you always have a home here too, remember that."

Na'om hugged Yakal, and he smiled. "Box is a good man; I hope you find him worthy."

"Maltiox, Tat, until we meet again."

The group leaving the city was up before dawn the following day, and Na'om hoped to make a quiet departure. But as soon as she reached the city center, she realized almost everyone was awake and waiting to see them off.

With Box by her side and Ek' Balam leading the way, Na'om, Ajkun, and the others walked through the copper gates and headed into the countryside to the stamping of feet, the clapping of hands, and the shouts and cries of safe travels from those who remained behind.

AJKUN

Ajkun cradled the earthenware jar that held Chiman's ashes in her lap as she slowly began to recognize the area of the river they were traveling on. *Almost home, my love*, she thought as she patted the urn. She breathed in deeply when the canoe rounded a bend, and she could see the small sandy beach and the path that led to the village center. Tears welled in her eyes, and she choked back a sob as the bow of the dugout bumped into the riverbank. Lintat hopped out of the stern and dragged the canoe farther up onto the sandy soil, then turned and helped Ajkun step onto the sand. He then helped Noy out of the bow.

"I'm going to tell everyone we've arrived," Lintat shouted before darting up the path to the village center.

Ajkun placed her jar on the ground, and then embraced Noy as tears flowed freely down their faces. "Itzamná, thank you for returning us to our home," Ajkun cried.

Na'om and Box guided their canoe onto the riverbank, and Ek' Balam nimbly hopped over the thwart and instantly began sniffing the air and dirt along the river. Na'om hurried to Ajkun's side. "Ati't, are you all right?" Na'om asked.

Ajkun patted Na'om on the arm. "Yes, my dear, never better. I am forever grateful to have made it back home after all the struggles we've been through. I shall never leave this place again," she said. She wiped her tears with the back of her sleeve and gave Na'om a big smile and then a hug. "We'll come back later for our things. Right now, I can't wait to see everyone."

Ajkun picked up Chiman's ashes and headed toward the village center.

Na'om looked around for Ek' Balam. "Hey, old boy, are you coming with us?" she asked. The jaguar swished his tail and twitched his ears, then leaped into the river and began swimming across the water.

"Hey, where are you going?" Na'om cried. She hurried to the water's edge.

Ajkun turned back at the sound of Na'om's voice. "He'll be fine, my dear. Come on, we need to go greet everyone."

By the time they reached the clearing near the temple, many people had assembled, including Setesik, Pempen, and Sijuan.

Setesik stepped forward. "Ajkun, thank the gods you've returned," he said as he bowed to her.

"It is good to be home, old friend," Ajkun replied. She motioned to Pempen with her one good arm and the woman came forward for a hug. Their daughter, Sijuan, nodded and bowed respectfully but remained at a distance. Setesik looked around the small group. "Lord Chiman, is he not with you?"

Ajkun thrust the urn toward Setesik who took it. "He died in the great battle. We must honor his courage and sacrifice with a proper ceremony."

The older man nodded. "Of course, of course, we shall arrange it right away. And Tz'? What of him?"

Na'om came forward. "He didn't survive the battle, either. I have his ashes in our canoe."

Then before anyone could ask any more questions, a young boy and girl of about three ran from their mother and straight to Ajkun. They wrapped their chubby arms around her legs, preventing her from moving, and laughed so hard that Ajkun had to laugh as well. She smiled at the children, wondering who they were.

"Ala, Ali, let go of Ati't so she may come sit by the fire after her long journey."

Ajkun looked at the children again in amazement. "They were just crawling when I last saw them." Two more children came running and joined Ala and Ali, who now held Ajkun by the hands and were slowly walking her toward the fire. "Don't tell me, Kab and Tuney?" Ajkun asked.

"Yes," Witzik' replied. She reached out and embraced Ajkun. "It is so good to have you back in the village. We've all missed you." She patted her stomach. "And there is a new child on the way who will meet you in a few moons' time." She pointed to the stool by the fire. "Sit, sit, you must be weary."

Ajkun nodded, but turned to look over her shoulder. Na'om and Box were still standing at the edge of the clearing, talking quietly together. "First, Witzik', you must meet my granddaughter, Na'om." She raised her voice. "Na'om, Box, come and meet everyone." She gestured with her hand and was glad to see the couple approach.

Witzik' bowed to Na'om. "It is a great honor to meet you, Lady Na'om."

"Please, no more formalities, I've had enough of them for a lifetime," Na'om said. "Just call me Na'om, and this is Box." The three embraced and Witzik' gestured for everyone to sit down, but before they could, another villager appeared.

"Chuch," Tuney said and ran toward her mother.

Tzalon smiled as she scooped the girl up in her arms. She hurried to Ajkun and gave her a long hug. "Oh, Ajkun, how we have missed you." She looked around. "And Ajaw Chiman, is he here as well?"

Ajkun pointed to the urn Setesik still held. "Chiman is with the ancestors now. We lost him in the great battle against Satal and her army from Xibalba. And his son, Tz', was also lost."

"We shall honor their sacrifice with a special ceremony tomorrow morning," Setesik said. Ajkun nodded and watched as he carried Chiman's urn over to the small temple and placed the vessel on the stone steps. She felt the pain of his death in her chest and took a deep breath. Then she turned to Tzalon, who was speaking,

"I'm so sorry to hear of his passing," the young woman said and briefly touched Ajkun on the arm. "If there is anything we can do to help you, please let us know." Then she smiled at Na'om. "We've heard bits and pieces of your story, but we all look forward to learning of your trials, if you care to share them with us, of course."

Na'om smiled. "Perhaps, after we've all settled in a bit." She reached for Ajkun's hand and squeezed it. "I'm going to show Box the rest of the village and take him across the river. I want to see what remains of my home and look for Ek' Balam."

"Yes, dear, I'll be fine. We're among family here," Ajkun said as she sat down. Lintat appeared with a stool for Noy, and she also sat. Instantly, the four children began vying for a seat on Ajkun's lap, and she turned to them. "One at a time, one at a time." Then she awkwardly picked up Kab with her one good arm and gave him a big squeeze as he settled comfortably on her knees. Noy, reached out and Ali climbed into her arms.

Witzik' walked a few paces with Na'om and Box. "Tzalon, Xoral, and I took turns maintaining your home while you were away. We all felt certain you would return to it one day."

"Maltiox," Na'om replied. She took the older girl's hand in her own. "I hope we can become good friends."

"Yes, I believe we will. Please, if there's anything you need, let us know. Now that you've returned, I'll gather some food together and have it brought over to fill your larder. And we must have a feast tomorrow to celebrate your victory and safe return."

"Maltiox," Na'om said.

Ajkun waved again to Na'om before turning back to the children. She set Kab on the ground and was about to pick up Tuney when the little girl screamed with fright. She pointed toward the liana vines, and Ajkun saw the face of a jaguar poking out from among the bushes.

"Shh, my love," Tzalon said as she bent down and lifted Tuney up in her arms. "It's only Sia." She turned to Ajkun. "She comes every few weeks and sniffs all around your hut before going back into the jungle. She's been waiting for your return just like the rest of us."

The big female jaguar stepped from the bushes and sidled past most of those gathered. She drew near Ajkun and began to purr but didn't approach, even though Ajkun held out her hand. The jaguar quickly crossed the clearing and then when she reached the path to the river, she bolted, and Ajkun laughed. "She's not been waiting for me, I suspect, but for Ek' Balam." She leaned down and tickled Ala in the belly. "Perhaps there will be jaguar kittens to play with in a few moons' time."

The shadows lengthened, and everyone kept asking questions, which Ajkun, Noy, and even Lintat took turns answering. In a lull in the conversation, Witzik' brought the travelers bowls of soup filled with chunks of turkey, manioc, and corn, and Ajkun felt the tension in her body gradually release. As she slowly ate the rich broth, she looked around the clearing at the familiar huts and the temple, and suddenly she wanted nothing more than to lie on her ceiba-filled mattress in her own hut and sleep. She looked at Noy and could see the tiredness etched on her old friend's face.

"Come, Noy, I think we should rest. Tomorrow, we can tell everyone more of our adventures. Right now, I want nothing more than to sleep in my own bed!"

Setesik walked Ajkun to her hut. "Will you be all right tonight?" he asked as he lit a candle and helped Ajkun into the main room.

She looked around and nodded. Someone had kept the place clean and organized while she'd been away. "Yes, I'll be fine," she said. Setesik bowed and quietly left. As soon as he was gone, Ajkun walked around the two rooms, looking at everything. A pair of worn sandals was near the door, and empty bark containers that had held foodstuffs lined the wall under the set of shelves filled with baskets of herbs and pottery jars of salves. Several pieces of clothing still hung from the row of pegs in the wall, and she picked up one of Chiman's shirts and put it to her nose. It smelled faintly of copal smoke, other herbs, and his sweat. She sat on the edge of the bed and felt a rush of tears fill her eyes.

"Oh, Chiman, we've made it home," she cried as she fingered the fabric in her hands. "I miss you so, my love," and she let out a large sob before lying on the bed. She clutched the shirt to her face and cried into the pillow for some time, and then, emotionally exhausted and physically spent, Ajkun fell asleep still dressed.

The sun had been above the horizon for many hours before Ajkun finally woke up. She was disoriented at first as she took in her surroundings and then realized with a strong sense of relief that she was finally, truly home. She sat up and patted at her hair. She needed to bathe and change her clothes and remembered she had left her basket of belongings in the canoe. She headed to the door and was surprised to see someone had brought her things to the hut and also started a fire in the firepit. A large pot of water bubbled gently on the rocks and several bark containers of cold water from the river stood nearby.

It's good to be back where there's plenty of water, she thought as she quickly mixed hot and cold water together for a shower. Her water dipper still hung from a peg in the wall and the bowl of jasmine-scented soap sat on the shelf underneath it. She removed her dirty clothes and took a long shower, washing her long gray hair, and luxuriated in the use of so much water. She looked closely at the deep were-jaguar scratches on her arm and was pleased to see they were healing well, though they would leave permanent scars.

She was just getting dressed inside when she heard a knock on the doorway.

"Yes, just one moment," Ajkun said as she rubbed her hair with a rough cotton towel. She stepped outside and was pleasantly surprised to see a plate of tamales had been left for her along with a hot mug of herbal tea. "Maltiox," she cried out as she looked for someone nearby.

When she had finished eating, she took Chiman's old shirt and hurried down to the river to see if there was a sign of Na'om or Box, but the area was empty. Someone had built a bench from thick slabs of mahogany near the riverbank, and she sat on it for several minutes with her eyes closed. She listened to the gurgles of the river as it flowed by and the croaking of some frogs hidden in the grasses at the water's edge.

How I have missed these simple sounds, she thought. More of the tightness in her shoulders let go, and Ajkun sighed. *Itzamná, thank you for bringing me home safely. I only wish Chiman were here with me.* She clutched his shirt as her grief rose inside her, filling her belly and throat with pain. Tears appeared and ran down her cheeks, but she hastily wiped them away when she heard voices on the path.

"There she is, see I told you," Witzik' said to Xoral, who was followed by their children.

Ajkun smiled at the two women and laughed when the toddlers saw her and came rushing over for hugs. "Oh, my sweet turtle doves, how I have missed you all," she said. She squatted down and gave each of the children a hug.

"Everyone has gathered at the temple for the ceremony for Chiman and for Tz'," Xoral said as she helped Ajkun to her feet.

"Yes, of course, I should have come there directly," Ajkun said. "I'm sorry to have kept everyone waiting."

"We wanted to give you plenty of time to rest," Witzik' said. "Tonight, we shall have a feast, thanking the gods for your victory over Satal and for returning you safely to us."

Ajkun nodded. She walked arm in arm with Witzik', while Xoral corralled the children and helped them all back to the village center.

Na'om and Box stood directly in front of the temple steps with Pempen and Sijuan. Lintat and Noy were beside them. Each of them held an item that had belonged to Chiman and Tz'. The rest of the villagers had created a semicircle around the group. Pottery braziers filled with burning copal and eucalyptus leaves flanked the small set of stairs, sending spirals of smoke into the air. Setesik stood on the small landing outside the doorway to the temple. He was dressed in a ceremonial cape made of honeycreeper feathers and wore a carved green jade necklace on his bare chest. He'd circled his eyes and drawn streaks across his cheeks with black and red paint and plastered his black hair with peccary fat, sculpting it into a mohawk on the top of his head. He smiled when he saw Ajkun and motioned for her to come forward.

She took her place beside Na'om and was grateful to have her granddaughter slip her arm around her waist.

Setesik picked up the urn with Chiman's ashes and held it chest high. "Ajkun, Na'om, friends, we are gathered to pay our respects to our beloved shaman and leader, Chiman, who willingly placed himself in harm's way in order to save the woman he loved." Setesik nodded and smiled at Ajkun. "I knew Chiman from when we were young boys, and I never saw him happier than when he partnered with you, Ajkun. Although your time together in this world was short, your love for each other filled every moment of every day, and it was a pleasure for all of us to behold. Today, we shall bury Chiman's ashes under the floor of the temple, a place he cherished and considered his home. Ajkun, the honor of placing his ashes inside belongs to you." He held out the urn and Ajkun stepped forward to take it.

Then Setesik reached down and picked up the urn that contained Tz's ashes. "Today, we also honor Tz'ajonel, son of Chiman, who also willingly gave his life to protect the woman he loved, our own Lady Na'om. Without Tz's intervention, the battle with Satal might have ended quite differently. It is with a heavy heart that we bury this fine warrior alongside his father." Setesik held out the urn to Na'om, who grasped it in her hands.

With Na'om on one side and Box on the other, Ajkun climbed the steps and entered the temple ahead of Setesik. A hole had been prepared in the middle of the floor and Ajkun knelt beside it. She kissed the lid of Chiman's vessel before gently placing it inside the hole. She felt the familiar pain of grief gather in the back of her throat and her eyes welled with tears. She held his old shirt to her face and sniffed it one last time. "Until we meet again, my love," she whispered as she folded the fabric and laid it beside the urn. She sighed and looked up at Na'om, Box, and Setesik. Pempen, Noy, and Lintat had also entered the small building. "How shall I ever carry on?" she cried and let the tears flow freely down her cheeks.

Na'om knelt beside Ajkun and wrapped her in a hug as her own tears ran. "We shall help you in any way that we can," she said as she inhaled deeply and swallowed. She placed two pottery mugs and a water gourd near the shirt, then put Tz's urn next to Chiman's before stepping aside.

Box added two new pairs of sandals, Pempen placed a large bowl of red, yellow, and blue corn kernels in the pit, and Lintat contributed a bundle of feathers. Noy positioned a chunk of copal near the other items, and then Setesik squatted and added two intricately carved obsidian knives with leather scabbards.

"All the items they shall need in Xibalba," Setesik said as he stood back up.

The group moved back outside where Setesik and Pempen stopped to talk to Ajkun. "When you left the village so many moons ago, we moved into Chiman's home in order to keep it from falling into disrepair," Setesik said. "Now that you've returned, we shall move out right away so you may live there."

"No, my friend, I have no wish to live in that house. In my mind, it always belonged to Chachal. My old home suits me, so stay where you are with my blessing. I know Chiman would be happy to have you there as well."

"Maltiox, Ajkun," Pempen said as she gave her a hug.

Noy placed her hand on Ajkun's shoulder. "Come, Ajkun, let's go have a cup of tea."

Ajkun nodded. She was grateful to have her old friend beside her and the two women left the temple area together.

"My grief comes and goes in waves," Ajkun said as they made their way down the path to Noy's hut. "I am so thankful to be home, and yet I expect to see Chiman at any moment," she sobbed.

"With time, you'll be able to let go of some of your grief and look to the future, as I did after Mam died. Playing with the children will help; together, we'll rejoice in the life energy that flows so freely through them, and teach them what we know so they grow into capable adults. And we have Na'om's own child to prepare for as well."

That evening, the two women joined the villagers in the main plaza and feasted with everyone, celebrating that they had returned home. Ajkun sat surrounded by the people she knew and loved and felt at peace. She laughed at the antics of the toddlers and looked forward to holding Na'om's child, her great-grandchild, in her arms. She listened to Na'om tell the villagers the full story of the great battle and shook her head, amazed that any of them had lived through it all.

The moon was on its way down when Na'om, Box, and Ek' Balam walked with Ajkun to her house. She wished them all a good night and entered the quiet building. Suddenly, she was exhausted, and as she looked around the empty room, she felt the mantle of loneliness slide over her. She crawled into bed, but as she closed her eyes, she heard something outside. She got back up and looked outside. Sia' lay in a patch of moonlight and her eyes glowed bright yellow when she lifted her head.

"Sia', you're back!" Ajkun exclaimed. She rummaged around indoors and found some dried fish, which she tossed to the jaguar. "I don't feel so alone now, maltiox," she said. "You're welcome any time."

The jaguar thumped her tail on the ground several times and settled in to eat the fish while Ajkun took another of Chiman's old shirts off a peg and slipped it over her nightshirt. Wrapped in the comfort of his smells, she went back to bed and fell into a deep sleep, knowing both Sia' and Chiman would watch over her while she slept.

Na'om

Nine full moons had passed since Na'om had entered Xibalba in search of Tz', and her time to have the baby had arrived. She stepped out of her small hut, quickly filled a ceramic pot with water from the gourds hanging near the firepit, and banked the fire so the water would heat but not boil away while she was gone. She rubbed her full belly as she slowly waddled down to the riverbank to her canoe in the moonlight. She needed Ajkun, but her grandmother was asleep in the village on the other side of the river. With difficulty, Na'om maneuvered into the bottom of the canoe and pushed off from shore. She took long, deep breaths as she paddled the short distance to the sandy beach on the opposite side and took her time getting back out of the canoe. A sharp contraction forced her to hang on to the gunwale of the dugout, and then she carefully walked up the path toward the village.

Once she left the river, the moon was hidden by the tall mahogany and mango trees that grew along the path to the village, and it was full of dark shadows. *The last thing I want is to trip and fall right now*, Na'om thought as she paused and bent over with her hands on her knees. She breathed through the next wave of pain and wiped a bead of sweat off her cheek.

A sudden light in the distance forced her to raise her head, and she smiled when she realized Ajkun was coming toward her with a lit torch in one hand and her basket of medicine in the other. "How did you know?" she asked as she stood upright and held onto Ajkun's forearm.

"I've been delivering babies for a very long time, and if there's a chance they'll come when the moon is full, they do," Ajkun replied. "How often do the pains come?"

"Often enough that I didn't want to wait any longer to see you," Na'om said. She gritted her teeth as another spasm went through her body.

"Do you want to continue to the village or go back to your own hut?" Ajkun asked.

"Is it silly of me to want the baby to come in my own house?" Na'om said. She took a deep breath and let it out slowly.

"Come on, then, I don't think we have much time," Ajkun replied.

Na'om leaned on her grandmother, and together the two of them walked the hundred paces or so to the river. Ajkun placed her basket in the canoe, helped Na'om get settled, then handed her the torch. "I'll paddle, you just keep breathing slowly and deeply."

Na'om nodded and dragged her fingertips in the water as the canoe slowly moved back across the river. The light from the moon bounced and reflected off the surface of the water, magnifying the colors everything around her. "It's so beautiful out here," she said as the bow of the canoe ran up onto solid ground.

She stepped into the shallows, then helped Ajkun drag the canoe a bit higher onto the shore. Arm in arm, the two made their way back down the path to the hut in the circle of mahogany trees.

"Good girl," Ajkun said when she saw the pot of water bubbling away.

"I remember some of my training," Na'om said and laughed, then cried out as a sharp pain forced her to bend over again.

"Come on, we haven't much time," Ajkun said as she helped hurry Na'om into the one-room hut.

While Na'om settled herself on the ceiba mattress on the floor, Ajkun took her bowls of special salves and ointments out of the basket. She also brought out her pottery statue of Ixchel and quickly poured some ground corn from a leather bag into the goddess's outstretched hands. "Please help my granddaughter deliver this child, Lady Ixchel," Ajkun prayed as she placed the small statue in a corner of the room. "Where are the blankets you want to use?" she asked Na'om.

Na'om pointed to a large basket in the opposite corner. "There . . . along with . . . the binding boards and the . . . cloths to use to clean . . . and wrap the baby. And a knife to cut the cord," she added as she slowly let out another deep breath.

Just then, the two women heard a noise outside, and Ajkun poked her head out the doorway. She laughed. "It's Ek' Balam, Sia', and the kittens. I guess they want to be the first to meet the newest member of the family." She turned and helped Na'om remove her dress and get more comfortable on the floor.

Suddenly, they heard footsteps running along the path, then a nervous voice called, "Ajkun? Are you there?"

Ajkun stuck her head out the door again. "It's Sijuan," she said over her shoulder to Na'om. "Do you want her to help?"

Na'om smiled through the pain. "Yes, of course, she's training to be the new midwife of the village."

"Come in, Sijuan, come in," Ajkun said and beckoned to the girl.

Sijuan pointed to the large cats lying near the doorway to the hut. "It's safe?" she questioned as she remained standing in the same spot.

"Yes, yes, girl, they'll do you no harm. Fetch me the hot water; we'll need it soon. Then take the water gourds to the river and refill them. Oh, and use this dried thistle and brew some tea."

Sijuan nodded and quickly filled a turtle shell basin with hot water, which she handed to Ajkun through the doorway. Then she poured some of the remaining water into a ceramic mug with the thistle and left it to steep next to the fire before she disappeared back up the path with the three water gourds in hand.

Na'om groaned and Ajkun quickly reached for her small bowl of sapote salve. She rubbed it on Na'om's belly, easing the pain away with each rotation of her hand on the skin.

Sijuan stepped through the door and handed Na'om the tea she had made. "Take small sips between the waves of pain," she directed as she helped Na'om drink.

"Maltiox, Sijuan, it tastes good," Na'om said and licked her dry lips. Another contraction bent her double, and she cried out a bit. "Oh, oh, I need to push," she cried as she bent forward again.

Ajkun quickly washed her hands in the hot water and dried them on a clean towel. "Let me look, Na'om," she said. She motioned to Sijuan to step behind Naʼom and hold her from the back.

Sijuan squatted behind Naʼom and linked her arms through Naʼom's elbows, giving her as much support as possible.

"I can see the head," Ajkun said. "At the next pain, push as hard as you can, Naʼom," she instructed.

"Trust me and lean into me," Sijuan added. "I'll hold you."

Naʼom nodded as sweat dripped down her face. She gritted her teeth, scrunched her eyes closed, and let out a howl as she pushed with every ounce of strength. And as she pushed, a faint bluish glow formed around her body and then faded as quickly as it had appeared.

"Here it comes," Ajkun said. "The head's out, now one shoulder and one hand and there, it's a boy!" she cried. And then she gasped as the other hand and the feet popped into view.

Sijuan sucked in her breath, and Naʼom opened her eyes.

"What's wrong?" she asked as she reached toward her child. "Let me see him." Ajkun placed the newborn in Naʼom's arms, and she looked down to see her child. And she gasped as well. "Itzamná! What happened to you, little one?" she said. She looked closely at her son, then reached out and touched his left hand, which looked less like a hand and more like a jaguar paw. The flesh was darker brown than the rest of his skin and was covered with fine black hair in the form of rosettes. Each tiny finger was stunted and ended in a small claw rather than a fingernail. She sighed. "I guess I shouldn't be too surprised, considering how you were conceived," she said while she nuzzled the top of the baby's head. She breathed in his sweet smell, like honey in water, and he looked up at her with his dark brown eyes. Naʼom instantly felt herself fall deeper in love. She put him to her breast, and he began to drink greedily. "Well, he has no lack of an appetite," Naʼom said as she leaned back into the pillows and mattress.

"Sijuan, bring more hot water so we can wash the baby and Naʼom," Ajkun said.

Sijuan nodded and left the hut without speaking.

Naʼom's legs trembled, and she was so tired, but it felt good to hold her child. And then suddenly, she felt another contraction and she gasped with the pain. She clutched the baby and he stopped nursing, releasing the nipple in a jerk that allowed milk to dribble down Naʼom's breast.

"Atiʼt, it hurts, oh, it hurts again!" Naʼom cried as she bent forward.

"Shh, child, it's just the afterbirth releasing and coming out," Ajkun said as she grabbed a large pottery bowl to collect the placenta.

"No, no, it feels like another baby is coming," Na'om cried and she screeched as the contraction hit her.

"Let me look," Ajkun said as she settled on the floor in front of Na'om. "By all the gods, there's another head," Ajkun cried. "Sijuan, hurry in here, we have another child coming!"

Sijuan raced through the doorway and hurried to take the firstborn child from Na'om. She wrapped the baby in a small blanket as he began to howl. "Shh, little one, your mother is right here, shh," she said as she rocked him back and forth. He quickly closed his eyes and fell asleep as she continued to sway him back and forth. Sijuan gently placed the infant on the far side of the ceiba mattress out of Na'om's way.

"All right, on the next contraction, push, Na'om," Ajkun instructed. "Sijuan, come here, you should catch this child. My knees are too old to remain squatting like this for long." She struggled to stand up and let Sijuan take her place. "Nice and easy now, just let the pain push the child out," she instructed.

Na'om nodded and concentrated. Tears leaked down her face, mingling with beads of sweat. She pushed and pushed and pushed. And the bluish glow reappeared, brighter and stronger this time.

"What's happening?" Sijuan cried as she looked at the light.

"Itzamná, I do believe Na'om's power is returning," Ajkun stated. "Now, push, that's it, just a little bit more," Ajkun encouraged. "I can see the head and the arms and oh, look, there he is, another sweet boy."

Sijuan smiled as she held the child up toward Na'om.

"Is he all right?" Na'om asked as she took the baby. She quickly looked him over and saw ten tiny fingers and toes, two eyes, two ears. "He's perfect," she said and kissed him. Then she glanced at her sleeping first son and leaned over to kiss him on his tiny forehead. "And you are too, my love." She placed the second boy on her full breast and he began to nurse.

"By all accounts, two healthy children," Ajkun said. "We'll have to discuss your firstborn with Setesik, though, so he may ask the gods why his hand is the way it is."

Na'om laughed and pointed to her own skin covered with spots. "The gods of Xibalba planted these children in me, so it's no surprise that he has a jaguar paw for a hand. All that matters is that he is my son. I think he could be a great shaman and ruler someday." The infant opened his eyes, and she awkwardly picked him up with one hand. "I shall name him K'ab Balam."

"K'ab Balam, and your second son?" Ajkun asked.

Na'om took him from Sijuan and looked at him closely. She noticed a tiny dark spot on his forehead. "Ch'imil, for this mark on his head that looks like a star."

She handed K'ab Balam to Sijuan and Ch'imil to Ajkun, then went outside to bathe. As she mixed the hot and cold water, she smiled at Ek' Balam, Sia', and the three kittens that tumbled about in the brush. It was good to have them nearby. *Maltiox, Ek' Balam, I know my sons will be well protected.* Ek' Balam purred, then went and picked up the one black kitten by the scruff and laid it gently at Na'om's feet. "Is this one for me?" Ek' Balam purred in response. Na'om picked up the baby jaguar and held it close, watching as it thrashed his big paws about, so reminiscent of Ek' Balam when he'd been a kitten. "Will you be a fearless jaguar like your father?" she asked and then she set the kitten down.

The warm water washed away the sweat and blood, and she quickly pulled on a clean shift before heading back inside. She watched as Sijuan bathed K'ab Balam in a pottery basin of warm water with pericón flowers in it. The yellow blossoms filled the hut with the scent of anise. Sijuan swaddled him and handed him to Ajkun, and then she took Ch'imil and washed him as well.

"K'ab Balam and Ch'imil," Ajkun repeated as she handed the babies to Na'om. Then she turned to Sijuan. "Tell your father we have two new members of the village and tell him their names, but don't mention K'ab Balam's hand. Let me show him to Setesik."

Sijuan nodded as she gathered up the last of the used towels and rags. "Shall I let Box come over, Na'om, or do you wish to wait until you've rested a bit?"

"Box has a lifetime to spend with her. Let's give Na'om some alone time with her children," Ajkun said. "Unless you want to see Box right now," she added as she turned to Na'om.

Cradling her sons on either side of her, Na'om felt content and just wanted to relax with them tucked in beside her. "I think I need some sleep, if that's all right. Tell Box I want to see him, but that I must rest a bit first."

"I'm sure he'll understand when he learns you have *two* sons," Sijuan said and smiled. She ducked through the doorway and was gone.

Ajkun sat down on the foot of the bed and gave Na'om a weary smile. "You'll have your hands full with these two," she said.

"Box will help me, Ati't, so I think we'll be all right. One day, he and I will have a child of our own and until then, we shall raise these children as best we can." She stroked K'ab Balam's soft fur on his left hand and wondered what really lay ahead for this child who obviously had jaguar blood running through his veins.

"The day shall begin soon, and we must bind their heads," Ajkun said. She walked over to the basket in the corner and pulled out the wooden planks and the strong leather cords that she'd use to hold the boards in place on the babies' heads.

Na'om held her firstborn son still while Ajkun nestled one board behind his head and the other on top of his forehead. Then she watched as her grandmother bound the planks to his skull with the thick leather thong, creating pressure so that the baby's head would conform to the slanted shape. Then she did the same with Ch'imil.

Ajkun bent down and kissed both children, then pecked Na'om on the cheek. "I'll return in a few hours with some breakfast for you. Try to get some sleep while you can."

Na'om smiled and settled back on the mattress. "I'll be here, don't worry."

Just as Na'om was about to drift off to sleep with the boys nestled against her chest, she sensed a presence in the room. She opened her eyes and looked about, but the hut was empty. And then she heard a voice in her head.

Na'om, it's me, Tz'. I heard the baby has arrived. May I visit with you?

Na'om pushed herself up on the bed and leaned against the wall. "Yes, come see, not just one son, but two," she said. She moved the blanket away from the babies so they were more visible.

A greenish glow began to form in the corner of the room and quickly solidified into the image of Tz'. He floated over to the bed and peered down at the children. *What have you named them?*

"K'ab Balam and Ch'imil," Na'om replied. She pulled the swaddling down from K'ab Balam's hand so Tz' could see it. "I don't know what this means for my son," she said as she touched his paw gently.

He'll certainly face some hardships, but with you by his side to guide him, the boy will do fine. And his brother will play a large role in his life too. Teach them everything you know and when the time is right, send them to Mayapán to study with the shamans. Tz' glanced toward the doorway where the first rays of sunlight were lighting up the sky. *Dawn is almost here, I must go.*

"Wait, before you leave. . . ." Na'om paused and swallowed hard as she felt a lump form in her throat. "I never got a chance to say good-bye or to thank you for saving my life." Tears ran down and dripped onto the blanket, narrowly missing K'ab Balam's cheek.

I was a fool in so many ways, especially thinking that becoming a were-jaguar was my destiny. I see that I missed out on so much of life in my pursuit of power. Know this though, I always loved you, and I will continue to love you until we meet again in Xibalba. And I will watch over you and your sons until that day arrives.

"So, you're not upset if I choose to live my life with Box?"

No, Box was a good friend to me, and you shouldn't be alone if you've found someone you care to be with. Especially since he loves you in return. I only wish things had turned out differently between us so I could be the father to these boys and be by your side as they grow. Tz' glanced again at the doorway and his light began to fade.

"Maltiox, Tz', you shall always hold a special place in my heart," Na'om sobbed as Tz's essence began to dissipate.

Blessings upon you, Na'om. Be well, be happy. Call on me if you should ever need my help and I shall come at once.

The greenish glow disappeared, leaving Na'om staring at the opposite wall of the hut. She sobbed and let the tears roll down her face, which woke the twins, who began to cry. "Shh, little ones, it's all right, I'm here," she sniffled as she kissed each boy in turn. They stopped their crying and looked at her with bright brown eyes. "Oh, I can see I'll have my hands full with you two." Na'om wiped her face with the edge of the blanket and laughed. "We're going to have some adventures together, that's for sure. And the first place we shall go once you're old enough to travel is to see the vast ocean and stay in this wonderful little hut on top of the sand dunes that a dear friend of mine left to me." The murmur of Na'om's voice sent the twins back to sleep, and she closed her eyes as well, slipping quickly into a dream about living by the sea.

Glossary

Ajaw: Owner; boss; lord.

Akab Dzib: The Red House or house of the shamans in Chichén Itzá.

ati't: An affectionate term for grandmother.

balché: A fermented, honey-sweetened drink made from the bark of the *Lonchocarpus violaceus* tree.

ceiba tree: The sacred tree of the Maya. Considered the world tree, its branches reach into heaven and its roots extend down into the Underworld.

cenote: Natural sinkholes that appear in the limestone terrain and are the source of fresh water in northern Yucatán. They are interconnected by a series of underground caves and tunnels, and many of these tunnels eventually lead to the sea. The Mayans considered cenotes the entranceways to the Underworld.

chacah: The *Bursera simaruba* or gumbo-limbo tree; it has yellow flowers and leaves used to draw out snakebite venom.

chac mool: A stone sculpture in the shape of a reclining man, whose head is turned 90 degrees from his body and who holds a rounded vessel between his hands on his abdomen. This bowl is used to hold sacrificial blood for the gods.

Chichén Itzá: A city in northeastern Yucatán, ruled by the Xiu tribe, and childhood home of Satal.

ch'om: *Bromelia pinguin* or piñuela plant. It grows up to one meter tall with red and white flowers.

chuch: An affectionate term for mother.

Cocom: The leading tribe of the city of Mayapán and the enemy of the Xiu.

copal: An aromatic tree resin burned as incense during ceremonies for purification.

dzudzuc: *Diphysa carthagenensis,* a very strong tree with yellow flowers that grows up to 15 feet tall. The leaves are believed to offer protection against evil.

huipil: A loose-fitting tunic shirt for women, made from cotton, often heavily embroidered around the square neckline.

Itzamná: Supreme god of the Maya; often used to express surprise, agitation, or other exclamations.

jequirity beans: A hallucinogenic bean, toxic in high doses.

Kini: A small village that Na'om passes through on her way to Mayapán.

Kukulcan: The feathered god of the Maya. Many pyramids are built in his honor.

maltiox: Thanks.

Mam: An affectionate term for grandfather.

matzaqik: Good-bye.

Mayapán: A city in northern Yucatán ruled by the Cocom.

noy: An affectionate term for grandmother.

ox: *Brosimum alicastrum* or breadnut, a flowering tree in the same family as mulberries. The leaves are used for vitality and good health.

Pa nimá: The village where Na'om was born; a phrase meaning 'by the river.'

Popul Vuh: The sacred book of the Maya, which included creation stories and other important events.

q'inomal: Riches, wealth, used as a toast when drinking.

sacbe: Raised causeways made from white limestone that connected Mayan cities, temples, and plazas.

saqarik: Good morning.

Silowik Tukan: The name of the bar in Mayapán; to be drunk; blackberry.

tat axel: An affectionate term for father.

to'nel: A witch who helps.

tzompantli: A stone wall covered with spikes where the heads of sacrificial victims were put on display.

utzil: Goodness, gracious, often used as an exclamation of surprise.

Wayeb: The five unnamed days at the end of the calendar year when the portal to the Underworld stands open.

xabalam: *Croton flavens*, an evergreen shrub from 3-9 feet tall; the leaves are used to draw out snakebite venom.

Xibalba: The Mayan Underworld.

Xiat: Small village that Na'om passes through on her way to Mayapán.

Xiu: The leading tribe of the city of Chichén Itzá and the enemy of the Cocom.

yax che: The giant ceiba tree that the Mayans believe grows from the center of the world. Its roots reach into the Underworld, and its branches hold up the sky and the heavens.

Acknowledgments

Many, many thanks to my husband, Jeffrey, who encouraged me to keep writing even when other interests drew my attention away from the blank page.

A big thank you to my editor, Jennifer Caven, who waited patiently for me to finish this manuscript. Several times I told her I was close to being done, and then months went by before I actually wrote anything new. I'm grateful she was available to edit this book on short notice and that she enjoyed it.

Thank you to my faithful readers who waited and waited and waited for this book and encouraged me to keep typing away at the story. Your patience and desire to know what happened pushed me through some serious writing blocks that lasted for years. Without your continued support, I doubt I would have finished this manuscript.

Thank you to my grandchildren, Jenson and Riley, who bring me such joy. I can't wait until you're old enough to read this series. I hope you'll enjoy them.

Thanks to all the archeologists and authors who have written about the Mayan people. Researching ideas for this series has been a great passion of mine, and I look forward to learning new things about the Mayan culture and people as more discoveries are made.

ABOUT THE AUTHOR

Lee E. Cart is an award-winning author, illustrator, editor, and publisher for Ek' Balam Press. Her first two novels in *The Mayan Chronicles* series have won awards in the Annual Latino Book Awards, which celebrates worldwide achievements in Latino literature.

Ms. Cart lives in central Maine, but lived in Guadalajara, Mexico for over seven years as a child. The time she spent in Mexico created a deep love for the Mexican people and their various cultures.

Ms. Cart enjoys writing, reading, weaving, creating surface pattern designs, gardening, and traveling to Hawaii and Mexico. One day, she hopes to visit New Zealand and see the penguins. When she's not writing or playing with her grandchildren, Ms. Cart can often be found curled up in a snug place with a good novel, a cup of hot tea, and a piece of very dark chocolate.